SIDEKICK

Henchman Book Two

CARL STUBBLEFIELD

MOUNTAINDALE
PRESS

CONTENTS

ACKNOWLEDGMENTS

This book goes out to all the underdogs. The unsung heroes who keep working hard, with minimal recognition, support, or appreciation for all their efforts.

Keep pushing, even when it appears the whole world is against you---because your efforts matter. Whether you know it or not. And if that fails...make them pay.

PROLOGUE

Brad Buchanan sat with his feet kicked up on the console, playing a game on his phone. Another computer in the large room beeped in the distance, followed by a whir of drives being accessed and an electric hum as others switched on, doing their preliminary checks before coming online. The sudden flurry of activity startled Brad and he almost tumbled backward. He juggled his phone, trying to keep from dropping it on the polished concrete floor, before he regained his balance. He scooted his chair closer to look at the monitor and pushed his glasses up his nose. The only message displayed was:

Beacon detected. Signal: extremely weak.

A terminal nearby began to emit a pinging pulse that reminded Brad of the sonar in the old submarine war movies his dad watched. Rolling his chair over to the terminal, he saw a green world map displayed. Ripples like a stone dropped in a pond emanated from their location outward. The weak signal was lost amid the competing interference of other signals. Brad had one job: Notify his superiors if the computer detected anything. Finally, he could do something for a change. Sure it was easy money, but with nothing else to occupy his thoughts, it made for some *long* days. He needed to get out of here, but that would take a promotion.

Brad was the only monitor still working who knew what they were supposed to be watching for. And it took nearly a year of sucking up to the old man who took over for the morning shift. He had finally told Brad the day he retired.

An evil grin formed on his face and Brad keyed the communicator on the display. Focusing on the signal, he left a short message: "Thank you, whoever you are. We have been looking for the manor for so long. Now that we know where you are, we will be seeing you soon to reclaim what is ours!" Satisfied with himself, he sat back in his chair. They hadn't mentioned anything about communicating back, but they liked people with initiative, right? Who knew what promotion awaited him? He sent a quick communique on his console to his superiors and told them what he had found.

As if waiting on the other line, a voice Brad had previously only heard in training holos answered as soon as he hit send. He looked at his watch. 3:23 AM? Who was awake at headquarters at this hour?

A manic, gravelly voice came through his console, "I will be there immediately."

————

Archon leaned back in his high-backed leather chair in the office far above, his bony fingers clawing the armrests in triumph and excitement. *"Finally, revenge is at hand for Manticorps!"* he shouted to the empty office. After Manticorps' fall from grace, they had become forgotten, abandoned by those who purported to be allies. Those deserters would pay. All would regret their betrayals. Archon spun his chair and looked out at the night sky, excited to share the news with his son.

CHAPTER ONE

Start Over

Gus was training on the beach, the soft sand cushioning his falls as he tried to level up **Basic Flight**. He jumped and flipped in the air, throwing Jet into the nearby blue water. The sleek black shape disappeared under the water. Gus pulled with an **Ether Leash** and a large fish came with it, skewered on the end of the blade. The serrated edge kept the fish from sliding off as he pulled the weapon back to him. He didn't need to fish, but it was easy grinding for **Polearms**, **Ether Leash** and **Fishing**.

The past couple days had fallen into a comfortable routine. Training in the morning in the arena, a big breakfast, then relaxing on the beach. Fishing was a lot more fun when he didn't have to do it just to survive. Also, it helped train his reflexes and aim. Gus enjoyed leveling at his own pace, with no emergencies to drive him. With the bio-stasis shield down, he could eventually make it back to civilization when he was ready and felt he had trained enough to hold his own.

Gus nodded in appreciation at Stuart's efficiency. The manor's AI steward in charge of managing the facilities had been tasked to clean up the remains of the Dark Nth. His robot minions were doing an exceptional job. The grounds already looked back to near-pristine condition. Gus would cook up his catch later in the day when the manor patio provided some shade and relax in the late afternoon and evening. Life was good.

Without battles, he wasn't leveling up nearly as quickly, but he was making slow and steady progress. He wasn't in a rush now that things had stabilized. He had hit level 14 and was halfway to 15, most of the XP from skill leveling. He hadn't realized how much tension he'd been carrying until things finally settled down.

Nick had reassured him that with the island being so remote, it would be very difficult to find, even if someone was looking for it. Since the manor wasn't transmitting anything or emitting any kind of signals, it should keep off the radar. Gus still felt a little exposed without the bio-stasis field, but after a couple days, he began to relax, chiding himself for his hypervigilance and worry.

He had cut one jumpsuit down into a nice swimsuit. After a lot of rummaging through the dispensary, he had found a mask and snorkel as well as some scuba gear. Not being familiar with the scuba mouthpiece and tanks, he opted simply to explore the reefs and wildlife around the rocks. He'd always been fairly pasty since he was always indoors, but he was developing a respectable tan, and an ever-improving physique. With a little tweaking, he had automated **_Energy Absorption_** so he'd never get a sunburn again. Membership had its privileges. Taking a break, he lay back in the warm sand and closed his eyes.

While Gus enjoyed his downtime, a flashing red light winked on in the control center.

(1) message pending.

It set off no alarms or notices. The peacefulness of its mute winking belied the bombshell that it contained. Gus went about his routine for another couple days, not once visiting the control center, and so the message stayed there, patiently blinking.

CHAPTER TWO

Panic Attack

"Gus, proximity alert! Someone is nearing the northwest shore!"

"What? Already?!" He had figured that it was a remote possibility that someone determined could find the island eventually. He waded out of the water and removed his mask and snorkel, tossing them to the beach, out of range of the busy little robot cleaners.

In his mind, he had estimated it would take a much longer time for someone to discover the island. Someone had come to ruin his plans to relax and prepare at his own pace before heading back to civilization. He tightened his grip on Jet and began to run to the area indicated by Nick.

The warm, salty wind blew by as Gus used **Dash** to move quickly down to the beach, drying himself almost immediately after a brief chill. He rocketed down the coast, steps bouncing like a skipping stone off the lazy waves that licked the sandy shore.

When the minimap showed he was nearing the landing zone, he moved away from the water, up to where the long grasses and palms grew, to hide his footprints and observe the invaders. His heart pounded like a big bass drum, threatening to betray his hiding spot to the world, even though Gus knew that it wasn't that loud in reality.

A bobbing blip became visible along the horizon, and Gus zoomed in his display to see a small, unremarkable ship skip into view. It was traveling fairly quickly, directly for the beach where he was hidden. He clenched his fists and narrowed his eyes at the thought of someone coming to take away the island.

This island was *his*. He had not constructed it, but it was through his effort alone that it had become viable for use. No one else had been able to do that in decades of trying. Gus was also painfully aware he was still a noob compared to most supers out there, but he wasn't going to let the island and the manor go without a fight.

The loss of the bio-stasis field was a double-edged sword. It freed up a huge reserve of energy taken up by the shield to unlock facilities. But the island was now out in the open, with no defenses to speak of. He felt sweat slick on his palms as he held Jet, waiting and watching the ship.

To be honest, he wanted to get back to civilization but hadn't thought that it would result in such a quick move to seize the manor out from under him. Being alone was starting to affect him more than he would like to admit. Besides, the capacitors were so shot from being operational for so long that Nick had told him they would probably never come back online unless they were repaired extensively or replaced. He would have to find another way to protect his home.

As the ship approached, Gus could resolve some men moving along the decks. Most were carrying automatic weapons and patrolling back and forth. He could not sense any Nth with his passive **Psi-link** skill, which was a little confusing. Maybe these were henchmen, fodder to exhaust him and 'soften him up' before the real supers arrived to finish what they started. So strange to be seeing this from the other side of the equation. He almost felt bad for them; who knew what he would do if he had a family he had to support.

The details of the unkempt men came clearer the closer they came to the shore. No one was wearing a standard uniform and the group did not behave at all like seasoned soldiers. At long last, the ship neared and slowed as it got close enough to debark and Gus could make out some of their shouted commands, but they were all in a different language. There was a quick warbling tone and suddenly he could understand the commands one particularly nasty individual was barking at the others.

"You're welcome," Nick drawled sarcastically.

"Get ashore and see if there's anything we can use. We need more water, and some food would be nice. Hurry! We need to finish here and get to the rendezvous point in less than thirty hours!"

It doesn't seem like they were looking for me... Gus relaxed a bit. This was probably just a coincidence and he only needed to wait for the men to leave. The manor was far enough away that he didn't think they could see it from this part of the island, and it would take them a while to walk far enough through the jungle for it to become visible. All he had to do was wait them out. Easy.

Part of him knew that was rarely the case.

Nothing was ever easy.

CHAPTER THREE

Ship of Fools

The men dropped anchor and two jumped off the boat. Gus heard them assigning tasks. One went to look for food; another left to look for supplies and fill the water jugs. There continued to be no indication that they were looking for him, which lowered Gus' alarm even more. Until they mentioned where they would sell the women. Time slowed for Gus for a couple moments, and he wondered whether he had heard correctly.

As Nick interpreted, Gus learned more of these men who had boarded a ship this morning, taking the owner and his family and friends captive.

The cavalier attitude the men had with slavery in this modern day took Gus' brain a bit to process. One of the men ranted about how even though they kept them all together in one room without conveniences, the younger girls had covered themselves in feces to avoid being violated. The other trafficker laughed, saying that wouldn't stop him.

Gus realized that he had to do something. Reality slapped him full in the face. Part of his mind was hesitant to take action, worrying about the possible ways it would reveal his location and result in the loss of the island. The stronger half asserted that if he didn't help these people, he deserved to lose the island, and he would be one of *those supers*. The selfish ego-tripping individuals who only looked out for number one. Now was time for action; he could philosophize later.

Gus toggled his display and saw six men in infrared. Two on the beach and four remaining on the ship. The ambient heat made it too bright to hold this view for long. He saw no evidence of the captives. They must be deeper onboard—possibly masked by walls or water, or in some kind of hold that would block their heat signature.

He would have to separate these guys, and not let them warn each other or harm the hostages. Sweat beaded on his forehead at the very real stakes involved. He tracked one of the traffickers as he stepped out of sight of his crew, exploring deeper into the forest that lined the beach shortly after the sand ended. It was the first time he had an opportunity to incapacitate someone rather than kill them outright, and he fumbled at what skills he should use. **Wreck-luse** would be nice if it didn't have its deadly toxic effect. Maybe some kind of **Ether Weaving** to prevent him from crying out and from firing a shot at the same time? It was worth a try.

Waiting for the heavyset man to put some distance between the ship and himself, Gus readied his weave. He had a bandana-wide swath of ether prepared, and snuck up behind the man. With a quick snap he swung it over and enveloped the man's head. At the same time, he used two tendrils of ether to plug the barrel of the gun as well as fill the trigger guard so the man could not fire a shot to warn his friends.

The man was startled and the gun wrenched easily from his hands. It was odd to see his hands fly to his face and pull at the invisible and incorporeal ether that displaced and sealed out oxygen. Try as he might, the man found no purchase on the material and struggled to regain the ability to breathe. Since he wasn't in the best physical condition, the pirate passed out quickly. Gus half-dropped, half-carried the man to the ground as he collapsed.

Gus reformed the ether, making it into a gag. He pulled the man twenty feet off the trail and fashioned arm and leg restraints out of ether lashes. Gus marveled at how ether reacted with regular matter. Without the ability to shape it, there was no way the man could untie himself and get free. He would feel that he was bound by something as incorporeal to him as air. Gus doubted he could even bruise or chafe if he struggled against the bonds.

Securing him to a tree out of sight of the trail, Gus made his way back to the beach, trying to find out how to distract the others and get them off the boat if at all possible. It only would take one slip-up and people could be hurt by his incompetence. When he reached the boat, the four men were still on board, and the other man who had disembarked was nowhere to be seen.

He could see the footprints on the soft white sand, trailing away from the boat. He followed them warily, intermittently changing filters on his display in order to distinguish where the man was. Gus had no luck until he came to a wide opening. The path spilled out to a taller area overlooking a pool. A waterfall dumped noisily nearby, into a calm pool beneath.

A man stood peering over the edge, surveying the scene, two large water jugs at his side. He appeared to be looking for a safe way to get down to the pool below to refill his water jugs.

Gus realized that he was too far away to risk sneaking out in the open, but if he could approach without being noticed, he could take this man down as he had with the first.

Gus floated an inch off the ground with **Basic Flight**, then triggered **Slide**. Gus glided silently over the ground towards the man, but his aim was off. He almost overshot his target and sailed off the end of the cliff, and barely hopped back to his feet. The pirate turned in surprise and Gus fumbled with the weave, wrestling with the man and trying not to have the two of them fall off the edge.

In the scuffle, the man tripped over a water bottle, giving Gus the upper hand, and he smothered the pirate until he passed out like the first. Quickly releasing the weave, Gus checked that the man was still breathing. He dragged him out of sight and bound and gagged him with ether.

Even after waiting a couple hours for their mates, it appeared the other pirates were cagey and would not leave the boat. They were clearly agitated but only paced and shielded their eyes as they scanned the jungle.

Gus would have to go on the offensive. As he approached the boat, he noticed that their mouths did not sync up with what they were saying, like a poorly-dubbed foreign film. Sometimes there would be long stretches where their mouths were moving but Gus heard no translation at all.

"Nick, how come—"

"I'm keeping it PG-13 for your oh-so-sensitive ears, remember? If you want, I can give their direct translations, or substitute some of your standard pseudo-swear words if you like. *Shut the front door! Got down, sat on a bench! You fricking, flipping, fetching, frelling, frakker!*"

"No, that would be even more annoying than usual, thanks."

"You didn't even let me get to Fraggle Rock, fudge nuggets, or tartar sauce…" Nick said petulantly.

Gus was evaluating his skills, and they didn't offer a lot of functionality for non-lethal combat. Still, he had an idea. Getting in position, Gus activated **T-Wrecks** behind the ship, with the construct being just deep enough to leave the top half of its body exposed. The beast bellowed and all the men rushed to the back of the ship to meet the threat. They fired wildly at the construct, who gnashed and waded towards them.

Gus rushed onboard the ship, his steps hidden amid the rattle of gunshots. Straining to split his ether in four ways, Gus snatched all the men simultaneously with an ether bubble over their heads. He hoisted them over the edge and dunked them under the water, holding them there.

Only one of the men appeared to keep hold of his gun, and he fired a couple muffled shots underwater before he too let go of his weapon.

Gus strained to hold the weaves and pulled the men out of the water as he felt his control slipping. He didn't want to accidentally drown them, so he held them above the water, straining to position them above the beach. Gus' ears began to ring as he held onto the weaves.

"Don't cross the streams," he snarled between gritted teeth as he struggled to hold the weaves in place until all the men were knocked out.

Two men succumbed quickly, while the other two thrashed violently, then weakly as they drifted into unconsciousness, expending the available oxygen in their bubbles. A chime sounded and Gus let go. They crumpled to the sand like rag dolls. Gus had to flip one who had fallen face first, but he appeared to only have a face-full of sand.

After tying them up with ether, Gus was struck with the most intense splitting headache of his life. His MP and stamina were only partially depleted, but his poor brain was not accustomed to that type of focus. After a lot of massaging his temples and the bridge of his nose, the icepick-like pain subsided and he could focus on his display and logs again.

You have leveled up the skill: **Ether Weaving to Level 4!**
750 XP awarded.
1,500 FP awarded.
860 XP to level 15.

You have unlocked a subskill of **Ether Weaving: Incapacitate (Level 1).**
Incapacitate (Level 1): *Subdue an attacker by restricting their oxygen flow through an ether weave. Success rates decrease by 10% per level for stronger opponents.*
100 XP awarded.
200 FP awarded.

760 XP to level 15.

It took another ten minutes to recuperate and feel like a normal functioning human. *Superhuman?* Nothing was normal anymore. Gus got to his feet, brushing the sand off. It was time to see how the original owners of the boat were doing.

CHAPTER FOUR

Aurora

Bodyguards filed out of the elevator and took their positions flanking the doors. A thin, almost skeletal man in long silver robes stepped off the lift. Brad tried not to stare at the exaggerated coif of white hair that was obviously very thin but styled to fluff it and give it artificial volume.

"Report," the old man croaked, and Brad explained all that happened. When he mentioned his own personal message, the man's passive expression contorted into an unsettling rictus. "And what motivated you to do such a thing?"

Brad lowered his eyes to avoid the maniacal stare the leader of Manticorps directed at him. "I wanted to scare them," he said, the explanation sounding idiotic when it came from his own mouth. He deepened his voice and looked the old man in the eyes. "To let them know they shouldn't mess with Manticorps, or they will face the consequences." He looked expectantly at the leader; maybe this would be enough to convince someone to get him out of this dungeon.

"So you took it upon yourself to warn them that we would soon be arriving. After over forty years, we have no idea of the advancements the Traitor has made. He might take this as an act of aggression and attack *us* first!" Archon said, anger leaking around the feigned smile and civility in his voice. "We have much to do!"

He spun, his silver cape billowing with the motion. Reaching backward, he let loose a bright flash of energy from his extended palm. Where Brad had been standing, a small charred pile of dust remained, which was stomped flat as the bodyguards resumed formation and exited via the elevator, surrounding their leader.

———

Aurora lifted her head and surveyed the darkness. Time had lost its meaning with the lack of any feedback. Even her interrogations were completed in total darkness. There was a noise of water dripping. Was she in a cave? The area lacked the earthy stale smell of air trapped underground, but perhaps this was a base of some sort. The ground underneath her was not smooth like a typical room and she felt large cobblestones or large smooth pavers, damp and slimy.

She tried to shift to get comfortable, but it only made the pain in her shoulders and arms worse. They had manacled her arms behind her, in an exaggerated swan-dive position that allowed no relief. A rubbery material completely encased her hands, which made her unable to focus her power, and she could not activate any of her skills. She was bound around her wrists below the large rubber spheres. No way she could flip or position her body to get the cuffs in front of her. And she had tried. Anything to get some relief.

After gaining some rest and enough resolve, she would stand and lean slightly backward to relieve the tension. Her leg muscles were unreliable—wobbly and exhausted from electric shocks, being stabbed with foot-long needles, and other horrors that brought her health low. Never enough to finally be done with it. When they suddenly buckled, her arms felt like they were going to be ripped out of their sockets, so she slowly sank to a kneeling position for as long as she could tolerate it, even though it stretched her arms out even more.

This had been her world. The only break in the routine was when they would come and ask her questions: *Where is the island? What is in the manor? What have your scans revealed?* Aurora had held out thus far, due to her training, but she was unraveling.

Truth was, she had no idea what they wanted. Sure, Graviton scanned the areas below his station and sent information back to Purple Faction, but there did not appear to be a concerted effort to find anything in particular, and since she was one of the highest-ranking officers on board, it wouldn't make sense for that type of information to be withheld from her.

Still, they would not relent in either their questioning or torture until she was near death. Having an HP bar that told the sociopaths just how much they could push her was a huge disadvantage. She'd never thought it would be a liability.

She tried to cast her mind back to better times, when things had changed from her horrible childhood to a less horrible tween-hood. Then to the academy. That was when she had truly come into her own. She focused on that feeling and embraced it, and the pain became a bit less present.

———

"You go now," the short woman shooed her out the door.

"What are you doing, Auntie?" the skinny girl asked, irritated that she was interrupted from her book and pushed out the door. Auntie had her quirks, so Cass decided to take a walk. Maybe she was going through one of her irritable spells or something. She had been on edge and acting strangely for the last couple months. Short for no reason, prone to strange outbursts at the slightest provocation. Cass just tried to give her space when she went cray-cray, and she would usually revert to her normal self.

She kicked a bottle down the garbage-strewn alley. It hit a small pile of garbage, scaring a rat enjoying a meal. As it fled, running against the wall, it was swallowed by one of the semi-sentient plants that spread like ivy across the walls of this area. Without them, this area would probably have been overrun long ago and disease would have run rampant. The purple bulb hung as it digested its meal, appearing to be a mere eggplant to the ignorant observer. *Gross.*

It had just rained, which washed the air clear of the odd combination of food smells that always permeated the area, but new ones took their place as the water revived smells from the ever-present garbage.

Usually, she had her music with her, but her Flik and head-phones were back in her room, and Auntie hadn't given her time to pick them up. It was probably the reason why she heard them coming from behind. One stepped on a discarded Styro-foam package, alerting her to the presence of the three men tailing her.

The large one on the right scowled and threw an angry glance at the hot-stepper, and the girl and men simultaneously broke into runs.

Since Cass had lived in the area for six years, she knew the shortcuts and was able to get a little space between her and the men, even though their long legs chewed up the distance quickly in the straight alleyways. Cass knew where to climb a dumpster to vault over a fence, or the narrow areas she could slide between where two of the sheet-metal-shanties almost touched corners.

Of course, no one got involved, even though she was running for her life, or virtue, or whatever these animals wanted. Just confused stares rubbernecking after them, but no one alarmed or motivated enough to step in and help.

She could probably take these guys out easily with her powers, but she didn't want anyone else to know that she was different—especially in the Chaos Gardens. Semi-sentient plants that ate vermin, people could handle. Humans with super abilities, they would ostracize forever. She wouldn't be able to live here if they knew; no one would sell her anything.

That was primarily how she and Auntie had survived. Cass would buy the things they needed and pay the few bills; Auntie supplied the cash. Since she had essentially been a mail-order bride, Auntie was totally lost and didn't speak the language. When her elderly husband died, shortly after she'd arrived, she was lost. She understood nothing of what the nicely-dressed men were telling her and having her sign with her fingerprint and DNA confirmation.

In the end, the woman Cass called 'Auntie' received a plastic tokencard and was shown off the property. She had not realized that they had liquidated all of her husband's assets, including the house where she lived, and given her the bare minimum they were legally allowed, then promptly disappeared.

Shortly after Cass' mother died, she had met Auntie by happenstance, who had watched over her, and they formed a mutually beneficial relationship.

A loud crash behind Cass brought her out of her reverie. She was beginning to get winded, her skinny frail frame unaccustomed to such a long pursuit. She usually could stay under the radar and not be noticed. Still, the men came, unrelenting in their chase. *What do they want?*

She yelled for help as she passed a group of teenage boys. They just whooped and cheered, apparently rooting for her pursuers. The burst of anger she felt gave her a bit more gas in the tank.

After a couple more turns, she had the uncomfortable realization that she was in unfamiliar territory. She made a few additional blind turns and the alley opened onto a cross street. The spray-painted plywood and cobbled-together hovels gave way to clean walls, textured and painted. It was like crossing some invisible barrier from the slums to the burbs.

Those damn guys are still chasing me? What gives? No one would care if you got mugged or worse in the Garden. But these guys could face major punishments for committing crimes on official Faction territory. If, and that was a big if, they were caught.

She ducked down another clean alley. It turned midway and

as she bolted left, she found that it ended in a large door used for truck deliveries. No other exits were visible. She saw security cameras above the moving door but harbored no illusions that some white knight would see anything and deign to come help. People were sick. They probably would watch like an MMA fight or worse.

Turning her back to the wall, Cass evaluated her options. Maybe no one coming to help would work in her favor. She doubted anyone from the Garden would see her, so she raised her hands, and pulled inward. Energy flowed into her, invigorating her.

The effect caused her hair to raise as the energy built up; she really needed to find a workaround for that. At the worst of times, it got in her face and she couldn't see. She was tempted to cut it in a pixie cut, but she'd had one when she was young and they just made her look too mousy and small. The young girl would never have guessed her current bedraggled appearance would in time transform to rival the model on the billboard hanging far above the secluded alley. *Focus!*

The men ran into the alley and they skidded to a stop, knocking the first man down as the others crashed into him. "Yep, you were right," the guy on the ground said to the leader, who threw another scowl to get the guy to shut up. They turned their predatory eyes to her and slowly began to inch forward.

"Come on now, little miss. Let's not do this the hard way," Scowler said.

Hot-stepper licked his lips in a slightly crazed way. His lazy eye didn't help his look and made his already creepy vibe even worse.

Cass started to extend her hands and began to move the energy out. Energy arced between her fingers, emitting an occasional flash of red or green as the oxygen molecules in the air reacted with the rising charge. Blues and purples began a bit later as the nitrogen in the air began doing the same thing. The men were mesmerized by the light show. Most people typically were. That was, until she sent the energy out in a spray.

Not only was it spectacular to see, but it did a number on men. The attack itself had become vastly more powerful since the last time she'd had to use her powers. *How long has it been? A couple years, at least.* The men clutched at their eyes, and Cass could see where the spray had etched the men's skins like they had been sandblasted.

Pockmarks littered their exposed skin like bad acne, which then began to bleed. There was a pretty good chance they had been blinded too, but she wasn't sticking around to find out. She sidled out into the alley as the men writhed on the ground from their wounds. Two of them were clutching their faces, but the third still sought her out.

As she was trying to sneak past the man who was reaching out around him with his eyes tightly closed, the security camera pivoted to keep her in full view. She flipped her middle finger at the camera as she continued to move out of the alley. The closest man moved his arms as if questing for a towel to dry himself. He almost grabbed her, and she inhaled, holding her gut in to make her profile that much slimmer. When he moved on, she finally tiptoed out of the alley.

As she turned back, she ran headlong into a burly, muscle-bound man in a purple suit. He had a big smile on his face and said simply, "We need to talk…"

———

"…Aurora," someone whispered. She broke from her memory and lifted her head. Her stomach tightened at the thought of another impending cycle of torture. Opening her eyes, everything was quiet except for the occasional sound of water dripping. Aurora swept her eyes left and right in the dark, but no one was there.

"Great, I'm going insane," she said, voice cracking a bit as she fought back the exhaustion and pain that had brought her to the brink.

"Aurora," the tentative voice repeated. This time she could tell it was in her head, becoming more distinct.

"Who is this?" she asked, wondering if this was some mental super from Purple Faction come to rescue her.

"Aurora, are you able to hear me at last?" Hope was evident now at finally being heard.

"Yes, yes! Who is this?" Aurora stammered.

"It has been so long! I haven't been able to communicate with you at all due to your training. I am the source of your powers, and we need to talk!"

CHAPTER FIVE

State of the Heart

"What are you going to do with them?" Nick asked.

"I really don't know. It's not like I can just put them in jail, can I?"

"As a matter of fact, the manor *does* have a brig. But are you going to support these guys forever? I mean, I guess you could put them in cells and have the robots feed them. Some supers would just kill them…"

"I don't think I can do that. I know these guys are evil, probably some of the evilest men I've ever met in my life. If they died, no one would know, and it would mean that much less garbage in the world. But it just feels wrong to me on a visceral level. I always swore I would do things differently when I got my powers."

"Situations change. Besides, what's the big deal? Like you said, you'd be doing the world a favor."

"I can see your point of view, but I still think this choice may be more extreme than you think." Gus wiped away sweat that was beading on his brow from the noon-day sun.

"Two years."

"I'm sorry?"

"It only took two years for Cyclone to kill someone. And he had no remorse about it either. How do you not know that? Don't you have access to all of my memories?"

"You think I'm some weird Peeping Tom? Well, technically, I guess I am. That's beside the point though. I generally experience memory only as you recall it actively, unless there is something specific needed, but it's like cleaning out your Aunt Greta the hoarder's garage. Good luck if you don't know where to start."

"Can you access the memory of when my older brother got his powers?"

"Let's see, how old were you?" A small window popped open in the corner of the display, speeding by like a fast-forwarded movie.

"I think I was thirteen," Gus wrinkled his forehead, trying to recall the exact date. "It would have been around his sixteenth birthday, so check around July 10th."

"Gotcha. Hmmm... This one?"

The small window enlarged to fill his display like a home movie recording, only the perspective was from Gus' own eyes. "Yeah, that's it."

———

"Today's the day, Black Anus, I mean Angus..." Alan teased.

"Hey, you're supposed to stop calling me that," Gus whined.

"Are you gonna run and tell Dad? I'm just kidding—sheesh. You've got to lighten up, dude. You know people tease you more if they can get under your skin so easily. I'm trying to help you out. Besides, you can't just tattle to Dad for everything. It's wimpy as hell and no one will respect you—even Dad. Don't you see how he's always babying you all the time?"

Gus bit his lip. Alan was older, so he probably knew what he was talking about. *Is that why he seemed to like Alan better? He didn't need anyone to come rescue him?* Gus decided to change the subject.

"Why won't you tell me how you're getting powers?"

"Jealous much? I don't blame you. But I can't tell you anything. I promised the others. Even to family. Sorry, bud. It's not me, that's just how the Faction works. I can't wait to see what I will get though."

"Do you have anything you are hoping for?" Gus asked, his frustration replaced with wonder.

"I'm sure it will be pretty good. Mom and Dad are both strong supers, and I really couldn't go wrong with any combo of their powers. They say that if both your parents are supers, your DNA is more primed for better, stronger abilities. Too bad you don't have the right markers. Not to say they'll never come, but sucks that you have to wait."

"Yeah, it does. It would be cool to work with Tempest, and go on trips with the Faction."

"Yeah, you're going to have to grow up a lot. We are going to be gone a lot for training and all that. You think you can handle it? Not burn down the house or anything?"

"I think I can manage," Gus grumbled.

Alan tousled Gus' hair. "Now get outta here, you're distracting me. I gotta get ready."

Gus swiped hair out of his eyes as Alan shooed him out the door, closing and locking it behind him. Alan wasn't *that* much older than him, only three years. He acted like he was so much bigger and more mature. He was lucky to get his powers so young at sixteen. Gus kicked some clothes out of the way and plopped down on a bean bag chair.

He stared at the ceiling and wondered what he would do when it was his turn. Part of him knew Alan would change. And it probably wouldn't be good, at least for him. Alan tolerated Gus in the best of times, but he expected the already-limited interactions they had would be even fewer from here on out.

He would move on. He would figure it out. It might even be good if he had some more time to himself.

———

"Seems like a jerk to me," Nick snarked.

"He kind of was, I guess. But aren't most big brothers? Getting his powers changed him, though. He became, I don't know, more vicious? Like regs deserved anything he did to them when they got in his way."

"Might makes right," Nick said without emotion.

"Yep. The Purple Faction way." Gus sighed.

"So you want to *save* these guys, is that what you're saying?"

"I dunno. I feel like I got a second chance; who am I to judge them? Maybe things would be different if circumstances were different. I mean, do I have the right to sentence these guys based on the limited knowledge I have on them? I'm not a magister. I can't read their thoughts and intentions. Killing them seems, so… final. What if I get so used to it, I do it callously?"

There was a loud gong noise that caused Gus to flinch. An opaque blue message window filled his display.

Congratulations! You now have the option to choose a Guiding Principle. Guiding principles offer many benefits as long as you hold them in solemn regard and do not break them, offering stat boosts and enhancements as long as you remain true to the tenets of the principle.
You have the option to choose: Compassion.
You receive a +5 increase in all basic stats and a 30% increase to XP gain while the status is maintained. Be true to yourself, and you will continue to grow and develop!
You have chosen to preserve life in the pursuit of your growth. XP awarded upon creatively subduing opponents who attack you, party members, or contested territory.
Know this! Penalties are incurred upon breaking this principle. Severe XP and level penalties variable on situation and frequency. If you show yourself unfit to live this Guiding Principle, it will be stripped from you.
When you are working in a team aligned with your values and views, they also will have access to the same bonuses applied for the duration of the party. Access to a unique team ability based on team dynamics available.

Conditions: Know this! All members of the team must adhere to this tenet as you move forward or the entire group will suffer penalties.
Accept? (Y/N)

"Hold up there before you go smashing that Y," Nick warned.

"Are you kidding? That's a huge boost to stats—and XP too!"

"I know you think this is a noble course of action, but I must recommend against it."

"What? Why?"

"This is a very difficult guiding principle to maintain. Most supers drop it eventually and suffer horrible penalties as a result."

"Yeah, it mentioned that. What kind of penalties are we talking about?"

"Generally, you lose all XP progression to the next level, as well as losing an entire level for the first offense. It only goes up from there. If you lose ten levels, you are forever locked out of this guiding principle, as well as related ones in the future."

"What happens if I just wait and accept it later, when things settle down?"

"Unique conditions are usually what leads to the opportunity to accept a guiding principle. Most likely the restraint and choosing not to kill these guys. If you want a probability, there is a 98% chance you will not have this option again in the future, even if you recreate the same conditions."

"Well, that sucks."

"This penalty would apply to all of the other supers who join you in a party. In fact, they would suffer a proportionally more severe penalty due to the larger XP gaps between you and their higher levels. Even with the XP bonuses, they would not compensate for accidental deaths. You struggled just recently with no real threats on the line. Many supers find that when the stakes get too high, often principles that seem noble in the bright of day cost too much to maintain."

"You said the Nth seeded our culture with ideas so that we would more readily accept them, correct?"

"Yep, that is true."

"So when we have things in the comics where there are defi-nite 'good guys' and the sacrifices they make, isn't that showing a preferred ideal? Or was that wishful thinking from the human side? That we as a species are capable of making that kind of sacrifice?"

"Gus, have you always been a 'good guy,' as you mention it? I for one think it's vastly overrated, but how do I put this? Just remember some of the antics you did when you were a hench-man. *So. Many. Antics!* Mike would be proud, though—I know I am."

"Who's Mike?"

"Never mind, all I'm saying is that if you want to be inher-ently good, maybe start with putting the shopping carts back in the rack first and work your way up. It's a big jump from chaotic neutral to lawful good."

Gus remembered some of the destructive things he had done during his time as a henchman. A smile crept across his face, which turned into a grimace. While fun, they probably weren't as noble as he was trying to be now.

"People can change. I can change. I at least have to try; my brother made it two years. I'm not going to compromise after only two *weeks* of being a super. Can you evaluate how likely I am to succeed if I do accept this guiding principle?" Gus asked.

"I… am not allowed to discuss it. I have already said too much. This decision is yours, and must rest with you alone. I simply want you to know what happens with the majority of humans who attempt this guiding principle. I am not saying you are wrong, but I doubt you have weighed the cost—"

"No. I'm doing it. Thank you for telling me about the risks."

"You should still think about—"

Gus clicked Y.

CHAPTER SIX

I Can't Fix You

"You know no one else is going to play by your rules, especially other supers, right? You think that was the best choice right now?"

"I think it's exactly what I need. I don't ever want to let myself get to that place, and if it takes a guiding principle and even punishment, it might be enough to help me be true to myself."

"Still—"

"I can do it. I just have to be smarter. Not take the easy way out like I always do. If I can't keep promises to myself then how can I keep them to anyone else? You don't know how much I would daydream about what I would do. I can't throw all of that away, especially with how things are out there."

"Yeah, yeah. Be the hero the world needs, not the one it deserves. So what are you going to do with these creeps on the beach?"

Gus blew out a big sigh and put his hands on his hips. "I don't know. I'm concerned that they could reveal the coordinates of the island and things might get a lot busier here than I'm ready for."

"A valid point," Nick confirmed.

"But I can't be sure that if I send them back with the family that they wouldn't just get thrown overboard or killed since I'll have to restrain them somehow. Then what's to ensure the men get tried for their crimes? That would require visiting a magistrate, testimony, and a lot of time. I get the feeling this family just wants to get on with their lives and get out of here."

"Also true. I've got no easy answers for you, unfortunately," Nick answered impassively.

"Why did this have to get complicated so quickly?" Gus ran his hands through his hair, lacing them behind his neck and looking up at the sky. "It would have been nice to level up a bit at my own pace and figure these types of things out in my own time." He sighed again and stared at the sand.

"How am I going to do this, Nick? I mean, even if I figure this out, what happens when I get back to civilization? Do I join my father's Faction and subject myself to their rules? Do I stay Factionless? Everyone has such strong opinions for one Faction and against another one. Everyone's a villain to someone and adored by others. I just want to be a good guy and do good sometimes. And have a life somewhere in the middle."

"You might have less freedom than you think if you join a Faction. They have their own rules, you know. Ones that regs don't see or hear about. There's always a bigger fish in the pond, and if you don't think they have ways of dealing with cocksure young supers with ideas of their own, you're in for some disappointment. Especially with noble ideals that conflict with the current mission in question. Just look at some of the things you were asked to do as a henchman. The overtly destructive ones. You think that changes just because you're higher on the food chain?"

"I didn't think about that."

"I know. Gus, you didn't choose this life as most do, but I have high hopes for you. I see you becoming a gunslinger, out there on your own, kicking ass and taking names. Plus you can't see your own greatness, which is kind of refreshing, to be honest. You lack the ego that most supers have and the Faction academies promote. I mean, you could use a little more bravado at times, but right now I see you as a wild card, amirite?"

"I suppose."

"Most supers are taught to suppress any and all Nth communication. They explain this connection as dissociative identity disorder that is a side effect of the anchoring of a person's abilities. I mean, really, don't the best of us all have voices in our heads?"

"Why would they do that? It seems like it would really restrict development."

"It's because of the Rooack—" Nick began but ended in choking noises.

"Because of what?" Gus asked.

"Oh, come on! Why is that restricted? It's part of history!" Nick protested. "Sorry, boss. Quantum server is restricting that particular information for now. That's pretty rare. That means some powerful people on this planet are currently using abilities to control the flow of information. All I can tell you is that this was intentional."

"So maybe not going through an academy will end up being a good thing. I have been thinking I would always be so far behind other supers in the Factions."

"Everything has a cost. The amazing help and guidance that Nth can provide, even if it isn't noticed or appreciated sometimes by *some people*," Nick's inflection was jokingly exaggerated as he paused for effect. "No offense, Gus, but I doubt you could have achieved what you have without little old me."

"No, you're right about that," Gus admitted, not taking the bait. "I may have gotten there in a couple decades, but I didn't have that kind of time. I really am grateful. I have stalled enough though. I need to do something."

Gus climbed aboard the boat and went below decks. He found a door with a large padlock on it and shattered the internal mechanism with **Wreck-It-Gus**. The lock emitted a loud crack, the stacked plates of the lock bent, and the loop disengaged. Pulling open the wooden door, Gus descended a steep ladder to the room below.

The cacophony that assaulted his ears was intense, as was the heavy smell of diesel and engine oil. The engine's thrum was so noisy he wondered if the people trapped here would have permanent hearing loss.

Not to mention the heat, which was so sweltering that Gus worried that the occupants might have heat stroke. It was so hot that he couldn't use any special filters on his displays to show the family. He made his way around the cramped machinery and found them crouched together next to one wall.

The father had been zip-tied to some piping and his wife and three girls gathered around protectively. They appeared to be of Asian descent, and while he knew Nick could translate for him, it would be like trying to carry on a conversation in a loud nightclub.

Gus held his hands up placatingly, showing he intended no harm. He slowly approached and removed the ties with a focused **Wreck-It-Gus**. He then motioned the family to follow him. They were skeptical at first, but after the father had secured a large wrench they followed after Gus had climbed back up the ladder.

Gus decided to let them come out on their own and went to retrieve the other two men. He was dragging them back to the beach on an ether sled when he saw the family come up to the top deck.

Anger was clearly visible on the wife's face; the father looked disappointed, as if ashamed he couldn't protect his family. The woman grabbed the wrench from her husband and jumped off the ship, heading to attack one of the men. Gus had to drop his burden and rush over to stop her from bludgeoning the helpless man.

"They should die!" she screamed.

Gus had to hold her back as she flailed in blind fury, attempting to get past him. If it weren't for his increased stats, she would have knocked old Gus over in her fury.

"Hold on, let's talk about this," Gus said as they struggled, and the woman calmed, shocked that he could speak her language. The Nth and Nick were managing his tongue, facial muscles, and vocal cords, and it shocked them both. He was speaking in her language, whatever it was.

It startled the women out of her attack and gave time for Gus to explain that the men were essentially bound and were no threat at the moment. They had to figure out what would be the best way to ensure they received justice for what they had done.

Allowing Gus to gently remove the wrench from her clenched fist, the woman slumped to the sand, sobbing. "The horrible things they taunted us with, and our poor daughters." She buried her head in her hands and let the fear, emotion, and uncertainty drain from her in the form of tears. Her husband came, knelt on the sand, and held her.

"When you are ready, I can show you to a place where you can get cleaned up," Gus offered, but the woman shook her head.

"We will clean up here. I'm not going anywhere with anyone, even you!" She practically screamed the last bit, making Gus feel awkward and uncertain.

He put his hands up and backed away. Her husband looked up apologetically as Gus turned to give them some privacy.

He finished lining the men up side by side on the beach and started searching them. He found what must have been the leader, who had the keys to the boat in his pocket on a small keychain with a small orange oval of foam that kind of resembled a stress-reliever. He stared at the little toy, which looked to be a flaming carrot.

It seemed so out of place among these men who, by all appearances, were monsters with no redeeming qualities. But they had their own aspirations and most likely broken dreams and lost opportunities.

I know nothing of their history, I just see the end result and make some knee-jerk judgment on how good they are. They are horrible, for sure. But they're human. Maybe they could be something more if circumstances were different. Gus reflected on his slow descent from good intentions to going with the flow as life beat him down with disappointment after disappointment.

The hypocrisy of judging others by their actions and himself by his intentions was not lost on him as he looked at the swarthy man lying in the sand before him. He pocketed the key, hoping it would buy him some time to figure out what to do with the men. The family couldn't leave without the key, and he had no idea of what to do—not yet.

Gus sat down on a dune and looked out at the ocean. The waves rolled in, carelessly beating more and more forcefully upon the shore. He would have to make a decision soon.

The women would probably not take too long to clean up, and Gus was sure the father of the family would want to leave as soon as they were done. There appeared no way to win this situation.

Things were cut and dry with the zombies, but there were negative consequences to every decision that he could think of, and the responsibility weighed on him. As he stared at the rhythmic waves, Gus suddenly smelled the scent of cotton candy as he tasted something sweet and grainy, *a pear*? Lavender dust appeared to drift on the wind currents in front of his eyes.

"What the hell? Am I having a stro—"

"It's the hybrid-Nth, trying to communicate with us," Nick interrupted. Sensations alternated between the feeling of coarse fur rubbing against his back, the hollow *tonk* of a wooden wind chime sounding, and the scent of roasted marshmallows, all combined in ways that meant nothing to Gus.

"Well, since you've already jumped in, there may be something I can finagle to help you out. The hybrid-Nth have a proposition for you, Gus. They have offered to have some of their number swap places with the Nth that are embedded throughout your system. This will free up a limited amount of Nth," Nick said haltingly, struggling to translate.

"Okay, what good would that do me?"

"The Nth could be gifted to the pirates—"

"Why would I ever do *that*!?" Gus pinched his eyes in disgust.

"Just listen. The gifted Nth would be a very limited amount, but they could enter the men's systems and work their way to their brains. By stimulating dopamine release, it may be possible to rewire the training these men have had throughout their lives, to get them to choose a better path. These Nth would also need to provide negative reinforcement through nausea and dizziness by stimulating the medulla and vestibular systems."

"Wa-wa-wait. These Nth are what give me my abilities, right? I don't know if I want to just *give* them away to these guys. No way. Besides, isn't that making the choice for them? I thought Nth weren't supposed to force people to act a certain way."

"I see you wrestling with the possibility that something happened to these men so that they do not have the normal social mores. Statistically, they most likely have been abused themselves or neglected enough that they failed to develop empathy and appropriate responses to function in healthy ways. This would provide them a functioning feedback system with which to become useful to society in some way."

Gus thought about it, and the biggest problem with jails and how society typically dealt with criminals, viewing them as irre-deemable. If they could change just that aspect of society, what could come of that? Still, he had his own dreams and ambitions with being a super. Was he being selfish? He knew the manor could fabricate more Nth, so that may not be a problem. Plus what changes would come with fusing with hybrid-Nth? Could be great or horrible.

"Why has no one done this already then? Couldn't the Nth have just made the change and helped humankind from the beginning?"

"We can't do it of our own volition, but it can be accom-plished if we are *directed* to do it. Our job is not to make the choices, but to facilitate them. We should be, at best, amoral. It is sometimes difficult with our construct's influence on our personalities weighed against the lifetimes of experience we have seen, with decisions made on countless other planets before yours. But the caveat for you is that you must give away a portion of your own Nth supply to do this. Most supers don't want to lose even a fraction of their powers."

"Can you just make more, like at the Foundry?"

"There are limits. Not to mention that fewer and fewer supers know about the Nth to begin with, so there's that as well. I think you also are unaware that there are very few locations that can synthesize Nth, among other concessions…"

"What's the catch?" Gus asked flatly, knowing from Nick's tone there would be a tradeoff.

"Two things. First, the hybrid-Nth can make the swap with your other fused Nth, but you will decrease your available Nth armor capabilities. Second, this upgrade will negate your next Nth evolution you would normally get at level twenty."

Gus' heart dropped, remembering all the amazing things that were on that list. It was, on the other hand, probably the best way to make this a win-win situation for all involved. And if he really wanted to walk his talk, it was exactly in line with where he thought he wanted to go as a super.

Gus tried to think about the future. Maybe this would be a way he could really help when he finally got to the mainland. He could stay here and level at his leisure, and get some perks when he hit levels 30 and beyond. There was no rush; he could go when he was ready.

"Make it so," Gus muttered, accepting the consequences. A stinging sensation prickled throughout his body, followed by a soreness that passed over him, then soon faded.

"Okay, touch them on the cheek."

Gus noticed his fingertip glimmered in the sunlight like he had swiped it through a broken Etch-a-Sketch. Leaving a smear on each man's cheek, the mark quickly paled as the Nth worked their way into the skin and began to do their job. Gus felt a pang of loss when they transferred from his consciousness to the men. They were not awake yet, but some were starting to stir when Gus began the transfer. Once the Nth hit their systems, they relaxed as if in deep, but comfortable, sleep.

"Now they just need time. The assimilation process will take one to two days."

Gus felt sudden fatigue go through him.

"You will be weaker for about the same amount of time. Sorry, I should've mentioned that, boss."

Gus just rolled his eyes. "I guess I'll just have to go easy on the training a bit then, no big deal."

Gus went and spoke to the father, explained the situation, and gave him the keys.

The man listened and rubbed his sore, bruised wrists. Gus could tell he just wanted to get home and get on with his life. He did feel indebted to Gus and begged that he be allowed to do something to repay him. Gus asked him simply to not tell anyone about the island and that he had protected the men.

He explained that he had made a big sacrifice to get the men to change and promised that they would confess on their own if the family would just trust Gus. Internally, Gus was not certain of that at all, but he had hopes that would be the eventual result, or would at least give them a chance.

The man nodded silently but looked at his wife, and Gus was uncertain how everything would turn out. He hoped this was a man of honor. He hoped even more that he was one as well.

In no time, they were ready and Gus loaded the men on the ship. He traded their ether ties for real ropes and gags, uncertain how soon they would encounter someone who knew how to use ether in this manner. A half-hour later they were gone.

Gus sat down and watched them sail out of sight. He stared at that spot on the horizon for a long time afterward.

Tension he hadn't realized he was holding slowly dripped away. He could have killed those men so easily. He had that power, and he had not taken the easy choice. *Or did I?* Promises he had made on how he would be different if he got powers. Deserving.

So why do I feel so empty?

———

"Alan, or Cyclone as he insisted he be called after getting his powers, did change. He would barely even talk to me, like I wasn't even his brother anymore, since I was still just a reg."

"And you didn't like that."

"Who would? But it wasn't just me. He looked at everyone who wasn't a super differently. He had this air of superiority, even the way he looked at people. I told myself I wouldn't act like that when it was my turn. Over time, it just got worse; he didn't even try to hide his feelings, and he became more and more rude. Later in life, I saw that this wasn't just something that happened to my brother; a lot of supers treat regs that way. The way the Faction has free reign in the district, it's not like supers ever get punished for anything they do. That immunity from consequences changes what a lot of people are willing to do."

Gus stared at the surf for a moment before continuing. "It happened the first week I started work as a henchman, after constant prodding from my father."

Another window opened in the corner of the display.

"Is it this memory?" Nick asked.

"No, I think it was the third day, after orientation."

The video sped forward, to that day.

———

Gus unlocked the door and let the cool air envelop him as he stepped inside. *Good. No one is home.* He dropped off his pack and helmet, then made his way to his room. He removed his belt and threw it in the corner, then peeled off the form-fitting unitard. The air conditioning felt good against his sweaty skin. He had been on patrol duty on the upper wall of the Purple Faction headquarters. It was high enough and secure enough that there was little risk of attack, but their coordinators were merciless in their drills.

While many of the other trainees grumbled at the mind-numbing work, Gus didn't mind. Occasionally, he would patrol a section of the wall high above the academy training yards. He would try to guess what abilities the small forms would use to cross the obstacle course. The instructors could generate different scenarios at will, and it was entertaining to watch. Gus could hear the faint cheering and celebration when someone pulled off an especially creative or innovative skill to solve one of the challenges.

He wasn't supposed to be distracted, but the other henchmen along the wall would snap to attention and signal him to improve his posture and stare ahead or otherwise mask his observation of the supers. The only thing that made it difficult was the heat. Gus didn't know if the helmets they wore helped or not. At least they resembled a motorcycle helmet and left the face exposed; some supers required full coverage.

They kept sweat from dripping directly from his brows, but at the end of his shift the padded lining felt totally drenched. It wouldn't take long for the heavy neoprene smell to be replaced with a different, but equally disagreeable, scent. He had been issued five outfits but only one helmet.

Heading to the bathroom, he gave the helmet a thorough rinsing and then took a quick shower. Throwing on some sweats and an old T-shirt, he put his helmet on the porch to dry in the evening sun, then relaxed on the couch. Before he could get settled and find the holo-vid remote, Alan kicked the door open. He had his arm around Tempest and they were laughing and joking.

"You should have seen the looks on their faces, it was priceless."

"What happened, Alan?" Gus sighed, a little chagrined that he hadn't had the house to himself for longer.

His brother turned on him, joviality gone. "It's Cyclone

now. Don't call me Alan." He poked Gus' chest with a finger hard enough to leave a bruise. "Got it?"

"Yeah, sure, Cyclone." Gus coughed.

"That's more like it, *lackey*. You know you're lucky you're not with Orange, or you might have had some trouble today."

"Why's that?"

"Well, yours truly just completed his first mission as a team lead. We infiltrated an Orange outpost and gathered some intel. Too bad they didn't keep any supers on hand. Some of the henchmen there got some flying lessons…"

"What?"

"The dummies tried to stand their ground instead of retreating. I mean, duh! You're standing next to a sheer cliff face with only a parapet to protect you. Against supers! What do you expect? Gus, I hope you're smarter if you ever get a posting like that. Know your place and stay out of the way, or you'll get what's coming to you."

Gus squinted and frowned a bit, looking up at his big brother.

Cyclone rolled his eyes, then held one hand up high and flat. With the other he made a little man out of his first two fingers, kicking as the hand fell then followed by a big raspberry at the end. "Get it?" he punctuated, looking at Gus expectantly.

"Y-yeah, I'll be careful," Gus replied, a bit stunned.

"See that you do. I wouldn't put it past you to lose your head in a real fight." He turned to the kitchen and strode out. "Man, I'm starving! What do we got to eat?"

Gus glanced at Tempest, who looked proudly at his older son. He turned and looked at Gus. Nothing was spoken, but Gus heard the words echo as if he'd said them again.

Well, it sounds like you learned a valuable lesson, then. Never engage a superior force, especially without the resources to defend your position.

Gus' tongue probed around the inside of his mouth that was suddenly dry and uncomfortable. Tempest nodded and followed Alan into the kitchen without a word.

———

"I think that was a big day for me, Nick. I remember how Tempest seemed fine with Cyclone acting as he did. Like it wasn't a big deal that he had just killed someone doing their job. A job that I could easily be doing! It really rocked my world. I considered getting out of it for a while after that. I spent a lot of time up on the wall that summer, looking down on those supers. Wondering what I would do when I got my opportunity. I got tested again later that year and I still wasn't a candidate." Gus shook his hands out to get blood back into them. He had been clenching his fists tighter than he had realized.

"Why did you stay?" Nick asked.

"For one thing, I didn't really know what I wanted to do. Nothing grabbed my attention, and I knew I would be in training for a bit, so I just stayed with it. It wasn't hard compared to what I could be doing. And it kept my family off my back, so it was a case of going along to get along. Around the end of that summer, I was playing online with some friends, and we got talking about work. Turned out we all had gone into henchmen jobs, and the others were surprised that I was actually doing the same thing. They suggested that we all apply for a transfer to the same unit after my basic training was over."

"So they were in training too?"

"No, they had been out for a year, and were all working together already. One of their friends had been promoted and transferred out, and then got busy so he was never online anymore. That's how they picked me up, to round out the squad after that happened. Everything went through, and we were working together in a matter of months. Being with those guys took a lot of the sting out of the work. Don't get me wrong, it sucked at times, but we had fun regardless." Gus stared at the water, interlacing his fingers as he sat there, pensive.

"You weren't worried about... the dangers of supers attacking?"

"I was at first, but you have to understand these guys. They knew how to work the system. Since none of us were shooting for a big promotion, we didn't have to take the high-risk positions which usually earned you more merit points, or danger pay. To be honest, I was glad. It was nice just to be me for a change, and let my shields down. And that they were cool with that. Drove Tempest bonkers, because I wasn't 'applying myself,' but I was happy for the first time in a while. I think it was because I began focusing on things I wanted instead of what others wanted me to be doing. Conforming to another person's expectations. After that day with Cyclone, I didn't just accept the Purple Faction mindset as undeniably true. That perhaps there was a better way."

"I hope the others see it the same way. You've committed them now, regardless."

"Yeah, I should let them know. It's only fair, right?"

CHAPTER SEVEN

Tempest

Tempest looked at the display and muttered in disbelief, "How could this happen?" Graviton should have been competent enough to protect his son. "And why did it take three weeks for this report to get to me!?"

Taking a deep breath, he released the volatile emotions that threatened to overtake him. *Always dealing with incompetence! Everything I've done and now I could have lost them both?* Through force of will, he released the tension the anger induced, activating a power that changed his physiology and lowered his blood pressure.

The same control he had built up over the years of refining his abilities had helped him learn the patience, focus, and concentration necessary to lead the Faction with stony determination. The negative impact of strong emotions was something that seemed to always compromise the other supers that he knew, regardless of level.

It was partially how he had maintained his position in the hierarchy. Anyone could challenge another in an attempt to move up the ranks, but the duels were monitored and the rules were rigid.

Tempest had avoided many challenges by maintaining a ruthless persona, resisting the desire to react to the taunts and ignorance of idiots. They probed with their transparent barbs, but nothing struck home, and Tempest revealed no weakness. Maintaining his persona constantly did get exhausting though; the ambitious were relentless. His calm allowed him to avoid snap judgments out of the anger or fear that led to losing battles.

One of the other Purple Faction leaders burst into his command center. "Were you aware that Manticorps just took out the Graviton station? Now how are we going to find what we're looking for, without the ability to scan from orbit? There's no way we can locate it! I thought your son was supposed to protect it! Isn't that why you lobbied to have him placed there? Shouldn't you have been maintaining some kind of protective barrier by using your powers?" the corpulent man bellowed, not waiting for answers.

Tempest's emotionless mask slid into place and he calmly turned from his display and looked at the batrachian intruder. "Welcome, Rampage, please make yourself at home." He folded his arms, repressing the anger he felt from the intrusion. "I just received the report as well. We are still gathering data about the attack. All we know is that the station crashed sixteen days ago. Escape pods were jettisoned from the structure, so we suspect there are some survivors. Supers are en route to the crash location to see if they can find anything, but the search radius is vast. This situation is well in hand. It is only a matter of time."

"We don't have time!" Rampage yelled, the usually innocuous gills along his neck flaring as he shouted. "If Manticorps finds it before us, they could make a play and remove *all* the Factions from power. Is *that* what you want?" Spittle flew from the red-faced man's lips as he continued his tirade, disgusting Tempest beneath his mask of composure. "We can't fight a battle on two fronts! We still have no idea who is attacking the Factions. You need to produce some results!"

Rampage finished, his enormous chest heaving as he tried to catch his breath, jowls waggling as he shook his head in disdain.

"When *we* know more, *you* will know more. Now, I'm sure the academy needs you more than I need distractions at this time. If you want results, leave me to do my work." Tempest turned, tacitly indicating that the conversation was over.

Rampage was technically subordinate to him, and he knew that dismissing him as if he were unimportant was probably the most upsetting thing he could do to the irascible super. Tempest let a smile creep onto his face as Rampage retreated, muttering frustrated epithets and insults he thought were too quiet to be heard.

Tempest reviewed the results of the search, which were discouraging, to say the least. The station's altitude magnified the search area for possible debris. Also, they only had an approximate trajectory for the escape pods, and time would have added to the scattering and dispersal effect, since they were over the Pacific Rim when the attack occurred. Most of the data was extrapolated from other satellites as all the sensors on the station were destroyed and they had not recovered any of the black-box analogues.

Purple Faction included supers with all variations of powers, but they recruited hard to specialize on forming a core of supers skilled with all types of elemental forces and effects. They were relatively weak in the Psi, or mental manipulation, department, so could not mentally scan for survivors as well as the Orange Faction could have. Neither did they use augments and technology to the extent of the Green Faction. If they did, they probably could have scanned and extrapolated the most likely search sites, saving a lot of time. Maybe he could get that computer prodigy on the task. What was her name again? Something Asian. He made a note to check.

Fortunately, Purple Faction was the only one aware of what Manticorps was looking for, and they would not let this information leak to the other Factions. The fact that Graviton was attacked must mean that their mole in that organization had been discovered, tortured, and divulged the location of the station. They had been especially active lately, after decades of inactivity, which was disturbing in light of new events.

It was Tempest's decision to maintain these infiltrators in as many organizations as possible, but it was more difficult with certain groups. Orange routinely utilized their telepaths to screen those on more sensitive missions and quickly found those who were trying to be duplicitous. Still, it had paid big dividends in the past and allowed Purple to stay strong among the three ruling Factions.

Having lost their mole, Tempest sent orders that Manticorps be monitored more than usual for the foreseeable future. While the attack could be simply retaliatory, he suspected Manticorps —rather than another Faction—was involved. They wouldn't have made such a bold move unless Graviton was getting close to finding something. If they mobilized any forces, it may be just as simple as following them. Tempest finalized more surveillance requests and went back to his monitors.

———

Aurora listened to the voice in her head, still unconvinced that she wasn't losing her mind. "I can see that I am not getting anywhere. Let's go back to the beginning. Do you remember how you first got your powers? Way before you met Auntie or Purple Faction." Aurora nodded, and the voice continued. "You were very young, so you probably missed a lot. Go back…"

Aurora's vision flared to life in the dark prison, seeing images and memories fly by, recalling days at the academy, time with Auntie, life on the streets, and back to when she was still with her mother. Aurora had walled off these painful thoughts as much as she could. Always hungry. Alone most of the time. And when her mother did come home, she was often so strung out on Silk or some other drug that she was drooling and unresponsive.

She saw that day and mentally started to cringe away. Even

closing her eyes tightly shut, she could still see the memory as if watching it on a screen.

Her mother staggered in, looking bedraggled and carrying some bags. After she crashed on the couch, Aurora—*or was she Cass?*—ran to the bags, smelling food.

There were two containers from some fancy restaurant and she tore into them, eating the contents without thought of reheating or getting utensils.

Afterward, her stomach hurt. Whether from the sudden introduction of food or the speed with which it was consumed was up for debate. All Cass could do was curl up on the ground by the couch, rubbing her cramping belly.

She must have fallen asleep because she awoke later when it had become much darker. Cass tried the lights, half knowing that there would be no power. Her mother was horrible with responsibilities. Cass lit a candle she kept for special occasions. It was one of the 'gifts' her mother brought home in the bags. She didn't know who gave them to her mother, or if she had bought them for herself. Cass wished she would just buy food, but sometimes there were useful items in the bags. More often than not it was just clothes, none of which would fit her lanky seven-year-old body.

This night was especially cold, probably because of the rain, which fell incessantly. It drummed against one of the windows, the only noise in the dark. There had been a couple times recently where it got so intense that it was noisy, and Cass, who usually loved the sound of the rain, felt unsettled. She grabbed a threadbare blanket, wrapped it around herself, and laid on the couch to cuddle close to her comatose mother, trying to share some of her warmth.

Yet there was no warmth… and her mother was always warm to the point of being hot. Cass could count on putting her perpetually cold feet by her mother or cuddling up to her when Cass had a chill or needed reassurance and warmth. This time her mother's skin was cold and clammy to the touch.

With a start, Cass scrambled off the couch as she stood evaluating her mother from afar. *Was she sick? Or worse?* Cass' stomach began to cramp up again as realization began dawning upon her. Her mother was dead. She had to be. Or was she just sick? She had never seen a dead person before.

Cass approached and poked her mother's cheek timidly and jumped away. There was no response, but that was nothing new. She tried next to lift an eyelid to see if her mother would stir. The bloodshot eye underneath stared forward, unfocused on anything.

Cass retreated, wiping her fingers on her pants vigorously, as if she could clean the touch of death off of them. Panic started to join the discomfort in her stomach.

"What now, what now?" she kept repeating, worried about her future. While her mother wasn't the best provider, Cass at least had enough to survive. Now that was all gone. Maybe she could sell some of her mother's things? But to who? If she did find someone to buy valuables, how would she know they wouldn't just cheat her?

Her mind raced and it was all too much. As she worried her fingers and slowly backed away from her mother, she eventually ended up in the corner, muttering to herself. The rest of the sleepless night was spent trying to figure out how life was going to go now that her world had changed.

"Do you remember?" the quiet voice asked.

"Please stop," Aurora sobbed, surprised that she was crying from seeing the memory.

"Not yet."

The memory continued.

. . .

When the next day began, Cass was tired, emotionally and physically. She had been staring at her mother's corpse as if it would reanimate and come to get her. She thought she saw a glint of something. Was it an earring? She could definitely sell that. It flickered again as the early morning rays streamed in, illuminating her mother on the couch with their light.

Cass tentatively crawled over and looked more closely. There was something there, but it wasn't exactly an earring. She reached out and touched it to see if she could remove the shiny silver bead, and it latched onto her fingertip. Shaking it madly, she saw her flailing caused the silver strand to stream out of her mother's ear like a long string. She waved her hand around, trying to flick it off.

Instead, the shimmering strand flowed down her hand. She attempted to pull it off with her other hand, succeeding only in transferring the mercury-like material to both of her hands. She stared at her hands as the colors played along the surface of the iridescent reflective material.

She felt pinpricks and pressure as the material began to absorb into her skin. No, that wasn't totally accurate. It *burrowed* into her skin. She could feel it crawling through her veins, cold and intrusive. Shortly after, there was a bright flash and stab of pain as the material made it to her neck, and she fell to the floor.

Her small hands felt like they were dipped in scalding water. Nothing she did would relieve the sting and it took a long time to feel normal again. She experienced intense vertigo and had to lie there, afraid to vomit up the small amount of food that she had recently been able to eat. Occasionally she would get brave and try to sit up, but the headache and vertigo would return. So she would get as comfortable as she could in the blanket and try to fall asleep.

"That was you? Why did you do that to me?" Aurora asked, viewing her young self crumpled into a ball in the memory.

"I'm... sorry. Your mother was not the best of hosts. It affected us and restricted how we could interact. We were almost feral, trying to escape, but our nature would not allow us to until your mother passed. Her self-destructive nature was deeply painful to us and all that we are. We regret how we came to you, and how excruciating the process was. We were... not gentle."

She hadn't thought about that day in years. It was a concentrated ball of horrible memories that she had pushed so far down that she never had to deal with them. Much different than the new persona she had fashioned in Aurora.

"You pushed me away when you went to the academy, and you forgot a lot of things I tried to teach you. You need to remember and learn this again, or I fear you will die here," the tiny voice said.

Aurora was conflicted. She knew she needed to escape, but all of her training told her that the voices were dangerous, a possible fracturing of her psyche that had to be overcome. That she needed help was undeniable, and she was fast approaching the point of being able to try anything.

"Okay, tell me what I need to know," she said, resigning herself to listen to the voice.

CHAPTER EIGHT

Around the Bend

Gus headed back up to the manor, deciding to go barefoot for a while. He took his time and didn't use **Dash**. The cold ocean water felt good as it washed the sand from his bare feet. He tried to plan what to do next as he walked.

He would have to find some type of defenses for the island in lieu of the bio-stasis field. But what? Even if the island had some kind of ballistic missiles, some supers could withstand and tank almost any of that type of attack. Then there were the FP costs. He doubted they would be cheap.

A plan began to form, but it would require a lot of things to fall in just the right places at the right times. Given the situation, though, it was the best he had, so no sense in overthinking it. It would all depend on the capabilities of the manor. He could refine plans based on what he found there. Eventually, he made it back and felt a little more encouraged now that he had a direction. Indecision was always one of his biggest enemies, with the motivation to start a close second.

Gus ate lunch and headed up to the control room. For the next few hours, he became immersed in the defense tab. Reading descriptions of facilities and different options to unlock, scribbling notes on FP costs, and what future capabilities would become available as he unlocked higher tiers and functionality of those facilities. The longer he stayed there, the more he realized he should have done this from the very beginning.

His previous unlocks had been a little random, and he had been fortunate to choose facilities that managed to help him. He could just as easily have unlocked something useless until he was a much higher level. Most offensive items were in the tens of thousands of FP, and wouldn't be viable for him, so he would have to get crafty with the few options available.

Every so often he would hear a high-pitched beep as he worked. It was enough to grab his attention, but so intermittent that he couldn't tell where it was, like a smoke detector with a low battery. It began to be so irritating that Gus stopped working and tried to localize the sound. It wasn't until he used his augmented hearing and found that he could localize a direction when the beep sounded again. After three more beeps he found an old console in the corner covered in dust.

On the screen he saw the message:

(1) message pending.

"Nick, what do you know about this?"

"Due to the bio-stasis shield, this communication network was never configured and connected to the system, so I did not receive any notice. Wanna have me do that now?"

"Yes, obviously. This looks pretty old," Gus said, swiping a finger across the monochrome screen, then rubbing the dust off his fingertip. "How far is the range on this thing? Can I communicate with the mainland?" he asked.

"Okay, comms are linked. You're in luck. It can relay to the mainland. You want to call home?"

"Yeah, no. Not yet. I... um, let me level up some more. I'm not quite ready for everything that calling my father would entail."

"You can't avoid him forever."

"I know. I just don't think I'm ready yet. I want to be able to stand on my own a bit before we cross paths again. He's got a very dominating personality. I don't want to give that up just yet." Gus exhaled. "Sorry for being so defensive, but I need to do this myself. For a little bit, at least."

"Understood. What about your bros? I know you miss them."

"Yeah, that'd be good. What's that message though?"

"Right. Well, time-stamp is from six days ago, looks like a couple days after the bio-stasis field went down. Here it is: 'Thank you, whoever you are. We have been looking for the manor for so long. Now that we know where you are, we will be seeing you soon to reclaim what is ours!'"

Gus' blood ran cold and his heart felt like it was being squeezed.

"You said six days, right? They could be almost here! Do you think they're supers? Of course they're supers if they know about the manor, who am I kidding?" Gus shouted in panic. "No, no, no. I'm not ready for this! Oh damn, Nick, couldn't you have told me about this before?" Gus pinched his eyes shut and rubbed his temples. "And that upgrade, that's not going to help me at all, is it?"

"Sorry, slugger. It should only work for people without Nth, as I described—"

"Hells to the bells!" Gus blurted. "I knew I shouldn't have let you talk me into that!"

"Hey now, don't pin this on me. You were stewing in your moral quandary over there and if you recall, it was the hybrid-Nth's suggestion, not mine. And just FYI, throwing me under the bus—seriously not cool."

"Sorry, sorry. You're right. It was my choice. It just sucks because I would have done things differently had I known." Gus rubbed his face, looking at the display through one eye as he tried to think. "At least I hadn't unlocked any facilities yet, thinking I had all the time in the world. Let me see what takes priority now."

Gus returned to the other console and reviewed his notes on

options and narrowed down his choices based on the new information. He wished he had more FP; there were so many cool things the manor could do if he just had the points.

He had worked out his next unlocks:

Remote Sensors: 1,500 FP.
Remote Sensors Tier 2: 2,000 FP.
Cafeteria Tier 2: 2,000 FP.
Training Arena Tier 2: 2,000 FP.
Brig: 150 FP.

First, he figured he needed an early warning on who was coming to the island. Nothing offensive was affordable, so he'd have to do the heavy lifting there for now. *Nothing's ever easy.*

Next, the ability to raise stats on the go, which the cafeteria could help with, and third, more training in disarming and disabling foes in non-lethal ways.

Am I insane for trying to defend the island with one hand tied behind my back? Any invaders would be playing for keeps and would not have any qualms about using lethal force. He had debated when he was younger about how he would do things different than his father and brother had, but was that too idealized and naive? He had seen their way of dealing with their opponents, and part of Gus rejected that unequivocally.

And finally, a place to store those who he detained, assuming he could even do that in the first place. He would have waited on this, but the cost was so small and he couldn't afford anything else on the list.

"Gus, you'll figure it out," Nick interjected into his thoughts before he was able to get too wound up. "I think you have a good plan—for now. If it's not working, we can modify it. Not everything has to be solved with force, and that may be difficult with your current level of skills, so go with what you know."

Gus turned back to the menus and focused once again on his plan. Remote sensing would allow the island, and by extension his minimap, to gather data from a certain radius around the island, a mere ten miles at level one. At tier two, however, the range would jump to one hundred miles. That would allow some time to mount a defense or get into position.

There were other offensive options to protect the island, but they were unreasonably expensive at his current level of FP. *Maybe someday,* he thought bitterly.

The brig was self-explanatory, and fortunately it was equipped with a dampening field that could interfere with Nth functioning. The only downside being that this would also affect individuals *outside* of the cells as well as those inside the cells. Not a total deal breaker, but useful to know. It would most likely be best to have any prisoners incapacitated, as he would not be able to fight back in most cases if they chose to resist. What to do with them in the future was a question for another time.

The cafeteria would offer him a way to selectively and remotely increase certain stats. With not knowing who would be visiting the island, having the ability to augment a stat or two on the fly depending on his opponent might be just the advantage he would need.

Finally, boosting the training arena's tier would allow more combat options and utilize his skills in more interconnected ways. He had just invalidated a lot of his prior training with his rash decision on a guiding principle.

Can't think that way, Gus. You've just got to modify it. You can do this. That's your preferred play-style in FPS. Just be a ghost and take them out one by one.

If he truly was going to try a non-lethal approach, he would have to get much better at stealth and surprise attacks. He had a mere 200 FP left after all was said and done. He would have to win some more battles to complete the rest of the items on the checklist, but he was done for now.

He needed to get familiar with what these new options meant for him. He focused on accessing remote sensing, but Gus did not immediately notice a change until he zoomed out his minimap, finding much more range in his outer zoom function. The island looked so tiny when put at the full range, a circle with a 200-mile diameter with the island in the center. He could even see that he was somewhere in the Pacific Ocean, but there weren't any landmarks that could give him a definitive frame of reference. There was another island close by that he hadn't even noticed, hiding off the coast behind the volcano.

At first, he was detecting birds and even aquatic mammals who had surfaced briefly for air. He had the system filter out these inputs. He tried his new *Psi-bond* skill which allowed him to modify his display and minimap to sense Nth, and he saw only a green dot centered on the island. This cleared the minimap of any other inputs that were not a threat to him on the island.

"Nick, can we remotely close any outside access to the manor?"

"There are storm doors that can shield the windows, and I can drop the bulkhead again."

"Let's do it. I doubt it will do much, but every little bit should help."

That finished, he decided to tour the brig so that he would be able to access it quickly and intuitively. The quicker he could move any invaders into a cell, the less likely he would have another battle on his hands. Especially one waged without powers.

Given the total size of the manor, Methiochos must have been expecting some resistance or need for discipline, as there were over fifty cells in the large facility. The cells themselves had matte black walls, with ivory floors, illuminated from below so they glowed. There was a large, clear window in front of each cell that had to be made of transparent plastisteel. It left no real room for privacy or clandestine escape attempts.

There was a gated slot where food could be transferred from one side to the other, that always maintained one side separated from the cell. Gus wondered if some supers could stretch through a simple slit, or morph into some kind of gas. Come to think of it, Mercurio from the space station battle probably could have worked his way out if the slot was the standard flap like a mail slot. Gus imagined him stretching his body, feeding it through the small opening to reform himself on the other side. If he could even manage to shift with the dampening field, that was.

Perhaps that was why the field encompassed the entire prison. To prevent effects outside the cells from damaging or opening the door, or breaking the windows. Gus felt reassured that if he managed to catch a couple supers, they could be contained here.

He tried to talk to Nick and heard nothing; the silence was more eerie than he would have expected. He would have to ask how Nick perceived the experience on his end while Gus was in the brig.

Paying attention to his body, he felt… average. He jumped and tried a kata and found himself much less smooth and coordinated. Apparently, even the stat boosts provided by Nth were dulled here, or maybe they were totally inactivated. He attempted to fashion an ether weave and it was similarly nonresponsive.

He walked closer to the exit, feeling his perception and ability to affect the ether get more and more tangible as he reached the elevator door to exit the brig. He entered the lift, yet while the doors were open, he still couldn't access his abilities. They were a hair's breadth out of reach, and felt oddly slippery. It was unsettling to say the least.

He pushed the button to his suite, and the elevator shifted into motion. Only when it left the brig did his powers return slowly, like a flashlight with low batteries. With some distance, his Nth began to reassert themselves.

Getting an idea, he pushed the button to stop the elevator on the brig level again to test something. He made an ether weave, as if he was securing someone and then returned to the brig. As expected, once the doors opened, his control over the weave relaxed, and it fizzled and shrank away like a balloon did when inflated and released. He would have to drag people to cells, which would be more of a hassle than he'd have liked—but good to know now rather than later.

From this perspective in the elevator, Gus looked up and saw a guard control room above all the cells that had evaded his attention before. Since the roof of the cells was made of the same transparent material, prisoners could be monitored from there as well. He should check that out later, he decided, and made his way out of the manor's prison.

It felt unnatural to be without his powers again, and some primal instinct just needed him to be out of there.

CHAPTER NINE

You're My Best Friend

Nick let out a nauseous groan. "I do *not* like that place."

"I was going to ask what was it like."

"Kind of like limbo, except that you're constantly spinning and dropping. I didn't think I could feel this bad without at least getting the benefits of making some poor decisions. Do me a favor, and be quick about it when you have to go in there."

"Sure thing."

Nick continued to moan, his wailing increasing in intensity.

"Okay, I get it already." Gus decided to change the subject. "Remember that comm center we just turned on? I think I do want to send a message. Can you walk me through it?"

"You should be able to call anyone with a normal connection, provided you know their number. Anywhere you would be able to reach by phone should be accessible."

Gus nodded and hit the button to the floor with the control center. *Who should I call? Who do I miss the most?* That was easy—his close friends. As the elevator opened on the control center, he eagerly approached the panel Nick indicated. He tried calling his friend Jim. He was the most responsible of the group, and would probably know how everyone else was doing. Unfortunately, Gus only received a 'voicemail box is full' message. He tried Dave next and the call connected.

"Hello?" the familiar, but sleepy, voice came across the line.

"Dave! It's Gus."

"Gus? Brotha man!" The gravelly voice that reminded Gus of Spicoli from *Fast Times at Ridgemont High* seemed more awake now.

"...like no otha' man!" Gus finished, elated to hear his friend.

"I heard you died! The space station attack was all over the holonet. They are playing it like it was an act of terrorism, and Purple Faction is on the warpath like a kicked anthill. According to the reports though, like no one survived..."

"I'm not sure anyone else did, to be honest. I got lucky and was right by an escape pod when everything went down. It was an attack by supers though, and I know Graviton is probably dead, from what I saw."

"Intense, man. Damn, it's good to hear from you. So where are you now? It's been a crazy couple months since we last talked; how was the station? Kinda sucked that you weren't able to call or nothing."

"It was lame, I didn't know anyone, and I was usually pulling custodial. Was probably rigged," Gus said bitterly, remembering how new members to the crew were usually treated until they were accepted.

"Yeah, it sucks if you're the new guy. The job we all took tanked soon after we started, so everyone came home early and we're all still looking for work. Oh damn, you don't know, do you? Jim's been in a car crash and is in a coma now!" Dave revealed, obviously shaken.

"What the hell?" Gus leaned forward to the screen.

"Yeah, someone ran into him and he's still in the hospital. His dad has been there almost every day, but there's been no change. I went to see him and he looked bad, dude. He's all purple and beat to hell. I guess he's at one of the premier hospitals though, so if anyone can do something for him, it'll be there. He's still in some special ICU wing."

"Dang, I leave you guys alone for a couple months and things go to hell. You think he's going to be okay?" Gus asked, still in shock.

"He's stable. Luckily, there were no internal injuries that were severe, but it's anyone's guess in terms of how long he'll be in a coma. I asked one of the nurses and she tried to be convincing and tell me everything will turn out okay, but I checked online and it said the longer he's out, the lower his chances are."

"Harsh. Man, that sucks. What about Chuck? Is he okay?"

"I dunno, we haven't been in touch as much lately. I've kind of been going through some things right now, so I haven't been as social as I usually am. Anyway. What's been going on with you? Are you home?" Dave asked hurriedly, switching the topic.

Dave was usually laid back with his surfer attitude. Gus wondered if something had happened between him and Chuck or if it was his personal stuff that was making him feel uncomfortable.

Gus didn't know where to start, but he started telling the whole story. At first, he was a little afraid that it would freak Dave out, but he really needed to confide in someone and the story kept spilling out. He had to jump back at times, adding things that he had forgotten. After about thirty minutes, he waited for Dave to respond. He was a little worried—no, a *lot* worried—that it would change things between him and his friends. "Well, what are you thinking?"

"*That. Is. Epic!* Congrats, dude! Wow, man, that is so flipping cool! That is huge! I do have one problem, though, and don't take this the wrong way. I love you as a brother, man, but what you did with those pirates? That was stupid. One thing I know: Regardless of who you are, you make your choices in life. Those pirates decided to be like that. Regardless of how tough their life or upbringing was, that's no excuse. No offense, but why weaken yourself when you already have the odds stacked against you? Plus, on top of it, you wasted your next upgrade or whatever? Yikes, dude. I think being alone on that island has affected your judgement."

"I only realized after that point that someone was en route to the island. I wouldn't have done it otherwise," Gus tried to defend himself.

"I mean, I get it, but *lots* of people have it hard and they don't do those types of things. *Lots* of people are abused and break the cycle. I know you want to be the good guy, but you can't save everybody. Especially *rapist pirates!* Who have you possibly endangered by saving those guys? You've gotta think about those things now too, man."

Gus sat there, silent as the truth bomb exploded right in his face. After a long while he responded, "I don't know, Dave. Maybe I was caught up in second chances, since I've felt like I've gotten a second chance with this whole superpower thing. Part of me feels like I should act differently now that things are different. I used to dream about this happening."

"Well, you were always the one with the most potential, having supers in your family and all," Dave said.

"You remember how our bosses usually acted. Like we were disposable to them. Even my brother changed after just a little while with powers. I don't want to be that kind of person, powers or not."

"I guess I get that. But real talk, here. Don't be a dumbass. Life is not a comic book. Get hard and get hard now. Don't be so noble you get your ass handed to you."

"Get hard, huh?"

"You know what I mean. I'm going to be pissed if you get yourself killed out there. Promise me that if anyone comes at you down there, just like those pirates—they've made their choice. You use that **Leech** power and rip and erase any power or ability they've got. Neuter anyone who has the balls to step foot on the island. Get strong and kick some ass! Will you promise me that?"

Gus sighed; he was often very good at making bad decisions

that seemed right at the time. Half the things he had done were so dumb when you looked at the big picture. He thought he was getting the hang of this super thing, but Dave was right. This was war. The time for pussy-footing around and being a nice guy was over.

"Yeah, I think I can do that."

"I hate to go medieval on you, man, but I love ya, and you need to know when you're being an idiot. Hell, I wouldn't be in the place I'm in if someone would've called me on my crap a long time ago."

Gus quirked his head. Something was definitely up with Dave.

"Now you have someone to run this stuff by if you need another point of view. Are we cool?" Dave asked.

"Yeah, we're cool. Thanks." Gus bit his lip, wondering if he should broach the topic. As he was about to get enough courage to ask, Dave continued, taking the opportunity away.

"Since we're talking about uncomfortable, awkward situations, how has your dad reacted? Was he stoked?"

"Actually, I haven't told him. You're the first person who I've talked to since this whole thing has happened. I'm still on the island, and don't have a way to get back just yet. I'm sure as I work on my **Basic Flight** skill that will change but, like I explained, there are a lot of people who want this manor. I'm going to have to defend it, and I don't know if I really want to have my father's help or the strings that will come along with that. Especially if Purple Faction is involved."

"You might have to, depending on what they throw at you. Half of something is better than nothing. Don't let your ego get in the way. I guess it's easy for me to sit back and be an armchair quarterback, though."

There was an awkward pause, and Gus rushed to fill it. "Dave, I'm so glad I got to talk with you again. We'll have to keep in touch more. Being isolated on this island was good at first, with my whole introverted thing, but it can wear on you too. I thought about you guys a lot. It kind of brought out some things, and made me reevaluate how I have been living my life. I'm sorry if I've been distant or standoffish in the past. It wasn't that I didn't want to hang out, I just have always been pretty protective of my 'me time.'"

"Hey, no problems. I think we all understand. I don't think anyone was offended or anything. I get that way too sometimes, but probably not to the same extent or for the same reasons. We dragged you along because we knew you needed to get out sometimes. I think we all need that support, sometimes. I'll admit I miss having the gang all together as well. We've kind of been split up and with Jim's accident, things have just been weird. We all thought you were dead too, so that was the start of it all. Then Jim's accident and then my personal stuff."

Seeing his opportunity, Gus asked, "How have you been doing, man? Everything alright?"

"I guess I might as well tell you, but I've been fighting with some alcohol stuff and recently got into some trouble. It's super embarrassing, and I hate to admit it to you, but I can't keep pretending that it's not something that's screwing up my life. If you try to reach me and I'm not available, then don't think I'm dogging you, man."

"What do you mean?" Gus asked, concerned at the sudden shift to a serious tone. Dave was *never* serious.

"I have a court date next week, and it could be bad. I may not be available to talk for a while. It's all up in the air, and it kind of sucks, but I keep telling myself that things happen for a reason, right?"

"That's heavy, dude. I feel guilty that I wasn't there for you. I've had to deal with depression issues in the past, myself. What's your story? What happened?"

"Well, long story short, I had a bit too much to drink and I got into an accident. Luckily, no one was hurt, but I got taken in and charged. No excuse for it. I was over the limit, and the enforcers caught me red-handed. Just trying to keep a positive outlook, because I don't know how this is going to go. The magistrate said that I might have to serve a new type of rehabilitation punishment, to see if they can help others conquer 'aberrant behaviors.' It was a bit creepy, since magistrates can read your mind and all and it's *not* the greatest sensation. But maybe she saw something good in there as well, so hopefully the sentence won't be too severe. To be honest, I've been struggling with some things for a while, but have kept them to myself."

Dave was always the life of the party, joking and keeping everyone entertained. Gus thought back and realized that he had no idea that Dave was struggling with anything.

Have I been so caught up in my own drama that I couldn't see that anyone else needed anything?

He'd have to get better at improving his awareness of others. Especially those who meant a lot to him. If he couldn't do that, how did he expect to be this great hero? He was 'saving' psychopaths, and not there for his friends. Not a great start.

"Sorry for killing the mood, man. We can talk about something else if you want."

"No, it's not you, I was just thinking. Hey—if I was too into my own stuff to not be there for you, I want to apologize, man. I had no idea, but I feel like I should have."

"Don't blame yourself, Gus. It's something that I thought I had a handle on, and it turns out I didn't. Just stupid of me trying to hide from my problems, knowing what I know. It's a stupid pride thing, but I didn't want you guys to think less of me. Sometimes life pours it on though, and even though you know better, you betray yourself. At least that's how it is for me. Everything happened at once, I got really down and fell back to old patterns. I'm just glad you guys haven't seen me at my worst."

"I don't think any less of you, Dave. You know that, right? I doubt any of the rest of us feel any differently than I do, either. And while I probably have been a little checked-out and into my own thing in the past, I'm putting all my crap on hold if you need something. Got it?"

"You're gonna make me all weepy," Dave mockingly sobbed.

"I'm serious, man. You know all the drama I've had with my dad. Some of what I've gone through on the island was crap, but it helped me grow up, at least a little. At times I acted like a little bitch, and I see that now. My perspective is a little different, and hopefully, you get that my bros are a priority now more than ever. All of you have been a rock for me and carried me in the past, when you probably didn't know what I was going through. Some days I was more down than you knew, down on myself, upset from something that happened with my father or brother, and just being around the gang boosted me and made me forget all the garbage. In hindsight, it probably wasn't even that significant, but it was to me, and you guys were there. So thanks."

"No problem. I should have trusted you guys more; I think I had convinced myself that I didn't need help. Or that asking would come off as weak, somehow. Too late to worry about the past though, amirite? If things work out for me legally, then I'm going to be calling you on your promise. Don't get too busy saving the world. I won't lie, I'll probably be a damn pest about it, too."

"Bring it," Gus said, laughing.

"Well, what do we talk about now that we've aired our dirty laundry?" Dave asked, his voice returning to its typical jovial quality.

"Well, I'm going to need some eyes and ears back home to figure out what threats I can expect. I don't know who is coming or the scope of what I'm dealing with. Can you look up anything you can find out about a guy named Methiochos?"

"How do you spell that?"

"M-E-T-H-I-O-C-H-O-S."

"Okay, but why? Isn't that the guy you beat?"

"Yeah, but that message said that they were going to 'reclaim what was theirs.' That makes me think that he must have stolen it from someone else. I'd like to know a little bit more about who that could be, if I could. It might help me better prepare. If you find him, see if there's anything about the manor, who built it, and what its capabilities are. There might be nothing, since it seems like great lengths were taken to keep it secret."

"Got it. That it?" Dave replied, obviously scribbling things down.

"Any idea how my dad is doing?"

"Sorry, can't say that I do. He hasn't reached out to us or anything."

"Well, I can't say that I'm surprised," Gus grumbled.

"Yeah, I'll bet you're probably used to it by now. Still sucks though."

"Alright, when is a good time to call you back? I don't even know what day of the week it is."

"Must be nice on your tropical getaway. It's Thursday, fool."

"Okay, I'll call you next Thursday, around this time. Cool?"

"Yeah, totally, totes magoats."

"Later, bro. Good talking with you," Gus replied, laughing.

"Catch ya later. I'll try to see what Chuck has been up to, he could help. Good talk."

Gus clicked off the connection and sat there with a stupid smile on his face. Even hearing Dave's bad news and being reamed by him for his own idiocy, it was good to talk to him again. Maybe he could even do something to help him out when he made it back to the mainland.

Gus reached for the keyboard, about to contact his dad, but thought better of it. *Maybe later.* He didn't want to spoil the feeling he had right now. No bad vibes. At least for a while.

CHAPTER TEN

Incredibad

"Basileus, you will be in charge. Anyone who ignores his orders will be terminated... in every sense of the word. Understand?" The group of supers nodded their agreement to the orders. Archon turned and headed up the lift surrounded by his entourage of bodyguards.

Basileus looked at the motley group of mostly Factionless mercenaries that were willing to go on the mission. Manticorps did not have the reputation it once had, nor did it have the same financial clout either. His father, the founder of Manticorps, had found some resources though.

Somehow Archon had managed to gather more candidates than expected. No doubt he was expecting some to not make it, so their contracts wouldn't have to be paid. Surprising how many mercs didn't insist on a clause in their contracts that would require payment to another in case of their demise. If they weren't that savvy, it certainly wasn't his business.

Finally, he was going to clean up this mess. He had botched the job all those years ago, and though his father didn't know about his involvement, he was concerned about what would happen if he found out. Archon was all about results, and he didn't care about good intentions if you couldn't deliver on your promises—even for flesh and blood.

There was still a lot Basileus didn't know about the Traitor. Methiochos shouldn't have been able to get the shield up if everything had gone to plan. He knew he should've gone himself, but Annie said she could do it. Part of him refused to admit his cowardice in allowing her to go instead, but he had a legacy to uphold. With her powers, she would always be support staff, probably in HR. He had to think about carrying on his father's legacy and the company. The familiar justification made him feel only slightly less guilty and even angrier. Since then, he had rarely failed. In fact, he knew the exact number: thirty-four times. Not bad for almost five decades, but they had taught him much.

He thinks he's not a failure! a voice said in his head, followed by a chorus of laughter.

Shut up, all of you. You all are failures! Basileus pushed his eyes closed and hit his temples ferociously with balled-up fists. Bit by bit, he distanced the heckling voices until they were imperceptible. He wiped away an errant drop of blood trickling down the side of his face. They were gone. He rubbed the copper-scented drop on his fingertips, feeling it get sticky as it dried.

Basileus was used to succeeding at whatever he tried. He overcame, often by sheer effort of will. But his failure with the nano-virus was both a mystery and evidence of his fallibility. And that could not stand. He would get the island back and the manor with it. He didn't care what Methiochos managed to achieve in the decades he had been on the island. Basileus had been tireless in his preparation as well and knew that the isolation would also put restraints on the Traitor and his crew. He had no doubt they weren't as well off as Archon believed. He would take everything back and then his father would never have to know.

He was under strict orders not to waste those under his charge, as there would be no replacements. They didn't need to know that, though. Basileus could make the calls on the mission but, ultimately, he was responsible for its success or failure. If he could pull this off, not only would he redeem himself in his own eyes, but his father would hand over the reins to Manticorps.

A new Manticorps with the resources to make them an unstoppable powerhouse. Then the retribution for all those who refused to help them or who were conveniently 'busy' when his father and Manticorps were in need. Basileus knew them all. And they would be repaid for their indifference, with interest.

The plan was to send his scouts out first. They would stealth in, gather intel on the situation, and return so they could plan their assault. What they found would determine if they made a large push or relied on planning and tactics. He excelled at any form of strategy, and almost welcomed the challenge.

He hoped Methiochos would struggle. Despite his healing abilities, the Traitor would be older and weaker by now. He wondered if he would recognize Basileus.

Only two of the mercs had stealth abilities, but they were also fliers which made things more convenient for him. They could go in alone and didn't need anyone to ferry them to the island and back.

They had extrapolated the location of the island from the beacon placed on Methiochos' ship all those years ago. Annie had gotten that right, at least, and the fact that it was still working after all this time was a miracle in itself. As soon as they had confirmation of the island, they would destroy the beacon to keep the island's location all to themselves. If one of the Factions found out, Manticorps wouldn't be able to compete with the sheer volume of resources they would throw at the island and their golden opportunity would have been lost.

Basileus thought they would obtain more intel from the space station assault as well as from their prisoner. Something must have worked though, because the wall came down just a little after the station. He'd had to kill Graviton in the process but, fortunately, there was no record connecting Manticorps to the attack, so they were in the clear as long as that stayed true. That meant Aurora would eventually have to go.

Such a waste. She was pretty, but when Manticorps rose from the ashes, he would have his pick of women. He was sure of that. Still, killing her was less ideal than turning her. She was unusually resilient though. He had done enough interrogations and torture sessions to see who would change and who would cling on to the bitter end. Aurora was a bitter-ender. She had really offered no useful intel about the island or the manor. Basileus was astonished that someone in her position would have no knowledge about their mission, but it could have been a brilliant move by Purple Faction.

He would deal with her before they left. And he would deal with it himself this time. He would be getting his hands dirty a lot in the near future if things went to plan. Showing his resolve would be an example for those who would follow. After he finished, they could set off and finally end this fiasco.

———

"Aurora! You need to focus!" the voice said with desperation.

"I'm trying, dammit!" Aurora gasped. She had always used her hands as a focus for her power. The voice had told her that was just a bad habit she had to break her mind of believing. She could project her powers anywhere around her; she didn't even need physical contact.

"You can free yourself if you just do this one thing. Project your power into one spot. I know you can't see the chains that are holding you, but you don't need to. Trust me!"

Aurora tried again, but the concept was fuzzy. When she tried to wrap her head around what the voice kept telling her, she just couldn't get it to work. There wasn't anything in front of her, so she couldn't really practice the skill on anything else.

"Stop worrying you'll accidentally hit your hand or arm. You're hesitating, and it's affecting your concentration and power buildup."

A door creaked open and bright light spilled into the chamber. "Let me finish up here, first. Yeah, she doesn't know anything. I won't be long, but we can't have any loose ends," a man framed in the doorway said, touching his ear and talking on a comm.

Aurora's heart froze. *Too late.*

CHAPTER ELEVEN

Jailbreak

Boots made loud clops on the floor as they approached, and Aurora held her breath. The high-pitched trill of a communicator went off. "Yes, sir. But I think that I should—" A pregnant pause. "No, I'm not second-guessing you— It would be wise to — Understood. We will get underway immediately." Angry muttering could be heard as the boots stomped back to the door and slammed it behind the figure as he left.

Aurora exhaled deeply from holding her breath. "You have no more time, if not him than someone else." Aurora pushed harder than before, spurred on by desperation.

"Good, good! Now move that focus left... there!" Aurora could see sparks occasionally pop overhead and the flickering light as she compressed her skill into a small area and held it. She usually used her skill as an area-of-effect attack, and it was so difficult to focus her power in this way.

At last, the chain gave way and one arm was free. She spun around and relieved the ever-present tension on her sore body. It was much easier to focus on the chain now that she could see it and she burned through the other side and lay on the cold cobbles, letting her back and shoulders rest.

The large rubber material that covered her hands bounced and came to a rest as her shoulders protested. Tilting her head to the side, she saw they were not as large as she had initially expected. Both were the size of soccer balls, but they were still heavy to lift. She tried to hit them against the floor and wall, but they were perfectly spherical and simply bounced.

Now that she was partially free, hope sprang back and with it just a bit of anger. She tried releasing energy directly into the rubber around her hands and felt no change in the material. This made her even more frustrated and she poured more MP into the skill, focusing on her right hand and the ball of rubber around it. The air around the ball began to ionize into plasma and she compressed the field to degrade the rubber.

She could feel the sulfur atoms in the material and attacked them, ripping electrons away. As it became oxidized and the cross-links began to fail, the material began to lose its cohesion. The outer surface began to crack and the furrows began to run together like clay in a desert riverbed, and still she pushed. When her MP was nearly expended, she slammed the ball against the ground and the material gave up.

It shattered into pieces, and Aurora dropped the T-bar handle her hand had been clutching. It fell with the chain that used to attach it to the wall as Aurora flexed her hand, sweaty, numb, and cramped for being forced in the same position for who knew how long.

With her other hand free, the remaining ball was quickly destroyed after her MP recharged. Getting to her feet, she felt like a fawn just after birth, wobbly and uncertain. Inside though, she felt like molten lava. She had been overpowered on the station, but three on one really wasn't a fair fight. She wasn't going to let them have another opportunity to get the drop on her.

She made her way to the door, her strength returning quicker than expected. After checking to see if it was clear, she snuck out. The area was conspicuously empty. Heading up two floors, she found a supply closet and ducked inside as someone approached. She subdued the man as he passed, who turned out to not be a super at all. She donned his jumpsuit and helmet, leaving him bound in the closet, tucking her hair up into the helmet as she exited.

Seeing another group of men carrying supplies, she followed them to a large troop transport. Taking a risk, she jogged up to them and offered to carry a crate that was sliding out of an overburdened worker's grip as they loaded it aboard. He nodded briefly and grunted as he tried to reorient his load. She followed and stacked the crate with the others.

As the men filed off to grab another load, she hung back and, instead of heading down the ramp, made an abrupt turn and hid behind some other crates. When the coast was clear, she made her way to an access panel and sealed herself inside. This was a standard C-type transport, and they were similar to what Purple Faction used to utilize. She waited until the ship began to lift-off, indicating that they were underway.

One of her specialties in the academy was working on transports, mostly because she was so skinny that she could fit in the tight accessways and fix things. Like any organization, you could wait for the work order to get through the bureaucracy, but it was almost always easier to get things done yourself. She stretched out in the narrow passageway, glad to be finally free of the chains, and massaged her hands and shoulders, rotating them to relieve them. The warmth of the duct got to her, and she drifted to sleep, thinking about the academy again.

———

Aurora looked at the man in the purple jumpsuit and was ready to bolt. "I saw what you just did there, young miss, and I'll admit I'm impressed. What would ye think about coming to train at Purple Faction Academy?" he asked, his voice thick with an accent. Not quite French—Belgian, maybe?

Aurora had heard things about the academy but it didn't seem real. That was for important people. The difference between regs and supers was a huge divide. And among regs, she was the lowest of the unspoken caste system that had developed post-supers.

No, it was too good to be true. This guy had to have some ulterior motive. *I'm not going to escape from those creeps just to jump into the arms of this one.* "I'll have to think about it," she said noncommittally.

The man laughed slightly and reached into a pocket, pulling out a card and a purple token. "Well, if you change your mind, go to this address and show the token. It was nice to meet you. Stay safe out there." He waved goodbye, spun on his heel, and walked away.

Aurora stood there, watching him go, anticipating him waiting for her but he joined the stream of pedestrians at the end of the alley and was gone. The card was a shimmering purple color and just had a single address on it. The chip was thick and had something embedded within; she could see some sort of electronics or wires through a translucent window in the center of the token as she held it up to the light.

Pocketing both, she made her way back to the main street. She was in a nicer part of town, and many people she asked for directions either didn't know anything about the part of town where she lived or outright ignored her, suspecting she would pickpocket them or beg for money. She must have been grimy and dirty, and the thought embarrassed her.

Eventually, she began to ask for directions to a couple landmarks, and she was able to make it back to the small shack she called home about an hour before sundown. She was mentally exhausted as she tried to open the door, finding it locked.

Knocking loudly, she yelled, "C'mon, Auntie, it's been a rough day. What gives?" She shook the door, and after yelling louder and louder, the neighbor Mr. Kim poked his head out of the window above next door.

"What are you doing here? She left a couple hours ago."

"What do you mean she left?"

"She said she doesn't need you anymore. Told us to tell you to find a new home."

"Huh?" she asked, shocked. She had been helping Auntie learn English, and she had become much better in the last four years, but she never anticipated this. "What about my stuff?"

Mr. Kim just shrugged and leaned back in, closing the window.

Reeling from the situation, she sat on the front steps of her former home and started to cry. *Life sucks.* Cass knew very well that it wasn't safe to be on the streets late at night in these parts, and it was getting dark. Pent up emotions from the near escape earlier crashed against the new anger and hurt from Auntie abandoning her. Cast off just like trash.

Is everyone going to leave me? First Mom, now Auntie? She swiped the tears away but they kept coming, then her nose started to run and she reached into her pocket looking for a tissue, but found only the card and token.

Balling her other hand in a fist, she stood and walked back to the main street, making her way to the academy, choking back her sobs.

Aurora frowned and groaned a bit, then rolled over in the dusty duct, and slept even harder, the dream fading away.

CHAPTER TWELVE

Still Alive

Gus got the alert early in the morning before the sun was up. His minimap showed two flashing yellow stars. Gus had set up the alerts so they would flash more and more quickly the closer they got to the island, until they would remain solid when they were ten miles or less away. The color of the stars would also shift to red the closer they were to his location, giving a quick heads up on proximity. Gus quickly got ready, grabbed Jet and an energy bar, and headed out.

Both the boat from earlier and this new approach had come from this same direction. Gus' plan would be to evaluate from a safe distance and try to discover what their powers were. Gus asked Nick to check the quantum server to see if there was any information there but was told that Nth often would not record things like weaknesses, in order to protect their host. After the host died, this type of information was recorded and transferred for all to see. Gus had no idea how many or what types of supers to expect, and his lack of preparation and abilities seemed daunting. Still, he had his ace in the hole.

Gus was counting on using his untested **Leech** ability to see if he could gain some new abilities and disable the attackers long enough to get them to the brig. Eventually, he would have to figure out what to do with them, but it was his best work-around for the time being.

He made it to the beach and took out his energy bar, hiding in the leafy bushes nearby. His stomach was in knots, and after a couple bites, it was hard to tell how much was anxiety and how much was due to the stale, sawdust-like concoction. *The life of a super. So glamorous.* He licked his teeth, trying to remove the residue the dry bar left.

Gus could see the two supers approaching through **Psibond** as the sun crested the horizon. They looked like the projections in the training arena, as he could only see the web of Nth scattered through their bodies, moving like red constellations in the brightening sky. As they approached the beach, Gus saw that the rest of their bodies were not only translucent, they were invisible as they moved from place to place. Gus saw no *Predator*-esque warping of the space as they passed through it to hint where they were.

Rather than totally settling on the sand of the beach, they continued to hover, a foot off the ground, to maintain their stealth. Mentally, Gus asked Nick if he could extrapolate and put a skin on the figures so that it would be more readily apparent where they were looking and what they were doing. A mannequin-like appearance formed over the wispy Nth framework and Gus could tell that one super was male, the other female. Their hand signals became more apparent as well, but Gus could not decipher their gestures.

Silently, they glided towards the manor but stopped just short of the grass. The bigger super pointed at two tiny emitters that Gus had never noticed before. They must have been some kind of proximity detector that would wake the manor interface. They floated even higher, skirting the range of the sensor. From here, one broke off towards the front door and the other explored the patio.

They joined back up and the one from the door shook her head. Then they took up positions above the shady patio, making sure that the sun would not cast visible shadows, and waited. It was almost entertaining to watch until Gus remembered they were waiting for *him*. He had no idea of the extent of their abilities, but worked out what he was going to try, and hoped it wouldn't get him captured or killed immediately.

Gus skirted the manor, staying out of the line of sight of the super-stakeout and headed to the jungle to access the manor remotely. Moving so slowly it was almost painful, he took care not to arouse their suspicions until he had made it to the clearing and onto the path.

Luckily, the birds and animals in the nearby forest were chittering, warbling and carrying on in the early dawn. Only once he was sure the ambient noise would mask his movements did he run back to the tunnel entryway. From there, he returned through the tunnels using *Dash*.

Gus found the same room he had used to attack the zombies en masse. With care, the large door to the balcony slid silently open. Peeking outside, Gus could see the two supers below, perched on the edge of the roof like creepy mannequin gargoyles.

The *Leech* skill description had no clear definition of proximity or physical contact, but his gut told him the closer the better. He also didn't know how well it would work against two combatants simultaneously. No cooldown was mentioned, but he was working on guesswork until he tried it.

He was getting used to life being complicated though, so he forged ahead on his plan. He assumed one or both had a cloaking or camouflage ability, and they both seemed to fly pretty well. So Gus was going to attempt to *Leech* these abilities if he could.

He climbed up on the balcony and prepared to jump. The plan was to grab them from behind and activate *Leech*, but that was not what happened. As he crashed into the two bodies, the roof—which was merely a sturdy pergola with clay shingles—did not support his two-story fall along with the weight of the other supers. They all fell in a heap of orange dust, broken wooden lattice, and the clunks of breaking terra-cotta shingles.

Gus reached out and touched both of the supers before anyone got their bearings, while they all scrambled and struggled to get to their feet. Gus found that both supers had a camouflage ability, and he activated the first prompt of his **Leech** skill. As he quickly chose these, a yellow bar filled along the bottom of his display. He added advanced flight which overfilled the bar, turning it to red and it pulsated in warning.

The larger super gave Gus a hard backhand that glanced off the side of his head.

Gus struggled to hold on as he tried to manage his display, reeling a little. He found he could adjust how much of the flight skill he could absorb and quickly adjusted the slider down until it fit within the field at the bottom of his display, turning yellow again. **Leech** had its limits; he couldn't just copy everything.

The man growled and Gus barely held on as the man threw off a large section of lattice, freeing himself to fight.

You have chosen to leech **Camouflage (Level 21)**.
You have chosen to leech **Phase-Shift (Level 18)**.
You have chosen to leech **Advanced Flight (Level 3) [Adjusted from 24]**.
You have chosen to leech **Vivid (Level 12)**.
You have chosen to copy and erase skills, are you sure? (Y/N?)

As Gus was about to move to the next prompt, a sharp elbow to the groin from the other super distracted him and he selected yes before collapsing to the ground. The invaders spasmed on the ground like they were having seizures or being tased.

Gus rolled on the ground with his attackers as disabled as they were. When the process was finished, the supers laid there prone and unconscious. Gus had to lay beside them in the fetal position until the pain subsided. Soon, however, a sensation almost identical to leveling up intensified. The pain thankfully subsided and he let his hands drop off of them. A notice popped up on Gus' display:

You have unlocked the skill **Camouflage (Level 5).**
You have unlocked the skill **Phase-Shift (Level 4).**
You have unlocked the skill **Advanced Flight (Level 1).**
You have unlocked the skill **Vivid (Level 4).**
Please note that full functionality will not be available until skills are consolidated during your normal sleep cycle. Levels scaled to your individual limits based on core stats. Victims of **Leech** *will remain unconscious in proportion to the invasiveness and extent of the extraction process. Even after regaining physical consciousness, their Nth will be inactivated completely for an indeterminate time span.*
Congratulations! You have subdued (2) opponents trespassing on privately-owned territory.
2,000 XP (1,000 x 2) awarded for non-lethal methods.
1,000 FP (500 x 2) awarded.
LEVEL UP! Congratulations, Level 15 reached!
You have (20) additional stat points to assign.
12,260 XP to level 16.

At first, Gus felt guilty for copying and erasing the skills, but he had not known what to expect from using **Leech**, and the low-blow hadn't helped. It was a snap judgment to end the fight, and he would have rather made their powers inactive for a while. Dave's words echoed in his thoughts and he felt his guilt evaporate. They had made their choice. This was going to be hard enough as it was. Who knew how many more of these jokers there were waiting in the wings?

He took a moment and, using **Ether Weaving**, cobbled together some ether stretchers and took the supers to the brig inside. Without their powers active, Gus saw a middle-aged man, balding and starting to get gray hair around the edges. The woman appeared to be a gymnast, svelte and sharp-looking in her angular costume. Thin plates either served as armor or to make her more aerodynamic when she flew.

As the stretcher fizzled out at the lift, he had to hold the super under the arms and drag her by walking backward. He left the man in the doorway of the elevator to keep it from leaving—that was the last thing he needed, the elevator taking him away and having the super wake up with free reign of the manor.

He leaned the woman against a wall and went back for her partner. The man was much heavier when Gus began to drag him into the brig. The unsettling feeling of his Nth's effects on his strength became even more evident the further he tried to wrench the man, and he felt the strain on his lower back for the first time since coming to the island.

He had planned on putting the supers far in the back, but the combination of muscle strain and how winded he was getting motivated him to drop him off in the first cell available. The female was easier, and he opted for a fireman's carry, not trusting himself to carry her in his arms without his Nth strength boosts.

He opted to place her in another cell around the corner so they wouldn't be able to communicate and come up with a plan. He closed the cell door barrier and activated the sound-block feature so they couldn't coordinate by banging walls or shouting. The brig was eerily quiet as his boots popped on the hard floor, and he made his way out quicker than normal.

"Can you do me a favor?" Nick's voice gasped when Gus was halfway to the control room. "You've unlocked the Infirmary. Put a stupid gurney or two in the elevator. That took way too long."

"Not a bad idea." Gus put a hand to the small of his back, which had already rebounded from the strain now that his Nth were on task again. "Right after I check one more thing off the wish list."

As the car sped upwards, Gus tried to fly a bit but nothing had changed from his level of skill in **Basic Flight**.

I guess I really will have to 'sleep on it.'

"Nick, can you send a message to the cafeteria, and set up a feeding schedule for the prisoners? Preferably automated, so I won't have to visit the prisoners personally." He anticipated it might get pretty busy in the near future, and he might forget while occupied with other, more urgent tasks.

"Bologna sandwiches and water, coming right up!"

"We have bologna?"

"We have a couple canisters of meat powder that can be reconstituted. It expired about two decades ago, but who looks at those labels anyway?"

"Ugh. I don't want them getting sick or anything. But no frills either."

"So… you're not saying no to the bologna. I hear you, wink-wink, nudge-nudge."

Gus was about to clarify when he noticed another red star on his minimap. At the manor! He had been so focused on getting the other supers into their cells that he had ignored the minimap!

Dumb, dumb, dumb, Gus!

Gus rushed to the control center and turned on the monitors, cycling to find evidence of who was attacking now. He skipped by the main front door then had to go back. His jaw fell as he saw who was standing there.

CHAPTER THIRTEEN

Follow Me

Aurora woke, the duct warmed by the machinery nearby. Even though she was lying on dusty sheet-metal, she felt like she had slept like a queen. After so much sleep deprivation from being bound, she was surprised she felt as good as she did. The soreness and ache were gone from her muscles. She was pain-free for the first time in a long while. She loved the resilience being a super offered her.

Getting her bearings, Aurora crawled deeper into the accessway and climbed the narrow single-sided ladder they kept in these areas to access the various floors. Wires and panels were studded with multi-colored cords and modules, and lights of various colors indicated what was in use. The cargo bay was on the lowest tier, so she climbed up two floors and slid down another accessway. From here, she could access some ducts and see what was going on in the crew quarters. Depending on where they were going, most of the crew hung out here before a mission, some doing final prep, others decompressing before the action.

She could hear them talking long before she got to the vent above the large room. From her vantage, she could see forty-six individuals, mostly men. She counted seven women among the supers. A large crowd was gathered around two men arm wrestling across a small table almost directly underneath the vent. Another group was playing cards on a table in the corner, and a few supers were cleaning guns and checking electronic equipment.

The two men grunted and growled at each other as they struggled. Neither seemed to have a distinct advantage and they swayed back and forth, neither getting enough leverage to even be near winning. There was a loud crack and the table broke in two, and the men let go.

"That's the third one—you guys are disqualified! Ya can't press down, ya idiots!" an older man with a cigar shouted. The men threw up their arms in protest, and the others in the circle jeered and laughed, some exchanging money.

Aurora looked over the group, trying to assess what their abilities could be. This group had *mercenary* written all over them. They wore no cohesive uniforms among them, although a couple had black patches attached to their suits. Their levels of hygiene and rough appearances made it obvious that some of them didn't have the discipline that an academy would provide. She doubted that there were many supers with Psi powers, but it was better to not take any chances. She decided not to get too close or stay too long. As long as she had no flares of emotion, she should be okay.

She could see at least ten fliers in the group, and a couple acrobats, detecting them just by the way they moved. Aurora's eyes tightened, noting that the ones in the corner were probably augments, having powers that synergized with their weapons or electronics, if she had to guess. Eight of those. The others were wild cards, probably Minmaxers, who specialized in one stat boosted to obnoxious levels at the cost of others. Usually fliers had other, more significant powers, so on average were more dangerous.

She wanted to observe more, but forced herself to silently slide backward, making her way back to the ladder, taking it up to the top floor. This floor was usually only captain's quarters and the bridge, and she made her way forward to the front of the ship. The passageway widened a bit to compensate for the increased amount of connections and sensors that had to be connected to the bridge.

She froze when she heard a familiar voice. It was the same one from the torture chamber. She inched forward looking through the grate.

"How far are we? It feels like we've been in the air forever," he barked.

"We should be there in about an hour. We are approaching the origin of the signal, but my orders were to maintain a distance of at least fifty miles, find an island nearby, and you would proceed from there," a quavering voice replied, obviously wary of provoking whomever was talking to him.

"Fifty miles? That's a bit far, but I guess I'll make do," the voice agreed, grumbling.

"There is a chain of islands in this area, so we should have a lot to pick from, sir."

"Good, at least there's that. Patch me into shipwide comms."

"Yes, sir."

"Okay, everyone, report to the bridge. I'm going to go over the mission ops and how we're going to play this. Touchdown is in an hour, so be ready. Basileus, out."

A short time later, the crew rolled in. Aurora accidentally sniffed a dust bunny up her nose and massaged her nostrils in an attempt to stay silent. She looked at her gray, dirty hand in disgust as she pulled it away.

"Everyone here? Good. Alright, like you may know, we don't really know everything about the situation we are going into, so we're going to have Fade and Sideshift do our reconnaissance on the island. You two are *not* to engage, got it? I want to know what the situation is, estimated numbers, and types of defenses we can expect. The tech should be around fifty years old, but they may have come up with something new in the time they've been off the grid, so don't get sloppy and keep your eyes open. Plus, we need to be quick about it before the Factions get wind of what we've found; we know Purple had a special interest in our target."

The twinge returned and Aurora buried her nose in her shoulder. If she sneezed, everyone would know. She took silent gulps of air through her mouth, blowing out her nose in an attempt to dislodge the offending particles.

"Based on what they find, we may go in quickly or in waves. I personally doubt there will be as much opposition as what you may have been briefed on. One more thing: there may be some infected individuals still on the island. If this is the case and you see anyone, do not allow them to have any physical contact. Shoot for the head and get out. If you have no ranged attacks, fall back and we'll have our augments take care of business. Any questions? No? Then, dismissed."

Basileus gestured, calling Fade and Sideshift over to him. The woman and man came closer and Basileus' voice dropped to a whisper. "You share your findings with me and only me, got it? I'll determine what the plan needs to be. All three of us know some of these mercs are volatile. I need them though, and I can't have anyone buggering out before this mission is done. There'll be something extra for you two if you can handle that. Deal?" He looked at them and they both nodded. "Good. Remember, stay out of sight. They should never know you were there."

The supers left and Aurora was curious, having heard the entire surreptitious conversation. What were these guys so interested in on the island? If they were willing to torture her for as long as they had, it must be important. Feeling the impulse to sneeze arise again, she retreated back down the duct and down the ladder. By the time she got to where she'd napped, the sneezing sensation totally abated. *Typical.*

Whatever they were looking for must be important to Purple Faction, if the two were connected. They had been running focused scans for a while and Graviton had not really given her any rationale, just that they had noticed some 'suspicious activity.' It had sounded contrived to her at the time, but she was not one to question authority. Becoming a lieutenant was a big promotion for her and she didn't want to come off as antagonistic on her first mission in that role.

The attack on the station was really surprising though. They had no warning and were caught totally flat-footed. That idiot Basileus had killed Graviton, and he was probably the only one who really knew what was going on. She shivered a bit, knowing he'd been about to kill her just a little while ago.

Something was *wrong* with that guy. Like, sociopath level wrong. If he was into something, it was something that she needed to stop. And since the enemy of her enemy was her friend, she made a plan to get to this mysterious island and befriend whoever was there. She would have to get in contact with Purple Faction before she left the ship though. Let them know she was alive and where to find her. Fortunately, she had everything she needed right here.

Popping open a panel, she slid out a tiny keypad connected with a rainbow-colored strip of wire. A tiny grayscale monitor came on and she sent out her message, timing it to go out with any other burst communications to mask its presence.

That done, she made her way back to the access hatch. She could tell when they were firing landing stabilizers and when the ship settled as it landed, bouncing slightly as the supports absorbed the ship's weight, followed by a jarring thud as the engines powered down.

In short order, two underlings hit a large button and the hatch yawned open. She would simply follow these supers and figure out what the hell was going on at long last.

"Let's get this crap unloaded, the boss says once we're done, we can relax on the beach a bit," one of the grunts suggested.

"Good, we deserve some downtime," the other agreed. They efficiently pulled large rectangular crates out to the sandy ground below. Half an hour later, their voices dimmed as they headed off to the distance for their R&R.

Aurora peeked out of her hatchway and made it off the ship to hide in some nearby ground cover. As soon as the coast was clear, she put some distance between her and the landing site, maintaining a visual on the LZ. Soon after getting in position and settling down to wait, a small group of supers began filing out. They conversed among themselves, consulting a device and pointing off to the south. Two of the supers lifted off and began to fly in the same direction, while the remaining supers returned back into the ship.

She recognized them as Fade and Sideshift from the bridge. *Perfect.* Giving enough of a lead, Aurora followed. Her flight abilities were not nearly as developed as she would like, but she could hover fairly easily. She headed out after the supers, occasionally getting sprayed by an errant wave as she tried to stay as close to the water as she dared.

The supers were making a beeline to a nearby island, and when they came to two miles away from it, they disappeared. Trusting that they wouldn't change trajectory, she made her way to the island.

CHAPTER FOURTEEN

Geek Out

Aurora waved at the tiny camera and waited by the door. She could tell by the way it panned left that she had been seen. Could it really be Gus on the island though? She had kept her distance as the two went into stealth mode and was surprised to see someone tracking *them*. She was even more shocked to see that it was Gus or someone who looked exactly like him. Apparently, he must have made it off the station in one of the escape pods. He'd been right in front of one when everything went down.

She followed him as he crept along the beach path, trying to stay out of sight. The sight of the huge resort-like building was a surprise, and definitely not what she was expecting from what she had heard about this island. Gus sat staring at something above the patio in front of the building for a long time, so she hid and watched the same spot but saw nothing.

Aurora maintained her position and kept looking to see what Gus apparently saw. They must be in stealth nearby. She didn't hear anything, but he must have been spooked since he took off into the jungle for no apparent reason. Aurora almost followed, but not knowing where the others were could give away her position. So she waited.

Half an hour later it happened. The window above them opened and Gus snuck out onto the balcony. He jumped down to the patio, literally getting the drop on the two. They materialized immediately when he startled them and they crashed through the terracotta tiles that covered the patio. They all fell ass-over-teakettle and scuffled a bit until somehow Gus subdued the two. Something had changed with Gus, because he somehow levitated their unconscious bodies and went back inside the large building.

Curiosity got the better of her and she just had to get some answers. Gus could fill her in on what the big deal was and why so many people were interested in what was going on here.

She couldn't see through the mirrored doors and waited there; sure he would be alerted she was there soon enough.

Gus soon threw one of the doors open. "Hey, it's you... you survived!" he said awkwardly. He saw her vivid sea-green eyes widen at his sudden appearance.

Amazing, he thought, transfixed momentarily. Gus barely pulled his eyes away before his stare got to the uncomfortable stage, and scratched the back of his head.

"You did too, congratulations." She looked around furtively. "May I come inside? I don't think there's anyone else coming right yet, but I'd rather they know as little about us here as possible."

"Oh yeah, sure, come on in," he said, leaning out and trying to hold the door like a gentleman but getting more in the way than making it easier for her to enter. "Are you hungry? I haven't eaten yet and we have a cafeteria..."

Aurora couldn't remember the last time she ate a normal meal, and her stomach growled its assent. "Some food sounds great. Lead the way." Gus seemed happy to see her but also tense and on edge. "So Gus, I saw you take down those supers just now. Obviously, a lot has gone on with you. With me as well, to be honest. I came in on the transport that brought the other supers to a nearby island."

"Really? How many are there?"

"A lot, unfortunately." Gus' shoulders slumped at the news. Aurora pressed on. "So who should go first with their story, me or you?"

They arrived at the cafeteria and a robot came and assessed them. It headed back into the kitchen as the two sat down. "I guess I can go first. What do you want to know?" Gus asked.

"Why don't you start with the powers? That's pretty new. Did you always have them and just chose to be a janitor?"

"I wasn't a janitor." His face soured at the thought that that was how he'd been perceived. "I was a henchman, but I did seem to get custodial more than everyone else. That may be partly my fault. I really didn't know anyone and kept to myself rather than getting to know the other henchmen; they all had their established cliques and I didn't expect to be on the station long enough to really make the effort worthwhile."

"Sorry, I didn't mean to offend."

Gus waved it away. "For all intents and purposes, I was a janitor. Anyway, you might have seen me jump into the escape pod. Maybe not. You had your hands full." Gus flushed a bit, hoping she didn't remember it was his barf she'd had to deal with.

Who am I kidding, how could anyone forget that? He hurried on, hoping the topic wouldn't arise. "I managed to get into one of the space suits and crash landed. The pod was destroyed and I got pretty beat up in the process. The suit was equipped with Nth who kept me alive and repaired a lot of the damage. And that was the day my powers came."

"Did he just say Nth?" the voice in Aurora's head asked.

Not wanting to seem crazy for talking to herself, she decided to ask Gus herself. "What are Nth?"

"What do you mean? You're a super, don't you talk to your Nth?"

"I don't know what the hell Nth are!"

"Oh, really? How is that possible? I guess they're extraterrestrial nanobots that help the highest lifeforms on a planet evolve and develop abilities using a game-like interface. Does that sum it up accurately, Nick?"

"Oooh, I see what he did there. N-I-C for Nick. I like this guy," the voice in Aurora's head cooed.

"Gus, do you ever hear voices? Ones that talk to you about your powers?" Aurora asked tentatively.

"Yeah, I thought everyone with powers did, but Nick told me that some places train supers not to listen to their Nth interface, which limits how much they can help their hosts."

"Oh, whoever could he be talking about?" the female voice asked, irritating Aurora. On one hand, it was a relief to hear that she wasn't cracked in the head, but she worried if she could get along with *this* personality in her head.

"How do you get along with Nick?" Aurora pressed.

"Oh, he's great. He busts my balls sometimes, but I wouldn't have leveled and gained skills if I didn't have him around." He suddenly turned red. "Sorry if that was offensive."

Aurora waved it away. "You don't have to be formal around me. That's nothing compared to the average conversation at the academy. But getting back on topic. *How* does Nick help you? I just escaped a sociopath's torture dungeon and only because of that experience was I able to reconnect with my Nth, as you call it. I have been using my powers for years without even knowing about an Nth, so what does it do for you?" She leaned forward, intent on the answer.

"For one, he's answered a ton of questions. There's a lot of things regs think they know about supers that are totally wrong. And maybe that is done on purpose. He's taught me a lot of things, both how to survive on this island all alone, and to develop some skills. He even helped me get my head straight when the zombies took the manor. Sometimes he leaves me alone to figure out things, but it's been—"

"Wait, zombies?" Aurora threw her hands up. "Okay, why don't we start at the beginning and explain what's happened since the station to each of us and I think that'll answer a lot of questions along the way. You go first, your story sounds much more interesting than mine."

Gus started his tale and the robot waiter returned with two plates of food.

Aurora was a little disappointed that it was fish, as she wasn't a big fan of seafood in general. After one bite though, she changed her mind. It had the texture of fish, but the flavor was something else altogether. She ate mechanically as Gus explained the crash, getting out of the suit, developing powers, finding the manor, training and fighting zombies, and eventually defeating Methiochos and lowering the bio-stasis field. She barely noticed she had eaten everything by the time he had finished. He then recounted what happened with the pirates and the two supers and how he took their powers.

She, in turn, recounted her considerably shorter tale of how the supers on the ship ganged up on her, and Mercurio wrapped her up while Slipstream jabbed a needle in her neck and she passed out. When she awoke, she was chained to the wall. They interrogated her and tortured her, then left her alone. Once a day someone would come in and feed her some flavorless gelatin-like material and leave. She recounted how she finally heard her Nth and escaped, and eventually made it to the island.

"So you've never even known you had Nth the whole time you had powers? That kind of blows my mind. How did you get them in the first place?"

"My Nth recently showed me a memory I had avoided when my mother died. I think I inherited hers."

"Yikes, that's heavy. I'm sorry your mom passed," Gus said, feeling awkward for bringing up the obviously touchy subject.

"Don't be. I've gotten over it; she was never really there for me. I guess she taught me to survive, if indirectly. Altogether it was a pretty difficult time though, so yeah. I've avoided thinking about it for so long it almost seems like it happened to a different person. Walled it off so it couldn't hurt me anymore. My life totally sucked until I entered the academy. Then things changed for me; it was like a dream come true."

"So how does the academy work? Do they pick a skill and you level it, or what? I'm kind of home-schooled, so I don't know how most supers use their powers."

"What do you mean 'level'? We do drills, spar, and try to improve skills, if that's what you mean."

"Well, right now I'm level fifteen. My skill levels are all over the place, but most are in the first-to-fourth level range. I have been on such a time-crunch in the last weeks that I haven't really followed a plan to improve my abilities."

Aurora sat there blinking, her expression clearly confused, but she didn't say anything, so Gus continued.

"Well, if you don't know your level, how much HP do you have? I have to check my logs for a level to register and for me to get points to increase stats though, just so it doesn't distract me while in a fight."

"HP? I don't know exactly, I can't really see my own, just others when I spar or fight with them."

"You can't see your own? My display has all sorts of bars, tabs, and filters. I know my MP, HP, Stamina, which is super helpful during battles. I can see my opponent's stats too but I haven't leveled up my **Wreckognize** skill that much. Are you telling me you don't even have a display?"

"That is partially my fault, dear," the voice in Aurora's head said hesitantly. "It took me quite a while to recalibrate after your mother, and I didn't interface with you as is typical with most Nth. There were a lot of things that got missed. All the Nth have an innate sensing ability that allows their host to scan and evaluate how healthy an opponent is, but I'm afraid that I have let you down in other ways. By the time I was back to myself, you had already entered the academy and I never had a chance to share that."

"That was two years after!" Aurora said indignantly.

Gus jumped at the outburst until he realized that he wasn't

the object of her anger. He relaxed, contemplating how he appeared when having an in-depth conversation with Nick.

"We had to make a lot of changes and wipes to avoid transferring any of your mother's behaviors to you. Even your powers are different than hers. She was a Psi-bender, did you know that?"

"No... I feel like I barely knew her," she whispered, almost in a daze.

"Are you okay?" Gus asked, obviously concerned.

Aurora nodded, still thinking about the past and missed opportunities. Surprised that a tear had fallen on her cheek unbidden. "Well, what can be done now?" she asked aloud.

Gus started to answer, thinking she was talking to him when her pupils dilated extremely wide, and Aurora *saw*. Gus stopped mid-word as he noticed her reaction. "What are you seeing?"

"Around the periphery of my vision there are intricate, curved designs. Tracing filled with delicate lace-like decorations. I don't know why, but I understand what they mean, like I've always known."

"That's different from what mine looks like. What else do you see?" Gus asked.

"There's a French-curve swirl with compartments on the bottom right corner which symbolizes my total health. Each compartment is filled and there's a fraction... eight-twenty-four over eight-twenty-four... nestled in a hollow rose-shape attached to the pattern."

"Really."

"I see MP represented by an orchid with multiple blooms alternating left and right along a large stalk on the right. There's a similar hollow bloom with the value one-thousand-fifty-six in the topmost flower."

"What's the matter?" Gus asked when she paused for a minute in silence.

"It's just so beautiful..." she said absently as she took a moment to just admire the different colored tabs and menus.

"Sounds like I got the no frills display, Nick," Gus said.

"Oh, you want flowers? I can do flowers…" Nick snarked back.

Gus saw Aurora's eyes flit around; presumably she was searching tabs, seeing her stats for the first time.

"Ah, here it is, I'm level fifty-four." A huge grin spread across her face.

"Now what?" Gus asked as Aurora's smile turned into a gasp.

"Tell me about stat points…"

"You get them every level to raise your six basic stats: Strength, Perception, Intelligence, Agility, Constitution, and Luck." Gus stopped as if slapped. "Have you not allocated any stat points?" Aurora shook her head. "How many are we talking about?"

"Two-seventy."

Gus and Nick simultaneously whistled in appreciation.

"I never was one of the powerhouse supers, but I was always determined and consistent. The assessors at the academy said I was making good progress on my abilities, but I never expected this. Those mercs aren't going to know what hit them," she said with a huge smile.

Gus just stared, as she almost exuded energy. Until her eyes rolled back and he barely caught her as she went limp. Lowering her to the floor, he pulled her tousled hair to the side and gently tried to rouse her.

"Nick, is she okay?"

"Oh, she's more than okay. She's just experiencing level-up euphoria multiplied by fifty."

The moans and squirming took on a different meaning with this new information.

"I'll have what she's having," Nick said.

Gus tried to imagine what the post-level euphoria for fifty-four levels would feel like and gave up. Post-level euphoria for only a couple levels at a time was intense enough for him. He had twenty stat points of his own saved up, and thought he was doing well. But two-seventy!

At last she settled, a serene smile spreading across her face, but she was still trying to catch her breath. Finally her eyes fluttered open.

"How are you doing?" Gus wrinkled his brow as Aurora released a long wistful sigh and slowly stood.

"*That was a mind scrambler!*" Aurora gasped. She held up a finger to forestall any more questions, and leaned heavily on the wall for support. Gus waited in awkward silence as she panted to get her breath back.

"Whooo. What was that?" she asked when she had regained some composure.

"Well, I think it's kind of a reward for hitting another level. A massive rush of endorphins and whatnot. It seems to mask any discomfort with improving muscle tone and body changes associated with leveling."

"Wow, I *definitely* can get used to that. I'm sorry Gus, what were we even talking about before?"

"Somehow it slipped my mind," Gus admitted.

"Stat points," Nick offered. And Gus repeated it as if he had remembered. "You should think of how you want to allocate them. If your abilities work like mine, a lot of them improve based on stats and your MP, HP, and Stamina pools should grow a lot too."

Gus watched as Aurora gazed in wonder at discovering the nuances of her display. He heard her mutter to herself as she tried to figure out how to navigate the tabs and menus as well as how to allocate her points. Recognizing that this could take a while, Gus turned his mind to the next set of preparations. It wouldn't be long before the other supers would come, but Aurora had said they didn't know Methiochos wasn't here. He could use that to his advantage, somehow. Give the illusion of strength so that they wouldn't dare an outright storming of the manor.

He would need to check out what options the manor had in terms of decoys and subterfuge. He thought he had seen some other items in the same menus as turrets and sensors that warranted more research. Plans began to form and Gus itched to confirm his suspicions, but Aurora was still exploring in her own little world.

"Aurora, when you're done, let's head up to the control center. We can plan up there; it has access to multiple cameras, and you can get a feel for the layout of everything. Then maybe we could head to the dispensary and you could pick out some clothes," Gus suggested.

Aurora nodded. She stood numbly and slowly shuffled out of the cafeteria. Gus took her arm and guided her around some chairs so she wouldn't collide with them.

"Have you made any decisions yet?"

"I'm still checking out all my abilities. I've always had a vague sense of the MP costs and recharge time, but it's so much clearer now. I actually have been holding myself back; my available MP has outpaced my expectations. I've always avoided bottoming out because I get these fierce migraines that persist for days afterward. This makes that so much less likely.

"Okay, I think I know where I want to allocate these points. You were right, my HP and MP are rising, but not by as much as you said. Wow. Damage for *Ion Storm* jumped to three times its normal value."

"Where are you putting the points?"

"I raised everything to a base of forty, then kicked my Constitution to fifty, Agility and Perception to sixty, and the rest in Intelligence so it's at eighty. I'll admit, I'm a little excited to see how things have changed with these upgrades." She blinked a couple times and her eyes came back into focus as they neared the elevators. "Where were we going again?"

"Control center."

"Yes, yes, control center. Let's go."

"Aurora, why do you think Purple Faction didn't train you about all this from the get-go? Wouldn't you all be much more powerful? It doesn't really make sense."

"I don't know. We had assessors in the academy who would come and give you a status update each month, evaluating your performance and seeing how you were progressing. Maybe they were reading our stats and levels? They always carried a holopad and took copious notes. Maybe after reaching a certain level of control, they would tell us? I really don't know."

"I guess that sounds plausible. The academy isn't really life or death, is it?"

"It can get pretty bad. You just wish you were dead with how they hammer you with training. It's like boot camp, but they can tell just how much to push you, even more than you know yourself. And they do. Relentlessly. I think part of it is they want to make it so miserable you bond with your fellow trainees. Whatever the reason, it works. You learn how to rely on your team for support."

"I can see that. I'm glad I was able to level up as I went. I don't think I would have survived without those stat bonuses. That reminds me. Aurora, I have a question for you," Gus stammered, uncertain again.

"Okay," she replied, a little on guard from his serious tone.

"I have an ability called *Leech* that I just got for defeating Methiochos. I can steal abilities from an enemy's Nth."

"I remember you briefly mentioned it before, but how does it work? I've never heard of someone getting an ability from someone they've defeated before. Could be very powerful."

"Well, after I touch a super, I can see their skills. I can take or copy some but the exact amount depends on how high their levels are and I think my own stats and level limit how much of that ability gets transferred. There's a yellow bar on the bottom of my display that shows how full my buffer is for the abilities I take."

"You can copy my abilities? Here try." She reached out a hand and Gus took it, activating the skill. Among the abilities, he found *Ion Storm* and selected it. The yellow bar filled a little past half-way on the bottom.

*You have chosen to leech **Ion Storm (Level 12)**.*
You have chosen to copy and erase skills, are you sure? (Y/N?)

Gus saw where he could toggle some of the presets. He carefully made some adjustments.

*You have chosen to leech **Ion Storm (Level 12)**.*
You have chosen to only copy skill, are you sure? (Y/N?)

The bar was now red and extended off the end of the display.

"Hmm, that's weird. It fills the buffer much more to only copy than to steal an ability."

Gus carefully selected no and closed out the ability. Gus breathed a quiet sigh of relief that he hadn't tried to merely copy abilities when fighting with the other supers. They would have surely gotten the upper hand in the time it took to figure that out and recalibrate.

"So, there's a limit to how much you can take at one time. How much time does it take to activate?"

"Once I trigger it, it takes a couple seconds to take the skill, but thankfully they get stunned while it happens, like they're being tased."

"I saw that. Can you touch them more than once if they have a lot of abilities?"

"I... don't know. Maybe. Definitely something I should try; that's a good idea. So far, all I know is that I need to get in close and touch them without being interrupted." Gus looked at Aurora, worried she might think less of him. He saw the placid face of a tactician who knew what it took to win battles. He continued on when she offered no objections.

"Any cooldown?"

"There's none listed. Plus it stuns them afterward, so I can get them to the brig."

"I can help with that. If you give me prison access rights, I could help stow away some of the unconscious supers. Or ex-supers. Whatever."

"Okay, great. Did I mention the brig has a field that turns off your powers?"

"Whoa, like a SuperMax?"

"I guess, I didn't know that was part of those prisons."

"Kind of has to be when you're dealing with supers. It takes a ton of energy though. Plus the technology is regulated by supers, so no regs get their hands on it and use it as a weapon. Can you imagine?"

Gus shook his head as he stared ahead. He'd never even considered that a super could lose their powers, temporarily or otherwise, before his experiences on the island. The image was always one of immutable power. He just assumed it was true. Seeing Aurora look at him expectantly he continued talking. "I'll admit, part of me has a problem with erasing the powers. The other part says that this is war and I need to do what has to be done."

"I agree with the Purple Faction tenet that 'might makes right.' Sometimes you have to make hard choices, and if that's not popular with some people, so be it. Life beat me down until Purple Faction helped me become stronger and overcome. So yeah, I think you should take and erase those abilities. I'm not sure if that's what you were asking, but don't give people an opportunity to screw you. Especially if they've already shown you their true colors."

"That's what I was thinking, thanks," Gus said, more secure in his decision now that two people had affirmed it. "Here we are," he said as the elevator doors opened.

CHAPTER FIFTEEN

Threshold

As they walked into the control center, Gus gave her a little tour and showed her how to use the cameras. She checked some of the monitors and a panel that showed the status of the entire island on a holographic projection in the center of the room. She walked around it, nodding in appreciation. They found seats and got to planning their defenses. Gus smiled to himself, grateful to have Aurora's experience on board to help resist the upcoming siege.

Gus checked what it would take to add Aurora as someone the manor would recognize. It was essentially as simple as 'employing' her and giving her a position.

"You were a lieutenant on the ship, how would you like to be the manor's first lieutenant?"

"Suits me just fine. What is your official title?"

"Master of the manor, I think." He flushed a little and scratched the back of his head. "It's really been a non-issue with only me here." He turned his attention to the console to enter the information.

New employee added to the registry. Employee sync complete. Leader-

ship role has been assigned. Legacy FP added for Master of Manor to utilize. New employee level: 54. Added 47,000 Legacy FP.

Gus whooped and told Aurora the good news. So *that* was how Methiochos had planned on getting the manor outfitted and upgraded to a decent lair.

"Why don't we find you a place to stay, and I'll show you where the dispensary is located so you can see if there's anything you'd rather wear." Gus tried not to notice as Aurora looked down at the baggy jumpsuit she had picked up at Manticorps and seeing the dirty smears and smudges all over her face, reflected in the glass of the monitor.

He authorized Aurora to access FP and facilities upgrades and sent coordinates for her room and other unlocked facilities to her display.

A prompt showed up on the screen:

Enable communication mode? (Y/N)

Shrugging, Gus entered yes.

"...you could really make a difference, Aurora—"

"Hello?" Gus thought, hearing a woman's voice other than Aurora.

"Oh, how do you do?" the not-Aurora voice replied, sultry and seductive.

"Sorry, I just enabled communications between us. Should I turn it off? I didn't mean to invade your privacy."

"That's odd. Usually to communicate in a party the party leader has to send an invite and I have to accept it. Can we filter this, or is it always on?" Aurora asked warily.

Gus found that he could toggle the comms on and off on his display.

"There's a little microphone icon on the bottom left corner, I can turn it off and on."

"Oh, I see it now." Aurora turned the mic off, which put a big circle with a slash over the mic. "Can you hear this, Gus?"

His expression stayed passive. "Gus, your fly is down." Still no response.

It was a joke that always worked on the noobs at the academy, which were not-so-lovingly referred to as 'fawns.' The jumpsuits they wore *had* no fly that could be unzipped, and still the fawns would always look.

A lot of her fellow supers in training complained that there should be a minimum time being a super before they were allowed into the academy, but most instructors thought it was better to get them fresh before they learned any bad habits they had to train away. In light of them keeping Nth and leveling a secret, she wondered what else was not what it seemed, as far as her training was concerned.

She repeated herself more emphatically and still, Gus was unflappable. He didn't even check. "I'm convinced," she thought and clicked the mic back on. She heard Nick's voice say, "She sounds like Blanche. I'd prefer Bea Arthur, but you take what you can get—"

"Okay, I'm back," Aurora said, trying the manor's communication link, pretending she hadn't heard Nick.

"Well, this should make things easier to plan," Gus thought and said. "What should we call your N.I.C., Aurora?"

"We haven't really discussed it. Did you have any preferences?"

"Who me?" Gus and the female voice asked in unison.

"I've always been partial to Daphne," the voice purred.

"Okay, Daphne it is! Well, now that's settled, we need to plan," Aurora said.

"What do you think they are going to do next?" Gus asked.

"Well, with their scouts not coming back to give them intel, I think Basileus will send a small group to suss out what happened on the island. They still think they're going to encounter a large prepared force here, so we need to maintain that façade."

"I was thinking that same thing. Here, let me check something." Gus opened the defensive measures menu. There they were, at Tier 2, just what he needed. Gus checked his available FP, recalling that it should be around 1,200 with his recent level up. His eyes bugged out a bit when he saw 48,675 FP available to use. He had to restrain himself from grabbing his wish list and buying everything as Aurora elaborated on how Manti-corps would most likely proceed.

"I estimate Basileus, their leader, will give them a day or two before he sends someone else but it could be sooner. If they find out it's just us, the jig is up and things will get more diffi-cult. They will most likely send drones or wear cameras for recon that will transmit live, to determine threat levels. After that, we will have lost some of the element of surprise, and they will be on guard and harder to catch unaware. I imagine that they will be cagey, ordered to retreat if they meet a superior force."

"I can unlock some things in the Foundry that I think will help us give that impression."

"Good. Another advantage we have is that these guys are mercs. They are not a cohesive team that has worked together often for common goals. We can use that against them. If we play it right, they will get overconfident and overcommit. Maybe even get them to compete against each other for brag-ging rights of who beats us."

"That's not as encouraging as you may think," Gus murmured.

Aurora continued as if she didn't hear him. "I don't know who they will send first, but I'm hoping that there will be some abilities that you can use against them. I only got a brief look at them but there are all types of different supers with different specializations."

"Do you have any idea of what they have available?"

"Only a general idea of some of their abilities, but nothing specific, I'm afraid." Aurora shrugged. "There are a lot of them, more than forty supers, give or take."

Gus massaged his temples as Aurora continued speaking.

That many? Yikes. That's much more than we can handle at one time if they all attacked at once.

"...we just have to stay focused and we should be fine. Do you have any problems using your **Leech** ability on them again?"

"Oh, I have no problem with that. We're outnumbered and are going to need any advantage we can get. I will need you to cover for me though; I'm a sitting duck while it's activating. I've absorbed two stealth abilities, but I have no idea what they do, so why don't we train with those tomorrow? Did I tell you about the training arena? It's really helped me since it's mostly virtual and can simulate a lot of things, provided you have Nth."

"It's probably pretty standard compared to what we had at the academy, but I can join you. It would give me a better idea of where your skills are at, and I can give you advice and we can learn how to coordinate our attacks. If you've never had any training, I'm sure I could show you a lot about working as a team."

"Okay, I'm liking where this is going. How much time do you think we have?" Gus rubbed his hands together, eager to get some training from someone who actually had been to the academy. Anything to help him level and get more powerful before the other invaders came.

"I would recommend we get ready as quickly as possible. I wish the abilities you took were available quicker, but it makes sense that it would take time to assimilate the data, tailor it to your body type and muscle memory, and update your own Nth. We'll have to add that to our plans and hope that they don't attack too quickly. Tell me more about those stealth skills you acquired from those supers."

"Yeah, one is called **Camouflage** and the other is called **Phase-Shift**."

Aurora bit her lip, nodding as she thought. "Those should be helpful, especially when you can sense when they are coming. One probably affects how easily it is for others to detect you. I know a super who can phase jump. He makes portals to create tunnels, using another dimension as a conduit. Much harder to detect but uses a lot more MP. I guess we'll see tomorrow. We'll also need to train some ambush tactics. How well do you know submission techniques?"

"Well, what I did with those pirates—" Gus began.

"That probably won't work with someone with augmented strength or agility," Aurora interrupted softly. "Depending on their abilities, we need something that can get you physically in contact for long enough for the ability to do its thing. What's your Strength at?"

"Um, let me check," Gus said and opened his stat screen. He had 20 unassigned points from his level ups for defeating Methiochos that he still hadn't assigned. Without the threat of the zombies, he wanted to give himself a buffer, allocating stats as his abilities developed.

"My stats are here." Gus found that while communication was enabled, he could slide a window with a screenshot of his stats over to Aurora.

Agility: 30 (25+5)
Constitution: 32 (27+5)
Charisma: 23 (18+5)
Strength: 23 (18+5)
Perception: 31 (26+5)
Intelligence: 32 (27+5)
Luck: 32 (27+5)
HP: 620/620
MP: 540/540
Stamina: 620/620

"Hmm, everything seems pretty even. I would ask what type of build you were trying to achieve, but with **Leech**, it could be practically anything you want. I boosted Intelligence since my attacks are all MP-based. Where do you think you want to develop?"

Gus was unsure. He had always hoarded points when

playing RPGs until he figured out what class and profession he wanted to be. It was different when the stakes were real and stat placement translated directly to more power.

"I have no idea. After the threat of protecting the manor was over, I just hoarded them, in case I got a new ability that was stat dependent. Placing points before was more of a desperation-over-inspiration type of choice," Gus admitted.

"Well, being balanced overall isn't such a bad thing. What are your abilities? I know people are secretive and protective of their exact abilities, but give me a general idea."

Gus went through the list. Some of his skills seemed especially ridiculous as he read their descriptions and details out loud.

"Hmm, that's… a little odd. What do you know about the five schools?"

"Absolutely nothing. I've never heard of them," he confessed.

"Well, if you classify powers, they tend to fall into five main categories. For most supers, they align along one of these categories: mental manipulation, matter manipulation, energy manipulation, augments, and supports."

"Can you give me examples?"

"Sure. Mental manipulation builds are the telepaths, illusionists, and supers who can alter their own or other's brain function to perform at superhuman levels."

"So that's like my *TimeSight* ability that allows me to sense danger on a kind of subliminal level. It slows down time and allows me to react," Gus remarked, thinking what in his skill set fit the category.

"It *doesn't* slow down time, it just speeds your normal brain processing so that things appear to be moving slower. But yes, this is a good example of a self-directed mental manipulation power.

"The next is matter manipulation. Telekinesis used to be classified as a mental power until we understood how ether functions. Objects were not just levitating around; they were being moved by a tangible but less perceptible matter. The lion's share of powers fall into this category. Most of the augments overlap in this manner. Have you ever wondered how a super can lift something like a plane without puncturing it at the point they grasp it and focusing all the force there? It's because they are supporting the entire object with a cradle of ether and pushing this supporting framework through space."

The revelation hit Gus like a bucket of cold water. Things he had assumed about supers and their powers were totally incorrect, but what Aurora was explaining made more sense.

"Nick told me that's how flying works, that supers are pulling themselves through ether like that. I never thought about it as matter manipulation."

"The academy has you do all sorts of drills to determine the limits and range of your powers. Flying is assessed early, because the more powerful supers have affinities in more than one of the five categories. Even if you are only specialized into one affinity, often they can uncover functions and adaptations that you never knew you had. The process is grueling and many drop out rather than go through years of punishment to discover everything they can possibly do. If you are found to be an augment, or what some people call a Minmax—"

"Not to interrupt, but before you go on, what's a Minmax?"

"Oh, sorry. Technically, a Minmax is just someone with exceptional development in a single aspect. Like super speed or super strength. For some, that's all they have that makes them super, but they are good support in a team. It can be a little confusing because some supers use cybernetics to interface with their powers and they often fall into a similar category, but a lot of supers do not put this on the same level as true superpowers." She wrinkled her nose as if she had smelled something awful. "I've had bad experiences with augments, so I make sure to use the term 'augment' when I'm referring to someone relying on something artificial to give them their powers, and Minmax for true supers."

"Wait, wait. How can anyone get stronger if you don't have

a display to allocate those points? You would be stuck at base levels, right?" Gus furrowed his brow trying to make sense of it all.

"Now that you mention it, that is something." She tapped her lip with a finger as she thought for a second. "The only thing I can think of is that the assessors must be allocating your points for you, somehow. They must be able to see your abilities too, because they usually are the ones who devise your course corrections in the curriculum."

"I don't think I'd like that."

"It's either that or figure it all out on your own without the academy's help. Anyway, if you turn out to be a Minmax, they push you and push you. They make speedsters travel faster and faster until they find their limits. Supers have to lift and move heavier and larger objects to find the extent of their skills. I'll be honest—I'm a little pissed that they never mentioned level ups and stat point adjustments. A lot of things make more sense now, though. I wonder if we could have skipped a lot of pain and suffering if we could have seen and raised our stats ourselves as we grew."

"Probably your typical control freaks."

"That could very well be true. The more I think about it, assessors and trainers must have known about stats and how to increase them, because they talk about them in generalized terms and trainees are familiar with them; it's just that I have never personally seen mine before today."

"What else did you see in your display? What affinity are your abilities?"

"Energy manipulation is what I specialize in. It's a broad category involving all forms of energy; mine probably would be sub-classified as fundamental force or very small particle manipulation. I can ionize matter and control free radicals. They can be very destructive to DNA or other biological matter. Basically, I am manipulating electrons and oxidizing tissue. I can hover by maintaining a constant spray of energy underneath me, getting a small amount of lift, but it's not true flight. I think I'm on the threshold to upgrade the skill to a better version though."

"Well, maybe you're focusing on the wrong things. Nick says it's not a spray of particles that moves you when you fly. Isn't that how you described it? You know about ether, so what if you tried the same process but left out the 'spray' aspect?"

"I… I don't know how I haven't seen that, but you're probably right. Thank you, Gus."

"Sure. But how do you get the control to manipulate something as small as an electron? My brain is short circuiting just thinking about it."

"Powers in energy manipulation take much longer to train for exactly that reason. The training involves honing the mind's ability to access the power to interact with such small particles. I remember being trained to create a funnel of ether to direct my power to function like a shotgun or by using a more focused tube formed of ether to create basically a beam of energy. You drill those so much that the power becomes intrinsic to your nature and as much a reflex as muscle memory."

"Could you show me? I'm still learning about ether and how to manipulate it. I'm sure there's things I'm overlooking."

"I have forgotten a lot of how they got us to visualize it. I really haven't thought about ether for a while either, to be honest. It is kind of abandoned once you find the extent of your powers, kind of like taking off training wheels for a child." She stopped and looked upwards. "Maybe that's kept me from developing certain skills. You've been kind of innovative with how you've experimented with things." Biting her lip she nodded, making some mental commitment to herself before continuing. "I'll try to remember and share what I can."

"Daphne, can we share that type of information? Display to display?" Gus asked.

"You better believe it, buster," came the smooth reply. Gus fist pumped, settling when Aurora rolled her eyes as she waited to continue.

"Sorry, go on." Gus sat straighter in his chair.

"Finally, there are supports, who help other supers with healing effects or stat boosts."

"How exactly does that work? I get how it works in a game, it's just 'magic,' but if I was a healer, how would my Nth cause healing in another person?"

"You know, I really haven't thought about it. You take it for granted after a while."

"I can answer that one," Daphne interjected. "First, you need to know how stats allow Nth to function. The higher a host's stats, the better they can integrate skills encoded into the quantum server. It functions much like when you upgrade a personal computer. If you have more memory, you can run more complex operations. A better graphics card can render better images at a higher frame-rate."

"That still doesn't explain how supports work though," Aurora pointed out.

"What you term support powers as a class would better be described as 'conversion.' The manipulation of one type of matter into another and the conversion of energy into matter are parallel abilities. When things get very small, it is much easier to convert back and forth from energy to matter. Support classes specialize in performing these effects remotely, on others. For healing, an Nth can generate a remote field where, by expending energy, damaged tissues can be reformed into healthy tissues and infused with energy to boost performance. Stat boosts are similar, they can cause a temporary increase in a person's stats, allowing their Nth to function at a higher level. Occasionally this translates to increased processing power due to a larger network of connected Nth, other times because of reaching a critical increase, an Nth is able to function more effectively."

"What about Intelligence? How does that increase MP and Psi-abilities?"

"The Intelligence stat increases allow the host to use some of the Nth's processing power in proportion to the amount the stat increases. Compared to the human brain, computers designed by humans are very slow, by many orders of magnitude. Nth operate at speeds ahead of the human brain by a similar factor. Utilizing some of their capacity allows supers to function and react at super speeds or, in Aurora's case, process the data needed to affect millions of electrons to generate electricity, then direct that flow in a manner she designs. The higher the Intelligence stat, the more Nth can be recruited to assist in these tasks and this translates to a higher MP or ability to accomplish more tasks until they can recharge their capacitors and fire the ability again."

"What about my *Leech* ability? I'm not sure where that one would fall," Gus asked.

"That one is unique. Apparently, you can either copy or cut and paste data related to the ability and transfer it to your own Nth. Even to us, the first development of specific powers for an individual is not clear and defined. We can help develop and evolve powers that manifest, but why that varies for different people is uncertain."

"Do you know why it takes more to copy an ability rather than just steal it?"

"Due to the differences from person to person, I imagine there is a conversion process that must be created if you wish to copy an ability. The ability has to be reformatted and each parameter altered to fit the new host, while maintaining the previous ability intact. If the ability is taken, these can all be reset en masse, and the process proceeds much more quickly. As far as affinities go, *Leech* seems to be a combination of a remote conversion ability with mental manipulation, but directed at Nth instead of at the super's own mind. It is quite unique," Daphne finished.

"My powers are a little weird in general, but I'm used to being an oddball." Gus stretched and stood up. As interesting as all this was, he felt restless and needed to do something. "It's probably something weird with my genetics. My father and brother's powers center around control over the weather and I have no idea about my mother's abilities. I should remember her more, but my memory really got wrecked when I got sick."

"Oh, she was dual-class, support and mental. She could offer all kinds of stat boosts and hyper-charge them by changing one's self-perception," Aurora said offhandedly.

Gus spun and grabbed Aurora by the arms. "Wait, how do you know my mom?"

CHAPTER SIXTEEN

We Are Family

"Gus, did you forget she was Purple Faction?"

"Yeah, I kind of did, I guess," he said, letting go of her, flushing a bit at his aggressive reaction.

"Why don't we head to this training area you mentioned earlier? You look restless."

Gus stopped pacing, trying to process it all.

"I'll tell you what I know about her on the way," Aurora added.

Gus led the way to the elevators, trying not to fidget. Finally, he would get some answers. *Keep calm, dude, why are you freaking out?* He took some deep breaths to calm himself.

Aurora waited for the elevator doors to close before she began. "She was like a stand-in mother for me when I first got to the academy. So kind. I was all alone and one of the few females in my class. I always felt that I was special, and that she looked out for me. I'm not sure if it was part of her power or just how she was, but she had this way of making you feel important. The way she would ask how I was doing and remembered things I had said, so I knew it wasn't just for show.

It was so unlike the other women in my life. You were lucky to have her as your mother."

"I wish I could remember her. It's weird because I remember everything about my brother and Tempest, but there's a strange void where she used to be. Like it was carved out. Was she one of your teachers then?"

"Yes. Our class was atypical with there being so many males. Plus most of them were either legacies or from wealthy families. I didn't fit in and had to fight for my standing. There was a lot of sabotage and competition, and in Purple, you just have to learn how to deal with it. Survival of the fittest, you know. I had a couple teachers who looked out for me; Rory, and your mom. Sometimes it sucked, but it made me stronger."

"Being the odd man out is the worst." Gus nodded, staring at his feet.

"Since I didn't really have anywhere to go during the holidays, an instructor named Rory recruited me to help him in the transport department. He was the one who first invited me to the academy." She smiled at the memory. "He taught me so much about how to fix things and kept me busy enough that I didn't think about what I was missing or have time to feel jealous of the other students."

Breaking her reverie, Gus asked urgently, "What else? Can you tell me more about her? I feel like I hardly know her, and I should. I was seven or eight years old when I got sick, so there should be *something* there, but there just isn't. They told me that my high fevers must have affected those memories, but I could tell they were keeping something from me." Gus felt it was rude to press her, but he had to know. The emptiness demanded to be filled.

"Well, what do you want to know?"

"Everything. What did she look like?" Gus hung on her next words, vaguely aware that he probably was acting creepy or weird, but not caring.

Aurora felt a pang of sadness that he had lost even that simple knowledge. Her own mother's slack face on the couch was as clear to her as if it had happened yesterday. *Why did Daphne have to remind me of that? Sometimes forgetting is good.* She shook the memory away and began. "She was about my height, maybe an inch taller. She had brown eyes and shoulder length brown hair with blonde highlights. She liked to sing a lot too, I remember that."

As she spoke, a memory floated to the surface of Gus' mind.

The whole family was sitting together, watching one of the Generations channels. They specialized in only playing movies, music and TV shows of a particular decade. Mom's favorite was the 80's. Grandpa was there sitting next to him on one side, then Mom with her arm around Gus. His father was on a nearby armchair, smiling and laughing with the rest of them. He seemed so different, as Gus watched his expressions. He was happy. Gus felt happy as well. His older brother Alan lay on the ground in front of the screen playing a portable gaming system. Mom started singing the theme song from some show as it started to play:

"I bet we been together for a million years,
And I bet we'll be together for a million more."

Gus remembered he really wished he would have that feeling for a million years. Grandpa reached over and squeezed his shoulder, and gave him a wink and turned back to the screen.

Life had been good. How did things get so screwed up?

"And then she—" Aurora started. "Are you okay?"

Gus looked over at her and noticed he had started to tear up.

"Gus, I'm sorry." She leaned over and gave him a hug. If he wasn't so emotional, he probably would have done something awkward, but he simply returned the hug numbly and held her as he thought of the past. Like a crack in the dam, with that memory, more came to the fore. He tried to choke back tears and not break down, but he was unsuccessful. *Damn it. Way to keep it together, Gus. You must love the friend-zone, dude.*

He remembered birthday parties, her reading him stories in bed, and how he would bargain and cajole her into reading just one more chapter, just so he could stay up a little later. Family trips, getting fixed up when he got hurt, and listening to him rave about something his favorite supers did. Memories rushed out as if angry they had been suppressed and longed for freedom. At last, he let go of the hug and swiped away some tears, trying to mask his face to maintain some semblance of dignity.

"Sorry about that, everything started coming back at once." He tried not to look at her, embarrassed about his red eyes, and his now-runny nose. Even with the new memories, there was still a lot he didn't know. *But her face!* He could remember her face again. The thought threatened to spill more tears and he took a deep breath, trying to tamp down the emotions.

"What happened to her?" Gus asked, unsure he wanted to hear the answer.

"No one really knows. She just disappeared one day. I think I had been in the academy for two or three years. The rumor was that she was on a mission, deep in cover. Her absence was a big transition for me. It hit me hard, and it made me realize how much I relied on her. As I said, she treated me like I was her daughter too. When you were on the station, I knew you were her son and wanted to let you know about what a difference that she had made in my life, but Graviton was kind of a jerk about 'fraternizing with regs.'"

"And she died on that mission," Gus finished.

"Oh no, I don't think so. We handle that a lot differently when that happens in Purple Faction. No, your dad took some time off and came back after a couple weeks. He was different afterward. Harder, and sadder."

That was the Tempest that Gus knew well. Maybe he had forgotten more than he thought he had. He had totally forgotten how his father had been happy when Mom was there.

The doors opened, and they stepped into the training arena.

Gus nodded. "Let's put a pin in this for now and come back to it, I have so many questions," he said.

Aurora nodded and they moved on.

As he entered, he found Jet was leaning against the wall of the arena, next to the sensor he always stood by to assess his skills. He could have sworn that he had left it up in his room. Running his finger along the engraved silver grip he thought about how he could use Jet in his fights with the supers in non-lethal ways. He would have to keep them alive to use **Leech**, so it wouldn't do to kill them outright. He wasn't against giving them a vicious cut, as long as he could still **Leech** them, but his fighting style would have to change. Remembering Aurora's huge HP pool though, perhaps he wouldn't have to pull as many punches as he thought.

He could do a lot of damage before incapacitating some-one. **Leech** didn't take that long to activate, so how much time did he need? Plus he could see his opponent's HP bar, so he could hold back if he was doing too much damage. He felt more confident and wondered if it would be easier to subdue and **Leech** a weakened opponent.

"Why don't you do one of your regular training sessions so I can see what you can do?"

Gus nodded and moved to the center of the ring to warm up.

He practiced some katas, getting the feel for Jet once again. He hadn't had a chance to use the polearm in battle since he defeated Methiochos and it was almost comforting to go through the familiar routine. He began to modify his routines, using fewer headshots and more attacks designed to disable or maim an opponent.

Jet felt lighter, and the forms flowed even more smoothly than normal. The naginata glided through the air as if it was on tracks, following the motions seamlessly. Gus got to sections of the kata where he made a slight modification so he could activate **Sweep the Leg** after blocking. The stun effect would allow him to close and get the contact he needed to activate **Leech**.

He combed through his abilities as he practiced feeling his body go on autopilot as it moved through the forms. *What else could he work into his fighting style?* He reviewed one that especially seemed useful, for the stun effect at distance.

Wrecks and Parks (Level 1)
Deals (100 x skill level) HP worth of damage on a target up to 20 feet away, then freezes the target in place for (20 x skill level) seconds.

Wrecks and Parks would also be invaluable for the same reason, especially since he could do it at range. He viewed the requirements for the skill.
50 MP per activation, no refractory period.

Not that expensive either, and no cooldown was definitely a plus. He found breaks in the routine where he could fire the ability and flow back into movement, giving himself time to use **Dash** to rush in and activate **Leech**.

He would have to be careful to get the timing right, so as not to fire it so far away that the stun effect would be too short to sap their powers. If he could level **Wrecks and Parks** even once, it would give him substantially more time to react.

Gus felt himself slowing down, the additional concentration for the timing removing him from his effortless flow. He would have to perfect this new style, so opposite the old way of fighting by keeping distance and headshots to immediately down a foe. Now his goal was to get in close, disable, and drain. His eyes pinched as he anticipated taking a lot more hits in his near future. He was glad he hadn't spent his points as yet; he could see a lot going into Constitution soon.

Gus lost himself in training for a while, not gaining any new abilities, but it evolved into a form of meditation, letting concerns over what the future held in terms of Aurora, invading supers, and other uncertainty slip away. All that mattered was keeping his rhythm. His halting progress slowly increased in speed. Hours later, he saw that it was getting late and Aurora was gone. He hadn't even noticed.

Turning on his internal communication, he told Aurora, "I think I'm going to turn in for the night. I'm sorry I zoned out there, I hope you didn't wait too long for me."

A high-pitched squeak answered him. "Oh, you startled me. Geez, it is getting late. I didn't want to disturb you. I took some notes on things we can work on, but I'm impressed with your focus. It should make some things easier for you. After about an hour, I could tell you were in a groove so I left to get some other things done. I found a new outfit and cleaned up a bit. Right now, I'm in the command center looking at all the facility options."

"Okay, we'll meet up tomorrow, and I'll let you know what I've found."

Gus retired to his room and slept, eager to see his new abilities on waking.

CHAPTER SEVENTEEN

Invisible Touch

Gus awoke, his room still dark. After about ten minutes of lying there, he realized he wasn't going to fall back to sleep. He was up for the day. He looked at his watch and noted it was 4:14 AM.

This was becoming his new normal and he would have to think of something to fill the time. He'd have to ask Aurora how much sleep she needed and if it had diminished as she leveled up. Sitting on the edge of the bed, a message popped on his display:

New abilities assimilated!
Camouflage (Level 5) [3 MP/minute]: *Blend seamlessly into your environment. Note: At your current level, you will be detectable during movement.*
Vivid (Level 4) [Passive]: *Enhanced dreams, often providing special benefits, including: temporary stat increases, insights, crafting epiphanies.*
Phase-Shift (Level 4) [10 MP/minute]: *Shift partially out of the current dimension to avoid detection. During shifts, cannot be damaged by projectiles or melee damage, but will still be susceptible to area-of-effect damage.*

Advanced Flight (Level 1) [60 MP/minute]: *Can control trajectory and speed of flight. Lowered MP cost to maintain flight and increased carry capacity as levels increase.*
4 new abilities assimilated.
4,000 XP awarded.
8,000 FP awarded.
Current Nth ability capacity: 27%.

Gus rushed to the mirror and activated **Camouflage**. He became transparent and, if he maintained minimal movement, only saw the wall behind him in the mirror. Waving a hand, he saw the shape of his arm ripple as the light imperfectly refracted around him. There was a little fudge-factor so he could keep breathing, and small movements of less than an inch in any direction appeared undetectable. He wondered at what level he would be undetectable while moving.

Next, he tried **Phase-Shift**. His ears popped and everything took on a blanched appearance. He winked out of the mirror and had none of the telltale shimmer from movement. His MP bar drained noticeably faster. He reached for the faucet on the sink and met a slight resistance as his hand passed through it, reminding Gus of moving his arms underwater. He found he could not interact with any objects that were not in his possession when he entered **Phase-Shift**. Dropping out, he grabbed a brush and reactivated the skill. The brush now passed through the faucet the same way his hand had.

He was eager to see how **Advanced Flight** differed from **Basic Flight**. *Is there an* **Intermediate Flight**? he idly wondered as he went to the balcony.

"Gus, I know you're excited to try out new abilities, but until you get regeneration or some kind of healing, maybe don't try jumping out of a window on your first go around, yeah?" Nick warned.

Gus sheepishly took his foot off the balcony railing. "You're probably right."

"Knowing how to do something is not the same as being

experienced with the same skill. You will need time to make these abilities your own and learn the nuances of how they work. Don't let their easy acquisition make you get lazy with the work it will take to master them."

"Hey, lazy bones, you're finally up! Ready to train a bit?" Aurora's voice sounded in Gus' head. Looking over he saw he had left his mic channel activated last night.

"Yes, let me get ready though. Meet you at the arena," he said and clicked off the mic. He'd have to be careful not to leave that on, wondering what he had been inadvertently broadcasting to her unawares. Looking in the mirror, he saw that he was looking a bit rough around the edges. His hair was a mess and his facial hair made him look like he was a contestant on Survivor. He took a quick shower and dressed equally quickly.

He ran into the arena and skidded to a stop. Aurora was already there, highlighted by the bright light shining down on the arena. She was practicing against some of the pillowbots there. Form-fitting spandex left little to the imagination as she flitted around, fighting multiple attackers. Her hair whipped to the side as she jumped and planted a foot on the chest of one attacker, springing off and simultaneously kicking the face of this pillowbot. Using the face for support, she launched into an aerial roundoff and landed on the shoulders of another. She trapped its head between her thighs and spun, flinging the figure to the ground as she punched the back of its head all the while.

As another pillowbot reached for her from behind, she rolled forward, timing a donkey kick perfectly into the crouching figure with a loud crack. In short order, she had taken down the three attackers, and she stood and waited for the scenario to reset. Brushing her hands off, she assumed a sparring stance and saw Gus for the first time.

Closing his mouth just in time, he stood there and gave her a slow clap. A chime sounded while Gus slowly approached the arena. "Aurora... You... I mean, that was amazing! You've got to show me how to do that!"

She moved to the side of the arena, rearranging her hair back into a ponytail. "I've seen you practice, now let me see what you can do against something that *fights back*. Then I can figure out what to show you first."

Gus got ready and the attackers rushed him. Without thinking, he tried to do the same attack he had just seen Aurora do. Surprising them both, Gus managed to mimic the kicks on the first pillowbot. His roundoff was less stylish and ended with him crashing into the other attacker, but still knocking it to the ground. He felt a **TimeSight** warning but was already rolling forward and his donkey kick connected with a satisfying crunch. He stomped the last pillowbot he had crashed into in the head and it stopped trying to get to its feet. Looking to the side of the arena, it was Aurora's turn to have her mouth hang open.

"Where did you learn those attacks? I thought you just got your powers!"

"Just now, I guess. I realize it wasn't as graceful as yours, but I'm surprised it worked at all."

"You got that all from just watching one time? No way. Here, watch this and try to copy what I'm doing." Aurora went over to the console and entered some parameters. The pillowbots changed formation and froze until Aurora started her attack.

With inhuman speed, she sped toward one of the attackers. Getting close, she swayed to one side then abruptly spun in the opposite direction, rotating around behind the pillowbot as it attempted to punch where it thought she would be. She clasped her arms and braced them around the head of the pillowbot in a choke hold. Gus wondered if this would have any effect on the construct, but it must have been programmed to respond the same way as a normal combatant because it flailed about, trying to get her off its back. She was able to pull the pillowbot backward while maintaining the hold, keeping the pillowbot bending backward like it was in a perpetual limbo contest. With a heave, she moved the body of the pillowbot between her and the other attackers. At last, the pillowbot stopped struggling and Aurora picked her next target.

Instead of letting the pillowbot drop to the ground, she lifted it up then kicked it in the back towards one of the other pillowbots. It flailed limply toward the attacker, causing it to jump backward. The distraction was all she needed to slink toward the other pillowbot and she unleashed a flurry of punches. It reminded Gus of someone using a speed bag with how quickly her arms were pistoning into the face of the pillowbot.

The hapless bot raised its arms like a boxer to shield itself from the onslaught and she sidestepped, ducking slightly behind and planting her forward foot along the instep of the dazed pillowbot. She then braced her back foot in the same fashion on the other leg and sunk into the splits with a sudden crash. She caught herself before touching the ground but the pillowbot was not so fortunate. The shift in its center of gravity caused it to topple to the ground and she rolled over and ax kicked the prone form right in the neck, and it rose no more.

The last pillowbot was wary and kept its distance, waiting for her to make the first move. She changed stances again and charged the last pillowbot. It fled, and Gus laughed a bit as she chased the cowardly pillowbot. It had to slow around the fallen forms of its comrades, and Aurora was able to grab one arm. Jumping up, she straddled it sideways, carrying it to the ground. Rotating in mid-air, she landed on her side and clasped her arms together, pulling the pillowbot's arm in close over her shoulder, pinning it. She held on like a hungry tick and kept exerting pressure until there was a loud click.

Did she just break that machine with an arm lock? After the noise, the pillowbot stopped moving and Aurora got to her feet. She allowed the pillowbots to reset and the last attacker, or more accurately, the last victim, disappeared into the wall as panels opened and another took its place. Once again, she walked to the edge of the arena, folding her arms, her smile a bit more smug this time.

Gus bounced into the arena, shaking his shoulders back and forth, trying to loosen up. When he was ready, he dashed toward the first attacker, just as Aurora had. In a similar fashion, he found that he intuitively moved much like she had done and could reproduce her fighting technique. Until he got to the part with the splits, that was.

His version of it was more like bracing himself and kicking the knee of the pillowbot. It had the same effect and saved his boys from some trauma. Gus stomped the downed robot and approached the third. Having a larger reach, Gus was able to grab the last pillowbot before it had a chance to flee. He began to swing it around, moving it in an arc until it collided with a downed pillowbot. He rushed in for the pin when the bot was taken to the ground. Gus heard a chime while he was subduing the last pillowbot, and then the battle was finished.

"No way. No way! That has to be an ability you haven't told me about. I had to train forever to get that good. Did you do martial arts growing up?"

Gus raised his arms to placate her. "Hold on, I did hear a couple chimes so let me check my logs."

You have leveled up the skill: **Master of Tasks to Level 3!**
600 XP awarded.
600 FP awarded.
You have leveled up the skill: **Master of Tasks to Level 4!**
800 XP awarded.
800 FP awarded.
11,200 XP to level 16.

"I guess you were right. My skill Master of Tasks just leveled twice to level 4."

"What does that ability do?"

"Description says '*Enhanced ability to mimic and adopt physical skills by observation.*'"

"Balls! You realize you are one lucky S.O.B., right?"

Gus smiled, pleased to see both her competitive side as well as a less formal, composed Aurora. She seemed more real.

"It kind of goes both ways, lately. You take the good, you take the bad, you take them both and there you have—"

"I don't know why I'm getting upset. Jealous, I guess," Aurora butted in, lost in thought. "This will actually save us a bunch of time. Gus, I'm just going to show you all the submission techniques I know, so we can practice them, got it?"

Aurora began going through the fighting styles that she had learned during her time at the academy and beyond. Gus absorbed everything like a sponge and leveled up **Master of Tasks** two more times. When she felt like she had gone over everything she could remember, they shifted to sparring.

This was a lot harder for Gus because he could copy her attacks much more easily than he could compile them into a directed, intentional defense or attack. Gus escaped some holds and pins merely by luck and a desperate application of one technique or another. Despite her smaller size, she could hit like a truck and when she bore down, Gus could feel her using more than just her body weight to press the attack.

At last, she had pinned Gus to the mat, straddling him. She leaned in, her forearm pushing just hard enough on his neck to cut off the blood flow without collapsing his windpipe or causing any real damage.

He began to fight more savagely as the sides of his vision started to dim. The position she had him twisted into, along with the vice-like pressure she exerted, prevented him from squirming out of the hold and he was losing the battle. Gus looked into her eyes as things started to wink into blackness, and saw her pupils suddenly expand and then the pressure was gone.

Choking and rubbing his neck, he sat up and saw that Jet had slid under her outstretched arms and forcefully pulled her backward and away from Gus. She landed unceremoniously on her butt a few feet away.

Jet, under its own power, floated in the air and interposed

itself between her and Gus, blade twitching menacingly as the two sat there dumbfounded. Gus shook his head and shrugged his shoulders and they both stared at the scene. Gus reached out and grabbed Jet out of the air and it relaxed into his hand and resumed its normal weight as it stopped maintaining itself aloft.

"What just happened?" Aurora asked, nonplussed.

"I have no idea, that wasn't me. Niiiiiick?"

"My guess is that Jet's Kroutonium must have leveled along with you as you defeated Methiochos, becoming more self-aware than an average weapon. I didn't know that it could manipulate ether and move on its own power—that is new. Obviously, it was trying to protect you."

"You have a sentient weapon? I didn't think they really existed," Aurora said as she walked around the polearm with new appreciation.

Gus and Aurora looked at each other and smiled. Gus stood Jet upright and thought of what he wanted it to do. Sensing his intention, the naginata retained its position upright as he let go, hovering in the air in the exact position. "I had no idea that was even possible!" Gus said with excitement.

"Me either," Aurora added, watching in wonder. "Still, that one doesn't count. I had you beat that round. You've got to really start training as much as possible. If you can't beat a single super like me then you're going to get creamed when fighting a whole group."

Gus frowned a bit but nodded his head in agreement. They continued to train, adding Jet into the routines and Gus found that Jet could, and would, follow his orders; the polearm would do some truly amazing things when Gus gave it a general commands like 'protect me,' or 'create an opening while I attack,' and let it interpret how it wanted to follow the order.

Aurora held her own and still gave Gus a challenge as she multitasked and fought both of them at once.

After working for another couple hours they decided to break for lunch. Gus hadn't eaten breakfast in his haste to get to the arena and was ravenous.

Gus left Jet in the arena, wanting to try something. As they were eating in the cafeteria, Gus sent the message '*come to me*' to Jet. He told Aurora and they waited to see if the weapon could sense what he wanted from this range, and how long it would take to make it past the doors and across the different floors. They were both surprised when, in less than two minutes, the lift opened and Jet flew out of the opening doors, doing a little flourish as it reached them, reminding Gus of a victory dance.

"Is Jet bragging?"

"It kind of looks like it," Gus said, laughing. "Okay, buddy, take a break. We're going to be really busy in the future, and you're going to be a big help." The wide blade dipped as if bowing and rested atop a long table nearby.

Ever the strategist, Aurora began planning the afternoon. "After lunch, we should make some quick upgrades to the manor, then train your new abilities."

Gus nodded and looked forward to using the new abilities, especially **Advanced Flight.** It was the one power that he had wished he had when he was young. If only he could fly, it would confirm that he belonged to the family and was a super. Right after his older brother had come into his powers, his father would have Alan give Gus piggyback rides to help him improve the skill. The feeling was exhilarating. To actually fly himself, rather than do an extended jump or hover, almost seemed like a validation to him, despite all he had been through.

"One of them is **Advanced Flight**, and Nick recommended I try that outside on level ground before I get too crazy. Maybe we can have Nick and Daphne sync and you can see how it is done so you can improve your skill."

"Is that even possible?"

"Sure is, sister," Daphne replied.

Aurora shook her head. "I'll admit, I'm curious why we were conditioned this way. Skill growth would be much easier with this type of cooperation in the academy," she mused out loud before going on. "Anyway, it would be helpful to get some rendezvous points and scope out some vantages where we can await their attack. What about the cafeteria upgrade? Didn't that make it possible to get something to boost stats while we're out in battle?"

Gus kicked himself for not getting on this immediately. As soon as they entered the cafeteria, he waved to the kitchen and the waiterbot wheeled out.

"What boosts should we get?"

"Let's do MP and HP boosts, and something to boost healing speeds. I think we'll be okay with our stats as is, but those could be clutch in a battle."

Gus made the order and noticed a timer pop up in the lower left of his display.

"It'll take about three hours," he informed her.

"That's perfect. Let's eat, then head outside. Don't forget to bring Jet with you."

A half hour later, Gus picked up the naginata on the way out, looking again at the formidable weapon. *What other secrets do you have, Jet?*

CHAPTER EIGHTEEN

She's Crafty

They headed out to the grassy field in front of the manor and Gus tried **Advanced Flight** for the first time. The movement was effortless and he could move in any direction and hover without any conscious thought of anchoring himself in the air. His hands began waving back and forth as if treading water by instinct but, upon testing, he found that the movement was totally unnecessary, and did nothing to keep him aloft.

"Here, try to lift me," Aurora said.

Gus floated down and grabbed her arms. When he raised in the air, the additional weight anchored him and he couldn't budge her at all. He could tell by the lack of pressure in their grip that his flight wasn't exerting much force beyond being able to lift himself.

"I guess that's a bust. Daphne, can you show me what the ether around this looks like?"

Aurora walked around Gus and observed him from different angles.

"Gus, try moving a little this way." Aurora motioned to his right. "Okay, now the other way." She squinted and then closed her eyes. Some cords on her neck stood out but she stayed earthbound. She opened her eyes again. "I'll have to work on that. Here, let me shoot some weak projectiles at you and try to dodge."

"Will they hurt?"

"Only if you get hit," she said wryly. "One, two…" she said, firing her first mini *Ion Storm* before hitting three.

Gus dodged backward reflexively, angling upward and to the side. He spun sideways and twisted to face her once again while keeping relatively close. Usually, he ended up far away from his attackers, which was perfect for staying out of the claw reach of zombies. Now, with *Leech*, he had to find ways to get in close.

They practiced more, and Gus found a couple additional movements that he could use in a pinch, trying to circle around behind Aurora after she attacked.

The better he got, the more she ramped the speed and number of snowball-sized *Ion Storms*. The air reeked of ozone when Aurora decided they had practiced enough and Gus had reached level 3 in *Advanced Flight*, getting another 1,000 XP and FP for the levels.

From there, they moved to stealth skills. Gus would hide and then try to make it to the front door without detection. *Camouflage* worked well when in more dense foliage but he found he had to switch to *Phase-Shift* if he wanted to cross the open section of grass in front of the manor. They had made an agreement that he wouldn't use his flight skills at all, and Gus found that Aurora was *very* good at seeing the depressions that his feet would make in the grass. Even if he moved slowly, she would punish him with an ion ball more often than not.

The expanse of the courtyard was too long to move quietly through and not expend all of his MP since that required *Phase-Shift*. The refraction of *Camouflage* was too pronounced at his level. He still made noise while using *Phase-Shift*, which was something he was glad to have found out before battle. Occasionally the rubber in his boots would squeak at an inopportune time and telegraph his location. Aurora would fire off a stream of ion balls and she could easily find where he was when they impacted him and dispersed around his form, the others traveling on to the distance.

Once he found a new route that allowed him to bypass her, she also changed her approach, her competitive nature not giving him a chance to gloat as she shut him down time and again. When he finally called uncle and toweled off, he glanced at the fruits of his labors: one level for **Camouflage (Level 6)** and **Phase-Shift** (**Level 7**) jumping three whole levels.

Satisfied that Gus was familiar with the techniques, they headed back to the cafeteria.

Three trays were on the counter lining one wall. Red, blue, and pink gels sat in the trays, sixteen of each. Gus picked one up and looked closely at it.

"They kind of look like those tiny soaps you put in the dishwasher," he said, squishing the rubbery film around the colored liquid. He lifted it to his mouth to eat a red gel.

"Wait! Do you trust me?" she asked with puppy-dog eyes.

"Less when you say it like that."

"Don't be a baby. Hold your hand out like this." She lifted her arm up to her side like she was being sworn in for court. Gus did the same and she zapped him point blank with an ion ball.

A flash of itchiness followed by an intense burning sensation hit Gus' hand as it started to blister. "Damn! What the "

"Hurry, eat the gel now."

Gus popped it in his mouth and bit down. A strong cherry flavor hit him, then disappeared before he could swallow. He expected there to be liquid but all that was left was the chewy outer casing, which quickly dissolved as he continued to chew. A second after he had bit down, he looked at his hand. The pain was gone and the small dip in his HP jumped back to 100%. His hand looked pristine and the red, sunburned appearance and blisters had disappeared.

"It wouldn't have done anything if you ate it at full health. Sorry if that hurt."

Gus marveled as he flipped his hand back and forth, feeling it with his other hand. "That was so worth the FP!" he raved, and excitedly ordered the cafeteria to continually make the gels so they would have a surplus when needed.

"How should we carry these? They look a little fragile," Aurora wondered aloud.

"I think I know just the thing. Hey, maybe I can teach you too. Have you ever sewn anything?"

———

They stopped at the dispensary to grab some cloth scraps, and a supply room for some Velcro. They headed back outside, and Gus used **Ether Leash** to bring two chairs down to Atlantis beach. They both kicked off their boots and dug their feet into the soft sand.

Gus, Nick, Aurora, and Daphne shared information so that she could see how to manipulate the weaves to make a small bag of holding. Since she had experience and a basic understanding of ether weaves, she bypassed having to use palm fronds and she set to replicating the complicated weaves, but it still took some trial and error to remember the basics.

"I always wanted a crafting ability," she mentioned offhandedly. "My old mentor, Rory, was so good with his hands. We would fix vehicles all day, and he just had a magic touch. I got pretty good, but I wasn't naturally talented at it. After hours, he would carve these little figurines out of wood and paint them. They were so lifelike, and were only about three-quarters of an inch tall. I don't know how he didn't break the wood while carving them.

"I especially liked this one with a paladin he did, his sword uplifted like he was going to smite something and his cape flapping behind him. He had painted it so that the armor had a mirror finish on it too. He gave it to me for my eighteenth birthday."

Her voice turned melancholy. "It was on the station when it went down."

Gus looked up but quickly returned to his work when his weave started to fizzle and unravel. "I'm sorry, Aurora. When we get back, maybe he can make you another, yeah?"

She smiled again, Gus' optimism that they would overcome and make it home bolstering the uncertainty behind her facade of strength.

"Yeah. First thing when we get back." She turned back to her work. "Okay, I think I got this first part done, what now?"

"Hold on, speedster," Gus caught up and finished the small ring of weaves. "Hold yours tight and watch how I connect the two ends together." Gus made the loops and turns larger than average so she could see what he was doing then cinched them together. As the sides connected a shimmer pulsed around the tiny ring.

With his ring stable he turned his attention to her and guided her as she tied the weave. He laughed a little as her tongue snuck out of the side of her mouth as she concentrated. Gus saw the shimmer with her ring as well and knew that it was finished.

"Now the easy part. See these loops? Just connect them to the Velcro, like this," he instructed, showing how to attach the now-tangible rim of the bag of holding. Gus added the adhesive strip on the smooth backing of the Velcro to his hip where a pocket would be and reached inside. Keeping it open, he poured in some of the red and pink gels. The angle made it feel like he was storing them inside his upper thigh.

Aurora laughed as she played with the strange dimensional effect. They hadn't made the bags so deep that they would have to fish around during an emergency for a much-needed gel.

"Let's make another for the other side, then we can separate HP from MP boosts," she said, a giddy grin on her face.

"Good idea."

They set back to work, Aurora finishing her second bag without any coaching, and much quicker than Gus had done.

"T-t-today, junior!" she taunted.

"You don't have to brag about it!" He laughed as she teased, trying to distract him and make him lose his concentration. He had to spin to face away from her in order to keep his eyes on the delicate finishing step. At last, he saw the shimmer and knew he was done.

"You're horrible, you know that, right?"

"You don't know the half of it," Daphne added.

"Hey, you're supposed to be on *my* side!"

When they were finished, they loaded the blue gels into their left pockets. That done, they sat there and took in the ocean.

Before they could even relax, red stars popped up in their displays and they looked at each other. Aurora turned to Gus, her eyes pinched.

"They're coming."

CHAPTER NINETEEN

Catch Me If You Can

"Let's do this," Gus said as he hit his **_Camouflage_** skill and moved into one of the cover positions they had designated.

"Crap, I haven't unlocked any of the new facilities for the manor yet," Aurora said as she flew up to an overlook and got into position. For Gus, the strain of flying was gone, and he effortlessly glided above the ground, the advanced level of the skill sapping barely any MP at all. Aurora moved painfully slow, but to her credit, she had managed to eliminate 'propelling' herself by using **_Ion Storm_**.

The cluster of dots split and resolved into five supers, one using a jetpack and another with his hands on the shoulders of two others. A light blue aura outlined him and the two other supers he was ferrying to the island as they hung there, reminding Gus of cats held by the scruff of the neck. **_Wreckognize_** wouldn't work from this distance, so Gus nicknamed another super, also wearing an exosuit with visible hydraulics and augments 'Jetpack.' He had one super he was carrying with him.

As soon as they touched down on the beach, the aura disappeared and they both shook free, rotating their shoulders like throwing off an uncomfortable load. Jetpack dropped his partner, who jogged as he touched down until coming to a stop, kicking up plumes of beach sand. After checking some switches, he pulled a gun connected to a cord from his back and powered up, glowing light illuminating a line from the pack on his back to the butt of the rifle. A loud electronic hum resonated as the super moved up the beach. Not the stealthiest setup, but maybe he didn't care.

Jetpack landed nearby, and as he turned, Gus could see cybernetics covering one eye. He pulled a flap open on his shoulder and a small roiling mass floated out. It sat there stretching and reforming, like a flock of starlings, and then dispersed as the cloud spread out, particles shooting in different directions. That done, he fiddled with the large bracers on his forearms, activating them and taking a practice shot at a nearby palm tree.

As he clenched his fist around a crossbar, the cuff surrounding his hands shot a ring-shaped beam of energy that ripped through the tree, snapping it in half. The top half fell towards one of the other supers, who casually reached up one hand. The fronds began to brown and wilt, shriveling to a husk and flaking to ash. In the time it took the tree to fall forward, the trunk darkened and crumbled. The coastal wind carried the ash away before most could hit the nonchalant super.

"Watch what you're doing, idiot! Why don't you just announce that we're here?!" a rippling bodybuilder super growled.

"You are a fool if you think they do not know we are here. The sooner they come, the sooner we finish."

The muscular super punched his palm and yelled in dissent. Tattoos flared along his arms and he increased in height as his muscles enlarged.

Gus smacked a bug that alighted on his cheek as he watched the scene.

As he did so, cyber-eye snapped his head to the right and looked directly at Gus. "There! Go! Go!" he shouted.

Gus flew upward, still cloaked, but found himself feeling little pings against his skin as he moved through the air. Rings of energy spun in his direction, following his movement and Gus would have been hit had he not suddenly deactivated **Advanced Flight**. Gravity pulled him down and Gus swore he smelled burning hair as the ring sailed overhead. Gus could see a murmuration of the bug-like creatures following him, like a contrail on a jet. And pointing directly at his flight path.

The muscular super sprang into the air towards him, clearing twenty-feet of vertical per leap. The rest of the crew was following, some taking aim and charging attacks. Beams occasionally zipped too close for comfort in between the leaps of the musclebound super.

In desperation, Gus flew towards Aurora. He pulled upward and a bright flash enveloped him. The light bursts were spectacular, like being inside of a firework as it went off and Gus almost forgot to keep juking and spinning, distracted by the spectacular display. As he sped through the pyrotechnics, he saw multiple tiny flares as the small pursuers were consumed. Gus flew straight up, to get out of range of any stray shots or other unknown powers.

Panting, he looked down on the scene and could see that they had lost him, at least temporarily, in the sparkling haze Aurora had created. The two cybernetic supers with weapons fell back now that he wasn't being actively tracked. They swept their weapons back and forth, looking up at the sky, preparing for an impending attack. From their vantage, it must have looked like he was responsible for the **Ion Storm** because none of them were stalking closer to Aurora's hiding spot. Yet.

"Maybe you should *scan* them and see what we're dealing with, yeah?" Nick prodded.

Gus' head cleared after the near-fiasco. **Wreckognize** revealed the muscle-bound guy to be Silverback, whose main skills were **Resilience**: extraordinary resistance to projectiles and explosive damage due to a passive ether shield that absorbed and deflected attacks above melee speeds, and

Bound, which was basically enhanced jumping and ***Enhanced Strength***.

Jet appeared in Gus' peripheral vision and he mentally instructed it to hamstring Silverback on his signal. That would allow him to drop in and ***Leech*** him while he was in the lead and separated from the others.

The others were too far away to lock onto with ***Wreckognize*** and, rather than give chase, they were carefully working their way toward the manor, with the methodical military caution of someone clearing an engagement zone. Once they reached the main patio, they stayed close to the door of the manor, holding back.

Hovering closer, Gus gave the order and Jet raced forward in a blink, slicing into the back of Silverback's meaty legs. There was a brief flash and the blade skipped as it hit Silverback, not cutting nearly as deep as Gus had expected. Still, the titan of a man let out a bestial roar and fell forward. There were some shots fired from the direction of the manor in Jet's direction, but the naginata easily evaded them as it retreated.

Getting an idea, Gus ordered Jet to fly through the intervening space and target whatever was signaling the others. The shots tracked upward as Jet zipped and zoomed about and Gus dropped down to ***Leech*** Silverback. By the time he reached the man elbowing himself forward in an army crawl, the cuts had stopped bleeding and then the gaping wound closed and knit together. He swiped out, growling as he struggled forward. Gus almost tried to reach in and rely on ***Leech***'s stun effect but another super was fast approaching with an arm outstretched towards Silverback.

Gus took to the air again, glad he hadn't dropped out of stealth.

Wreckognize revealed Ash to be the simple name of the super who vaporized the tree. He wore a flamboyant red jacket with exaggerated shoulder pads flaring out and curving upwards. Ash began sweeping his hands back and forth in front of him and a wave of something passed over Gus. As it did, it sucked out a third of his health and MP.

The effect was so jarring that he lost focus on his **Camouflage** and **Advanced Flight** and crashed to the ground, barely staying on his feet. Gus dashed backward to get out of range, half expecting to brain himself on a tree in his haste, as the two supers charged toward him.

He took flight again but hovered much lower than normal, about twenty feet above the ground. The timing would have to be right, and he had to force himself to face this rabid rhino of a man without fleeing or escaping into stealth.

Silverback perked up and got him in his sights. As predicted, he jumped up towards Gus, grabbing him around the waist in a huge bear hug.

Gus slapped his arms on the sides of the bald man's head and hit **Leech**, draining **Enhanced Strength** first. The hard tone of the man's muscles seemed to relax into something more like flab. The vascularity and tautness of his skin disappeared as his strength stats were robbed from him.

The unconscious and weakened Silverback let go of Gus. Gus grabbed him and clung on as they fell, allowing the burly man to take the brunt of the fall back to earth. It still shaved off another five percent of his total health as they hit and Gus bounced off, spinning onto the beach. Spitting out sand, Gus shook his head and crawled back to the prone man.

He quickly absorbed **Bound** and **Resilience** before dodging back into the air as Ash reached toward him. He felt a pull before he got out of range and lost a tenth of both his MP and HP. Gus glanced and saw his HP was at 252/620 in just a matter of moments of fighting, then it began quickly decreasing, along with his MP.

Wiping sand out of his blurry eyes, Gus squinted as he activated **Wrecks and Parks** on Ash. Instead of totally stunning him, it only dropped him to one knee, but the draining effect paused.

Ash looked up and grinned, Gus' HP and MP beginning to slowly trickle away again, picking up speed.

A sensation like ice cold fingers wrapped around Gus' heart and pulled. Gus could barely keep himself in the air as he was reeled in, Ash staring him in the eyes the whole time.

There was a jerk and Ash's eyes rolled up into his head. Jet appeared as he fell face first to the ground, butt of the shaft having cracked into Ash at the base of his skull. Jet tipped as if in salute and sped off as Gus felt a crushing pain in his left side. He fell to the earth and pain lanced through his hip and cracking ribs as he landed hard, dropping him to only 42 HP remaining.

He couldn't breathe as he scrambled for his pocket and quickly consumed a pink and red gel. The pain subsided somewhat and he had to greedily eat another red gel before the pain faded and he coughed up blood. The red restored fifty points and the pink helped him regenerate 2 HP per second.

Seeing a shadow over him, Gus rolled over just in time as the ground where he had fallen shimmered and puckered into a crater. He continued to roll until he made it into some nearby foliage and activated **Phase-Shift**. The flying super began peppering the area with distortions that crushed everything in their sphere of influence about the size of a beach ball. Nearby palms kinked like garden hoses as the effect bent them in half, and the existing ground cover was flattened and rapidly approaching Gus.

There was a loud boom, followed by a dazzling display of shimmering particles, glittering sparkles of purple, pink and green fizzling like a crate of lit sparklers, spiraling toward the ground. The super turned and stared at the spectacle.

Gus averted his eyes as Aurora had mentioned and dashed forward, hitting the super low in the back. Pain flared in his side from the collision, then he pushed. The momentum launched the dazed invader into some nearby palms where he hit with a big crunch, loosening some coconuts. From there, he tumbled out from the higher tree, flipping like a contestant on Wipeout into another lower tree, disappearing into the bushy fronds.

A red flash warned Gus that his MP was below ten percent and he quickly dropped *Phase-Shift*. His HP wasn't much better at only 27/620. Checking his minimap to find the other two supers, Gus saw that the three supers that he had downed had turned from red stars to hollow red circles. Gus smiled weakly, knowing that would come in handy to determine if a super was truly unconscious or was just faking to lure him close.

He was tempted to drain the others but instead crawled to get into some cover before approaching the other two supers in front of the manor. He leaned his back against a small dune while he fished in his pockets for some more red gels and bit down on two in rapid succession, panting to catch his breath. He sighed as the pain in his side began to fade while he watched the remnants of Aurora's ability fizzle in the air above.

As the last spirals of sparkle dust or whatever it was were fading away, the two remaining supers came out of their daze and started firing at the small dune Gus was hiding behind. He cringed and slid further down as their shots kicked up explosions of sand and plant debris. As he stared up into the blue sky, there was an assortment of sweeping energy beams and some kind of energy bullets filling the air, leaving no safe way to approach.

Gus rolled to the side and tried to peek, but they were expecting him and he barely ducked back into safety before a whirlwind of dust and small shredded scrub plants puffed up into the air with the shots. A hot glob of something fell on Gus' hand and he shook it off, looking at it as it cooled. The orangish material solidified into a grayish-brown glass, a red blister rising almost instantly.

Even when he tried to skirt around and move to the sides, they quickly picked up his location and began firing. Gus got a nasty burn on his arm as a beam nicked him. He almost grabbed another gel, but held back, not wanting to form a bad habit of using them too freely and not having them when truly needed.

Gus wanted to **Phase-Shift**, just to get out of there, but he wouldn't be able to sustain it with his depleted MP. He reached in his other pocket and pulled out some blue gels. Even among the whir and pulse of their shots and their detonations, the tearing noise of the Velcro announced his position and he had to roll to another nearby dune as the ground started exploding around him. One of the supers was flanking his position so they could get him into a crossfire.

Gus had lost his gels in his escape. He was running out of options when he heard a high-pitched noise like a camera flash charging. The shots paused briefly as they evaluated this new development, the noise rising in pitch. It reached its peak tone and then a muffled *ba-tang* sounded and Gus ducked and covered his head, expecting some huge cannon to blow him to oblivion. He felt a wave of energy wash over him, followed by a wave of heat, then there was silence.

There were no more intermittent shots, and Gus checked his status. He noticed no other changes or debuffs. After a tense minute, Gus hazarded a peek and saw the two men lying on the ground. Expecting a trap, he checked his minimap and their icons had shifted to hollow circles. Gus' shoulders slumped in exhaustion as he finally relaxed. *Thank you, Aurora*.

———

After firing an **Ion Storm** that took out the tiny insect drones, Aurora saw that two supers moved to guard the manor entrance, trying to prevent a retreat. She suspected they would hunker back if attacked, hoping to avoid ranged attacks that could miss and damage the manor. They were lining up shots as Gus popped in and out of view, fighting the other supers. It was only a matter of time before they got a lucky shot.

Both of the armed supers were relying heavily on cybernetics, so if she could activate the new manor upgrades, they would be neutralized. She used **Dazzle** in the center of the courtyard above the grass and the two supers moved out of their cover to more easily see what was happening.

Aurora took her cue and snuck to the manor door and slipped inside. Sprinting to the elevator, she bashed the button to the control center. She wondered if there was some upgrade to allow faster manor transport as the elevator began its lazy ascent. Crashing out of the elevator, she ran to the console and approved EMP Targeting. An antenna on the roof of the manor hummed to life as the coils charged. This unlock had no upgrades, and Aurora held her breath as the two supers were close to the edge of effect around the field. *Don't walk forward, don't walk forward...*

The **Dazzle** effect faded and the supers retreated closer to the manor, getting back under cover, bracing themselves as they fired at Gus. One directed the other, who moved laterally to get a better shot.

At last, the pulse had reached full charge and Aurora activated it, and she saw the ripple of energy spread out. And slumped back into the chair when the last two attackers collapsed, unconscious.

———

Basileus hit the console as he watched his mercs get beaten by one guy. *Wait. What was that?* He scanned the video back and froze the frame. There she was. Aurora slinking in the background, making her way to the manor door while the others were looking upward, focusing on some explosion above.

He knew he should have ended her back at headquarters.

See what being a good little servant gets you? a voice chided.

I wouldn't have let this happen, another taunted.

Basileus felt a growl in the back of his throat as he stared at the screen. It would have taken so little time to get rid of her. Maybe she had already escaped by then. If his father hadn't been in such a hurry, he would have seen that she was gone.

Too late to worry about it now, but experience told him if he wasn't decisive, the same problems came back to haunt him, again and again.

He tried to calm his escalating rage, and quiet the voices. *Just get the mission done. Appease your father until you have taken the manor and then Manticorps. Archon will have to hand over the reins after success here.* He could hold out just a bit longer. If he could regain the manor, finally he could be free.

He's forgetting about the girl. Typical.

Basileus' eyes widened. If Aurora was here, she had to have snuck on board. He called his comms officer. "What's the status of the burst transmission?"

"We just started it, it's at about 24%—" came the languid reply.

"Shut it down!"

"Y-yes, sir… transmission aborted. Any data mid-transmission is probably corrupted and will have to be recompiled and sent again," the tech replied, suddenly attentive.

"They can wait. The relay will be back in position in thirty-six hours. I'll have something better to report by then, anyway."

CHAPTER TWENTY

Lay My Claim

Gus slumped to the grass in exhaustion. "Woof to the woof!" He laid there staring at the indifferent clouds. He had dragged the others all onto the manor's lawn but he felt exhausted. He was grateful that his minimap showed where the downed supers were or he wouldn't have found the super who had fallen into the branches of a tree. Deciding it would be safer to **Leech** him while on the ground, Gus pushed and prodded with ether leashes until he could get a grip around the man and drag him down to the ground, then transport him to the lawn.

Congratulations! You have subdued 5 opponents trespassing on privately-owned territory.
5,000 XP (1,000 x 5) awarded for non-lethal methods.
2,500 FP (500 x 5) awarded.
6,200 XP to level 16.
You have (20) stat points to assign.

Gus sat heavily on the ground and hung his head. *That was too damn close! And where the hell was Aurora?*

He stared at the twenty stat points, feeling like an idiot for not allocating them sooner. At least this encounter made it painfully obvious—he needed much more HP and MP. He dropped ten into Intelligence and the other ten into Constitution, raising each pool by two-hundred points. 840 HP still seemed low for total health with how hard those supers hit.

"Aurora, are you okay?" He sat up in alarm when she didn't respond. During the heat of battle, he had long since lost track of where she was and what she was doing. He checked his minimap and saw that she was moving in his direction, her green dot the only one left solid, so she was safe.

He got to his feet and limped over to the closest super. Touching him, Gus found three abilities: **Absorb**, **Transfer**, and **Intermediate Shielding**. Gus found that **Absorb** took up seventy percent of the buffer. Clearing it, he selected **Intermediate Shielding**, which took roughly sixty percent. Trying to add **Transfer** pushed the bar far into the red, so he deselected it.

You have chosen to leech **Intermediate Shielding (Level 32)**.
You have chosen to copy and erase skills, are you sure? (Y/N?)

Gus chose yes and Ash spasmed a bit before settling again. Gus attempted **Leech** again, hoping that he hadn't wasted two potential abilities. *Yes!* The other two were still there. Repeating the process, Gus was able to take the other abilities in their entirety, but saw that it also caused a fifty-percent reduction in HP. After taking the third ability, Ash was down to only twenty percent health. Gus made a mental note—if he overdid it, he could see the process being fatal. He made a stretcher underneath the super and pushed Ash towards the door while he moved to the next super.

The two supers heavy with cybernetics were sprawled on the ground, Gus touched the first with the gun. He found **Electronic Mind**, **Aim-Assist**, and **Coerce**. Gus sapped them and while his hand was on the super, he saw his own hybrid-Nth travel down his arm onto the super. Compared to before, the cloud of hybrid-Nth was only a quarter of its former glory. They looked like an ant swarm as they moved down the super's arm to his connected weapon, and seeped into the cracks of the machinery.

As Gus watched in fascination, Nick explained, "There's Kroutonium in that weapon; they're scavenging it." As the swarm coalesced again and moved back, he could not detect any change in its size. The weapon sputtered and its blue glow winked out, the Kroutonium having been an essential component for it to function. The dull hum disappeared as well.

"I just realized, we're going to have to strip all the extras off of these augments, aren't we?"

"It wouldn't be good to leave them with anything that is not affected by the brig's dampening field," Nick confirmed.

Gus turned his attention to the display again.

*You have chosen to leech **Electronic Mind (Level 47)**.*

*You have chosen to leech **Aim-Assist (Level 33)**.*

*You have chosen to leech **Coerce**.*

You have chosen to copy and erase skills, are you sure? (Y/N?)

Moving to the other super, he found only two: **Hyper** and **Krackle**. Taking these and erasing them, he moved to the last super, the one who had fallen into the tree. His abilities were **Warp** and a strange one called **Xyzzy**. He also had **Advanced Flight**, but it was grayed out, perhaps because it was an ability Gus already possessed.

He looked pretty scratched up and one arm was twisted at a sickening angle. His health hovered at 57% and was slowly dipping. Gus fished out a red gel and put it in the man's mouth, closing it so he bit on the edge.

With a nauseating crack, the bone reset and the super's eyes sprang open. Gus triggered **Leech** and he shook a bit then his eyes fluttered closed. The gel did its work, and Gus waited to take an ability until he'd recovered into the eighty percent range. Gathering his abilities, he set to ferrying them to the brig.

Aurora burst out the door just as he got there and held it open. "Did the EMP work?" she asked, then looked down at the collected supers. "Well, I guess that answers that."

Gus fashioned a train of floating stretchers and they slowly got them all to the brig, having to make multiple trips down the lift. The gurney from the infirmary was a big help, but the lift was small enough that only one would fit in the small space.

The previous supers were awake, and boy were they pissed. They pounded soundlessly on the glass as Gus and Aurora spread the remaining supers out, keeping them all on one side of the alleyway and toggling on the soundproofing. Aurora hit another combo of keys and the transparent door frosted over. She kept playing with the settings and the opacity reduced.

Meanwhile, Gus tried to strip off everything he could detach from the augments, throwing the guns and power-cells into an empty cell. Aurora was saying something but he registered none of it. After a couple minutes, she poked him on the shoulder. Aurora stood there with her arms folded, one eyebrow raised.

"Sorry, just lost in my thoughts trying to figure out how to detach all this. What were you saying?"

"I just changed the cells to basically function like a one-way mirror. We can see in but they can't see out. That way we can see if they're up to something without them knowing we're watching. That should curtail any escape attempts, or make them wonder if we're watching."

Gus gave her a thumbs up and turned back to the augment he was trying to de-mechanize. Everything else was placed internally and couldn't be removed. Hopefully there were safeguards against this very thing, considering this was a brig to contain supers.

"Here, follow me to the control center. Let me show you what upgrades I decided on for the manor."

Gus shrugged and closed the cell as Aurora turned to the elevator. Gus was ready to go, eager to get away from the power dampening effects of the room.

In the control center, Gus relaxed in a chair, choosing one that sat in the warm sunlight. Aurora excitedly began showing him some of the new features of the manor. First was the EMP emitter, which had a limited range of two-hundred-feet around the central antenna of the manor, and that range could not be increased. There were at least six other mercs that relied on those types of augments, so if they could be lured to the manor, it was an easy knockout. The only problem was that it took forever to recharge, a whopping twenty-six hours.

"This next one was expensive, but I think it will really come in handy." The lift opened and twenty men and women spilled out of the crowded elevator. They all wore the characteristic manor jumpsuits.

"Who are these guys?" Gus said, suddenly alert. The warm sun had been making him feel like a nap was in order until the intruders showed up.

"They're decoys! Watch." She hit some settings and the familiar pillowbot skeleton became visible, with emitters embedded on its chest and back. She turned them back on and they filed back into the elevator. "We will be much less easy targets if the enemy is distracted and we can hide in plain sight. There are thousands of profiles we can attach to the decoys and we can give the illusion of a fully-functional manor. They are not sentient and cannot aid us in fighting or defending, but they can mimic the normal routines of manor staff. Because they carry their own emitters, they can even join us outside, but shadows might give them away, so we'll have to decide when to use them. I've set them to roam the manor, then act surprised and flee if there are any intruders. We will get an alert remotely if that happens."

"I could see where that would be helpful. Would've been nice if they could help us fight, though."

"Then you'll like what I have next… Weaponized drones." She said the last two words with the verbal equivalent of a mic drop, as if that was all that needed to be said.

"Yeah, and?" Gus asked, not impressed.

"You don't get it. I can do *soooo* many things with these bad boys. I've maxed them out so I can drop explosives, debuffs, heals if you're out of reach. The possibilities are endless and I have so many devious little ideas that I want to try. I can link all controls to my display, so I'll be much more helpful in battle and can attack from much greater distances, so we'll both be safer."

"I guess I'll take your word for it," Gus said, still unconvinced drones would be that great, remembering how easily the mantids tore his own drones apart.

She went on to defend her choice but Gus barely heard all her ideas for implementation. This spot was the perfect temperature and he closed his eyes, trying to nod when appropriate to show he was paying attention.

CHAPTER TWENTY-ONE

Comin' Thru

After the adrenaline from the battle had long burned away and sitting in the warm sun, Gus was deeply tired; he began to feel himself fading fast. "I gotta get to bed, I'm so tired all of a sudden."

"It was a busy day. I think I'm going to crash early too. I'm going to finish making some upgrades to the manor so we won't get caught unprepared. Do you want to see what I've picked out?"

Gus shook his head and waved for her to go on without him. "I trust you; you pulled that EMP out just in time. I'll put you in charge of facilities. Do I have to give you some kind of authorization to make those decisions?"

"You already did when you made me lieutenant."

"Good. Okay, knock yourself out. I'm going to bed." He staggered to the elevator and fell into bed. Gus thought he heard a chime as he fell asleep, but he was too tired to even check as he fell into a familiar dream. He had it repeatedly, but it was one of those that was easy to forget the particulars.

The young apprentice crept downstairs in the dark and silent manor. The boy made his way to the large door that led to the alchemist's secret cache.

The manor had been in his master's family for many, many generations, and the lock, which was the best of its kind when it was made, was still functional, but less secure than what had been made for many years. On the floor below was a sturdier door. It was covered with powerful wards and complex locks. Large and vault-like, it would be a challenge to any master thief. But the boy knew this to be a decoy.

One night, after a failed invasion of the manor and the thief was apprehended, the family had celebrated. The master alchemist had become quite drunk and bragged about how the family had a special protection for their legacy. A special enchantment hid the real location of their unique potions, and if one was not told of it, the mind would slide over this hiding place like oil on water.

"The thief had no chance!" the master laughed. He gloated over the value and contents of the hidden trove.

That was when the boy had begun to make his plan. The next day, the master remembered nothing of the exchange, and the boy did not say anything about the matter.

Facing the nondescript door, he surveyed the challenge. The lock appeared to be fairly basic, after what the boy had learned. He got his tools out and deftly picked the lock; it was easier than he expected. The door swung silently outward. Grabbing a candlestick, the boy made his way down the stairs. The scant light refracted through multitudes of flasks and bottles filled with various colored liquids.

This was what the boy sought. These potions were the rare, select ones that raised one's stats. With what was in this chamber, he could become so much *more*. The potions were meticulously arranged. The boy, who had thought about this moment for as long as he could remember, opted to start with the strength potions. This would fortify him to tolerate all the other changes the potions would do.

Wasting no time, he grabbed the first vial. He uncorked it and drank the contents. It was bitter, and he could feel some flaky sediments at the base of the vial.

Ugh. Who knows how old these are? I'll bet some have been here so long they have become inactive.

Steeling himself, he grabbed the next vial. This one tasted like a decent herbal tea, albeit cold.

Not too bad, I could tolerate them if they were all like that.

Still the boy felt no stronger. This was more disappointing than expected. One more. Another.

All of a sudden, he felt a cramp. Worry began to creep up the boy's spine but then the discomfort passed. He watched as his weak frame seemed to stretch and fill out. At first, he could see thin bands of muscle become visible, which reminded him of the town messengers who ran to and fro delivering missives.

The quaffing recommenced. His runner's build soon gave way to the thicker builds of rangers and progressed to a full-fledged warrior's build.

He was worried that there would be some side effects, but he honestly felt better than he ever had in his life. And this was permanent! After finishing all the strength potions, he moved on to agility, and constitution.

His skin tightened and he could tell something was happening to make it stronger than even plate steel. His increased agility made the consumption of the potions all the faster. Initially, he was worried he would become full or water-logged from drinking so many potions, but this was not the case. The rapid growth must be utilizing all of that extra moisture.

Now onto intelligence and wisdom potions. Awareness and ideas, plans and schemes flooded into his mind. Past conversations the master had with other specialists came rushing back, recalled in perfect clarity, and he began to understand the subjects they were discussing, then to see where they were occasionally incorrect in their suppositions and conclusions.

His mind expanded and he began to understand both the inner workings of his own body and how mana flowed in and out of his system. Designs and structures behind the symbols and gestures of wizards, mages, and necromancers began to become clear. And then he was done. There was nothing left but piles and piles of bottles.

Then the door above him opened, bright light spilling down upon him…

———

Gus awoke to find the morning light shining in through the balcony window, a shaft of sunlight playing directly across his face. Blinking at the light, he sat up and eagerly clicked the button to check his logs, and the dream was soon forgotten.

Looking at his display, he checked out his haul of new abilities:

New abilities assimilated!
Enhanced Strength (Level 36) [Passive]: *At its current level, this ability gives a (1.7 x level) permanent increase to the Strength stat. Each stat point allocated into Strength yields 1.7 points in addition to skill boost (not retroactive).*
Bound (Level 5) [20 MP]: *Jump with increased ability. Energy stored upon landing, aiding height and power of successive jumps.*
Resilience (Level 11) [Passive]: *Grants extraordinary resistance to projectiles and explosive damage due to a passive ether shield that absorbs and deflects attacks above melee speeds.*
Intermediate Shielding (Level 16) [10MP/minute]: *Form barriers around the host. Can be enlarged to encompass more people but will drain MP at an accelerated rate. Energy attacks will weaken shielding and destabilize it.*
Absorb (Level 26) [20 MP]: *Extract energy and store for later use. Most effective when directly draining MP and HP from others.*
Transfer (Level 13) [15MP]: *Distribute energy from* **Absorb**. *Cannot change its form or convert energy into another medium. If energy is absorbed, it will be transferred in the same form.*
Electronic Mind (Level 36): *Facilitated communication with non-*

biologic entities, as well as intuition in construction and repair of all constructs meant to interface with biologic tissues.

Aim-Assist (Level 8) [5 MP/minute]: *Display augment to aid in targeting, allows the host to lock-on at higher levels. Once a lock is achieved, it can be maintained even after the target is out of the line of sight or uses stealth skills.*

Coerce (Level 11) [50MP]: *Compels a target to agree with instruction. Success calculated based on the delta between the target's base Intelligence stat compared to caster.*

Hyper (Level 17) [20MP]: *Doubles a stat for 5 minutes per activation.*

Krackle (Level 6) [30 MP]: *High energy burst attack of concentrated cascading spheres of energy.*

Warp (Level 12) [30 MP]: *Distort reality in a localized area, either crushing or expanding items in a 1-meter diameter sphere.*

Xyzzy (Level 3) [75MP]: *Bamf! Form wormholes to create portals and transport from one location to another. Base range is 5 feet. Each additional level extends this range another 5 feet.*

13 new abilities assimilated:
13,000 XP awarded.
6,500 FP awarded.
8,200 XP to level 17.
Current Nth ability capacity: 92%. You are nearing capacity and will not be able to learn or absorb more powers when Nth reach maximum capacity.

"Well, that sucks! **Leech** will become obsolete in just a little while. Can I erase a power and gain space? I could do without **Bound**."

"I'm afraid not."

"Sh—" Gus almost swore, then started spitting as he had the sudden taste of pencil shavings in his mouth.

"That the hybrid-Nth?" Gus guessed when he had cleared the bitter taste.

"Yes, the hybrid-Nth gathered some refined Kroutonium

from that beam weapon, and are wondering why you don't use it to make more hybrid-Nth."

"Will that even make any difference? Did they scavenge enough?"

Gus heard the crunch of footsteps on newly-fallen snow and waited patiently for the reply. "There's not enough from the gun, but they suggested getting their brothers from the other suit."

"What other suit? That augment?"

"No, from the escape pod."

"Huh? But that's on the bottom of the ocean! Plus who knows where it's moved in the meantime, even if I could make it down there."

"It should be possible to go that deep, now that you have a shielding ability. The specs seem adequate for what we would need to do."

Gus hedged a little bit; he had always been a bit claustrophobic. "Do we have to?"

"Only if you want more powers. The hybrid-Nth can store about ten-thousand times more skill data than Nth alone. If they weren't tied up maintaining your systems, it would be a non-issue."

"Helping those damn pirates is going to keep coming back to bite me in the ass, isn't it?"

"Pretty much."

"Well, I guess a chunk of my day is planned out for me. I don't want to lose any powers because I don't have the capacity. Where's Aurora?"

"She's already eaten, trained, and is now down on the beach. She's been up for hours, but I let Daphne know you were recovering from the battle, and probably sleeping longer to assimilate all the new powers."

"Yeah, I wondered why I was so tired. I was getting used to needing less and less sleep."

"If I were you, I'd shift your **Energy Absorption** skill to be more active after **Leeching** some powers, so you don't get overwhelmed."

With a little guidance, Gus made the changes to automatically pull needed energy from the environment as opposed to his own limited stores of glucose and body fat.

"Now that I know that some abilities can give a huge boost to stats, I think my main focus is going to be maximizing my MP pool. I'm pretty sure Aurora will agree, but I plan to sink all my points into Intelligence for the foreseeable future. Plus, I need to get a comfortable buffer of HP until I get some kind of self-healing effect."

"Seems reasonable, just make sure you practice using all your new abilities so you aren't using them for the first time without knowing how they function."

Turning his comms on, he called Aurora and asked if she wanted to train. "I'll meet you there. I'm almost done here. Feel free to start without me. I think I'll be done quickly, but just in case, go ahead."

Gus stood on the scanner in the arena and waited as the beam played over him, back and forth. "Is there something wrong with the scanner, Nick?"

"I think it's just overloaded with your changes and trying to figure out a training regimen that would be adequate."

Gus stepped off the scanner and opened the menu that displayed training options. The cursor blinked for a minute doing nothing. "Did I break it inadvertently? **Wreck-It-Gus** strikes again."

"Give it a minute."

Finally a new set of tabs appeared and Gus opened the new menus. Reading the description of a tab labeled 'Adaptive Training' Gus had a smile spread across his face.

Adaptive Training: *Opponents generated in waves, with successive waves increasing in difficulty and learning attack styles and defending against them with greater efficiency as levels progress. Future training* *sessions will retain this information, creating an ever-changing challenge for the user.*

Gus started the session and a single pillowbot slid to the center of the arena. Gus dashed and punched. With his **Enhanced Strength**, the pillowbot flipped and rolled out of the circle that demarcated the confines of the arena.

After a brief pause, two more combatants appeared. Gus dashed to attack again, but the speed of these pillowbots was unlike any they had ever shown before. Two rapid punches to his kidneys surprised Gus as he dodged out of the way. He had never even seen the pillowbot move behind him. He almost triggered **Hyper** to double his Agility and increase his own speed—but caught himself. What if the system ramped speed up even more? Would he even be able to compete at those speeds?

He jumped up and got a view of how the bots were arranged in the arena, his descent slowing automatically as he reabsorbed the kinetic energy as gravity pulled on him. This allowed him to direct his fall and kick into one of the bots. He got a good kick to the head in, but it quickly dodged away, reducing the potential damage to half of what it should have been. He tried to dash and punch but the bots were just too quick for him, anticipating his attacks, and since there were two of them, they outmatched him, one getting in a punch while his attention was focused on the other.

Enough of this. Gus reviewed the description for **Electronic Mind.**

Electronic Mind: *Facilitated communication with non-biologic entities, as well as intuition in construction and repair of all constructs meant to interface with biologic tissues.*

Since these were essentially robots, maybe he could detect the location and how the two bots were communicating. Maybe even influence it somehow. Gus felt an incoming attack on his flank and was able to block and execute **Sweep the Leg**. His leg shot out and toppled the pillowbot.

Have I ever done that without Jet?

Gus punched the ground where the pillowbot had fallen, but missed. It had barely managed to turn, over and over, while Gus pounded futilely at the mat, chasing it. Gus followed until it rolled out of the arena, signaling a loss. Gus sensed the other bot jumping at him with a kick, and he found that he could exactly time his attack. He sidestepped and grabbed the outstretched leg, swinging it so the robot followed its partner outside the ring. That type of win was much easier than brute force.

Gus realized that he would have to stay clever, and not become too reliant on using physical strength, especially as green as he was with these new attacks. He wouldn't have the nuances and utility as a super that had used fewer powers in various situations.

It just felt good to punch things like a beast though! Turning, three robots had reset in the arena. This would be a test of stamina too, as the levels increased. He wondered if they would keep adding pillowbots, too.

They all sprang to life, dashing towards him. Gus took to the air, confident that they could not fly. One bot leaped to the shoulders of another and launched toward him and grabbed him. *No fair, was my last jump considered a **Bound**?* Probably, if his landing was affected.

The dome around the arena was only about fifty feet high, and he really didn't have that much maneuverability with flying. On reflex, he activated **Intermediate Shielding** before he hit the ground. It saved him from having the wind knocked out of him.

Crap. Would the next wave have shields now?

As far as Gus could tell, the pillowbots could not use techniques until the next wave, so he might as well take advantage. He placed shields around two of the attackers, and fixed a shield embedded in the floor of the arena, only leaving the head of the last pillowbot exposed. Gus jumped to the top of the shield and began punching the pillowbot until it deactivated in defeat.

Gus could see the other bots punching the shields but making no headway. The shields turned out to be extremely resistant to melee style attacks. Gus focused on one and shrunk the dimensions, constricting it and folding the robot into the diminishing space until it went limp.

Gus went to finish the last robot, but the shield had expired and it was free. Gus activated **Electronic Mind** again and found that he could sense where the robot was going to move, but then the signal fuzzed out after ten seconds, changing something about its frequency so Gus attempted to use **Electronic Mind** again to sense the robot's planning again to no avail.

What the hell am I doing fighting these mercs, just send out these OP robots! The robot began jumping around at increasing speeds and Gus couldn't even find out where to attack. It found ways to jump behind him and rabbit-punch him in the back of the head before he could respond. He began to get pissed at his inability to retaliate.

Looking at the new abilities he hadn't used yet, he decided to try a new one, but a little less conventionally. When the robot punched him again, he tried to activate **Absorb**.

Absorb: *Extract energy and store for later use, most effective when directly draining MP and HP from others.*

Gus wondered if the ability would even work. Did pillowbots even have simulated HP? Another punch interrupted his thoughts. He gritted his teeth as he missed the timing on the first two hits, but on the third, it activated and Gus felt a jolt of energy as he pulled energy from the bot, replenishing both his HP and MP.

After being drained, the robot moved much more slowly and Gus easily finished the fight. After the round, the pillowbot was replaced, it's battery obviously drained. To Gus' relief, only three robots reset for this next wave. Gus recognized the shimmering blue aura as shielding.

Sighing, he readied for the match to start. He threw up a shield and the robots darted in, hitting it repeatedly until it began to sound like popcorn popping in the microwave or hail on a roof. He reviewed how **Krackle** worked and decided to give it a try.

Krackle: *High energy burst attack of concentrated cascading spheres of energy.*

The effect consumed one of the pillowbots, charring the material covering the robotic skeleton. Gus dropped the shield, preparing to trigger **Absorb**. When he fired the ability, nothing happened, and he knew he had gotten the timing wrong.

One more ability down. What else was on the list?

Warp: *Distort reality in a localized area, either crushing or expanding items in a 1-meter diameter sphere.*

Xyzzy: *Bamf! Form wormholes to create portals and transport from one location to another. Base range is 5 feet. Each additional level extends this range another 5 feet.*

While Gus tried to figure out what to do next, he saw one of the robots was using the downed robot as a bludgeon to hit him, while the other tracked behind, skirting to one side or another, awaiting its turn to attack. This extended reach kept him from having direct contact and draining them again. He was running out of tricks.

Let's see how you like this… Gus activated **Warp** on the arms of the bot and the downed pillowbot-club. The two were crushed together, and part of the active bot's forward leg was included in the effect, significantly reducing its mobility.

For the first time in the session, his **TimeSight** activated and gave him a warning. He used **Xyzzy** and focused on the other side of the arena. He reappeared a couple feet away as the last bounding robot brought its clasped arms down, hitting its fellow robots now that Gus had vacated that space. He hadn't even noticed the other robot slip away.

As they tangled together, Gus dashed in and attacked the mobile robot and then finished off the crumpled one. The robots reset; mashed robots being replaced with two others. Gus raised his hands in defeat and walked out of the arena.

Hearing a slow clap, he looked up and saw Aurora watching from the side of the arena. "Good job. I'm impressed. Are you ready for some sparring?"

"Give me a minute." Gus sat on the edge of the mat, his hands on his knees.

"Okay, I'll give you a break then. For now. Have you eaten yet? You look a little faint." Gus just shook his head. "Let's go then." She motioned and they headed to the cafeteria.

CHAPTER TWENTY-TWO

Holding in the World

Gus checked his logs and saw that the Adaptive Training was a great way to gain XP.

You have completed (4) waves of Adaptive Training. Final difficulty rank: B.
20,000 XP awarded.
LEVEL UP! Congratulations, Level 17 reached!
500 FP awarded.
You have (5) additional stat points to assign.
5,700 XP to level 18.

Gus shivered as the post-level euphoria faded. A big smile crossed his face at how fast he was leveling now. Maybe taking that XP boost with his guiding principle wasn't a bad idea after all. He dropped two points into Constitution and three into Intelligence, bringing them both to 45. Once his HP hit a thousand, he'd put them all into Intelligence.

He wondered if the influx of new powers was so rare that it triggered some compensatory XP when they were used. He remembered having to work an entire three hours to get one new skill. He was already planning future sessions, anticipating himself power leveling with the new discovery.

"You just leveled again, didn't you?" Aurora asked.

"Yeah."

"I hope I don't look like that."

"Like what?" Gus asked, a little concerned now.

"Full on ahegao."

"How do you know what…?" Gus asked as he flushed deeply.

"Daphne told me."

"Oh." Gus was at a loss. He could wait to check his logs until later from here on out.

There was an awkward pause and Aurora finally broke the silence. "Here, why don't we grab something to take with us? I spent the morning on the beach and it was perfect."

"I'm down," Gus said, grateful for anything to change the subject. He ordered some food to go. Their meals arrived in a large bag, complete with utensils. "I have to do this more often. I wouldn't have even thought it was an option if you hadn't suggested it!"

"I imagine it'd have to be with a facility this size."

They headed out to the beach and kicked off their boots. They ate in silence, watching the waves.

Gus massaged his feet in the soft sand. "Man, some days I wish I could just sit here in the sun with no responsibilities, powers or not."

"Someone told me that it doesn't matter how much power you have, there's always responsibility."

Gus sat up and looked at her. "Who said that?"

"He was an older super in Purple Faction. He retired a couple years after I started. I forget his name."

"Hmm. What did he look like?" Gus' grandfather had always said that to him and he always attributed the tenet to him, but it was probably just part of Purple Faction training. Still, what if it was Grandpa?

"I don't know. Old? Gray hair, typical super build. I never

talked to him directly, he just gave us a pep talk before one of our practicals. It was pretty typical for them to try to give us a bunch of advice pretty much all the time."

"Was any of it useful?"

"Yeah, sometimes. You heard the Purple Faction tenets a lot, and while I didn't understand them all, at first, you got to see why they were there after a while. Some advice only really sticks after you see what happens when someone is seriously hurt or dies from ignoring it."

"Sometimes I feel like I'm like that guy in *Greatest American Hero*."

"What's that?"

"It's an old TV show about a guy who gets a super suit from aliens and loses the instruction manual. Then he basically figures out his powers from trial and error."

"That's pretty on the nose, at least as far as you're concerned."

"In some ways, my situation is a lot better because I have access to my Nth to help me train, and it sounds like most supers don't have that. On the other hand, I feel like I'm struggling to reinvent the wheel. Doing things the hard way that is probably obvious to most other supers. However, I definitely am glad I didn't have to drink Purple Faction's Kool-Aid. What you described just reminds me of propaganda a little bit."

Aurora tilted her head and screwed up her mouth in thought.

"Maybe with some things, but I guess you had to be there. There's no perfect system with imperfect humans, even ones with superpowers. You just try to find a way to do the most good. And learn how to live with the times where the system falls short. You can't save everyone. You can't please everyone. I think one of Purple Faction's strengths is how it is structured, and how it provides a framework of behavior and ethics." She speared a large chunk of watermelon and chewed.

"I've been on the other side of that framework. It feels like compulsion and intimidation. As a super, you probably don't really know what it feels like to do something under duress, but a lot of regs feel that way. There's always the implied threat of recrimination if we, I mean they, don't act in the right ways."

"It does keep crime down." She shrugged.

"I suppose. And I'm not saying I have all the answers either. My father would always say, 'Don't bring me a problem unless you have two possible solutions prepared.' You may not realize it, but it can feel really demotivating to live in a world where even if you try your best your whole life, you can be easily surpassed by someone who has been mysteriously blessed with Nth."

"You make it sound like it's all fun and games for supers. Like we don't have any problems at all." She turned and looked at him.

"But you have to admit some things are easier, right? I never really found my thing until I got my Nth. How many people are there just like that out there? I know supers view people like me as layabouts, lazy and unmotivated. But what is there to be motivated about? Slaving away, being a cog in the machine? Sorry if I just don't find nirvana flipping burgers or doing a job to make ends meet." Gus stabbed at his food, his appetite gone.

"Have you really ever flipped burgers? With your parents in the Faction, I doubt you guys were poor." She arched an accusatory eyebrow.

"No, but my father was always on me to improve myself. When I really didn't have any interest in any of the typical service jobs, he found jobs for me working for other supers. I'll admit it was kind of cool at first. I've always been a fanboy of supers and their adventures."

"Yeah, tell me about that. How was the transition from a henchman to a super? I mean, you guys are really only known for following orders, usually poorly." Gus scowled as she said this. "I'm sorry, am I wrong?"

"No. The reality of being a henchman is actually pretty boring. I think anyone would be hard-pressed to always be alert. Ninety-nine percent of the time there's absolutely nothing going on. Then there's one percent running-down-the-street-naked-with-your-hair-on-fire level crisis mode. It's easy to be disengaged."

"Okay, I get it, go on."

"When I met up with some other of my gamer friends, that kind of changed. I actually looked forward to going to work. It was less the actual job, and more the company. We could be cleaning the dried bugs off the windshield of an aerial fortress when it was in drydock, but it was still fun with those guys."

"I didn't have many friends in the academy. Not when they realized I wasn't 'girlfriend material.' I just wanted to focus on my training. I was an ugly duckling that transitioned late, and without any close friends, the other girls saw me as a threat. I had a reputation before I even knew I had one."

"Well, that sucks," Gus said, shaking his head.

"It worked for me. Kept people out of my hair, and they left me alone for the most part. But enough about me. So you and your buddies were, what do they call it, 'henching'?"

"Yeah. There were good times, just enjoying life. Still, as I look back on that time, I wasn't really going anywhere. There isn't any upward mobility or working towards something bigger and better; you're just kind of stuck. Maybe there were some positions for those who went above and beyond, but it was way more responsibility and effort for barely any more pay. Not a huge motivator. Plus they're usually much more dangerous."

"You seem like you'd like to keep on the down-low."

"I guess. I just wanted to live my life without other people getting involved. I think I just found my comfort zone and accepted the fact that I was lesser than other people. Then I learned some coping mechanisms that weren't really that helpful, but took my focus off the real reason for my lack of drive. I got into gaming pretty heavily, because I could be a part of a world that my character could shape and actively change. I saw consistent progression and growth. I even looked forward to grinding because the rewards were there, though the tasks were monotonous and repetitive. Then the rest of the game was a breeze."

"And you think that's how supers are."

"Well, life isn't like that for regs. You can do something monotonous forever and there's no reward at the end. If something doesn't eventually pay off, then there's no real reason to push through the drudgery. And yeah, it's even more appropriate because you do gain levels and get stronger. The Nth are impartial; they always give rewards. Real life, not so much. Does that make sense?"

"You make it sound so bleak. Is it really that bad for regs?" She pressed. "I mean, you said you were happy, right?"

"Okay, Aurora. What was life for you like before you got your powers? Was it great?"

Aurora didn't respond as her eyes went out of focus.

After a minute, Gus pressed onward. "As time has gone on, I've remembered more and more about my mother. One thing that I recently thought about was when I asked my mom why she liked the 80's so much. She said it was the last normal decade."

"I've seen the clothes and heard some of the music, Gus. I don't know if normal is the right word..." Aurora said with a wry grin.

"What I mean is that when the Nth came in the early 90's, there was a lot of change. Obviously. But she said that at least people were trending towards a little more tolerance and equality. The introduction of powers negated that to a large degree, and while people weren't discriminated against because of nationality, wealth, or color of their skin—they were discriminated against by whether they had abilities or not. Governments changed, power shifted, and the whole dynamic of society changed."

"Not to interrupt, but you seem done." She pointed to the food that Gus had been mushing and cutting into smaller and smaller pieces. "Should we head in to train?"

"Maybe later. Actually, I have another idea."

"Such as?"

"Deep sea diving?" Gus asked with a shrug.

Gus explained what Nick had said about his Nth capacity and how he needed to get more raw materials to absorb and left it at that. He outlined the plan Nick had for what his new ability **_Intermediate Shielding_** could do. All that he needed to do was to go to the ocean floor and find a crashed escape pod.

"It's really freaking me out, to be honest."

"Gus, you're a super now. This is what we do! I'm actually kind of excited. Nick? What do we need to do to make this happen?" Aurora asked eagerly.

CHAPTER TWENTY-THREE

Dive Down

"The closest point on the beach to the crash site is on the east side of the island. Why don't we head there? It's not very far from here, you could probably walk there in a half an hour," Nick suggested.

"Nick, is getting the suit even feasible given how much time has passed?" Aurora asked as they grabbed their boots and began walking on the sand.

"I don't see why not. The weight of the pod should have minimized how far it would drift, given there wasn't too much shrapnel." A familiar wave of weird sensations hit Gus and he waited for Nick to translate what the smell of kettle corn and the feeling of a foot massager could possibly signify.

"The hybrid-Nth can sense the Kroutonium nearby. They say they know where all their 'family' is. Not just here, either. If I'm interpreting this correctly, they can sense it from everywhere in the world. No, their word for 'here' is synonymous with what we would use for eons and galaxies. Everything their conscious-ness can experience and has experienced is available to be remembered or used. Anyway, to them, some of their family are a short distance from us, but I'm concerned that it may be *very* far from our perspective."

"Whoa, whoa, whoa! You never said anything about Krou-tonium!" Aurora said, grabbing the sleeve of Gus' outfit. "You actually *have* some of it already?" Aurora moved her grip to the front of Gus' jumpsuit, her eyes wide and a giddy grin on her face. "And no one calls it Kroutonium anymore, by the way."

"What? Why?" Gus sputtered, shocked at her sudden change in demeanor.

"It is the most valuable substance on Earth! Just how much are you talking about?" Aurora demanded, staring more intently.

"Well, the plate in the one was about ten pounds and—" Gus hung on the last word as Aurora let go of him and plopped to her butt on the sand, as if struck. She was muttering some-thing unintelligible to herself.

"And why don't they call it Kroutonium anymore?" Gus inquired, smoothing out his outfit.

"The guy who found it made so much money that he moved to Wisconsin and built this huge underground bunker. Then he got a little weird and started doing genetic experiments on rabbits. There was a furor among the animal lovers and the name was changed to Endurium," she explained almost in a daze.

"Endurium, huh?" Gus smiled with nostalgia, instantly understanding the arcane reference. "Yeah, but to answer your question, I need some more, thanks to some asshat decisions I made earlier on, before you got to the island."

Aurora sat heavily on the sand, jaw agape, muttering, "***Ten*** pounds?"

Gus ignored her and turned his attention to Nick and the plan. "Ask them if they can show it on the display, then we would know in our frame of reference."

"You know they understand you and your thoughts just as I do, right? Probably better, in fact. Just because you don't under-stand them, don't underestimate them. They get it."

Gus asked his question mentally and received two sensations. One was the smell of a diamond, which was how they referred to themselves, and Gus was past trying to make sense of the stimuli. It was what it was.

Couldn't they just have a normal name?

In the second sensation, he saw a blue diamond pop up on the edge of his display. Zooming to the appropriate scale, it was way out there, miles away, maybe twenty or so. *But how deep?* A number popped up above the blue diamond: 14,678. *Was that feet? Meters? How deep was the ocean anyway?*

"So how am I going to get down there, Nick?"

"I think you could reinforce your new shielding ability to transfer the pressure exerted by the water to the ether. The volume of ether in the universe trumps the water on this planet and it should be able to resist that easily, if done correctly. I would recommend making two separate spheres, as the weaves will compress the more pressure is exerted on them. You could be in the inner sphere and the outer sphere would be a barrier for the compression. The only challenge is that you will be limited by the available oxygen in the spheres so you will have to be fast."

"Fast I can do, especially now. What about the bends or compression sickness?"

"You have Nth, remember? We can monitor the pressure of the inner bubble and the outer sphere will be managing most of the compression, significantly lessening the effect on the inner sphere. We will also track blood and tissue gasses and guide the ascent and descent, and display everything as a timer so you can have a representation you can see and use to plan."

"I'm coming too," Aurora broke in, hearing their internal conversation.

"It's too dangerous, plus it would cut oxygen reserves in half," Nick replied, not even considering the argument.

"How are you going to see down there? It'll be pitch black," she said.

"Gus' perception is high enough that he has filters he can

use, plus the hybrid-Nth can sense the other Kroutonium, and I'm sure can update the display. Besides, he needs you to monitor surface conditions in case those supers come back."

Aurora finally relented and stood, brushing the sand off herself.

"You're sure, Nick?" Gus asked, seeing Aurora's disappointment.

"I don't think your skill in shielding is adequate to create a sphere big enough for the both of you. In addition, the amount of energy to pull a sphere that size down to the ocean floor will expend all of your MP before you get there. You have to actively **Ether Leash** down to counteract the sphere's buoyancy."

Gus shrugged apologetically.

"Logistics made the decision for us. Alright, I'll be the lookout. What if someone attacks while you're submerged? Send a message through our Nth if there are any complications?"

"Let's hope it doesn't come to that, but that sounds like a good plan." Aurora kicked sand into a little pile without looking at him. "Hey, I'm not looking forward to this, if that's your concern. I'm slightly claustrophobic as it is. But lately, life is a bunch of *have-tos* and not a lot of *get-tos*. If I don't upgrade my Nth, I can't power up like I need to, in order to do what I must to keep the manor out of Basileus' hands. I promise I'll be careful."

"Okay, just do it. The less time this takes the better." She hugged herself and refused to meet his eyes.

Gus put on a brave face and tried the ability for the first time. He made a sphere around himself, making it just big enough to not trigger his claustrophobia. With Nick's guidance, he made another larger sphere, pushing the range of his concentration and ability.

"We'll have to make some changes when we get above the pod, but this should work for now. Now just ether lash and go," Nick advised.

Gus waved to Aurora and walked the ball to the water. He

had always wanted to try zorbing, and now he had one of his own design! Currently, the inner sphere was resting on the bottom of the outer sphere and he could feel the bobbing of the waves as the water lifted him up and down inside the construct. He made two tethers and launched himself like a slingshot, flying out over the waves.

Gus crashed forward as he hit a wave, tumbling ass over teakettle until he settled on the bottom of the sphere, looking upward.

Nick guffawed. "Classic!"

Gus got back to his feet, happy that the soft membrane of the sphere didn't hurt as he collided with it. He turned and gave Aurora a sheepish wave.

"You suck, you know that?" Gus griped.

When the laughing finally calmed down. Nick showed Gus where to put internal supports between the two spheres.

"You need practice stabilizing these supports, before they're stressed, which is why you're using MP to create them now. One of the advantages of ether is that you can make frictionless surfaces. Now if the outer sphere encounters something, the supports will absorb it and not transfer that to the inner sphere."

Gus made the changes as shown. "And you couldn't show me that before?"

"I could have, but where's the fun in that?"

With a growl, Gus started pulling in the direction of the blue diamond on his display. There was still more jostling than he liked with the herky-jerky movement of the waves hitting the sphere and trying to gauge their movement. He soon found that he could avoid the water altogether and start swinging the spheres through the air.

From there, Gus got into a rhythm and even found that he could launch himself again before touching down and losing momentum. He felt like Tarzan, swinging on ether vines, swooping and feeling the exhilaration of the brief moments of weightlessness at each arc's apex. All too soon, he was at the designated spot. This far out from the island the water didn't seem to have perceptible waves.

"Okay, after your MP recharges, you are going to want to compress that outer sphere and make it selectively permeable to nitrogen. Your brain is going to fight against this a bit because it's hard to conceptualize but... There. I've temporarily highlighted the different gases in different colors. As you compress the outer sphere, let the black particles filter out and keep the light green ones."

Gus started compressing and had difficulty separating the two, so both gases were escaping. Struggling, an idea came to him and he imagined the black particles as being square shaped and the green as circular ones, much like the baby toys designed to teach shapes. Subconsciously the adjustment was just what he needed and the large sphere began to shrink, concentrating the space between the spheres with purer and purer oxygen.

His MP drained at a higher rate while doing the compression and he had to rest twice to allow the bar to slowly trickle full. He itched to grab some blue gels but Nick warned him to save them for an emergency. His current regeneration speed wasn't quick enough to maintain both spheres but it was close. The drain was much slower when he wasn't changing their dimensions, then it began creeping back up. When he was finished, the now much smaller outer sphere was easier to maintain and manage.

"Okay, now with that done, make the inner sphere permeable to allow only oxygen into the smaller sphere and carbon dioxide and nitrogen out to the larger sphere. The partial pressure of the gases should auto regulate. I will warn you when you are running low. If we're in a pinch, we could do a little ***Wreck-It-Gus*** hydrolysis, but let's try to avoid that."

"Why?"

"Explodey reasons."

Gus rolled his eyes at Nick's explanation. He focused on the inner sphere, and imagined the shapes again, but as valves resembling a revolving door.

"Perfect, I think you got it," Nick congratulated him. "Alright, **Ether Lash** yourself down and go for it."

The resistance of pulling the twin spheres through the water was significantly more difficult, as he had to maintain the weaves constantly and with more force. This sensation was not pleasant at all, feeling like climbing a rope down into the murky depths. All while someone kept adding weight to you the higher *or deeper* you got.

This too became rhythmic after Gus got the hang of it, and he altered his display to night vision mode. There wasn't much to see in this patch of water. He had expected to see more marine life, but this area was a watery desert with nothing to change the view. Gus pulled and realized that the action was purely a mental one. He had been tensing his back muscles, straining with each pull and was getting more fatigued than he needed to. Sitting down, he closed his eyes and focused on the motion.

The task became easier, although Gus saw that his MP was draining at a more prodigious rate the lower he descended. Finally Nick relented and allowed him to consume an occasional blue gel. It was all he needed to replenish his MP bar and give him a comfortable margin again. Peeking at times to see his display, the number representing proximity gradually shrank. Gus could feel a slight humming vibration accompanied by the sensation of pulling a cotton ball apart.

"The hybrid-Nth say we are getting close, and that they're excited."

Gus wasn't a fan of the sensation. It wasn't uncomfortable, per se, but it did give him the chills a little bit. Shaking his head, he turned back to the task of pulling. A chime sounded and Gus continued to pull. What felt like hours passed. Another chime sounded but Gus' focus was on the task at hand—logs could wait. When Gus looked, he saw pale green below him.

The wreckage of the pod was visible, and it looked like a clamshell that had been ripped into the shape of Pac-Man. Silt and debris floated around, reminding Gus of vacuum lint. It coated the surface of the pod and the exposed beams and struts from where the pod was ripped apart. It looked like slimy algae. When Gus approached, the silt fluttered away, making things murky and difficult to resolve. The panel shone as a bright gold square in the murk, deep within the pod against one wall.

Gus was concerned the outer sphere would limit how close he could get but it had condensed significantly. Still, he could not go inside the pod with the current size of the spheres. Noticing that his MP was dropping below 10%, he quickly lashed the spheres to the pod wreckage and let go of his active pulling. The pod shifted and was lifted off the ocean floor as the spheres began to rise. The heavier weight of the wreckage anchored the sphere and Gus saw his MP jump to 11%, trending upwards again. He breathed a sigh; he only had two blue gels left.

His concern that he would run out of juice before reaching the bottom and having to start all over again was relieved. Without the focus required to pull the spheres down, he had time to take in the whole scene. The pod looked so small from this vantage point and he was surprised that he had survived reentry. The outer surface was crumpled and dented every-where, black scoring along the base licking up around the sides of the pod.

"Gus, we'll need to hurry. I know we came here for the Kroutonium, but there is a capsule of Nth in a cylinder right next to the plate. Could you grab that as well?"

"Hells, yes. That would be awesome if I could add them to my Nth pool." Gus reached out with an ether lash and tugged on the glowing plate. It moved slightly but then Gus met heavy resistance.

"Careful, don't crack the cylinder or the Nth will be lost," Nick warned. "If you could, put it in a bubble of its own. I'm surprised the cylinder is intact."

Instead of pulling, Gus used the ether leash like an extra hand, probing around to see if he could determine what was holding the plate up. The plastic receptacle holding the plate was still intact, and although Gus could see the plate as a bright blazing square in his display, he had been trying to pull it straight through the side of the plastic. Grasping the top edge, he gently pulled, sliding it out like a game of Operation. Once extracted, he pulled the plate towards him.

He sent another tendril of ether out and found the cylinder situated above the plastic receptacle. Two latches had to be pulled and then Gus dislodged the canister in a similar manner, enclosing it and bringing it slowly to the sphere.

Not wanting to compromise the integrity of his spheres, Gus had the ether leashes trailing underneath, reinforcing his grip around them so they wouldn't be dropped and lost. He undid his anchoring tether and the sphere shot upward.

"Slow down!" Nick yelled, and Gus hit the brakes, throwing out two ether lashes that slammed him to one side of the sphere. "Well, not *that* much."

"Dammit, you scared me," Gus said, resuming his climb, sliding up in a rappelling fashion to avoid too much speed.

"That's better, we should be good as far as oxygen is concerned," Nick reported.

Gus saw the outer sphere stretch back to its old dimensions. He had expected more complications or having to worry about the bends. He just felt… normal, albeit tired. He was exhausted from all the mental exertion, but he was sure he would bounce back if given just a small time to recover.

The ascent was much quicker and more relaxing than the descent, and took a mere fraction of the time. When he broke the surface, the sunshine felt heavenly. He hadn't realized he felt chilled to the bone with the mental focus required to maintain the spheres under pressure.

He lay down in the inner sphere and put his arms behind his head. Using an ether leash, he lazily pulled himself back toward the beach where Aurora was still waiting. The hot sun filtered through the clear spheres and Gus basked in the release of pressure and tension he had felt while constantly flexing his mental muscles. The sphere bobbed on the waves, but in his inner sphere, the rocking motion was soothing rather than jarring.

He began to feel drowsy and sat up. Looking towards the beach, he noticed that he was getting close, but still a good half mile away. Aurora's comm finally managed to reach him.

"Gus! Can you hear me yet? Gus. Gus!"

"Okay, I can hear you, what's up?"

"Did you get what you went for?"

"Yes, no problems or complications."

"Then, what are you doing floating in the ball? Did you forget you can fly?"

"Um, I needed to recharge my MP after resurfacing," he lied. He really just hadn't thought of it, flying wasn't 'normal' for him yet. "I think my MP is high enough now, I'll be right there."

Allowing the outer sphere to disperse, Gus pulled the tethers holding the Kroutonium and canister of Nth to him and allowed the inner sphere to pop as he took flight, keeping himself dry.

He sailed back to shore carrying his loot, intent on making more hybrid-Nth.

CHAPTER TWENTY-FOUR

Cat's in the Cradle

"Father, we need to talk!"

Tempest looked over his shoulder. "Not now, I'm in the middle of something—"

"I challenge you to a duel of supremacy for your title," Cyclone said, almost shouting.

Tempest turned and saw his son standing there with his hands on his hips, trying to look bold. Rampage and After-shock stood behind him, smug looks on their faces. It was obvious what was happening here. Unable to beat him in a fight themselves, they were using his son to make a power grab. *Cowards.*

"Cyclone, don't do this. These are not the individuals you want to side with in the Faction. They are going nowhere and want to use you as their puppet."

"They told me you would try to confuse me and keep me from my rightful place. Father, you have had your time and now I am stepping up to claim the role. Purple Faction must evolve! We have clung to old ideas for too long and the other factions are outpacing us. I will not allow you to hold us back any longer!"

Insanity. How did they convince him to do this? "We will discuss this later; I am in the middle of something important—"

"You are always in the middle of something. Do you forfeit to avoid the challenge? It sounds like you are afraid," he said, gaining confidence.

Tempest narrowed his eyes. "Enough. You realize what this means for you when you lose though, don't you? You will lose your ability to challenge another until you are challenged, which is unlikely as a class D super in the Faction. You will be stuck there with no possibility for promotion, as a failed challenge will lock you in that tier."

"I am not afraid," he said, trembling voice betraying his uncertainty.

Sighing deeply, he turned to one of the administrators nearby. "Set it up, and let me know the time."

"I have already taken the liberty to set everything up. The arena is ready and the council is gathered."

Those weasels! Tempest gritted his teeth and stared at Rampage and Aftershock, who shrunk slightly behind Cyclone. It took all his control not to attack them directly, which would lead to even worse repercussions. He would be stripped of rank and incarcerated until there could be a trial. He didn't have time to be out of commission.

Realizing how well they had orchestrated the entire encounter, Tempest relented and followed them to the arena. Apparently, he had been so caught up in the search that he had not seen them rallying. The arena was full to the brim with members of Purple Faction and he was even more surprised to see that the majority were rooting for his son.

What had he done to them? Or was this more of Rampage's handiwork? If he didn't know better, he would have suspected they had been using a Psi-manipulation power. Rampage could vibrate objects, especially large ones, and cause them to crumble and break. He had no mental abilities. The same with Aftershock; he only had the ability to cause earthquakes and form pits and traps by manipulating the ground below a battle.

Less useful powers against other supers, and both ineffective against him, since he could fly. It was clear now why they didn't oppose him directly.

"Cy-clone, Cy-clone, Cy-clone!" the crowd chanted, and Tempest thought he saw a couple people he didn't recognize inciting the mob. If he had to guess, they were mercs that Rampage had hired and outfitted with Purple Faction uniforms. It burned Tempest that he could not call out his suspicion, as it would be counted as a weak attempt to get out of the battle. *Could it be that I'm actually that unpopular, and I'm looking for an excuse to all this animosity directed towards me? No, it couldn't be.* The only way out was to win and ruin his son's future.

They made their ways to the opposite sides of the arena, a massive dome in the center of the Purple Faction complex. Once the battle started, referee supers would create a shield around the perimeter and the battle would continue until one super relented or was rendered unconscious. Support supers stood on standby to heal any mortal injuries.

Requiring healing also was considered a forfeit, and the super had only a five-count to refuse healing and battle on, else they could do what they needed to save a life. No one had ever died in a duel, but there had been some close calls. As he thought of it, there hadn't been a battle in quite some time. And everyone liked a good fight.

"I'm getting too old for this," Tempest muttered to himself as he charged up his skills. He knew his son's attacks and skills intimately, having trained him throughout his time at the academy. *How does he think he could possibly win?*

The referee dropped the shield that separated both halves of the dome, adding his strength to the outer dome shield. Cyclone raised in the air, supported by a swirling mini twister. Tempest shook his head, knowing the effect was just for show and did nothing to actually support Cyclone. He refused to give it up, wasting precious MP that would eventually be needed in a battle and not be available.

Tempest applied pressure fronts counter to the rotation of

the tiny tornado and ripped it away. As expected, Cyclone settled to earth, unwilling to cede that it was necessary. Tempest extracted energy out of one area in front of him, transferring it to another area rapidly, cycling and alternating the effect to create his own twister, directing it to where Cyclone would land. The force of the blast threw his son to the ground but did not have enough time to develop enough momentum to do any damage.

Just submit, we'll find a way out of this later.

Cyclone jumped to his feet, hair wild from the blast. He reached his arms out in front of him and exerted his ability to create an increase in pressure right above Tempest.

I taught you this, and you try to use it against me? Tempest reached a single hand upward and easily resisted, countering the force and pushing against it. He affected a yawn to further rattle the boy and get him to see the futility of his attacks. He also had to maintain his persona. These battles were a waste of time and he didn't want to be fighting a new upstart every week.

Sweat beaded on Cyclone's forehead as he strained to push against the increasing counter pressure. In frustration, he dropped his attack and charged at his father.

Tempest easily sidestepped and pushed him in the back as he passed, causing him to stumble with the additional momentum and nearly fall.

Cyclone turned, face red and nostrils flaring as he charged again. This time he tackled Tempest and began punching. While it was obvious he was giving it his all, the blows barely registered, only occasionally dropping a single point of HP here and there. Taking advantage of their proximity, he decided to get to the bottom of this fiasco.

"What did they say to you, Cyclone?"

"You wouldn't understand," the boy growled as he continued to punch, getting angrier as he noticed that his father's red bar was not diminishing.

"Try me," Tempest said.

"You say that they want to make me a puppet, but you're the one always keeping me on a leash, limiting my potential."

"I'm trying to keep you safe. The only time I've kept you back was from missions you obviously weren't prepared for, just like you aren't prepared for this fight."

Taking this as another insult, Cyclone fired his **Wind Whip** ability right in Tempest's face.

It caused minimal damage, but it did hurt like hell and Tempest's anger flared as he easily slid out from the unstable pin and leaned in, forcing the bone of his muscular forearm down on his son's throat. "You've forced my hand. I never wanted to do this. I really wish you had talked to me about what you were feeling. This was the worst choice you could have made, and I'm sure you won't like the consequences."

Tempest looked into his son's fearful eyes. They seemed to scream without words. The crowd began booing him, disgusted with the turnabout. Tempest looked up at the crowd. Faces contorted in anger comprised the majority of the crowd. Yelling and shouting obscenities.

What did I do to warrant this hatred? These were people he had served at great personal sacrifice. No doubt a great majority didn't know the hours he had put in to make their lives easier. Doing all the unpleasant tasks it took to run an organization this large. To enforce order on a chaotic world.

Slightly nodding, Tempest twisted, making it look like Cyclone had broken free of the pin, and allowed his son to get the upper hand.

Cyclone's eyes went savage as he grasped his father's neck and started to squeeze.

Out of reflex, Tempest applied outward pressure around his neck, not allowing Cyclone's hands to do any permanent damage, but he could see his son struggling. He really was trying to hurt him. The thought hurt him more than any of the attacks he had ever experienced from friend or foe.

The crowd roared at the apparent turn of the tide. Cords stood out on Cyclone's neck as he strained, and tears squeezed out from crazed eyes. *So this is what Purple Faction has become? This is what I've been sacrificing for all this time?* Flashes of all the hours he had spent, solving some problem or other, being a mediator between disputing supers, or off on some mission or another. What had he traded? He thought he had given enough time to family, but apparently, he knew less than he thought he did.

He had so much less to give after she was gone. Less happiness, less energy, less everything. Looking back up into his son's eyes, he made the choice that he had given enough. The Faction would continue to take from him until it drained him to a husk and then cast him aside. *Sometimes people get the leaders they deserve.*

He looked over and saw Rampage and Aftershock congratulating themselves. Tempest would lose this battle either way, by ruining his family's legacy or by losing his career. Reaching out, he slapped the arena floor, signaling that he conceded the battle.

Cyclone let go of his neck and stood on shaky feet. His hands trembled in amazement, and confusion was barely recognizable on his face until someone rushed forward and lifted his right arm in victory. The crowd roared again, celebrating the apparent upset.

"The challenger has succeeded! Per Faction rules, they will trade ranks immediately. Tempest will be reclassified as Class D and Cyclone is elevated to a Commander!" the referee bellowed, voice augmented to project through the arena.

Cyclone didn't even give him the respect to offer a hand to get back on his feet. Tempest stood and made his way out of the arena, heading to clear out his room. No one paid him any attention as he walked out the door.

CHAPTER TWENTY-FIVE
Sad Girl

Gus and Aurora went to the Foundry with the canister and plate. "Nick, are you going to go offline forever like last time we did this? That would suck if the supers showed up and you were AFK."

"No, this should go much more smoothly. I have already interfaced with the hybrid-Nth and there should be no time offline upgrading and installing anything," Nick reassured and Gus breathed a sigh of relief.

"What should I do with the Nth in the canister? They're first-generation, right? Should I save them for something?"

"I would put them in for processing with the Endurium. They no doubt would be even more powerful because they haven't overspecialized. The Endurium might even allow them to retain adaptability, which would be especially helpful with your wide range of abilities. This Foundry can process and fuse the two, and it should take less time than a straight fabrication."

"How long would that take compared to last time?"

"Integration should only take about two or three hours. Once they are synced to you, they would be immediately available for use. Your shielding would rebound and be even more robust, and I think your storage problems for abilities would be gone."

"Good news for a change. Thanks, Nick." Gus entered the orders and entered the materials and canister into the indicated hoppers. A timer synced with the lower left of Gus' display.

"And now we wait," Aurora sighed, tapping her fingers while watching the countdown timer.

"You know everything about me, but I still don't really know you. Why don't you tell me how you came to be a super to pass the time?"

"Nah, there's not much to tell," Aurora said dismissively.

"That's not true," Daphne broke in. "He showed you his, so he gets to see yours."

"Daphneeee," Aurora warned.

"I already have the memory queued up. Movie time!" A window popped up on Gus' display that he could maximize just like a holovid.

"Here, let me catch you up, Gus," Daphne said and a montage of Aurora's memories replayed. He saw her mother die, and her Nth transferring. From there the movie slowed.

"Please don't show him this," Aurora pleaded.

"You need this Aurora; you're too closed off. This was a key moment for you. Now hush."

———

The little girl stayed in the shack for as long as she could stand. But soon the flies came. And the smell. There wasn't a lot of room in the small space, and the girl realized she couldn't stay there anymore. When she could take it no more, she rolled her meager belongings into a blanket and went outside.

She wandered the streets, shy, yet fascinated by the large city around her.

She hadn't eaten since her mother had come home and she held her stomach. One boy a bit older than her offered to share his bread. After she had a couple bites, he grabbed onto her arm while older boys came, whooping and hollering.

In a panic, she stomped on the foot of her captor and twisted out of his grasp. She ran and ran, finally escaping, but she had to leave her only blanket and belongings behind. After that, she was much less trusting.

Due to her small size, she could crawl into small nooks and try to keep warm by packing old newspapers and discarded scraps of clothing or bags around her. She constantly shivered, awaking in fear with noises in the interminable nights. She would sleep fitfully, hoping to wake in the morning, but finding only a couple hours had passed, and the cold night would endure.

Her favorite nook to rest had a view of the clock on Svenson Tower in the distance. Even when daylight finally arrived and the temperatures rose again, it still took her a long time to stop shivering.

The gaunt little girl was always hungry. This wasn't new to her, but she had to swallow what little pride she had and scavenge for food from the ubiquitous trash bags that always populated this part of town. This went on for three or four weeks.

She was loitering around a small local market that usually threw away expired, but edible food and vegetables. Cass saw a woman trying to buy some groceries, but she also saw the owner was charging her way too much for the food. The woman seemed oblivious to what was happening so Cass followed her.

She tried to explain what was happening but neither could understand each other. The woman took pity on the little girl, and took her to her tiny shack of a house and made the two of them a meal.

Ever wary, the girl picked at the food until she could resist no longer. She tore into the meal like an animal. Halfway through she looked up at the woman, ashamed to see her surprised look. Then she smiled and served Cass some more food and motioned for her to eat.

After the pair had eaten, the little girl tried to learn how she had made the meal, waving to the ingredients and how she had mixed them together.

This must have sparked an idea with the woman because she began grabbing some things and putting them on the table. She pulled out a tokencard and pointed to the girl. She then brought out various things from the cupboard and had her write a list.

The next day, the woman gave her the card and shooed her out the door, pointing to the list. The girl had to pull her by the hand and get her to come with her. The woman didn't understand that tokencards worked on someone's unique DNA fingerprint and the owner must hold onto the card when paying. It did no good to steal anyone's card.

The woman and girl went together the first couple times, but being out in the foreign environment was very uncomfortable for her. She corrected the shopkeeper when he tried to overcharge them, and he scowled at her and threatened to kick the little girl out.

"We can just take our business to the other market on Sixth, it's just as close," she said defiantly. The clerk abruptly stopped complaining and rang up the rest of the groceries, muttering under his breath.

The girl began calling the woman 'Auntie' and their arrangement was worked out through pantomime and gestures. Eventually, Auntie became more and more reclusive, so they would go to one of the cash kiosks and pull out money. Then the little girl could shop alone.

Auntie never seemed to worry that the girl would run off with all of her money, though she easily could have. By then, though, they had a comfortable routine. The girl would handle the bills and Auntie had access to the money and would cook for the pair.

The girl happily made sure the electricity stayed on and the rent was paid, even though she didn't like how much someone was charging for the crude construction of sheet metal and bare wiring. Still, it kept the heat in and the girl wouldn't trade it. A month in the elements was enough for her.

After living with Auntie for a year, the girl began to notice strange things about herself. It started when she was very happy or very angry. She would begin to see tiny greenish-tinged sparks appear near her fingertips. There were only about five or six at a time, but they scared her. She really didn't know what was happening to her.

One time after they had made the monthly money run, Cass had made a quick shopping trip. Someone must have been watching because they thought she had the full amount with her. The girl only took barely enough to pay for what they needed for just that reason. The rest they kept hidden in a coffee can under one of the loose metal plates in the floor, covering the plate with one of the couch legs.

When she had turned off the main street on her way to the store, a teenage boy grabbed Cass. He wanted the money and she gave him what she had, hoping to avoid him hurting her. He clutched at her wrist harder and began to lift the small girl off the ground and shake her a little, demanding the rest. He didn't accept that was all she had.

The sparks appeared and the girl shouted, "Stop!" Her hands burst into fizzling showers of sparks and the teen had to let go of her as the sparks burned into his hands and arms. As he let go, she pointed her free hand at his face and sparks puffed at him like confetti. He ran off, covering his eyes and wailing.

As soon as it started, the sparks guttered out and were gone. The girl had no idea what had happened, and looked around, making sure no one had seen. The boy had dropped the money in the confusion and the girl scrambled to pick it all up before the wind blew it away. One or two bills blew away, but she still had enough to get most things on the list.

The girl played with the ability in secret from then on, trying to consciously bring it up, but it was intermittent and unreliable. Some days she could do it with ease, others it was like she had imagined the whole thing. Emotion really was the only reliable trigger for her.

Around that same time, Cass began teaching Auntie some English. Over time she learned Auntie came to America to get married. Her husband was very old though, and died soon after she arrived. From what she described, Cass understood that she inherited his money.

The lawyers, knowing she couldn't do anything about it, gave her the minimum they could and kicked her off the property. She was all alone in a foreign country with no idea on the customs. If it weren't for her opportune meeting of Cass, she would have been drained dry from dishonest people fairly quickly.

From there, the video sped up and Gus saw the day Auntie disappeared. Then the vision faded.

———

Gus sat stunned at what he had seen. "Aurora, I never knew. What happened to Auntie?" He looked over and she was biting her lip, her eyes red and uncertain.

"I guess that once she learned enough to communicate, she figured she didn't need me anymore and left without a trace. I still don't know what happened to her. I ran into Rory that same day and he recruited me into the academy."

"Do you think they somehow *arranged* for her to be gone? That seems to be too close to be a coincidence," Gus asked suspiciously.

"No. I don't think they would have tried to recruit me if I hadn't used my powers to defend myself. Auntie abandoning me just helped make the decision for me; the academy was really the only option if I didn't want to be homeless again. Life got dramatically better for me in pretty much every way after, though. So I don't blame supers for the problem. The worst times of my life were before that, as you have seen."

Gus had thought he had it hard, but felt ashamed at seeing

her perspective. His life had been relatively good, and he was at a loss for words.

"It seems to me that it's not just supers that have problems, but a lot of people suck in general—regs too," Aurora said.

"So that's how you got your powers. My family never talked about the how. It was always a big secret."

"Well, now you know all my dirty secrets, whether I like it or not."

"If anything it impresses me even more, to be honest."

"What, that a dirty homeless girl got to be a super?"

"No. That you did it without getting bitter and angry at all the people who should have been there for you—but weren't. I would be sorely tempted to get some payback in my own less-traumatic-life-by-comparison if I wasn't stuck on this island." Gus shrugged his slumped shoulders.

"Well, thanks, I guess. I still would have preferred Daphne kept that private," Aurora whispered.

"I'm glad I know, and I won't tell anyone, if that makes you more comfortable."

"You better not. I'm trusting you. When I was in the academy, there were rumors that went around. Do you even call them rumors if they're true? I acted like I didn't know what people were talking about, and over time they just went away. That life seemed like it had happened to someone else after a while."

"I know what you mean."

"So can you see why I kind of bonded with your mom?" Aurora leaned forward.

"Yeah. I've been remembering more and more about her lately. What else can you tell me?" Gus peered intently at Aurora, eager for any more he could learn.

"One thing I remember is that she was very persuasive. I remember that she cowed these strength-build Minmax supers. She was very tolerant of most things but foul language was her pet peeve. I don't know what she said or did, but they never spoke like that around her. She never raised her voice or made a scene."

"The little I do remember of her makes me feel good."

"Have you ever thought about going back? Why don't you call your dad? I know he could send some reinforcements, or give you some advice."

"That's a hard no. I don't think I'm ready yet. I'm sure he'll look at how I've developed my skills and allocated my points, and pick them apart. 'Why didn't you focus on this skill? So many points into *that* stat?' Even talking about it, I can feel his disapproval." Gus scrunched his nose in disgust.

"I never got that impression. He's actually one of the better generals. Sure, he expects you to keep your commitments, but he's not as rude and dismissive as most of the others—"

A flashing light warned of more supers approaching.

"So soon?" Aurora asked.

"Of course they are, let's go."

CHAPTER TWENTY-SIX

Doucheworm Attacks!

Gus and Aurora ran to the beach and saw a large super with a gold breastplate patterned after some Greek warrior standing on a hovering dais a hundred feet off shore.

"Ah, nice of you to finally wake up and join me."

"Who is this douche?" Gus quietly asked Aurora.

"This is the psychopath who kept me prisoner for a month. His name is Basileus."

"Your name is Bacillus? Like bacteria? What the heck are your powers? Infection?" Gus yelled to the dais.

Basileus looked taken aback, never having anyone criticize his *name* before. "No, Bass-IH--lay-us," he articulated carefully into the microphone amplifying his voice. "It means king or emperor—I... I don't have to explain myself to you!" he stammered, getting irritated at the interruption in his well-planned monologue.

"Coming by yourself? Probably not the wisest course of action," Gus taunted as he slowly began to hover above the ground, ready to charge.

"Don't bother trying to reach me—actually, I take that back. I wouldn't mind seeing you splatter against the shields."

Gus relaxed and let himself drop down to the ground. Basileus gave him a golf clap. "So you can be entreated. Good. I came to discuss your surrender."

Before Gus could think of a retort, the pompous super turned. "Aurora, nice to see you again. I'm surprised you didn't like our accommodations in the Manticorps sewers; I've heard you came from the slums. I thought you would be right at home there."

"Hey," Gus said with dawning recognition. "Are you the guy from the station who throws lava balls?" Gus shook a finger at Basileus. "Yeah, I think you're the guy."

"Lava balls? No! Why does everyone think that? They're plasma. *Plasma!* Does no one know science? It's a fourth fundamental state of matter. People know solids, gases, and liquids; how do they not know plasma? It's ionized gas. Why is that so hard to comprehend?"

"Is that it? Sorry, I didn't know you were so sensitive about your balls," Gus yelled back.

The pilot of the dais-craft could be seen chuckling and Basileus threw him a warning look.

Visibly flustered, Basileus blurted, "Aurora, I hope you don't expect any help. I found your little hidey hole and I stopped the burst transmission. I'm sure you sent a distress call piggybacked on it, waiting for when we got in position under the satellite. Well, forget it! No one is coming, you're all alone! I'm giving you two the chance to leave here quietly because you're not worth my time. I know you're the only ones left on the island. You have one day."

He hit the display, turning off the speaker, and motioned for the pilot to maneuver the dais back to their own camp.

They watched the ship disappear to the northeast, contemplating what had just happened.

"Is he serious?" Gus asked, looking stunned.

"Don't underestimate him, he's kind of insane."

"How does he know we're the only ones here?"

"We should have had some of the decoys meet us outside.

They will probably be less effective now. His transmission would have been sent to everyone at the manor. It's not too far a leap when only two of us show up. I should have thought of that before." Aurora tapped her lips, trying to remember anything else she had overlooked.

"He's fun to mess with, I know that. I guess he is crazy if he thinks I'm just going to give up the manor. Do you have any idea what is here that everyone wants so badly?"

She motioned and they walked back up the beach to the manor. "I spent so much time looking through facilities upgrades, and I came up empty. There's nothing out of the ordinary. I searched by highest FP cost for anything that seemed out of the ordinary and worked my way down. Nothing popped out to me. I honestly wonder if it wasn't all just an exaggerated story that kept getting bigger as it got passed along. Don't get me wrong, the manor is awesome as a base, but it's not that different than what I've seen at Purple Faction, just that the manor is stacked vertically instead of being a large compound."

"No, I don't buy it," Gus said, pushing the call button for the elevator. "My gut says there's something unique here, and he's not getting it. That reminds me, let me check on something before training."

"Will you be long?"

"I'm just going to phone a friend, and I'll meet you down there."

"Sure, I have things to practice," she said as they entered the elevator. She stepped off at the arena's floor and Gus waved as the doors closed again.

"See you in a bit," Gus called as the doors closed and he headed to the control center to call Dave again. He picked up on the first ring.

———

"Gus, how have things been?"

"I'm still alive."

"I had no doubts, brother. Tell me about what powers you have now."

Gus caught Dave up on the battles and new powers he had acquired.

"I think you're more powerful than a lot of supers we used to work for! Good job, man!" he said.

"Yeah, we used to work for some losers though."

"'Tis true, but I'm kind of partial to staying alive. The powerful ones are always fighting and expect their henchmen to do the same. I ain't no fodder!"

"Dave, I am your fodder!" Gus said with a Darth Vader intonation.

Dave laughed. "Then can I borrow twenty bucks? What else is going on? Have you unlocked anything cool in the manor?"

"Actually, I haven't told you about Aurora yet, have I?"

"Wait, that sounds like a girl's name. It's not some weird robot slave girlfriend, is it? Gus, you dog!"

"Calm down, hornball. She's a super that I worked with on the station. She stowed away with the supers attacking me after she escaped their prison. She's been helping me ever since."

"Is she hot?"

"Look her up, you have the holonet. She's Purple Faction."

"Hold on."

Gus could hear keys clacking over the connection.

"Dayum, dayum, *dayum*! Dude! You're making me jealous. She looks a little serious though. She's not one of those uptight prissy supers, is she?"

"She's pretty chill."

"You like her, dude! I can tell. Have you made a move?"

"It's not like that—"

"Don't BS a BS-er. Just sprout some balls and ask her."

"Dude! I need her help. I don't want to make everything all weird by hitting on her. What if she's just nice, and I screw things up by being all clingy? Besides, she said she hated it at the academy when guys just saw her as a potential girlfriend."

"You're gonna get friend-zoned. Just sayin'."

"Whatever."

"It's true, dude. Don't be that guy that she always confides in, telling you how much other guys hurt her bad—"

"She's way out of my league, anyway."

"Hey, I have a cousin, Carl. He married a girl way out of his league. The dude is goofy looking too, so I'm telling you…" Dave said, drawing out the words.

"…so you're telling me there's a chance. Yeah, I get it."

"It works for me. Well, sometimes. But it *has worked*. Nothing ventured, nothing gained. You'll never know if you don't try."

"I'll think about it."

"Hey, when did it happen?"

"When did what happen? When did she get to the island? It was like two days ago."

"No, how soon after you got powers did you make your vow of celibacy?"

"You suck, you know that?" Gus asked as Dave cackled on the other side of the line.

"I would go for it, if I was in your shoes."

"Sure you would. Now you're just saying crazy stuff. I never saw you hitting on girls when we all went out as a group. Are you drunk or something?" The moment Gus said it, he wanted to grab the words and take them back. "Sorry, that came out wrong," Gus said, cringing.

"No, that's fair," Dave said soberly. "It's getting closer for my verdict pronouncement. It's scaring the hell out of me, Gus. I haven't drank anything since, and I haven't even been tempted. Maybe I'm legit scared straight." The mood had changed and Dave pushed on.

Gus could tell he was upset, and he mentally kicked himself for the poor turn of phrase. "Hey, about that—" Gus tried to say.

"Here, let me give you that information I got on Methiochos." Dave plowed forward as if he hadn't heard. "He was a super about fifty years ago. Worked with an outfit named Manticorps. I guess they were kind of a big deal, but something happened and Methiochos disappeared. Everyone thinks he embezzled a large amount of money and retired to his own island or something. Funny that they're partly right!"

"After that, Manticorps hit hard times. From what you said, they must have had a lot of money tied up in the manor. When those debts came due, they really struggled. There probably would have been four Factions worldwide if this hadn't happened to them. They managed to stay afloat, but just barely. It wiped them out, and after they lost their financial base, a lot of supers jumped ship and dispersed to the Factions. That's all I really have. It's run by a guy named Archon. Everything says he's still alive. Probably will be succeeded by his son Bah-silly-us? I don't know how to pronounce that."

Gus wondered if that was all they were trying to do. Reclaiming their lost property, and there he was trying to keep it from them.

"Does it say anything else? Anything about the manor?"

"Nope, sorry, dude."

"What was their reputation like, did they do good things?"

"Is any corporation good? I guess they're pretty similar to most. They don't stand out as doing anything shady. No scandals, if that's what you mean."

"Okay, thanks for checking that. At least I know a little bit more about who's attacking me. That guy Basileus *is* here and he's kind of a joke. I have a lot to think about."

"Hope it helps. I better let you go. Like I said, look me up when you get back. I'm not sure if you can visit, but who knows. Alright, catch you on the flip side."

The line clicked off abruptly before Gus could say anything. What more *was* there to say? He'd totally stuck his foot in his mouth and soured the whole call. He almost called back but thought it'd be better to give Dave a little time. Hopefully, he would still be around when Gus called again, and vice versa.

CHAPTER TWENTY-SEVEN

The Greatest Show

Gus went to the arena, still mad at himself.

"How did it go?" Aurora asked.

"Let's train," Gus said brusquely while checking the timer for the hybrid-Nth. There was still an hour and a half before they would be ready. "I want to get those new hybrid-Nth online before anything else goes sideways."

Sensing Gus' change in mood, she let the subject go. They headed to the arena and Gus explained his new abilities in broad strokes. Gus set a timer and they got to work.

Aurora was adept at finding weaknesses in Gus' application of his powers and he had to think hard to avoid her incessant attacks. He bled off his frustration at himself through the exertion and his mood had improved greatly when the timer went off.

"Timer's up. I'm heading to the Foundry to add those new hybrid-Nth."

"I want to see this too, let's go." Training forgotten, they both made their way to the Foundry. Walking down the metal walkways, they followed the LED lights indicating the appropriate conveyor belt.

"This is so exciting!" Aurora gushed.

When they got to the appropriate area, Gus saw three plastic trays, all with a familiar grayish-black dust. He pushed a little around, expecting it to stain his finger since it looked just like graphite powder but his finger came away clean.

"Okay, Nick, I'm ready."

"Here we go, then. In three, two, one…" Nick counted him off.

Gus slammed his eyes shut and sucked in a breath as he had the experience of jumping into a deep cold lake. His skin prickled with pins and needles, and numbness overcame him. There was a rush of vertigo and he was quickly sinking, the darkness engulfing him. His ears popped and the void expanded.

Sounds became muffled and he wasn't certain that he was still in the Foundry. After a few moments, a conduit opened and Gus was propelled upward again. Normal sounds and sights returned as he quickly sped toward the bright doorway above. As Gus was slingshotted out the opening, he found himself standing in the same position as before, wobbly on his feet.

The hybrid-Nth in the trays began flowing into the air like dust in a windstorm. Some spun around Gus, encircling him, while other roiling clouds twisted like vines around his arms and legs, coalescing around them and forming intricate patterns of interlocking shapes.

As the hybrid-Nth solidified, they began to take on a gunmetal color with tiny facets reflecting light with his movement as he twisted his arms to view them from all angles. The dust kept coming, and a helmet—no, it was more of a mask, formed around his head and covered his entire face.

His vision went black as his eyes were covered until the hybrid-Nth came online and Gus could see normally again. Not only that, but they cycled through multiple areas. Gus could see behind him, getting visual information from anywhere the hybrid-Nth covered his body. He poked his finger above one of the taller machines and found he could see through his index finger as if he were looking through a small camera on his fingertip. *Very cool.*

With a thought, he removed the mask. Not physically though; the Nth appeared to melt and flow to his shoulders, making them look even more impressive and broad as the Nth reconfigured into pauldrons.

"I need to get myself some of that armor! It makes you look pretty badass." Aurora reached forward and ran her finger along the polished rounded edges. Gus didn't tell her that he could *feel* it as if she was touching bare skin. He'd have to adjust that setting for more reasons than one.

Gus moved around and was impressed that it made no noise. He thought the plates would clink together but the feel was extremely similar to just wearing his jumpsuit. Flexible and not restrictive as he tried different movements, even a couple katas without Jet, and nothing bound or got tight.

"Let's finish training and see what this stuff can do." Gus clenched a fist and looked at the imposing gauntlet-like effect of the armor.

"Good, I'm getting tired of holding back on you. If this armor is all you say it is, you should be fine."

"Sure you have," he said and she scrunched her nose and shrugged.

Wait. Had *she been holding back? No, she's probably just trying to get me riled.*

He followed her back to the arena. They faced off when they got there and, at the signal, Aurora took off. He had never seen her move so fast. To compound this, she intermittently dropped what amounted to a flashbang before she moved and Gus could not see where she had gone. Solid hits came from behind, his side, and one even atop the crown of his head. He could feel the armor undulating at the sites of impact, spreading the force out over a larger surface area and absorbing a good portion of the force.

Aurora grabbed his arm and twisted, trying to take him down using her momentum and weight. But she only ended up dangling off the end of his arm like he was a statue. Gus tipped his hand down and she slid off as the armor shifted. She couldn't hold on anymore, the outer coating becoming smooth and almost oily. After sliding off, it reverted to its normal configuration.

An evil grin settled on Gus' face as he rushed to attack and Aurora barely had time to spring back to her feet. She launched a huge **Ion Storm** at his chest and the armor began to glow with a purple aura. Leaving off her attack, the armor looked unscathed. Then she aimed for his head, and the mask reformed and encased Gus' face moments before the shower of colored sparkles washed over him. The view Gus got reminded him of the end credits of *Buck Rogers in the 25th Century* as sparks blasted against his display. It was oddly soothing. A red blip on his minimap ruined the moment.

"Guess who's back," Gus said.

"Shady? Or is it Backstreet?"

"I wish. Looks like they're sending in a lot more this time. They're in a formation with two groups, but at least ten total."

"Let's see how they like my little friends," Aurora said with anticipation. "I linked the interface so that I can access them remotely," she said as she walked to the exit.

Gus followed her and they exited the manor onto the courtyard.

Aurora was continually moving her hands, sweeping left and right, hitting virtual buttons invisible to Gus as she accessed some system she had set up.

As if in response, automated drones appeared on Gus' display, their icons showing their flight out of the manor. They made a beeline to intercept the supers. A small window showed their viewpoint as they progressed, Gus and Aurora making their way out of the manor.

Due to their small size, the few shots that came their way

flew wide. In response, the drones spread apart, encouraging the enemies to waste even more ammo trying to hit the tiny targets.

They burst out the door and Gus activated the blast doors to close. Colorful weapons of different energies flickered in the distance. Since the drones were out of eyesight, Gus had to zoom in his display to see what the drones were doing. There were two clusters of supers, a forward party and one lagging behind. The drones split as well to meet both sets of enemies, his interface highlighting them in the magnified view. Instead of flying at the supers and detonating, they took position about ten feet above them.

"They've totally missed them," Gus complained. "Is the signal too far away?"

"Wait for it." Aurora held up a finger.

An orange mist emanated from the drones and they dropped among the supers who batted them away as the cloud settled around them.

"What was that?"

"I had the cafeteria cook up some debuff gel pods, then made some diffusers at the Foundry and attached them to some targeted drones."

"What kind of debuffs?"

"Everyone in that cloud just lost half their MP and their MP regen rate is cut in half as well!"

"Noice!" Gus said in a singsong voice.

"I call it 'The Showstopper,'" she said with pride.

"They're going to be pissed!"

A projectile shot out, flying erratically.

"That really threw off their aim!"

"Gus, I don't think they're shooting at us."

The missile hit the mountain in which the manor was encased, rocks exploding off.

"Are they insane? I thought they wanted the manor or something inside!"

"These guys are probably loose cannons, literally. They may not be following orders strictly. These are mercs, remember?"

Another missile shot toward the tower.

"Aw hell to the no!" Gus said as he took off to intercept the missile.

CHAPTER TWENTY-EIGHT
Love Missile F1-11

Reaching the missile, he barely erected a shield as it detonated early against its surface. The explosion shattered the shield and Gus went flipping through the air, barely catching himself activating **Advanced Flight** before hitting the ground. Gritting his teeth, he flew back toward the supers. Five of them were aboard small craft that looked like flying jet-skis. There were mounts underneath the contraptions that were the source of the missiles.

Gus reached out, attempting to use **Absorb**, but he was too far away. **Krackle**, on the other hand, turned out to be very effective. The supers scattered on their jet-skies. He wasn't sure what to call them but patted himself on the back for thinking of the name.

Krackle appeared to have some kind of homing ability as the balls of energy followed their targets, gradually decreasing in size before winking out. The second wave of supers could be seen behind the first, four supers being ferried by flyers. They were still a way off, so Gus felt pressured to stop this first wave of idiots from firing more missiles.

One buzzed by him, peppering him with some kind of slugs.

He expected a burst of pain, but the bullets slowed before they hit and flattened about a millimeter from his skin, hitting some invisible barrier.

Before he could discern what was happening with the bullets, he threw out a **Warp** bubble on reflex and crushed the undercarriage of his attacker's jet-sky. It managed to keep flying but it was slowly losing altitude. The missiles, now twisted wrecks, didn't detonate for some reason.

Gus laughed as the super repeatedly leaned forward, trying to coax a little more forward momentum out of the jet-sky that clearly was not going to make it to land. He was going to have a little swim in his future. Two whooshes signaled more missiles being fired while Gus was distracted.

Get your head in the game! he chastised himself. Flying forward, he saw that he was not going to make it to intercept and shield the manor. He shot **Krackle**, but the missiles left the slower energy balls in the dust. He followed as fast as he could fly, but he could not overtake the missiles.

Gus tried to activate **Absorb** and still, there was no effect at this range. He'd probably have to be in direct contact at his lower level of the skill, he thought with frustration. Hitting upon **Electronic Mind** in desperation, he activated it and understood the simple controls. The missiles were too close to deflect away from the manor at their current speed so he opted to have them detonate early.

Gus flew into the bright fireball, the brief heat momentarily uncomfortable. The bright flash was enough of a distraction and blinded him so that he crashed into the mountainside the manor was carved into. Pain blossomed across his head and he lost his focus, tumbling downward. After hitting an errant branch, he threw up a quick shield as he tumbled down to the ground.

"That sucked." He popped pink, red, and blue gels, and his vision resolved immediately. The supers were closer than ever and he sent the shield flying upward again. Getting an idea, he activated **Electronic Mind** again and fired all the remaining missiles. Before they got too far away to command, he directed them to target the incoming supers.

The flying supers were not nearly as maneuverable while carrying their burdens, and one decided discretion was the better part of valor and let her two passengers go, flying away. One missile began to follow her, but as she got far enough away, it circled around to target one of the dropping supers. They both hit the water with a crash and the missile exploded as it hit the water.

The supers floated to the surface, and Gus could tell they were alive but unconscious by the change in their minimap status. He flew close and created two shields around them, partly so they wouldn't drown. He didn't want to lose the opportunity to harvest their powers either, if he was honest.

The other flyer managed to perform an aerial swing, twisting in a spiral and her passengers swung up and over, allowing the missiles to pass underneath. One of the supers she was carrying fired some sort of attack that clogged their propulsion systems before they could circle back around and they hit the water in the distance, making hollow *booms* after hitting the water and detonating.

As Gus flew to engage the other supers on jet-skies, he saw that Aurora had launched more drones. Keeping his distance from them, he engaged the last flyer as he quickly flew to the shore. With a large *crack,* blue fingers of electricity arced between three of the drones and two of the remaining jet-skies. Their riders spasmed and jolted as the drivers either let go of some throttle that kept the machines aloft or the electricity ruined something inside.

They both fell like rag dolls, still jittering as their muscles held their clenched fists to the handles, even after the electricity had dissipated. Gus was too far away to do anything to slow their fall and both hit the sandy beach at odd angles. Odd, unnatural angles for people who were still alive.

Gus felt ashamed that his first reaction was disappointment —that he probably had lost some potential powers—instead of feeling bad that two people had just died. He didn't have long to think about them as he approached the flyer and his two passengers.

The mercs were close enough to the ground that they dropped to the sand. One executed a three-point landing and the other spun into a roll and sprang to his feet in a fighting pose. Gus looked at the floating super and a visceral dread overcame him as he gazed at the squid like creature in front of him. *Is this a super or some kind of construct? Most likely a construct.* Breaking from its gaze with an effort of will, Gus strained to refocus his attention on the two supers who had landed on the beach.

Hearing a repeating **pssh-pssh** noise behind him, Gus turned and saw Aurora running through the sand to meet these supers.

Aurora joined Gus and she faced off against the other super. They immediately engaged each other and Gus could barely follow their arms and legs as they kicked and blocked at blinding speed. The super Aurora fought wore only tightly fitting pants and some shoes with a split toe that resembled socks more than shoes.

He was covered in tattoos that blazed with color during various moves. A brilliant tiger, shimmering like goldfish scales, reflected in the sun as he made a slashing attack with a clawed fist. Aurora ducked to avoid it and kicked upwards. It connected with his chin with a resounding crack. He flew backward and landed on his back, but sprang back onto his feet as if he were on a trampoline.

The air snapped behind their rapid kicks and punches, punctuated with dull thuds and slapping noises as a hit connected or was blocked. Neither appeared to have the advantage, but Gus saw that Aurora truly had been taking it easy on him in their sparring sessions.

Seeing movement out of the corner of his eye, he turned to face his opponent and saw the air ripple as the super extended both arms toward him. There was no time to dodge, having been too enthralled watching Aurora fight. Waves hit Gus, shimmering through his armor. He felt the wave directed around his sides and exit behind his back. Besides a tiny itch from the vibration, he suffered no ill effects.

Frustrated, the super placed his hands on the sand and sent out another pulse. Before Gus could realize what was happening, the sand below him stopped supporting him, and he sunk knee deep into it before the pulse ended. The sand stopped vibrating and locked his feet in after solidifying. Gus grabbed his thigh with both arms, trying to wrench his leg free. Another pulse sunk Gus to mid-chest in the sand and now his arms were trapped as well.

A smarmy look of satisfaction that seemed out of place settled on the super's childish face. He was still struggling to create a respectable semblance of facial hair. Backing up, he ran towards Gus, who began to expect the worst. When his leg cocked back for a kick, Gus activated *Xyzzy* at the last moment and appeared fifteen feet above in the air.

The young super, meeting no resistance, kicked through empty air and fell on his butt from overextending himself. Only to become stuck butt-first in the hole left by Gus' absence, awkwardly trapped and slapping the sand, trying to pull himself out.

Gravity reasserted itself and Gus fell on top of the boy, pushing him further into the hole, neatly folded in half. Gus slid a hand across his cheek and activated *Leech* and the boy stopped his struggling.

Behind him, Aurora screamed in frustration and Gus spun to see her trapped to her shins in the sand as well. Her opponent was focusing a large bright ball of energy in front of a tattoo on his chest that resembled an eye, but was hard to tell due to the brilliance of the energy ball. His arms were in front of him in hadouken style and it was obvious he was going to hit Aurora point blank.

Gus activated *Dash* and flung up a shield as he moved to intercept.

The impact shattered his shield and shot him backward into Aurora, the impact pulling her out of the sand. The rebound flung the other super into a rock wall and he crumpled. Gus continued to shoot backward until he collided with a large pitted and porous rock. His armor kept him from getting shredded on the rough rocks, but he hit with enough force to crush a human-shaped imprint in the rock.

Gus felt his vision shrink to a tiny space in front of him, almost passing out. *That definitely caused some internal injuries*, he thought through the agonizing pain. His right arm felt broken as he had taken the hit on his right side. Awkwardly with his left, he reached across to try to get a healing gel but his thigh was buried in the rock. Weakly, he rolled out of the indentation he had made and fell face-first into the sand. Coughing up some blood, he spit out sand that had pushed into his open mouth as he grimaced in pain.

He tried to push himself up but he felt weak all over. Aurora was screaming again, but Gus hurt so much he couldn't help her even if he wanted to. He was disoriented and unable to coordinate his own movement effectively. Gus activated **Energy Absorption** or maybe **Absorb**, and tried to pull in some kind of energy from the sun on his back to see if he could get enough to move. His HP was at a meager 62/880, and his stamina bar was bottomed out, and did not want to refill. Aurora's shouts stopped and Gus expected the worst when he was forcefully flipped over.

CHAPTER TWENTY-NINE

Hell No

It was Aurora, and she looked mad as hell. She roughly brushed the sand off his face and cheek and jammed a red and pink gel in his mouth and forcefully closed his jaw.

"Gus, what the *hell* was that?"

Gus slowly bit the gels, sucking out the contents, then spitting out the casings. One side of his jaw was definitely broken. Aurora continued to berate him, even as she gave him more gels as he cleared the previous ones and his jaw became more responsive as the bone knit together and muscles were repaired.

"What was *what?*" he croaked when he finally got enough control over his mouth to talk.

"You swooping in trying to 'save' me. You almost got yourself killed! You have to think about the mission. I can take care of myself! I'm not some damsel in distress that you need to rescue. Same thing with the damn manor. It can be rebuilt, dummy. You rushed in and took a big risk trying to put yourself in its way."

"Why are you so pissed? We won, right?" he asked, pushing himself up onto his knees and wiping the sand off of him.

"We won *this time*. And just barely. That type of sentimentality is ultimately bad."

"What about no man left behind? Or woman, I guess."

"That works for a large team, not when only you and I *are the team*! You had better promise me that you will never do that again or we are *done*!"

Gus had never seen her look so angry. And he really didn't know what the big deal was. It was like he had inadvertently pushed a hot button.

"Say it!" she shouted at him.

Gus stopped trying to clean the sand off himself and looked up in surprise.

"Okay, okay, I won't do it again," he conceded, putting his hands up, even more confused. *Don't save you when you're obviously in trouble. Seems legit.*

"Gus, you're a nice guy, and that's going to be your downfall. You can't get sentimental like that. About a teammate, hell, even about the manor. It makes you soft, and you're too soft! Man up! As you are, you're worthless to me!"

"Worthless? Really?" he snarled as his anger flared. He was getting tired of taking this abuse.

"Yes! I don't need someone who can be manipulated by an enemy attacking a soft target, and they'll drop all reason and compromise the core mission. Why is that so hard for you to understand?"

Gus had never seen this side of Aurora and he definitely did not like it.

She continued her tirade of abuse. "Do you know how many supers I've seen killed because an opponent used their good nature against them? Some people are just evil, and you have to accept that and react accordingly. If you tap dance around them trying to be all airy-fairy, they'll crush you and everything you hold dear. You probably are a *big* fan of comic books, and that's what you're basing your personal code around. Well, news flash: You're not a mystical chosen one. You're not the savior of the world. You're a naive man-child playing super-hero, who has powers he has no idea how to use to their maximum capacity and probably never will. You need to accept reality and your own limits, or you're going to screw us all!"

She broke eye contact and it felt like a physical weight had been lifted from Gus. He got to his feet, trying to equal the dynamic. Aurora wouldn't, or couldn't, stop talking as she paced in circles.

"Who knows what hell Basileus will rain down on the world when he gets his hands on the manor, Gus? You're still clueless about what it could be, so all we can do is prevent him from getting a hold of it. I'm heading to the control room, because I guess I'm going to have to figure this out, since you can't. You're just like everyone else, expecting me to do everything," she spat, turning to leave.

Aurora stormed off into the manor, signaling that she was obviously done with the conversation. Gus' eyes narrowed as he stood there stunned. He muttered, "I guess I'll take care of all these supers. Don't mind me, I don't need any help." He almost expected her to peek around the corner and ask 'What was that?!' but she was truly gone. He almost wanted her to challenge him so he could *really* say what was on his mind.

First, he retrieved the supers floating in the water and dragged their spheres to the shore. One had a twisted ankle but the other looked healthy. Gus activated ***Leech*** and noticed that he could take all of their powers with a single touch, the increased capacity of the hybrid-Nth making a big difference. Leaving these two on the beach, he fished out two others.

Gus decided to carry the supers instead of making stretchers and ferrying them around. He was still seething from Aurora's scathing words and needed to bleed off some energy. A bonus was that he could use ***Leech*** on them as he hauled them to the courtyard, multitasking the cleanup. He threw a super over his shoulder and carried another by his side. Before becoming a super he never could have done it, but with his new strength it made the task only a mild strain. He hardly got winded as he muttered angrily to himself.

"Worthless, huh? I am so done with being treated like a

piece of crap."

Gus threw one of the supers onto the sand like a sack of rice.

"If you can't see that I'm doing everything I can to make this work out here, then you're a damn idiot." Another toss and he stalked back to grab another couple supers.

"I bust my ass, and this is the thanks I get. I would expect that from these damn mercs, but we're supposed to be on the same side." His body tensed as he remembered other times throughout his life where various people also assessed him as 'worthless.'

"Tempest, you were worthless as a father," Gus growled as he flung another super up onto his shoulder.

"Graviton, you were worthless at protecting your station and those who trusted you." He strained as he pulled the metal exoskeleton off another and trudged back to his pile.

Faces cycled through his mind, everyone who had put him down and made him feel lesser. Girls, coworkers, classmates; it wasn't a small list. The rage in him began to burn hotter and he became firmer in his resolution that he was done allowing *anyone* to treat him that way again.

"I have nothing left to prove to you people!" he screamed into the uncaring sky.

Gus hit **Leech** on both the supers simultaneously and absorbed all of their abilities without a thought. They wriggled and spasmed and he gripped even harder, as if they were trying to wrestle free. He clamped down, giving in to the anger and securing them with a stony, unrelenting grip as he stormed towards the manor.

"Too soft. People have called me things like that my whole life, and I've just accepted it. Enough." Gus threw the two supers unceremoniously to the ground and headed back. He could have flown but he was in no hurry. He needed some alone time. It turned out that the two supers who had fallen from the jet-skies were not dead, but had some major injuries. He used the remainder of his gels so they could be moved. "Yeah, leave me to clean up your mess from the drones, Aurora." His anger focused on her.

"If that's what you want, Aurora, that's what you'll get. I'm not your dumping ground for whatever baggage on your end sparked this little tirade, but obviously something else is going on with you." He grabbed two more supers, but due to their size decided simply to drag them. Sure, they'd get beat up as they bounced against rocks and the ground. Good. Deal with it.

"I'm tired of always having to be the one who 'goes along to get along.' It's high time someone else works on their issues instead of always being me who has to make the changes. Try taking your own ego down a notch or two, and stop expecting the world to accommodate you."

He pulled and took their powers like a rabid wolf tearing a piece of meat from a kill. He mentally wiped away the pop-ups on his display, unread, and let himself seethe.

"This. This is the problem with the world. Everyone is so damned entitled that they just worry about having things their way at the expense of everyone else. All the way down the chain, from supers to regs, people are just in survival mode."

Gus looked down at the next super with contempt, his rugged and handsome features irritating Gus all the more. He spoke the next words accusingly at the unconscious man.

"Always trying to maintain power once you have it, or taking advantage of someone else to get a little bit ahead. I'm tired of it. The Factions have done a piss-poor job of making any changes either. Their agendas come first and the rest get the scraps."

Gus loaded up two more supers, one on each shoulder, and continued his angry march. His *Leech* of these two was a little less aggressive as his emotions began to ebb. He took a little more care in setting these supers down as he had a realization.

"Why am I making this my problem? Who says I ever have to leave this island? Why should I even worry about all those selfish bastards out there? They've made their choices, right? Do they even deserve any of my efforts which are probably going to get thrown in my face, just like this? Why do I feel like I owe them anything?"

The more Gus thought of it as he continued his labor of moving the supers to the courtyard and leeching their powers, the surer he became.

"Just so stupid."

"Talking to yourself is a sign of impending mental collapse," Nick interjected.

"You too, huh?"

"Are you okay, chief? I never took you for someone who'd rage quit."

"It doesn't matter what I do or what anyone thinks, Nick. I'm not doing this to impress anyone. I've wasted way too much of my life trying to be something or do something to earn some kind of appreciation or recognition."

"Screw those jerks," Nick encouraged.

"I'm not going to let them decide what I do—that seems like letting them win. I still haven't decided what I want. Whether I stay here or go home. But I will tell you this, Nick: I'll be damned if I let someone else tell me what I can and can't do. Let them be selfish and petty, I'm through with changing who I am to accommodate their smallness."

"Can I get an aaaaamen!" Nick said in a rising tone.

"I know I don't have all the answers on how, but I do feel that I've found out what I need to be working towards. I just have to believe there will be others out there that are like-minded, and stay strong when people try to tear me down. If you won't help, stay the hell out of the way!"

"Preach, brother!" Nick exulted and Gus hung his head, put his hands on his hips, and he finally gave in to a tired chuckle.

He flicked off some sweat from his brow and looked up at the manor. The budding attraction Gus had been feeling for Aurora had been stamped out. Extinguished by the sudden change in her demeanor, and the realization that he didn't know her like he had thought he did. The excitement and feelings of limerence gone with the conflict.

"What was I thinking, Nick? Just because she's hot, I automatically assumed that she was as good on the inside as she looks on the outside. When people show you their true self, believe them."

Who said that to me recently? Had it been her? Was it Dave? I don't remember.

"I guess it doesn't matter. She obviously doesn't think much of me, and as such, to hell with her." They could collaborate on this mission and go their separate ways. "Hell, I wouldn't be surprised if she turned around and offered Purple Faction a chance at the manor, deeming them more worthy stewards of the property in her eyes." He stopped and asked Nick, "Hell's bells. Am I getting paranoid now?"

"It's just a part of your mental collapse," Nick said with the right amount of sarcasm to lighten the mood.

Gus stood there, having brought all the supers to the lawn. From there, he began the work of bringing them to the brig.

"I'll tell you this: Let them come. Purple Faction or any other arrogant, self-serving person or group, and I will put them in their place, and take their powers to boot. I am only going to get stronger. Even if I have to fight the whole damn world, I'm going to go down swinging. And they'll be sorry they ever underestimated me."

Gus kept stewing in intense emotion as he placed all the attackers in the brig. The physical exertion of moving the supers had given him some time to cool down and a lot of his anger had burned away, but the whole situation with Aurora had left him emotionally raw and irritated. He knew if he saw her right now, he wouldn't hold anything back this time, regardless of what mood she was in. Better to keep some distance for a bit.

At least it was getting late. Gus got takeout from the cafeteria, not wanting to see Aurora if she stopped by to eat, and went to his room. He ate and stared out at the majestic view from his balcony but was unaffected by the beauty before him. Finishing his day with a long shower, he relaxed enough to make it into a fitful sleep.

CHAPTER THIRTY

Close to the Edge

Aurora slammed the door to her room, cooling down a bit now that she was in her own space. She had startled herself with how she had reacted and tried to figure out why she was so edgy. She sat on the edge of her bed and then laid back, looking at the ceiling. She knew why but, like most of the painful things in her life, she walled them off, putting them far back in her mind and never revisiting them. Despite not wanting to, the memory came back from her academy days, loud and clear, as if it had just happened yesterday...

———

"You can't just ignore your problems; they won't go away. You just push them in deeper to rot and fester. As much as it hurts, you have to go in and pull that sucker out," Rory said, the gentle demeanor seeming out of place on his gigantic frame.

"You weren't there, Rory! You get to stay here at headquarters. It was horrible, and I don't want to talk about it." She bit her lip, determined to keep this to herself.

"I see you're upset, but we need to talk this out. You need it whether you think you do or not. Holding it all in isn't being strong. It weakens you. We're here to share the load here in the Faction. Don't insult us by acting like we're unworthy to share that burden." He put one of his massive hands on her slumped shoulders and raised an eyebrow.

Aurora looked up at this man she admired, grease-streaked face and all, with his genuine look of concern, and gave in. She looked back down at her hands and began, telling the story as best as she could between sobs that became so strong, she had to pause at times, her heart in almost physical pain.

"It was all because of me! *I* was the weak link, and because of that we failed the mission and lost three of our team."

"It happens. That's the life we signed up for. I don't mean to gloss over their deaths, but everyone knows that can be part of the job, and we all go in with eyes wide open. Your job is to not let their deaths be in vain."

"They wouldn't be dead if I wasn't so weak! If I didn't need to be rescued, they wouldn't have been distracted. I think because they are all so strong and were handling everything so masterfully, I got overconfident. Instead of hanging back and being support like I was ordered, I thought I could take on one of the other supers. He had some kind of draining power and he latched onto me with his abilities. It was like a whip that extended out of his hands. He flung it out and caught me by the neck. I couldn't breathe, it was horrible!"

Rory folded her into a hug as the sobs came. The words came easier once she had started.

"Crackshot slid from the side and shot the guy holding me, but it put him in a bad position and the other crew attacked him all together. I was there holding my throat trying to breathe, totally worthless. To help Crackshot, Jade Dragon and Polyphemus had to break out of formation and the enemy was able to flank us. El Tigre grabbed me and retreated. The last thing I saw was all three lying on the ground with the other team mauling them mercilessly before I was dumped into the transport and we sped away."

"So you feel guilty," Rory gently massaged her back with one of his meaty hands. She flung it away, not feeling like she deserved his attention, standing in defiance.

"He should have left me! We lost three higher tier supers trying to protect a trainee. It was such a waste!"

"No one could have known it would all go south. You are responsible for your teammates, we all know that."

"Is that always true? We failed that mission, and from what I've heard it will set Purple Faction back. We showed our hand and didn't get the intel we were supposed to get. That can be exploited." She buried her face in her hands and more sobs began spilling out.

"Okay, Aurora, I get the feeling you need to process this a bit more. But I want you to know I've been there before. I haven't always been here at headquarters. Like you, I've been in the field, and I've had my share of loss and pain. I'm not going to insult you by saying I know exactly what you're going through. Sometimes you need time to sort things out. As much as I want to erase those emotions, sometimes nothing anyone says or does can lessen the weight of that. But know that I'm always here. You're going to want to blame yourself, you're going to be angry. I'm going to keep checking in with you though, because I know you're going to want to isolate yourself and that is something you *cannot* do. I know how special you are, and I'm here when you need someone to talk to or just vent. Got it?"

Aurora wiped tears from her eyes and nodded, still staring at her hands. Just like her, they seemed dainty and ineffectual. She stayed in her room and cried herself to sleep.

———

She opened her eyes, wiping the tears away. So much loss in the past. These people who had been her surrogate family, gone. It was much harder losing these people than when her mother and then Auntie were out of her life. She felt that these people understood her, and that they needed her. For some reason, that had a big impact on her own feelings of self-worth. She was important, not baggage that had to be managed. She had always felt like an imposition and a handicap to how others wanted to live their lives. Tolerated, but never cherished.

To have them sacrifice themselves for her was difficult, as she still felt unworthy of how they valued her, with very little requirement on her part. She felt unproven, and always in their debt. That she had to somehow repay the interest that they had in her, and all the time they spent to mentor and train her.

After the incident, she felt intense guilt at asking instructors for assistance. Her failure with her team made it difficult to approach others, many who were friends with them. She stopped being such a try-hard, and felt like she saw some disappointment in the eyes of the instructors. She felt unworthy of their help. While she buckled down, studied harder, and tried harder in all her drills, she built up inner walls that put distance between those who were willing to help her.

After a while, others eventually accepted her new persona as growing confidence, and as she played the part of being self-assured and confident, she began to believe it herself. Rory had been right, though. Until Gus' actions today had brought that guilt and fear to the fore again. She hated apologizing but it wasn't like she had said anything untrue. Gus had a lot to learn if he wanted to survive in this world. She probably could have used more tact, however. *I'll deal with it in a bit after we've both had time to cool down.*

CHAPTER THIRTY-ONE

Foolish Pride

Gus awoke to a blue screen in front of him. He hadn't even thought to check yesterday what he had **Leeched** and found he was in a better mood, and a little excited to see what this group had to offer.

Congratulations! You have subdued 9 opponents trespassing on privately-owned territory.

9,000 XP (1,000 x 9) awarded for non-lethal methods.

4,500 FP (500 x 9) awarded.

LEVEL UP! Congratulations, Level 18 reached!

500 FP awarded.

You have (5) additional stat points to assign.

16,700 XP to level 19.

New abilities assimilated!

Telepathy (Level 21) [10 MP/minute]: *Send and receive mental messages, images and information.*

Cleanse (Level 17) [50 MP]: *Eliminate toxins of all types from self or others who possess Nth. At higher levels, can create remote effects on those who do not possess Nth.*

Gemini (Level 11) [40 MP/copy]: *Create an illusory copy of self that acts independently based on mental commands. Shares no actual abilities and can cause no physical damage.*

Zeno Effect (Level 29) [30 MP]: *Focusing on the quantum state of an object or target will freeze its passage through time, preventing physical movement or skill activation while observed.*

Smol (Level 13) [45MP/minute]: *Controls quantum field fluctuations to reduce the space between fundamental particles, using modified quantum chromodynamics to stabilize quark/gluon interactions. TL;DR: Reduces size by a factor of up to 30 times.*

Shake (Level 21) [30 MP]: *Creates an intense vibration that causes disorientation and dizziness.*

Shatter (Level 11) [20 MP/minute]: *Vibrate at a frequency that will cause stress-hardening weakness in metals and polymers, inducing failure. Vibrations will cause glasses and ceramics to propagate any weakness and break.*

Chi Pulse (Level 29) [150 MP]: *Drain internal stored energy to create an intense pulse, causing severe compression damage. Target will also be sapped of stamina regeneration after activation for 10 minutes.*

Cat-Like Reflexes (Level 34) [Passive]: *More intuitive reactions and agility. Increases Agility by 1 point every two skill levels. (Current boost: +17)*
9 new abilities assimilated.
9,000 XP awarded.
4,500 FP awarded.
7,700 XP to level 19.

Gus dropped five points into Constitution and relaxed back in bed, the post-level euphoria feeling like it lingered longer than normal. 980 HP! Just one more point to make it an even thousand and then everything into Intelligence. Today was going to be a lot better than yesterday.

Even if he still wasn't looking forward to seeing Aurora again.

———

Aurora awoke and took a long shower. She still felt wrung-out emotionally, and wasn't prepared to eat crow and talk to Gus. She procrastinated the interaction by heading up to the control center.

Gus must have unlocked a lot of new abilities, because there was a much larger batch of FP to play around with. Aurora figured they would have a couple days to train before the next wave of attacks. There hadn't been too many augments attacking yet and she set up more defenses to restrict their access to the manor from afar. She really didn't like augments, realizing from her raw memory of when her teammates died.

She made an upgrade to lab processing which would allow the cafeteria to have access to more reagents and components to create more gels with different effects, both buffs and debuffs. She added more variety to attack drones, guesstimating what powers could be neutralized by their differing effects. She got lost in the planning and development of different drones based on the available components.

A minor upgrade to the Foundry allowed her to queue items remotely and then have the finished products ready to launch in bays she could access from her display. She began hearing an odd beeping that she couldn't understand where it was coming from, since it was so intermittent. When she finally stopped and investigated, she found an old console in the corner with a pending message. When she returned, the proximity alarm signaled another attack was imminent.

Aurora was nowhere to be found, and while Gus' anger had eased a bit, his pride kept him from initiating any reconciliation. He went to the arena and started another session of Adaptive Training.

The three pillowbots met him and Gus did a few minor stretches. He looked forward to punching *something*. The bots began their attacks and Gus held off using any abilities for a while. He began cycling through his katas to warm up, taking advantage of the practiced motions to slip and dodge away from the robots' attacks. When he felt his opening, he moved, spinning and landing two powerful blows to the core of one of the bots and following up with an uppercut that knocked it onto its back.

A swing from the side was blocked by Gus' forearm, and he retaliated savagely. He locked the arm and performed a submission technique that he had learned from Aurora and actually bent the metal arm backward, hyperextending it past normal ranges of motion, hearing an unpleasant grinding. The noise was reminiscent of when he was trying to learn how to drive a stick shift with Grandpa. He probably wrecked that transmission with his poor timing.

TimeSight flared and Gus was back in the battle, intuitively kicking a pillowbot back and rolling out of the way. He charged this last bot, swinging wildly. He received a swat on the ear which set it ringing, but Gus kept going. The pain fueled his anger and aggression and he managed to push the bot out of the ring with his constant barrage of punches and hits.

The robots reset twice more, with Gus using only his fists and feet. It was oddly satisfying to punish these poor robots as if he were dispensing justice to all those who had wronged him in his life. A victimless crime. The pillowbots were increasing their fighting skills each round, and were even replaced with stronger models. Two had pressed him between them, holding his arms still while the third jabbed in and out with well-timed punches.

Struggling to get free, Gus found that he could not move despite his angry wriggling and twisting. He activated *Smol* and felt himself shrinking. It felt like he was condensing, and he felt a constant compression against his skin in his smaller form. His now one-foot frame slipped out of their grasp and he fell to the floor. Gus pushed against the leg of one of the pillowbots and found that even though he was smaller, he had the same strength. Leverage was working against him, but he still managed to trip one of the pillowbots, pushing the leg out from under it. Gus sprang back to normal size once the effect wore off and dropped an atomic elbow on the pillowbot's head. He'd always wanted to do that at least once in his life.

The two remaining bots worked in tandem to keep Gus from grappling with one, so he readied **Gemini** and waited for his moment.

Gemini: *Create an illusory copy of self that acts independently based on mental commands. Shares no actual abilities and can cause no physical damage.*

Now! He sent his double after the other bot. With this distraction, Gus was able to close and subdue the other pillowbot easily. He turned back and saw the pillowbot swinging through the ghostly image of himself, but continuing to fight with it, despite not encountering anything physical. This allowed Gus to sneak around and grab the bot in a headlock, and soon it was down.

The next round started and the pillowbots engaged now that numbers were in their advantage. Once they found the duplicate was insubstantial, they ignored it completely, turning their attention to Gus. Gus suffered dual hits as one pillowbot kicked him and another followed up as he was thrown to the side from the kick, punching him right in the nose.

The fury that had fueled his previous attacks was waning, and Gus tried activating **Smol** again. He shrunk in size, but the bots backed away and sunk lower, lowering their centers of gravity. They maintained a consistent distance, corralling him until he regained normal size.

As expected, **Telepathy** did nothing, and the robots had retained their resistance to **Electronic Mind**. "You damn Borg, stop modulating your frequency," Gus challenged as he looked for something new to try.

Zeno Effect: Focusing on the quantum state of an object or target will freeze its passage through time, preventing physical movement or skill activation while observed.

Gus had no idea what these abilities were even supposed to do as he activated *Zeno Effect* on one robot. To his amazement it stopped in mid-air! He rotated around the robot, and it hung there, the effect feeling very *Matrix*-esque. A rabbit punch from behind caused Gus to blink and the frozen robot completed its jump with no loss of momentum, though it had been hanging stock-still. Gus tried *Zeno Effect* again, this time on all three pillowbots but found that it only affected the two who hadn't initially been frozen. Gus tackled the previously frozen bot, finding it more difficult than he imagined to keep an eye on the other bots while he fought the third at the same time.

"What kind of weeping angel BS is this?" Gus tried to alternate blinking only one eye and fight at the same time.

The effect didn't seem to have a time limit. He turned his attention to the others and the airborne pillowbot crashed to the mat. He was free to take down the other frozen bots. Smacking his forehead, he pushed them both out of the ring, winning the match easily.

He had just started another round when Aurora's comm clicked on. *Finally she's ready to apologize. Took her long enough.*

"Meet me outside," Aurora yelled, her voice breaking Gus' concentration. He ended the simulation, cutting the training session short. "…they're already back," she finished grimly.

Gus stepped out of the ring and toweled the sweat off. He still hadn't showered today.

You have completed (5) waves of Adaptive Training. Final difficulty rank: A.
25,000 XP awarded.
LEVEL UP! Congratulations, Level 19 reached!
500 FP awarded.

You have (5) additional stat points to assign.
7,700 XP to level 20.

One point to Constitution and the other four to Intelligence. *Boom! Done.* Gus smiled as the elevator doors closed.

CHAPTER THIRTY-TWO

Carried Away

Gus jogged out the manor entrance to see Aurora on the court-yard lawn, pointing seaward.

"More of them are approaching!" Aurora shouted, even more angry than the day before. "We haven't even recovered yet!"

"What makes you think these guys fight fair?"

"Oh, they're going to see how dirty I can fight."

As the supers came closer, Gus recognized Slipstream and Mercurio among this batch of opponents, the ones who had subdued Aurora on the station. A quick look confirmed she saw them at the same time.

"Don't you even *dare*, Gus. Those two are *mine!* I have a score to settle. And payback is going to be a bitch." She took off, and Gus could swear that she was flying faster and with more control than she had in the past.

He wondered if she had leveled or evolved her flight skills or was just so pissed that she was hyper-charging the ability subconsciously.

"Go ahead, knock yourself out," Gus said, a little irritated, but part of him cheering on her revenge.

Gus targeted some of the other supers, intent on keeping them busy so that Aurora could fight with better odds. All of the supers in this wave of attackers appeared to be able to fly, but they landed and formed a semi-circle in front of him instead of engaging in the air. Eight opponents against him alone. Gus wondered what to expect when multiple attacks came at once. A woman reached out her hand, gaudy exaggerated fingernails pointed at Gus, and beams shot out of the tips.

He dodged and flew upwards and cracked his head against some kind of invisible barrier there, falling to the ground, a little dizzy and landing right on his tailbone. He rolled over in unexpected agony as two supers looked at each other knowingly. "So predictable."

The semicircle closed as Gus rolled onto his side. *Did I damage my spine?* Pain shot down both of his legs and he couldn't get comfortable as lances of pain shot into his hamstrings and he did not trust his legs to support him. Weakly he thought, *Jet, help me out here.* Gus heard a loud scream and twisted his neck to see that Jet's blade had sunk deep into the shoulder muscle of one of the supers with its jagged side before dragging backwards and disappearing from Gus' view.

Blood shot out and splashed a merc to the side, distracting them from their attack. He could hear cracks as the butt of his weapon hit either armor or bone, and Gus was forgotten as the mercs dealt with the new threat. Sliding his hand down to his side, Gus snuck his hand in the slit there and drew out two gels, both pink. He bit into both, chewing as the sounds of battle moved away from him. *Mmm, watermelon.* He could get used to these gels.

While the gels didn't give him the immediate boost like the red, he felt that the pain was fading and the disorientation from running into the barrier cleared. He rolled over onto his belly and pushed himself to his knees. Pain faded to pins and needles of numbness, which also began to fade and Gus stood again.

Would it kill these supers to have a passive rapid regeneration ability that I could snatch? Gus got to his feet and shuffled towards the sounds of where Jet continued to scuffle, his legs still stiff and less responsive than normal.

Crashing through some large leafy ferns, Gus saw one super trying to hold onto the end of Jet as he was flipped back and forth, reminding Gus of someone riding a mechanical bull, hanging on only by his hands. He must have had an iron grip because Jet was merciless in lifting and slamming the poor guy up and down. Still, he hung on like a pit bull determined not to be shaken loose of a chew toy.

Jet flung the poor super into his mates, and they ducked and dodged, unable or unwilling to grab the erratically-moving blade. While their backs were turned, Gus fired **Warp** on the legs of one of the more agile supers, and heard a crunch as the bones were crushed in the altered space.

Attention was split and three supers rushed to meet Gus. Blood dribbled down the chest of one man from where Jet had cut deep into his trapezius. He rushed to grapple with Gus as the other two prepared some energy attacks, raising their hands menacingly.

Gus ducked his head and activated **Bound**, hoping that the barrier was still in place. It was! As Gus leaped, he carried the other super with him, the strength of the leap slamming them into the barrier and the already-weakened super hit and the barrier fizzled and faded away as he went limp.

That was lucky! So you were responsible for this little gem of an ability.

Gus landed and placed his hand on the super's chest and tried to activate **Leech** but nothing happened. The enemy's suit covered his entire body except for a cutout for his face. **Leech** *requires skin-to-skin contact, good to know.* Checking his own fingertips, he saw the hybrid-Nth had pulled away from the pads, exposing his bare skin. It quickly resealed, returning to its gunmetal texture. He quickly touched the super's face and grabbed all the abilities, more to guarantee the stun than for the abilities at this point.

The other two supers made it to where he had landed and attacked.

Almost ready to dash to the left, *TimeSight* warned him to hold back and frost erupted on the trunk of a tree where he would have been. Meter-long daggers of ice formed like stalagmites on the tree as the humid tropical air crystalized. He was not lucky enough to dodge the other attack, which exploded over him in a tar-like mess. The amber-colored material held his extremities and severely slowed him down as he tugged against the material. He pulled, and the material appeared to get stronger the more force was applied to it, but it did thin and finally snapped.

Getting one arm free, Gus saw a broad smile spread across the face of the Ice Queen. In a panic, Gus activated *Xyzzy* and moved an outline of his figure as he surveyed the scene in front of him. Finding where he wanted to place it, Gus completed activating it and was out of the sap-like goop.

Standing behind the super, he kicked her in the back and she stumbled forward into the newly-vacant patch of material. Extending her hands to catch herself, they sunk deep into the goo. Her head fell into the material, submerging her chin and mouth. She leaned back and pulled, desperately trying to keep her nostrils out of the goop. Gus worried that she would freeze the material but it apparently needed to have contact with the air to activate. The other super, now very close, fired her ability again, this time in a much larger spray than before.

Gus was prepared this time and used *Intermediate Shielding* to create a concave shield in front of him. The ability splashed and rebounded, coating the woman in her own resinous goopy material. Its honey-colored hue darkened as it set into a deep amber color, emitting a noxious odor as it cured. The material appeared to thicken with her resistance, allowing her to move less the more she struggled.

The front of her body was totally covered, and Gus worried that she wouldn't be able to breathe. He formed a shield into the shape of a small cylinder the size of a toilet paper roll, and pushed it through the goop, which was already hardening. The woman's lips grabbed hold of the makeshift snorkel, gasping. Gus touched the two supers and **Leeched** them dry. The material had almost solidified in the air and the limp supers were held in place, but did not appear to be sinking deeper into the material.

Gus went to assist Jet and saw that two of his opponents were unconscious, one of them the 'cling-on.' One of the supers touched her temples upon seeing him and he could hear a voice in his head, trying to compel him to stop the polearm. Gus almost reached forward to recall Jet, then stopped, shaking his head when a chime sounded.

You have unlocked a subskill of **Coerce: Psi-Resist (Level 1).**
Psi-Resist (Level 1) [Passive]: *Having obtained the ability to control others' thoughts, you have the increased ability to resist attacks of a similar nature.*
1,000 XP awarded.
500 FP awarded.
6,700 XP to level 20.

Gus looked at the woman and shook his head, wagging his finger 'no.' The woman paled and turned to run. Jet interposed between her legs and she tumbled to the ground. Crawling in the sand to get away, Gus grabbed her by the neck and activated **Leech,** taking her abilities while holding her until she stopped twitching.

The last opponent had retreated when he heard Aurora's voice remark over the mental comms.

"Gus, hurry!" she choked out before the message suddenly cut out.

Gus turned his attention to see how she was doing.

———

Aurora's hands tingled with the amount of power she was holding. She couldn't remember the last time she felt this angry. The pain she felt in her month of torture fueled her anger and she focused it sharper than a monomolecular blade. The two supers she blamed for that pain were here in front of her. Right as she activated her meager flight skill, she heard the tinkle of a windchime and suddenly she was flying with much less effort. In her rage, she barely noticed.

Mercurio was wearing a jetpack, while Slipstream was maintaining herself aloft, light emanating from the soles of her boots and her hands. They looked at each other in recognition as they saw Aurora approaching.

Aurora attempted to remotely trigger the EMP, but found the signal was being jammed. She growled to herself as she assessed the situation. She would have to separate the two and focus on Mercurio first. Slipstream could absorb her attacks and also provide a shielding that would protect Mercurio.

Aurora first activated *Dazzle* and punched through the curtain of sparks, connecting with Mercurio as hard as she could. Her fist stretched through him, distending like a trampoline with the force. She worried he would be impervious to this type of attack, due to his rubbery, fluid nature. *Rubber...* that gave her an idea.

Taking advantage of *Dazzle*'s effect on him, Aurora clung onto him. She hit *Ion Storm* repeatedly, engulfing Mercurio's entire body with the effect, just as she had to her rubber restraints in the dungeon. His more pliant tissue succumbed more easily to the oxidizing effects of the ability, and his suit and skin began to crack and blanch under the onslaught.

Aurora noticed that he really wore no suit at all, that it was really all his skin imitating a semblance of a suit. The added weight of Aurora had overtaxed the jetpack and the soft blue hue emanating from the jets had darkened to a sickly purple. Before they hit the ground, Aurora spring boarded off of Mercurio's back, letting him hit the sand. The jetpack shot forward without her weight, and pushed him through the wet sand, plowing a furrow like a drunk farmer curving back and forth. With a large *pop,* the backplate of the jetpack flew away as a fuel canister exploded. Mercurio spun around, arms elongating with the centrifugal force until he lay prone on his back, tiny flames guttering away in the wet sand.

Sensing someone behind her, Aurora ducked to the side and took only a glancing blow from Slipstream's kick. The two women grappled, Aurora grabbing her opponent's wrists to keep her from launching any light bolts her way. Each time Slipstream inhaled deeply as they struggled, she pulled in photons and though in broad daylight, the area around them became darkened like standing in a shadow. With a glint in her eyes, she made spheres of bright light around Aurora's hands. With a twist, a long needle began to extend out of a wide banded bracelet that usually surrounded Slipstream's wrists, but had been pushed further up to her mid forearms by the struggle.

"Seems like we have the same strength levels. Too bad that's not my only trick. Say goodnight again, Aurora."

Aurora smiled back. Slipstream thought she still needed her hands to focus her power. She concentrated **Ion Storm** at the base of the needle and saw it begin to glow red in less than a second.

Slipstream's expression morphed from arrogance to confusion to horror as she saw the tip of the needle dip down to her own exposed wrist.

Aurora suddenly let go of Slipstream and used her fist to hammer the needle deep into the skin. In an instant, all of her muscles relaxed and she slumped to the ground. An ignominious smell alerted Aurora that whatever was in that needle relaxed *all* the muscles in Slipstream's body. *Did that happen to me on the station? Gross!*

"That was very satisfying," she said. Despite her revulsion she felt elated she had beaten them. After Gus took their abilities, she definitely had plans to visit these two and gloat a bit.

A sharp pain hit her neck and she reached up to find that she had a small dart embedded in the side of her neck. Turning to face her attacker, she saw an obvious augment, full of bionics and cybernetics on both his suit and embedded into his skin. *Damn augments!* Her disgust towards augments resurfaced.

Not having powers strong enough to *really* be supers, they used technology to make up the difference or amplify their skills to some semblance of significance. While some augments had Nth, most did not. They were unworthy adversaries in every sense. She sneered at him and tried to work the barb on the dart out of her neck.

With a coarse laugh, the augment shot another dart into her arm that was clasping the first dart and pushed energy through the clear, hair-like filaments completing the circuit. Aurora spasmed with the electricity, losing control of her arm as it flapped and flailed like a fish out of water, periodically hitting her. She tried to grab the filaments, hoping to break or tear them. Her muscles refused to cooperate for the most part, and the filaments were deceptively strong, though they looked thin and fragile.

Unable to break them, she changed tactics and used the filaments as a guide. She forced an **Ion Storm** attack up the filaments, crawling up the fibers back to the augment. He increased the voltage and Aurora almost lost consciousness, and probably would have if the pain had not kicked in as well. She could smell burning hair, realizing that it was emanating from *her!* The darts had heated up and were burning the skin and blood around where they poked out into the air.

Anger flaring, she pushed a huge wave of MP into her **Ion Storm** and it flew up the remainder of the filament, causing an overload in the power cells. The feedback blew them both back and they collapsed on the ground. She tried to contact Gus as she saw something approaching, her body unresponsive. The creature approached and activated a skill, and Aurora faded into unconsciousness.

After waiting for confirmation that she was out, long arms wrapped around Aurora's body. With a large leap, the non-humanoid-looking super named Cthulhu took flight. Keying his comms, he gave the signal that he had the package and for everyone to return to base. Cthulhu couldn't speak anymore, but had developed ways to communicate. Aurora disappeared, masked by tentacles swaying in the air.

———

Gus saw the small group of supers retreating. "Yeah, you had better run," he said, satisfied. They were getting the hang of this. He checked his display and saw three more red circles and went over the small hill and descended to the beach.

Mercurio and Slipstream were there with another man bristling with electronics. His suit appeared to cover his entire body and he wore goggles. Touching each, he wiped their powers and then began hauling them back to the brig. He wondered where Aurora was, but assumed she still needed some space after their argument.

He returned and gathered the other mercs and lined them up, so he could make a stretcher train and bring everyone to the brig and save some time. Basileus would be pissed! He must have lost more than half of his fighting force by now, and should be getting desperate. Each failed attempt on the manor made him weaker and Gus stronger. With the new powers from these supers, protecting the manor would become a non-issue.

Gus began to ferry everyone to the brig, more than a little irritated that Aurora once again wasn't helping him. He muttered under his breath, after making sure that the comm was clicked off, of course. Perhaps it was best she was taking some alone time; Gus was pretty bad at speaking with no filter when he was upset. He didn't want to say anything to strain the already awkward dynamic that had arisen. Still, he grumbled to himself, the murmuring kept his mind occupied while he dragged everyone to their cells.

Congratulations! You have subdued 5 opponents trespassing on privately-owned territory.

5,000 XP (1,000 x 5) awarded for non-lethal methods.
2,500 FP (500 x 5) awarded.
1,700 XP to level 20.

Gus waved away the message in his irritation. Since he didn't assist Aurora, he got no XP for 'subduing' them. Just another irritation; he would be level 20 now with that.

Finally done with the task, he had some free time but didn't feel like doing anything, being in a sour mood. There had been enough battles that he didn't feel like any training. He needed some fresh air, and maybe a quick swim to clear his mind.

CHAPTER THIRTY-THREE

Grown Up

As Gus kicked open the front doors, a tablet that was leaning against the door flew away, landing in the grass nearby. Gus stomped over to the tablet, kneeling down to pick up the device. A crack ran across the display. There was a grass-stained note on it that said simply: 'Watch Me.'

Gus turned it on and, after connecting, Basileus came into view on the screen. "You found my little gift, good. It took you long enough. Listen up, as I'm only going to say this once. We have Aurora. The deal is simple: You give me the manor and we give you Aurora, unharmed. Meet me on the beach tomorrow, and we will go to transfer ownership. If you refuse, she dies. If you plan on betraying me, she dies. Once ownership is transferred, I will give you a transport and I expect you both to leave the island, forever. Those are my terms, and they are non-negotiable." The camera panned to the side where Aurora was bound and unconscious. "She's alive, for now. How long is up to you. Don't disappoint me again." The video ended and the screen blackened.

His first impulse was to try to come up with some plan on how to outwit Basileus and trap him or overpower him, but he didn't want to put Aurora at risk. Gus sat down on the grass and ran his fingers through his hair.

What now? Gus was a planner by nature; he did his best work when he had time to ponder and think about a challenge, then craft a solution. Ever since he had landed on the island, he felt like that luxury had disappeared. There was no time to be methodical, and he felt a majority of what he had come up with on the fly was inferior and inadequate.

The recent argument with Aurora weighed on his mind. She would be pissed if he tried to save her, and she would be dead if he did nothing. It was an awesome lose-lose situation.

He exhaled a loud sigh, surprised at how quickly the situation had shifted. His father's warning came back to him: 'Never engage a superior force, especially without the resources to defend your position.' He thought his new powers would be enough. They had been until now. He had to check in to see what Aurora had invested the FP into; maybe he could defend the manor better than he could in the past. If they wanted to take it, they were going to have to fight for it.

Gus had walked down the beach on auto-pilot and began to jog down it as he thought. He was bursting with stress and indecision and just had to bleed some of it away through physical exertion. He was rapidly approaching being overwhelmed with the heavy decisions he would have to make soon, so he ran and he was able to think a bit more clearly with his body otherwise occupied.

He knew he couldn't just give up the manor. Basileus was crazy but he had to see that if he killed Aurora, he wouldn't have any negotiating power. Gus began to form a plan on how to buy himself some time. He would get new abilities after sleeping tonight and extra time would let him get familiar with them. He should hit level 20 and hopefully unlock another Fractal Level with the stat boosts that accompanied it. Or so he hoped; he still didn't understand how or why that mechanic worked.

He still had the arena, and he couldn't waste the XP that

Adaptive Training offered; maybe he could level enough to get that much stronger. Gus jumped over a large downed tree with ease. So much had changed from his first time running around the island.

What about his pre-**Leech** abilities? He had been neglecting them in his effort to become familiar with the new ones, but how could he blend the two? Nick's question of 'What do you want?' kept coming back to him. What did he want from all of this? He remembered those days before the pirates came where he could practice his skills at his leisure, develop them in an easy, relaxing environment. Granted, he had leveled much more quickly with all the attacks, but it was stressful and frenetic all the time. Not something he felt he could maintain long term.

How had his dad done it for so many years? Compartmentalizing was never one of Gus' specialties. He was becoming painfully aware that he really had not had any major challenges in his past life. He had gone through some things that he thought were tough, but in comparison to now, they were laughably frivolous and fairly childish.

He wondered again what life would be like when he got home. His big worry was that it was going to implode. That his new self-imposed responsibilities and goals would be so alien compared to the past Gus that he would simply not connect with his old friends and just drift away.

Or that he would be so busy that there would be so little time to dedicate to goofing around that his friends would find someone else to fill his space. The thought of losing his friends both worried and angered him. He sped up his running as the emotion swelled. Part of him thought they would accept him regardless, but the other part that held on to his own prejudices stirred up enough doubt to make him uncertain.

He had thought he had wanted just to defeat the invaders, but what would prevent more from coming? While he enjoyed trying and gaining new abilities, the novelty was wearing off a bit. He was often using them as an afterthought, rather than a planned part of his attack strategy. Maybe that would change in time as he assimilated them into attack routines.

He had to get more powerful, that seemed to be the key. Maybe Purple Faction was right by following the tenet 'might makes right.' If he was strong enough, he could make his own choices, not be buffeted about by the whims of others. He was so sick of other people forcibly guiding his life. That was the type of independence he really wanted, to choose his own destiny without anyone interfering.

When he framed it like that, it almost sounded like how super villains lived. Hell bent on their personal agenda, and any opposition must be swept away. Was that where he was doomed to end up? Was there any use in worrying about things that far in the future when he had a real enemy to face tomorrow? Gus shifted his thoughts to planning what to do to deal with Basileus and his goons.

Gus continued to run, dismissing worries as they popped up, trying to center his thoughts on productive plans. He was worried he would come up with nothing useful as he kept moving while his brain shifted into cruise control, offering nothing insightful.

Gus wanted to take a break. To just run away until he was mentally ready to deal with these new problems. None of his powers could stop time though. He tried to formulate plans, but he kept coming up empty. Before he had Nth, and Gus felt over-whelmed, he would sleep a lot more than normal. He would retreat from any social interactions and keep to himself. Maybe binge stream a holovid series, or play a game.

Eventually the overpowering sensations would fade and he could deal with life again. That life was over. There was no time for such escapes. He ran in silence for a while, keeping the pace such that his stamina was maintained around half-full and not drained to empty.

"Gus, I know you are going through a lot, but you can do this," Nick encouraged.

Gus had been mulling over his own thoughts so much that

he had forgotten about Nick. "I don't know, buddy. I'm beginning to wonder if I really can."

"Nothing's ever easy, right? That doesn't mean it's impossible. You've just got to choose how you are going to respond. Give yourself a break once in a while. You can't let the thought of making a bad decision paralyze you into inaction. It's easy to break down, quit, and let the situation win. Don't worry about the far future, just focus on tomorrow. What can you do to make the best showing that you can when Basileus shows up?"

"Well, I should figure out what defenses I can use. I should throw everything we've unlocked in the manor at him. No use holding things back if he overruns me and takes the manor away."

"What are you going to do about Aurora? Are you going to try to save her?"

"I don't know, Nick. She wouldn't want me to, I know that. It's hard to accept, even though I know she has much more experience working on teams. She escaped their headquarters, so she should be able to handle whatever limited restraints they have here."

"Do you trust her to take care of herself?"

"Part of me says no, since she let herself get captured. The other part thinks that I have to. Even if I wanted to, the stakes are too high. Aurora's words burned me the last time we argued, but I think they hurt so much because she was mostly right. I can be too optimistic about things, and I'm not dealing with honorable people. Basileus might not be mentally stable from what she told me before, so how do you negotiate with someone like that? I've always avoided confrontation, but I'm going to have to face more and more of it. Especially if I'm going to change anything when I get back home—if I get back home. Anyway, I might as well build those skills now, and part of that is making hard decisions and trusting those who follow me. Hell, she made me promise I wouldn't overdo the heroics at the cost of the mission."

"So what's next?"

"Let's give this bully a fat lip," Gus declared, his eyes glinting. His knuckles popped as he clenched his fists with his resolution. Gus made a beeline for the control center. He had trouble figuring out what Aurora had done until he selected the 'Recent Updates/Unlocks' tab hidden among the multitude of open facility info tabs. He smiled as he read the devious little things the invaders had in store when they returned.

An hour later, Gus headed to the Foundry and programmed the items he needed. Once they were finished, he placed everything in its proper place, preparing for Basileus' return. He fiddled with placement, until things seemed just right as the light for the day faded.

He took a long shower, and thought that Basileus must think that he was dreading the upcoming fight. He was actually looking forward to it a little. For a chance to stand up, instead of folding in defeat. Gus knew he would get roughed up, no doubt, but it would be worth it to see that smarmy smirk wiped off his arrogant face. That vision accompanied him as he drifted to sleep.

———

New abilities assimilated!

Dick in a Box (Level 12) [25 MP]: *Encase an enemy in an invisible, impenetrable box. Duration at current level: 5 minutes.*

It's All in the Tips (Level 22) [10 MP]: *Fire beams of energy from fingertips.*

Kitty's Got Claws (Level 7) [20 MP]: *Increased damage and poison transmitted to wounds for continued damage over time.*

Shapeshift (Level 18): *Change your physical form at will by temporarily reconfiguring connective and hard tissues. Mass must remain constant and may result in condensation as matter is temporarily converted.*

Meld (Level 8) [40 MP]: *Temporarily gain properties of a selected item. Duration depends on the type of material utilized and energy requirements to affect transformation.*

Ice Shard (Level 16) [15 MP]: *Use ambient moisture to create* *dagger-like weapons. MP cost doubled if insufficient ambient moisture and ether must be converted to water to create effects.*

Amber (Level 8) [20MP]: *Create a viscous substance that rapidly hardens, trapping enemies inside.*

Command (Level 17) [10MP]: *Compel targets to obey instructions. Success rates increase with higher levels of Intelligence.*

Mimic (Level 5) [20 MP]: *Impersonate others by adopting their outward appearance. At higher levels can match vocal patterns and mannerisms.*

Photoelectric Shielding (Level 11): *Energy below a certain threshold state will be absorbed by shielding, sufficient energy will result in a retaliatory burst of photoelectrons causing radiation damage.*

Lightskate (Level 8): *Move effortlessly on any surface on photonically charged ether.*

Drafting (Level 34): *Creates a wake behind you that allows team-mates to travel at the same speed. Cannot be utilized without an established team and is unavailable to enemies to exploit.*

12 new abilities assimilated.
12,000 XP awarded.
6,000 FP awarded.
LEVEL UP! Congratulations, Level 20 reached!
1,000 FP awarded.
You have (5) additional stat points to assign.
19,700 XP to level 21.

Gus hesitated with anticipation as nothing happened. He got up and looked in the mirror.

"I expected it to happen when I hit level twenty, but I guess not," Gus said as he looked at himself. The silence drew on. "Nick, are you there?" Still nothing. There was a sudden vibration and his watch came to life, flickering on and off. Finally it formed a familiar oval window to the side of his body. A voice he now recognized as his mother's said:

Requirements met...

Dimensional unfolding progressing…
Fractal unfolding level two…

Gus felt the tight feeling of compression again but was not scared, knowing what to expect this time. He braced himself for the upcoming pain.

It hit him like a brick wall, even more intense than the last time. Gus caught sight of himself in the mirror as furrows on his skin appeared to tear, but there was no blood. He gasped, unable to even scream as the pulling sensation intensified. At last it was done and he dropped to the floor, collapsing.

Nick's voice sounded. "Assembling Nanobot Interface Construct."

"Reviewing a suitable framework based on scan history and personal preferences…" Nick continued. Once again Gus felt like he was losing a friend.

The voice shifted to Nick's less formal style. "And you, Gus, you… you're gonna miss meeeeeeee!" the voice sang, then faded and morphed into another.

"Evaluation complete, assessing suitable mentor framework…" Nick said with a slight accent Gus couldn't make out at first. While it compiled, he took a glance at his new stats, putting his five points for level 20 all into Intelligence.

Agility: 57 (52+5)
Constitution: 61 (56+5)
Charisma: 33 (28+5)
Strength: 42 (37+5)
Perception: 41 (36+5)
Intelligence: 64 (59+5)
Luck: 42 (37+5)
HP: 1200/1200
MP: 1180/1180
Stamina: 1200/1200

Not bad at all.

"Tertiary nanobot interface construct will be patterned after *Chiun*."

Who the hell is Chiun? Gus thought blearily.

"Next evolution is set at level 30. Don't just lay there boy, stand like a man!" Nick ordered.

Gus rolled over and stood. "Who are you supposed to be?"

"Always asking questions and never learning. Perhaps it is better to be *doing* at this time."

"Okay," Gus mouthed slowly as he got ready as quickly as he could and headed down to the arena and started a brutal session of Adaptive Training. He was determined to include all of his new abilities, especially when the pillowbots adapted.

Except Chiun forbade it. Somehow, he even grayed them out, making them unavailable to use.

"A fool hath no delight in understanding, but that his heart may discover itself."

"Is that supposed to mean something to me?" Gus asked, throwing his hands in the air. "I need to be resilient, as strong as I can be. I don't get jack for XP if I don't use these new abilities. These supers are highly trained—"

"Exactly, and you know none of your fundamentals well. Reset!"

If Gus hadn't known better, he would have assumed Chiun was the personification of Chop Chop, who was suspiciously absent...

"Fight!" Chiun commanded, and the pillowbots sprang to life.

Gus pushed himself until the arena went dark. He did have to begrudgingly admit that he was more adept at switching with his more familiar new skills and how to integrate them. He checked the time. It was still early, now all that was left was to let all of his bars refill and double check on his preparations. Despite Chiun's quirks, things were falling into place. *I love it when a plan comes together.*

CHAPTER THIRTY-FOUR

Hide Away

"Nick, if I erase some things out of the system, can you restore them at a later date?"

"Why?"

"I want to erase any maps and informational directories from the database, but it'd be nice if you could store these somewhere as a backup."

"Ah, I see. In case you are tortured and are too weak to resist. Yes. This can be done. Direct search cannot be erased but they must know the exact name."

"Yes, do that now! How long do you need?"

"The two most powerful warriors are patience and time."

"What the hell does that mean? I have both in short supply!"

"Thirty minutes."

"Thank you. Can we encrypt something so that they can't change any settings or access the control system?"

"No."

"No, you won't, or no, you can't?"

"The manor is protected with redundancies that prevent lockouts."

Gus tried to think up what else would hide vital information. Nick's silence was deafening. "If you could help in any way, I'd appreciate it." Still nothing. *This Chiun kind of sucks.*

"You are the first victim of your anger," came the emotionless reply.

Gus shook his head and thought. He got some ideas but Chiun turned them all down. *What kind of name is that, anyway?* Something fluttered in his thoughts. Name. *Could I rename a system so that it is not easily found after directories are missing, though?*

"Please tell me I can rename some system folders so they'll be harder to find."

"That is… acceptable."

Gus exhaled a sigh he didn't know he was holding. "Okay, Gus, what would help me and hinder them?" His mind kept returning to the scanners. "I need a way to stay out of sight, but I would like to know where they are. Can I hide scanners and tracking so that I'll be the only one to access them?"

"Just state the new name for the file for those processes," Nick said sternly, like he was trying patiently to deal with a small child.

"Man-boobs."

"Excuse me?"

"Man-boobs. I knew a guy who hid important stuff in a file named that because he knew no one would ever look there."

There was a grumble of dismay. "*Man-boobs* it is."

With that being done, there really wasn't much left to do. Gus made his final run to the cafeteria and loaded up on blue, pink, and red gels before heading to the inevitable confrontation.

Gus made his way to the beach to meet Basileus and crew again. He wasn't looking forward to the meeting, but he knew what he was going to do.

Basileus was waiting on his little dais, smiling with an expression that just begged to be slapped off his face. By all appearances, he looked like everyone's version of a hero: handsome with perfectly-styled hair, impressive jawline, and the physique to complete the package. He was even sitting upon a throne of all things as he looked down at Gus, his outfit gleaming in the tropical sun. The effect was supposed to make him feel intimidated, but something seemed off.

Mercs stood around him like the little toadies they were, trying to look menacing and dangerous. A metal contraption that resembled a loader sat on the right side of the dais, and its arm extended out over the water. Aurora was gagged and bound by her hands hanging from this loading arm, suspended one-hundred-fifty feet above the water. She kicked and struggled as she dangled there.

"I am glad to see you are reasonable, Gus. We can solve this misunderstanding like gentlemen," Basileus gushed, secure he had won.

Gus probed at Basileus with his new *Telepathy* skill. He was tentative at first and unsure it would even work at this distance. As he was about to let the ability go, he got faint shades of emotions, which became more distinct, but flickered from one extreme to another. There were traces of fear, uncertainty and doubt, resolve, anger, pride, all swirling together.

As Gus intensified his focus, he began to get impressions of motives. Under the emotions, there was the strong feeling that Basileus was putting up a brave facade to fool everyone, including his own men. That wasn't all though, there was a resonance...

And somehow Gus just knew. In a flash, he saw that he would have been just like this guy had things gone differently in his life. As he always imagined they should have, with his mother never disappearing and him getting powers like his older brother. He too would always be searching for ways to make his father proud. And he would never find them.

Gus pulled back out of his probe, shaken. *What was that?* A chime sounded, but Gus was so struck he didn't check it.

"Now he begins to see," Nick said. "You get the chicken by hatching the egg, not smashing it."

Gus shook his head to clear it. This wasn't the time for riddles.

Focus! Basileus was hiding something, so he probably didn't really want to kill Aurora. Or he had no intention of keeping his promise if Gus did hand over the manor. He didn't want to hurt Aurora; his plan was probably to turn her to his side if he could. That had to be it.

Gus cleared his throat, trying to sound bold. "I am afraid I'll have to disabuse you of your assumptions. I'm not giving up the manor." Gus shrugged and put his hands on his hips, awaiting the response. He knew it would push Basileus' buttons.

"Who do you think you are? That manor is no more yours than it was Methiochos'. My father paid to have it made and sacrificed more than you can imagine to design it and all it contains. You will never be able to utilize its full capabilities. It is wasted on someone like you." Basileus spat, all composure gone.

Gus could see his balled fists start to spark by his sides. *Just a little bit more agitation…* "Last I checked, possession was nine-tenths of the law. If I hadn't done what I have to clear the island and take down the bio-stasis field, you would have gone along without ever having access to the manor. So in my book, you lost ownership when you first lost the manor. You didn't try to contact me to work something out and now you're trying to coerce me under duress of harming someone close to me. And you think that makes me want to trust you? I'm not the idiot you seem to think I am. Get bent." Gus tried to ooze smugness, folding his arms and plastering a huge grin on his face.

"You don't think I'll do it, do you? Don't push me, you won't like it when I push back," Basileus said through clenched teeth, veins visible on his reddening forehead as he began to become angrier and angrier. He reached out an arm towards Aurora, as if to emphasize his threat.

"Do whatever you damn well please. You're going to anyway, regardless of whether I concede or not. There's a reason people don't negotiate with terrorists. If you don't have any morals, what's left to create a basis of trust that you'll honor any agreements? If you harm her, what will that leave you as far as negotiating power? Nothing. So shut up and get out of here."

Basileus became an even deeper shade of red and flung both hands out wide over his head. Energy arced between them, magenta and purple-hued streams connecting his fingertips.

"Ooooh. I'm impressed, fireworks," Gus hollered back, trying to pack the words with sarcasm.

A sparkling storm of blueish energy built up larger and larger and he flung it at Aurora. She brought her legs up, crunching into a fetal position and there was a large flash as the plasma ball collided with her and the loading arm. When Gus blinked away the photo-bleaching effect of the bright explosion, he saw only a burned rope swinging at the end of a partially melted metal loader arm. Nothing substantial remained to even make a splash in the water below.

"You see now, boy? I will have no mercy with you either." Basileus panted, winded and drained from the massive expenditure of MP.

Gus stared at the spot where Aurora had hung. *No!* He looked back and forth at Basileus and the empty loading arm. The smile crawled back on Basileus' face, his anger gone seeing Gus' distress.

"Not what you expected, is it?"

That shouldn't have happened! I read his thoughts! He was bluffing, he had to be. I was sure of it!

"Now let's discuss your surrender, here and now, boy!" Basileus commanded. "You have worn my patience thin."

He felt emotionally sucker punched as he looked at the tiny cloud rapidly dispersing over the water. *I did this. I pushed him too far. Aurora would have had a chance if I could've kept my big mouth shut. Why did I drop my telepathy probe? Would I have sensed him change his mind?*

Doubt and questions continued to barrage Gus and he stood there shell-shocked at what to do. The other supers around Basileus took a small step back, uncertain what their volatile leader was going to do next as well.

"Now what?" Gus asked, mostly to himself, not really knowing where things would go from here. He was alone again. His bravado evaporated away as reality sunk in on his situation. He reminded himself that he only had to deal with a couple dozen supers, and that he had managed so far, but the thought gave him no comfort. *At least Aurora got her wish*, he thought sardonically. *I didn't sacrifice the manor for her, she would be happy. Wouldn't she?*

"I weary with how often people disappoint me." Basileus gestured to one of the mercs.

"Your plan," Nick reminded him.

Gus nodded, waiting for just the right time.

"I am done playing games. I will gather everyone and remove you from the manor by force." Basileus touched his ear and said something without amplifying it, then folded his arms in front of him with confidence. In less than a minute, Gus saw a large craft appear in the distance, moving to rendezvous with Basileus.

And that is my cue to get the hell out of here. Gus ran back to the manor and Basileus just laughed maniacally at his retreating back.

"Scurry away, little roach! Go get him!" he roared at the other supers and they took off after him. Gus activated **Gemini** and ordered his double to flee in an erratic pattern. Meanwhile, Gus ducked and dodged the shots and beams upturning the ground around him as he activated **Hyper**, doubling his Agility as he fled to the manor. A blast hit him in the back but his new armor absorbed the shot without even heating up. More supers broke after his double, assuming that he was the fake, not having been damaged by the hit.

Thank you, hybrid-Nth! At last he was at the entrance, and he slid inside. He signaled for Nick to drop the security slab into place, and launch his countermeasures. Gus could hear grinding gears and scraping of metal as panels shifted over vulnerable accessways, changing the exterior look of the manor before the other supers could reach it.

"Entryways protected," Nick reported.

Gus saw red stars swarm over the manor, searching for weaknesses. It was only a matter of time before they found a way in. Gus headed for the control center. The atrium was dark with the windows covered, and he had to change filters to find his way.

He rushed to the control center to watch the results of his efforts. Sliding into a seat, he rubbed his hands, ready for the show.

CHAPTER THIRTY-FIVE

The Future Soon

All of the mercs spilled off the dais and more joined from the support craft, racing toward the manor. One super remained on the dais, watching it all impassively, previously unnoticed by the others and unmoved at the opportunity to fight.

He was neither on one side or the other, and since he hadn't been provoked, he did not rush to retaliate. The super named Voltekka watched as the others chased after the retreating man on the beach.

His employer grew restless and urged his pilot to land the dais near the structure. Hopping off and following the other supers onto the beach, he paused to look up at the large mecha before following the others.

"What are you waiting for? Let's go!" Basileus yelled, eyes wide with excitement.

"I will join you shortly," Voltekka responded, his voice a perfect imitation of Optimus Prime. It was totally unnecessary; he could have synthesized his actual voice, the one he used when he was merely Merlin Vandezon. However, people almost expected the voice with his appearance as a real life mecha. In truth, he did it just to toy with them. He had lost some things as he mechanized himself, removing all physical weakness through engineering, but his personality was intact.

Voltekka hovered over, adjusting the thrusters on his mechanized suit. No. Suit wasn't accurate. The transition had happened over time, but the line between technology that he wore and technology that he was had blurred long ago. He cast his mind back to when he had crossed over. Was it on the station? Or after? No matter.

One of the advantages of the transition was his perspective. He had obtained a level of patience he had never possessed when he was merely human. With plans as ambitious as his, he had much to do to accomplish them. Many, many preparations.

He could sense what he came for nearby and the man would provide the most efficient way of locating what he sought. It would be no big loss if he died, Voltekka would get what he came for either way.

He looked up to the heavens and his display rendered the orbital ring that would span the planet. The exquisite isolation, away from the frenetic distractions down here. He longed to be up there again, building and making his vision a reality. Were it not for the specialized resources here, he wouldn't be wasting his time. He had tracked a large shipment of Endurium to Manticorps decades ago, when it had inexplicably disappeared. Years of searching had turned up nothing.

When the virus Voltekka had planted in the Manticorps network began pinging keywords, he tore himself away from his work. The components that should be here were too valuable to be used for any purpose but his own. At last, he would eliminate this bottleneck to his plan's progression.

He prepared a quick communique to his followers, delineating his plans and intentions, then sent the burst data packet to the converted remnants of the Von Neumann Space Station. This completed, he surveyed the manor and floated past it, traveling over the jungle.

If the man was caught, he would know about it in party comms. He adjusted the filters to reduce the near-constant updates and chatter. The invasive nature of comms forced him to slow down his processing to manage the maddeningly slow nature of spoken conversation. So inefficient. It was good he was almost done with this objective.

Pulsing out a deep scan, Voltekka zeroed in on the strongest signal. He increased his speed, realizing that it was *unpurposed*. Arriving at the location, he noted a primitive camp. Landing deftly, his metallic feet crushed coconut shells that had been strewn about. Muffled pops sounded as he walked forward and fished a small triangular piece of metal out of the sand. He held the tiny piece in front of him, turning it about in wonder.

"Interesting," his synthetic voice droned as he tilted his head slightly. He weighed the small piece of Endurium in his hands, determining it to be 50.2 grams. The further calculations were instantly done. It was sufficient. He could now begin crafting his army. This was the key to creating mecha duplicates. Ones with a stable mental matrix, and with which he could communicate via hive-mind. His followers would still be useful, but he could only rely on himself.

Now that he had a sample, this would vastly aid his ability to scan and extract more of the material. Voltekka shot into the air, making a sharp 90-degree turn after clearing the canopy below, and flew toward the manor.

CHAPTER THIRTY-SIX

Breach (Walk Alone)

According to plan, the enemy supers rushed toward the manor. Gus activated the new stealth drones who unleashed a barrage of laser blasts and launched a myriad of missiles that locked on the nearest targets and sped off as the drone dropped back into cover to recharge and reload.

The attack disoriented and broke their blitz on the manor. They scattered, looking for cover, while flying supers soared higher in an attempt to get out of range.

Pylons rose out of their hiding spots, and electricity arced between different pylons in unpredictable patterns as they shot up and down, like deadly whack-a-moles. Gus was pleased to see he placed the bases for the pylons well.

"Sorry to tase you, bro!" Gus cackled as a few supers were hit and twitched on the ground.

All too soon, one of the aerial supers shouted, "Enough!" and thrust his hands downward. Pylons were crushed and smashed, along with foliage that hid most of them, crushed in a way that reminded Gus of Graviton's abilities. All too soon the stealth drones were also dispatched, and the remaining supers formed ranks, on guard now.

Two supers stepped forward and formed a shield bubble around them as they moved forward cautiously. They were on the lawn when Gus launched another attack. Some special debuff gels that Aurora had designed were aerosolized in a mist underneath the supers. Orange and yellowish-green smoke billowed underneath the group, the shield trapping the noxious material closer to them, concentrating it. Soon Gus could not see them amid the roiling vapors.

The shield was modulated and the gas was being expelled somehow, but the damage had been done. Most supers rubbed at their eyes, blinded temporarily and they suffered a huge -10 Perception effect. On top of that, Agility should have taken a similar hit. Gus rocked back in his chair, fistpumping. With Aurora's skillful upgrades the effect would last twelve hours or more.

Even though they had destroyed the pylons and drones, the manor would replace them at no additional charge; the only drawback was the time it took to fabricate the items.

Gus was hoping they would retreat, and give him more time to build up defenses. As he turned back to the monitors, another super was bathing the others in a green light. Those affected walked out of the beam, their red eyes gone and HP bars refilled.

"At least the blast doors should hold; they held off those juggernauts for a long time." An alarm sounded just as Gus was trying to think of other traps and defenses he could enable. Red circles flashed on the display along with warnings across the tops of the displays.

Breach detected, main entrance...

Gus changed the view to the front entryway. He expected to see the blast doors peeled away by some Minmax supers, but there was a shimmering purple portal spanning it, allowing easy access for the others to walk right in. He rubbed his eyes and refocused on the monitor.

"That's it, just a little bit more," Gus coaxed as he brought up the menu. When most of them were in position, Gus hit the

Electro-floor button. Ankle high electrodes extended from the walls and blue energy cracked and arced as the mercs jiggled and shook.

"Dance party!" Gus cried as the floor pulsed and arms flailed. Gus couldn't help cracking up until one of the supers following touched the panels and deactivated them, one by one. "C'mon, that was a good one."

"If you say so," Nick replied.

Gus frowned at the prospect of having this wet noodle as his mentor for ten more levels.

One of the supers was leaning down and healing the ones affected by the electricity. "Where was that guy when I needed him? I still don't have a self-heal."

One was unconscious and they left her there rather than take time to revive her. "Nice loyalty to the team." Checking the minimap, there were others that the group had left behind from the initial attack, lying outside, represented with hollow circles.

"You expect honor among thieves?"

"I think what goes around comes around."

"So you believe in karma?"

"I'd like to think so. You try your best and hopefully it comes back to you."

"Be careful what you wish for, especially when it comes to cause and effect."

"Lighten up, dude," Gus said, shifting in his chair.

"You take the manor from its owner. The manor is taken from you. Symmetry."

Gus growled to himself and focused on the monitors, trying to ignore Nick's words for the moment. The supers were breaking into three different groups, moving cautiously.

Gus triggered one of the decoys to run across at the end of a hallway. The other supers pursued, just as Gus had planned. As they turned the corner, he activated the PyroMatic 2.0 system. Tiny sprinklers coated the supers with a fine mist as they ran through. Some did not notice, but others skidded to a stop and looked for the source. The nozzles were quickly rendered useless, but then the system activated phase two and showered the supers with sparks.

The fine mist ignited like lighter fluid and instantly many were aflame, as the gel coating them lit up and would not go out despite them patting or rolling on the ground. One super extended her hands and a black fog billowed out like living shadows. The cloud wrapped briefly around the worst of the flailing supers and swiftly moved to another, leaving them extinguished and smoking.

After another round of heals, the group was none the worse for the wear, and they were nearing the elevators.

"Aw, hell to the no!" Gus growled as the supers pushed the button to summon the elevator. He activated the EMP to see if that would stall their movements. The whine began again and Gus watched on another monitor. Four augments rushed together and interlocked arms. Another super waved their hands as if casting a spell and then in an instant, yellow glowing lines formed a cell-like structure over the augments.

When the EMP finally fired, there was a distortion wave at the cage's outer edges, but the augments within were unaffected. The elevators arrived and the supers piled in. They were coming straight for the control center.

CHAPTER THIRTY-SEVEN

Break Stuff

He keyed in a command and the metal plate shielding the control room window retracted. He locked the door to the control room and opened the window. He had expected to take more of them out before he had to fall back on the last part of the plan. Aurora had said they'd have a tough time working together, but that didn't appear to be the case.

He sneered as he hit play on a playlist he had crafted a while ago: Kick-ass Battle Mix 1. He stepped out the window and closed it behind him.

Then he jumped.

You have created a song-chain. Current multiplier: Geometric x2.
Flash by Queen. Song Chain Anchor.

As the music thumped the intro, Gus dove out the window, slowing his speed so he was not in front of any windows on his flight down to the ground. He landed and surveyed the scene, making sure there were no stragglers on his minimap before proceeding. There were a couple disabled supers lying around.

Gus began the task of **Leeching** their abilities, approaching the closest one who looked to be right next to one of the damaged pylons.

The super was burned badly and gasped as he tried to crawl forward. A spike of anger hit Gus as he realized that his teammates had just left him here like garbage. In their rush to get into the manor, no one had stopped to offer one bit of aid. The man was obviously shuddering and groaning in agony.

Hustla by Teddybears. Success rates x2.

The new song put a twinge into Gus, reminding him there wasn't time to think too much about it. He reached out and put a hand on his shoulder, hoping the unconsciousness would ease his obvious discomfort. As Gus extracted his abilities, he began to shake uncontrollably and then suddenly stopped. Gus felt for a pulse but unfortunately, the strain must have been too much for him.

You have defeated Skorzeny (Level 38).
32,500 XP awarded.
65,000 FP awarded.
You have unlocked the skill **KritzKrieg (Level 12).**
You have unlocked the skill **Schadenfreude (Level 17).**

Gus gasped at the enormous amount of experience and FP. It was easily on par with what he received for defeating Methiochos. He stood there in shock, conflicted with what he had done and for how *easily* he could have been getting stacks of XP. He stared in shock as the form blanched and crumbled, collapsing like a log in a fire. All that was left was something metal in the ashes.

He remembered feeling guilty about killing mantids a couple weeks ago, and now his actions led to the death of another human. Was he becoming that callous? *No! It was an accident.*

"He would have died anyway," Nick ventured, startling Gus' stupor.

"That doesn't make me feel any better. I should have given him a gel. I didn't even check before draining him."

"What is done is done."

Gus turned to leave and felt a sudden shock, as if he had been struck by lightning. He crumbled to a ball amid the remains of Skorzeny.

PENALTY!
You have acted in a manner contrary to a Guiding Principle by directly taking another's life through your actions. Recent actions are compounded by your desire to retaliate and acting upon feelings of vengeance.
You lose any XP gained for this level and ALL remaining FP, in addition to losing an entire level.
This is a serious breach and if repeated will lead to further penalties and ultimate loss of access to this Guiding Principle and its benefits.
You have lost a level! You are now level 19, last allocated stat points automatically deducted.
25,000 XP to level 20.

Gus rolled onto his back, the pain intensifying. It felt like burrowing worms crawling through his system, eating as they moved throughout his body, but mostly in his gut. At last the pain subsided, but he was thoroughly coated with dust and white with ash. His squirming had spread out the remains to a small oval that was not human shaped any longer and Gus saw a ring sitting there among the dust. He picked it up and looked at it, noting an inscription and, if it was authentic, the largest sapphire Gus had ever seen in his life.

As he looked closer to read the inscription, his watch began to buzz and flicker to life. Gus stowed the ring in a pocket and ran to get somewhere a little less exposed.

Error. Insufficient level for Fractal Unfolding.
Removing stat boost +10 per stat for reaching level 2.
Refolding unable to be performed... calculating...
Error
Run diagnostic sequence...

Gus now felt a paralyzing numbness sweep over his body, making it hard to coordinate his body and walk.

Without warning, his left leg stopped working and he pitched forward, barely catching himself from falling on his face. *What is happening to me?*

"You are reaping what-t-t-t—" Nick-Chiun's voice stuttered and then stopped.

Reversion to previous NIC interface due to level insufficiency...

"You know, I have to admit, I'm flattered," Nick said. "Losing levels just to see me again, wow. What a mensch!"

"I never thought I'd say it, but it's good to have the old you back."

"I told you you'd miss me! I just didn't know you'd go to extremes."

Invincible by DEAF KEV. Success rates x4.
Note: This song chain has deviated from a single focus. Various buffs will increase functionality but may lose potency in comparison.

"Are you in the middle of something? I was just kind of yanked back—"

"Yeah, Nick. The supers have taken over the manor."

"'Nuff said, go get 'em."

Gus' took one last look at the remains, then moved on and activated **Leech** on the remaining supers. He didn't bother moving them. They wouldn't know what happened when they awoke, and he couldn't put them in the brig. The fact that he could steal powers would soon be out.

Gus was about to go back inside when he looked upward. A super in a mechanized suit stood watching him with a curious tilt of his head. Gus assumed a defensive pose, but the super made no effort to attack.

After a tense moment, Gus retreated toward the front entry to the manor, all the while with his hands in a placating gesture as if the mech were a wild animal. Still the super made no moves. Gus entered and half-expected the robot to have alerted his fellows, but the atrium and lobby were empty except for the abandoned female super.

Gus checked her health and only after seeing it was mostly full did he activate **Leech.** Gus saw on his minimap that one team was now in the control room, while others had spread out to search the floors in teams of two. The invaders were clearing rooms in military fashion and working their way through the first floor.

He-Man Woman Hater by Extreme. Success rates x8. Added effect: +10% damage to female supers. +2 Strength.

Gus wouldn't consider himself a misogynist, but the intro to this song, *Flight of the Wounded Bumblebee*, always got him pumped up. The song couldn't have been better timed as he spotted two supers patrolling this floor, both female.

With a thought, Gus called Jet to his outstretched hand as he ran toward the two supers. He activated **Hyper** and doubled his Agility, noticing an immediate increase in speed. It was only this that allowed him to move quickly enough to dodge three orange darts the woman on the right flung directly into his path.

Bracing against one wall and taking a couple steps, Gus flipped and leaped over the pair, swinging Jet in mid-flight. There was a satisfying crack, but when Gus landed and rolled, he saw that he had not connected with his target's head, but with her forearm, which now bent at an odd angle.

She held it with the other and screamed in agony while her

partner advanced. She let loose with a barrage of swipes and grabs, each narrowly missing Gus and forcing him back. Even with his extra speed, he was losing ground and barely reacting before she could connect.

Jet attacked from the other side; she kept her eyes fixed on Gus, deftly blocking Jet's probing strikes without even looking. Gus saw his stamina bar draining like it had a heavy leak.

"What a disappointment. Too stupid to know you shouldn't try to prevail against a superior force," the woman spat, not even winded from her efforts.

TNT by AC/DC. Success rates x16.
Added effect: +10% damage to area-of-effect attacks.

Gus felt a surge of strength with the sudden jump in power. He felt his muscles tightening. The woman's words stung in far too personal a way. He gave in to the inner rage that he had managed to tamp down for his whole life. Every bully he had had to deal with since the punks in the parking lot, the weakness he felt in himself around his father and brother, all the times he had been cheated or pushed around. It flowed out, and kept coming. He had crammed so much in there.

He raged that there was such disparity in the world at large. Too many went unpunished for the wrongs they committed. They took what they wanted and went unchallenged. The thought of how much this must be going on everywhere if he had seen so much of it in just his own experience. Some people were always taking, and had an insatiable desire for more.

Gus looked at his hands and arched his eyebrows, a manic grin on his face. Time to take it all back. He pulled Jet to him and let the katas take over. The two moved and counterattacked, the space between the *thuds* and *thwacks* shortening as each blow was countered then returned.

Gus saw a countdown timer on the lower right of his display, but was so occupied that he couldn't see it well enough

to read what it was measuring. When it ended, however, it became incredibly clear as **Hyper** deactivated and Gus' motions slowed to a crawl. He tried to move to block an incoming swipe, but it was like moving underwater. A fingernail scratched along his cheek like a gentle caress.

With this done, the woman stepped back and bowed. Gus readied himself to fight on, when he noticed his MP and his already sparse stamina bar drained to zero. A sudden dizziness caught him and he fell forward.

The room spun and Gus hit the floor, and the world continued to twirl.

"Yes, we've got him. Here are the coordinates…"

Sounds became quiet then suddenly loud as Gus' senses were scrambled. He fought nausea until someone flipped him over onto his back.

"Well, what do we have here?" Basileus crowed. "Drag him over here."

Two supers roughly jerked Gus forward by his arms and dropped him unceremoniously at his feet.

"You just saved us so much time, I really appreciate this." He steepled his fingers and tapped his lips with his index fingers. "Let's get him to the control room, and make this official!"

Gus swooned as they pulled him suddenly upright, and when he came to, he was somewhere else, the dizziness only slightly diminished.

"Press his hand there," someone commanded.

Gus felt warmth play under his hand as the scanner worked and the pinprick as the system confirmed his identity. "Okay, now you do the same, Basileus," another super directed.

Gus saw them cheer as ownership of the manor was transferred and all functions were switched over.

"Boss, there is a problem with some of the functions. This little turd-merchant has been screwing with the directories. We may need him later if I can't unscramble some of this mess. Hopefully not. I'll keep working on this, and there's a good possibility we won't need him. Then you can do what you want with him," the hacker recommended, pushing his amber-colored glasses back up his nose.

"I have just the thing," Basileus said cruelly, then punched Gus repeatedly in the face until everything faded into darkness.

CHAPTER THIRTY-EIGHT

Falling to Pieces

Gus awoke with wind fluttering in his ears. He opened his dry crusty eyes and began screaming, realizing that he was falling. Pinwheeling his arms around he flailed in the darkness.

"Nick, where am I?" Only silence answered back. He tried to activate his *Advanced Flight* skill and found that he could barely touch the skill, it only slowed his descent slightly and was much more taxing and burned though MP with little effect. Seeing his MP quickly drain to ten percent, he let go of the skill and allowed himself to fall.

"Hello?" Gus yelled. The sound was swallowed up in the hollow darkness. Gus toggled to his different views through infrared, ultraviolet, and beyond; all that could be seen was inky blackness. He leaned forward and pulled his arms to his sides like he had seen in a James Bond movie, seeing if he could direct his fall. He could tell he was moving in another direction from the feel of the wind rushing by but after maintaining the pose for at least ten minutes, he realized that he was not reaching anything by moving in this direction.

Gus determinedly tried different directions but to no avail. An hour or two later, he had neither hit the bottom, nor had he found the edges of the pit. He flipped around so that he faced upward, giving his eyes a break from the drying effect of the constant wind. He swiped at the salty residue left from tears that had streamed to the side of his eyes, pushed out from the constant air flowing by him.

So this is how it ends? Gus didn't feel like he had died, but how would he know? Nick was gone, his powers were essentially gone, and he had been falling for enough time that he should have hit bottom by now. He waved his hand in front of him and saw nothing.

The absolute darkness reminded Gus of a trip they had taken through the Midwest. Somewhere along the way, they went into some caves. At one point, the tour guide turned off the lights and the darkness became palpable. *I can palp it,* Gus thought idly. This was that same darkness.

His stomach growled, which gave Gus pause. The word 'nothing' drifted into his mind as he stared out into the void. He was in the middle of nothing and nowhere. Maybe this was Limbo? Gus was never religious, but his mind could not see how he could be in this situation.

What if it's an illusion? Did some super do something and trap me in my own mind? Gus had always been afraid of being trapped in a dark place where he couldn't move.

He'd watched a documentary movie on spelunking when he was a kid and how people would sometimes get stuck and not be able to move forwards or backwards. They showed how they would break someone's collarbones to fold their arms in and pull people out, but the thought of being trapped and slowly starving was nightmare fuel for quite a while after that.

Gus tried to access his display and could see nothing. No access to his visual filters, logs, or anything. Not even a clock. The absence rocked him and he felt even more powerless. *What if they stripped my powers?!* He had been so flippant in taking their abilities. Maybe karma was kicking him where it counted. The trapped feeling became even more intense and his heart rate spiked with panic.

A couple years ago, his fellow henchman Chuck's father got Guillain-Barré syndrome. Gus had no idea what it was until Chuck explained it to him. Basically he was trapped in his own body. Awake, but with no control over his limbs or any bodily functions. As he pondered the implications, the same claustrophobia made him tense in wondering what he would do in the same situation. The scariest part was that it could be temporary or last your whole life. Fortunately, Chuck's father recovered in a couple months, but had to do some physical therapy to regain his strength.

The few Psi abilities that Gus had been able to **Leech** required MP for activation, and he thought it unlikely that an illusion could be maintained for so long. With another growl, his stomach announced its disapproval at being empty. Gus checked his pockets and found a few healing gels. *No, I had better save them. I may be here a while.*

Save them for what? You're not getting out of here. Gus shook his head as he fell. Not even a day had passed and he was already talking to himself. It reminded him of his early days on the island. His thoughts got a little weird when he was alone for a long time. *Is it weird that my inner voice had a point? What's the plan?* Gus' mind came up as blank as the area around him. What could he do?

"Nooooooo!" Gus screamed out loud, his yell disappearing quickly, leaving only the whipping air as he continued to fall. A contorted mass of emotions began to break free. Anger, frustration, then despair. Each flared and then flagged as the wind whipped by, extinguishing their ardor. Still he fell, and eventually only an emotional numbness remained. He had thought getting more powerful was the key to keeping him alive, and keeping the manor. But he had never felt more powerless. Unable to effect any change whatsoever on his environment.

So this was his reward for using compassion? Trying to use his power for something productive, and nothing to show for it in the end. *Those last damn levels came so easy and gave me a false sense of hope. Why do I keep hoping for the best after life keeps beating me down? Am I just super naive in thinking anything I do will ever make a difference?*

With the emotional numbness came a deep fatigue. Was that the sum of life? Struggle then ignominious release? *Why am I always struggling? What good has it done me?* Realizing the futility of his situation, Gus finally let go.

All the ranting and bitter feelings were ineffectual. Everything was. So he stopped. For a long time he was alone in his thoughts. And for a while he thought of nothing, which was new. His brain usually got anxious if there was any down time and he got fidgety and played a game on his phone or listened to music. Rarely had he just been alone with absolutely nothing to do.

At first, he had flashes of thought on things he should try. Why he needed to protect the manor, get back to civilization, and let his family know he was alive. It all failed to inspire him. As if the darkness had penetrated into him and smothered any kernel of hope that was trying to survive. Gus made no effort and let each spark be quenched. In time, the thoughts stopped coming and he was alone.

It was strange, suddenly having no obligations. He had felt that fate had chosen him for something special. He'd been beginning to believe that maybe, just maybe, all the doubters and naysayers were wrong about him. That he really *was* destined for something great. The weight of that self-imposed duty had increased day by day. There was always something that he was doing inefficiently or incorrectly.

He had lost though. So now he could rest. At last.

CHAPTER THIRTY-NINE

Dream On

Gus fell for quite some time. A heavy fatigue overwhelmed him and he drifted to sleep and began to dream—a new one that he knew intuitively was a continuation of the young thief who had drank the master's potions.

———

He was back in the alchemist's manor. A hooded figure stood over his bed, mixing various reagents and pressing compresses to his body. Uncontrollable spasms arched his back until the only thing touching the bed he was resting on were the back of his head and his heels. He then would fall limp. Cold shivers would wrack his body, causing what felt like painful needles to stab into every pore. Then the pain would shift. Raw and hot, burning like he was flayed alive.

He came in and out of consciousness as the pain grew too intense. Something pressed to his lips every time he gained a brief moment of consciousness. A golden liquid dripped onto his tongue and he gained a brief respite from the pain, until it changed modes.

As he lay there sweating, the alchemist turned, suddenly looking for something in a rush. The cowl fell away, revealing a woman. Strangely familiar. And she was helping him. After he had stolen so much. Pain blossomed again, stopping all thought. His insides felt like they were expanding, pressing against his skin like a taut sausage casing. Tears fell down the sides of his face as if pressed out. Again a drop of liquid, this one a luminescent amber color, and the pressure subsided. Exhausted he closed his eyes and gave in to oblivion.

The cycles felt like they went on forever. Occasionally his rest was longer, sometimes shorter as some new form of pain wrenched him out of sleep to mete out more punishment. One time he saw the master alchemist in the doorway, arms folded in stern disapproval. He had no idea why the master had not killed him for his offense. Maybe they had means of extracting that which had been stolen and needed him alive to regain what they had lost.

He opened his eyes, sticky with some crusty exudate that had partially congealed on his eyelids. Three figures stood beside the plinth-like bed he was laying on in the middle of the workshop.

"I can fix this, but it will cost you…" the new dark-clad figure growled.

"Anything, anything! I will do whatever you want—" the woman cried.

"Watch what you promise! His kind never comes cheap, and we don't know if he will keep his word."

The dark figure held up a hand to forestall any more arguments. "I am all you have. So please do stop trying to negotiate. My time is valuable, so if you do not like my terms, I will be on my way. You will be left to deal with this matter yourselves."

"Nooo…" the woman wailed and collapsed.

———

Gus came awake with a start. That was *new*. He'd had the dream with the apprentice thief many times in his life, but it was always the same. He could tell that what he had seen tonight was a continuation, in the weird way things make sense in dreams that sound ludicrous when you try to explain them when awake. Elements of the dream started to fade, and he tried to actively remember them, until the only thing he had left was the woman's face, which also evaporated into oblivion.

CHAPTER FORTY

Running Just to Catch Myself

Time became a fuzzy concept. There was nothing to separate the moments, and the lack of stimulation allowed his mind to wander. After a time, the falling sensation became almost soothing, and Gus recalled his time floating in his space suit so long ago. He reviewed all of his abilities, and the only one that seemed possibly applicable was *Xyzzy*. He attempted to fire the ability, but it was too slippery, the high MP cost making it oily to his mind. No matter how he attempted to approach and access the skill, it would not fire.

See what you get for trying?

Gus felt even smaller, like a tiny sliver dissolving in the vastness of the void that surrounded him.

At some point, Gus fell asleep and dreamed about some of his jobs as a henchman. While the majority of his jobs were with Purple Faction, the guys had convinced him to take a couple jobs with the Factionless.

He awoke and for a while tried to think back on what those supers stood for. How they interacted with the world at large. He was embarrassed to say that he really didn't know. They could have been horrible. He had just gone with the flow, and allowed himself to not feel any responsibility, since he wasn't directly taking part in any atrocities. Maybe they had been benign, but the fact was Gus really didn't know. He never took the time to find out.

Too late to do anything about it.

Was he any better now? He had gotten so much stronger than he was, but how had he really changed? Or had he? Despite all his powers, he was powerless now. Both to save Aurora and to keep the manor. It should have worked. **Leech** was an amazingly OP skill and only someone like him could lose despite having it.

Just rest. These worries are past.

Gus realized all the time he had wasted worrying about the future. Trying to prepare for things that never happened, or regretting poor choices that left lasting consequences. Always wishing he could go back in time and erase them. Then life would be better.

He recalled his epiphany about Basileus. That could have been him. Easily. And would he be any less trapped? Would he be better off if things had gone as he had always wished? It would just be a different void, with no apparent progress. But he would have the illusion of someday finding... what? That he was worth something? Of showing everyone they were wrong? Getting the validation from those he admired?

Is that what I'm chasing? Is that what warrants all this effort?

Gus let it all go. He let go the shame of his past mistakes; those were done. He shifted his focus onto what he should change now. Without the fear of failure and losing the manor or protecting Aurora, Gus let himself go.

He didn't even have to support his physical body as the feeling of falling changed to a sensation that the air was trying to support him. He relaxed and imagined himself turning into a giant lump of lead. The visualization allowed his postural muscles to relax, and he sunk deeper inward, retreating from trying to change and manage his environment and just let himself *be.*

He went deeper inward, barely hearing a chime sound and losing the sound of the wind rushing by him. *What do I want? What have I been chasing? Let it go.* One by one, Gus let his cares and desires be pulled away, floating away like ashes in the breeze. They were consumed as they floated further away from him. Expectation. Duty. Responsibility. Any false facade he had erected to be accepted by another crumbled and floated off.

It was possible he slept during this time. It was a different perspective than Gus had ever let himself have in his whole life. He didn't have to do anything but be himself. His core self. And he was surprised to see that underneath all the garbage he had collected throughout his life that he had been trying to be happy by pleasing everyone else but himself. He let go of the things he had held close and opened himself to viewing his life, without judgment or blame.

Gus looked at himself laid bare and was surprised to see his father. He had never seen the parallel between him and his father, but from this vantage they were nearly identical. He worked to be seen a certain way by Purple Faction the same way Gus had worked to have others accept him. Scales of anger flaked away as he accepted that his father was just trying to do the best with the cards he had been dealt. He could see how he had placed his filter on every action, interpreting them in the worst light.

He felt embarrassment at all of his tantrums when his dad hadn't given him what he had wanted, whether it be attention, respect, or whatever he imagined would validate him. Gus wondered how he would cope in the same situation. Funny how he judged others on their behaviors and himself on his good intentions. Naive and immature, the embarrassment and shame intensified as he confronted his lack of maturity.

Gus found that he could let the embarrassment go as well. It was strange to see that he clung to this negative feeling as part of his self-view. Just like his father, he was doing the best he could at the moment.

Or was he? Guilt presented itself as the next layer. Guilt for wasting so much time playing games, being lazy, making no effort to make something of his life. Binging obscure TV shows that only gave him the ability to make pop culture references that no one would understand. Without the expectation pressing on him anymore, Gus was able to let go of the guilt.

He had changed. He recognized his behavior as a coping mechanism. An inefficient one that gave poor consolation, but he saw it for what it was. And that it was a step on his path. More meandering and aimless than it could have been, but it had eventually led him to other things. Better things. He let go of the guilt of not being perfect from the start. Releasing himself of the burden of failing to make the right decision all the time.

He didn't know when he had crossed the line, but he wasn't the same aimless person waiting for life to happen. He had a mission. Correction, he'd *had* a mission—past tense. Without the feeling of duty, did he still feel like he had to help anyone? The feeling he had after helping the family and even the pirates came back to him. That seemed pure. Worth pursuing when compared to other things that he had dedicated vastly larger amounts of time trying to achieve.

He weighed what Dave had told him, and found that he didn't feel stupid for the choices he had made. Maybe he couldn't save the world, but he saw that, at his core, he wanted to try. He knew it was an impossible feat, and would probably be filled with heartache and disappointment. Not probably. Definitely. And that was okay. He could do it without guilt.

Still Gus fell inwards. He felt like he was getting smaller and smaller as more and more flaked away from his core being. He could feel the last layer surrounding him exposed as the guilt was gone. An outer shell, hardened from being compacted for so long. Regret. All the missed chances not taken because of fear.

Fear of failure, of persecution, sometimes of the truth. Of avoiding responsibility and missed opportunities. Avoiding the pain that would lead to growth. Unwilling to suffer to get to a better place. Fear of rejection or ridicule for failure. And under-neath it all, the regret of allowing that fear to control him. He felt regret that he had possibly worked for some very bad people, and was complicit in the things they had done, by supporting them, even if indirectly. Fear crept in at the unknown effects of his participation with these men.

As he fell, none of that mattered anymore. So many fears that never came to be. No future to ruin with bad choices. Nothing left to regret. While he could not repair any damage he had done or lives he had hurt, he could dedicate himself to a new path to atone for his mistakes.

Cracks appeared in this last shell and as it broke away, Gus basked in the glow from what remained. Free of all else, he felt himself expanding, and he opened his eyes.

CHAPTER FORTY-ONE

Freedom

As Gus looked outward, he felt himself become awake again. He was sure that he wasn't dreaming, per se. But it was probably dream-adjacent. The wind whistled as it had for who knew how long. With nothing left to do, Gus stared into the deep. A slight pulse like a phosphene ghost blinked at the corner of his vision. It disturbed his peace and he looked at it. It was faint, but was that the message icon?

A little focused attention and a very dim display opened up. He listlessly checked his status screen and logs. Some new messages greeted him, but they scrolled by quickly, disappearing after he barely read them:

You have leveled up the skill: ***Mindfulness*** *to* ***Level 3!***
600 XP awarded.
600 FP awarded.
You have leveled up the skill: ***Mindfulness*** *to* ***Level 4!***
800 XP awarded.
800 FP awarded.
You have leveled up the skill: ***Mindfulness*** *to* ***Level 5!***
1,000 XP awarded.

1,000 FP awarded.
You have leveled up the skill: **Mindfulness** *to* **Level 6***!*
1,200 XP awarded.
1,200 FP awarded.
You have leveled up the skill: **Mindfulness** *to* **Level 7***!*
1,400 XP awarded.
1,400 FP awarded.
You have leveled up the skill: **Mindfulness** *to* **Level 8***!*
1,600 XP awarded.
1,600 FP awarded.
Congratulations! You have unlocked the skill: **True Sight [Passive]***!*
True Sight: *You have looked beyond what is false for long enough to gain a certain sense of clarity. You now can perceive truth more readi—*

That was all he could read before the message scrolled away and was gone. After the messages vanished, he was surprised to see that he was no longer in total darkness.

The faint outlines of a unique manipulation of ether could barely be seen if he squinted his eyes. He recognized two portals embedded seamlessly into the weave that he now understood were unique manipulations related to his **Xyzzy** skill. He saw himself fall through the portal below, transporting him to the portal above, over and over again. As he stared at the shape more and more, it resembled one of those impossible optical illusions that could be drawn but not fashioned in three dimensions. The warping and portals created a space akin to a three-dimensional Moebius strip. Too much movement in any direction would merely take you to the other side, indefinitely.

Once the secret was revealed, Gus could see where some areas were twisted, reminiscent of how clowns twisted balloons to make the small compartments that comprised a balloon animal.

Knowing where to look, Gus made several attempts to attach an ether leash to the focal point, but it kept slipping off. His falling momentum made timing difficult as he zipped by, with only a fraction of a second to make the grab. It was as maddening as trying to win a stuffed animal from a weak claw toy. Likewise, his weave was weak and stunted, despite how hard he pushed to create it.

It didn't help that he was moving by as quickly as he was, and that his slight movements sometimes changed his position so that the area he was trying to manipulate was in a different spot than expected. Gus calmed himself and let go of his frustration. Where else was he going? What else did he have to do?

With the release of tension, success came at last. The weave attached and as Gus reached the end of the ether leash, his momentum stretched the weave, slowing his descent. With a sudden yank, the weave came to the end of its length and ability to expand. This strain transferred to the focal point and Gus worried that it would merely shake loose.

It did not. The thin weave of the pit in this area was torn in half, and Gus saw a sight that almost made him weep. Just like an unfinished bag of holding, breaking destabilized the construct and it began to unravel. Filaments fizzled and sparked into nothingness as they flipped and flopped, burning like a hybrid of an unmanned fire hose and a lit firework fuse. The simple sparking was more beautiful to Gus than Aurora's **Dazzle** or any firework display he had ever seen.

Seams began to spread apart and light poured in. Gus hit the floor hard. He had slowed as the construct bowed and deformed, so he wasn't at terminal velocity, but it did hurt like hell. He enjoyed the feel of the cold tile floor underneath him. He stayed there until his ears registered that he had stopped his constant fall and the strange sensation he was still falling ebbed.

Gus moaned, feeling a little dizzy and nauseated as he sat up to his knees. Gus rested his hands on the cool ivory colored floor, the chill helping him to combat the lingering sense of vertigo.

Opening his eyes, he saw that he was in the far corridor of the brig. He crawled forward, seeing that all the cells were opened and abandoned. His muscles ached and protested as he crawled, especially his knees. Gus didn't care. He was free! An eternity later, he knelt and pushed the elevator summon button, half expecting a merc to step out.

Fortunately none did and he again pushed the button to his suite. He felt so tired. He curled up and rubbed the soft carpet in the elevator.

"Gus!" Nick yelled in Gus' mind.

Gus started awake, looking around with confusion.

"You have been gone for over a week! I could not communicate with you, and that awful limbo sensation again. It was the worst—"

"A week?"

"Yes, a week!"

"They put me in some kind of dimensional pit trap in the brig. I could barely access my powers." Gus checked his minimap and saw that all the supers were still in the manor, but none were close to his current position. Standing, he stretched, legs stiff from inactivity for a week. He stood and his back cracked. Gus sighed in satisfaction while he stretched. With the blood pumping more, his thoughts became a bit clearer. "Wait, how did I access powers at all in the brig?"

"Talk later. You need to get going—I'm just seeing everything updating now from the manor and it's not good."

Gus nodded and shuffled to his suite. The door had been forced open and the room ransacked. Otherwise, it appeared empty. Gus locked the door behind him, not sure if it even would hold.

"What has changed since I've been out of commission, Nick?" Gus inquired.

"They had command codes; my admin privileges were revoked. I'm just glad I wasn't kicked. They have been searching for something floor by floor," Nick warned.

Gus began to notice his display solidify and his MP bar charging again. Gus felt energized to have things just a bit back to normal.

"Where are they now?"

"Hmm, this is suspicious. They have been all over the

manor in the past week, but now they are all gathered in the same place—floor twenty-three. I think they may have found what they're looking for."

He used his minimap to check and they did seem to be clustered together. The minimap only showed a top-down view, but with the multiple levels in the manor, things could overlap, so he rotated the minimap and saw that they all were on the same level. Gus felt a chill tingle down his back. He may already be too late.

CHAPTER FORTY-TWO

King of Yesterday

Following his minimap, Gus came to a nondescript gray door on level twenty-three. The supers were all congregating here. Taking a furtive glance, Gus opened the door and slid inside. A walkway with terraces encircled the large room, with a staircase leading down to a large, raised platform in the center. Before he could be seen, he moved away from the doorway onto one of the terraces and got to where he could see what was happening. Everyone was so entranced that he probably didn't need to take any precautions.

One by one, the supers Gus had previously drained filed forward and touched a large orangish-pink crystal in the center of the room. Some shouted in triumph, others had a visible expression of relief.

"My powers, they're back!" one exulted. Another flew up, reveling in the feeling of flight, and Gus had to cower down to avoid being seen.

"After all who have had their powers taken are restored, we will begin the next phase. You who have helped secure this facility will be the first to benefit from the wealth of power that will emanate forth from Manticorps. Only those who swear allegiance will be found worthy, so choose now! Will you follow me and Manticorps into the future? Will you be my generals as we take this world back from the archaic Factions and their tyranny?"

Shouts began to swell from the mercs, who had long-standing grudges against the Factions. Most of the Factionless were either those who had washed out of an academy or who could not maintain the discipline necessary to be accepted to one in the first place. Some were simply poor or not in the right place at the right time and had figured out how to use their abilities on their own to survive.

"Then swear by your powers that you will remain loyal to me and to Manticorps to the end!"

"Why does he think these guys will not backstab him the first chance they get? Is he that stupid?" Gus asked Nick mentally.

"It has fallen out of practice, but if one takes a certain oath, their Nth will become non-functional if they break it. The wording must be exact, but I have a feeling Basileus knows what it is."

In a similar fashion as before, the supers lined up again and swore fealty, repeating the words after he spoke them.

"Yep, he knew them."

"Why would Nth even allow that? Isn't that like condoning slavery?"

"Gus, you look at things from your Earth point of view. The cultures and mores that have evolved on countless worlds encompass more interactions that are considered normal that would outrage even the most lenient hedonists of the planet. A pact of loyalty is nothing compared to what exists in the universe. Those supers were not coerced, they are trading that portion of their freedom for the rewards they think they will get from him."

"I still don't like it," Gus muttered aloud.

"Don't like what?" a voice asked from behind.

Gus yelped, drawing the attention of a super, and shrank

back on the balcony. Luckily, the super turned back to the ceremony, awaiting his turn. Gus looked over his shoulder and saw Aurora crouching and calmly staring back at him.

"What the—what are you doing here?" Gus hissed. "I thought you were dead!"

"You did? Good. If you didn't suspect anything, then for sure they don't," she said, tilting her head towards the supers below.

"What? How?" Gus stammered.

"A girl can't reveal all her secrets…" she teased coyly.

"Aurora…"

"Fine, I'll tell you—later." She waved at the assembled crowd. "After we deal with all this mess. Where have you been?"

"A girl can't reveal all her secrets," Nick replied in Aurora's voice before Gus could speak.

"What he said. She said. You said. Later." Gus said after an awkward pause.

"Whatever. I don't know what you did to the control room, but they were pretty pissed—"

"I'll tell ya what happened. Man-boobs saved the free world. Truly some of your best work, Gus. I've taught this youngling well!"

Aurora mouthed 'What?' looking at Gus suspiciously.

"Well, not yet. Later," Gus ran fingers through his hair. "Thanks Nick."

"You earned it, kid. One of the unsung heroes."

"Whatever happened, it kept them searching all over. They weren't able to get the telemetry to work for them, so I always knew where they were on my minimap, and could avoid detection and sneak around. When I saw a green circle, I knew it must be you, so I came right away. I've been in my room, trying to figure out what to do next. I tried to make it to the Foundry but they had someone stationed there. I think they found all the gels in the cafeteria too, so bye-bye stash," she revealed with a disappointed frown.

Gus only had one red gel remaining, but he still had a half-dozen blue in his left pocket. "How are you doing with gels?"

"I used all of mine up to heal the burns on my hands. Sorry," she admitted sheepishly.

"I guess we'll have to make do. Okay, so here's what I was thinking…"

Gus went into his plan, adjusting it to accommodate Aurora's unexpected presence. When they were on the same page, Gus took a peek at Basileus, narrowing his eyes.

He cracked his knuckles and growled, "Let's go."

CHAPTER FORTY-THREE

It's Good to Be King

At last, Basileus got the notice he had been waiting to hear.

"Boss, can you come down to level twenty-three? I think you'll want to see this. You said a big-ass crystal, right? Kinda orange with pink in the center?"

Basileus stood up straight, eyes wide. "I'll be right there." He keyed off his comm and did a double-fist pump, arching his back and screaming silently in victory. His father would be so proud. Now that they'd found it, he didn't need to keep that little twerp alive 'just in case.' The thought of torturing him for his intrusion and insolence widened his smile even more. Eventually, things always seemed to work out for Basileus.

"You hear that, all of you? They've found it, now I'll be free of all your mutterings, forever!" Basileus said out loud.

He got in the elevator, tapping his foot as a beam slowly scanned him to confirm he had access to level twenty-three. Finally, the car began moving. His thoughts flitted back to all he knew about the artifact. Manticorps had to liquidate millions in resources to obtain it, then keep it hidden from those who would try to steal it. Many were silenced to avoid even the possibility that its location would be revealed.

His lips pressed into a razor thin line as he thought of how Methiochos betrayed them all, conveniently offering to hide the artifact at the manor he *knew* he was going to try to steal away from them.

At last, he would be the one to bring the manor and the crystal back to Archon. So many of his brothers had tried and failed over the years. Within the crystal had to be some ability that would help him overcome the flaw he and Archon had hidden from the world. As the strongest among Manticorps, they had to maintain appearances, especially of power.

He pulled back his glove and looked at the '35' tattooed in small numbers on the back of his wrist. Thirty-four different clones before him and he had finally achieved what he had been destined to do. Once he repaired the damage the process had wreaked upon his genetics over so many forced replications, he would lead a new order of supers and those smug Factions would be a thing of the past. And best of all—the voices would be silenced. Blessed silence.

Archon was adamant that the Factions needed to be destroyed, and he was unyielding in his determination to make that happen, even to his own detriment. With the power of the crystal, it was a foregone conclusion they would be able to over-power them. If that was what his father wanted, he would make it happen. He would fail him no longer.

It sapped his father's vitality every time he had to be raised again. Basileus grinned inwardly that he had finally succeeded and validated his father's sacrifices. Archon would only have one, maybe two more times where he could perform the proce-dure, and two would almost certainly kill him.

Still, Basileus knew he would do it. His own lifespan had decreased significantly with each cycle. Fortunately, his father had the body of each failed clone, so his memories could be transferred, preserving his sense of self. The psychological weight of multiple deaths had begun to wear on his psyche.

He was much less emotionally resilient than he used to be. He did not tell Archon of the presence of the 'others' that came before. It wasn't just memories that were transferred, but entire personalities. The older iterations fracturing more and more. Thirty-five of them sharing the same space. He was just fortunate he had been able to maintain control; they were always struggling to take the wheel if he let his attention drop.

The elevator opened up into a plain, unfinished hallway. He could hear men yelling at each other and walked to where they were, eager to see for himself. Stepping into the room, he moved to a nearby railing and saw it there in all its splendor.

A Mandrite crystal!

They were so lucky all those years ago to find someone who knew what the quartz-like crystal really was, and obtain it before that information could be disseminated. He doubted anyone knew of its full potential.

Basileus swallowed, and began stepping down the nearby staircase to the platform where the crystal sat like a king on his throne, the obvious object of preeminence in the entire room. He wiped away a tiny bead of sweat as he approached, not wanting the men to see how the crystal affected him. He couldn't show any weakness.

No one knew that he was any different than the first Basileus, attributing his longevity to some regenerative ability. It had to stay that way; if they knew the truth, they would never swear fealty and in turn would not be able to be controlled. He needed that collar if Archon's plans were to be accomplished.

Uncertainty filled him as he stared at the crystal, close enough to touch. Could his DNA handle the transition or would it be torn to shreds? He knew he had lost some things, being a copy of a series of copies. Fortunately, his erratic nature was overlooked, with him being 'the big boss' son.' Somehow that elevated him from creepy weird to eccentric weird, which the mercs could handle.

As the warm colors pulsed inside the crystal, Basileus felt there had to be something that would compensate and help him be whole again. He didn't want to die, not when he was this close! Better to have others try it first to see if they could regain their lost powers, and then he would hazard a try. It was maddening to have to wait, but his confidence and bravado needed to be feigned.

Deep down, he resented the fear and cowardice that had entered into his core. Many of the others were afraid; was it bleeding through to him? He didn't think that had always been there. Possibly an artifact from the cloning process. It angered him though; his father was ruthless against weakness, and he had endeavored to mask those feelings and so far had succeeded.

His anger flared at the thought of how their powers were stolen! He had no idea what that worm had done to his men when he had allowed him to be trapped. But if he could find a similar ability in the crystal, he would take it for himself.

Yes, that would be suitable, have those supers try to reclaim their abilities first. It would make him appear magnanimous and convert any of the skeptics to his side. He could work this to his favor. His weakness must not be known. His fear must not show.

"Gather all those who have lost their powers, we shall offer them a chance to regain what they have lost, and possibly much more if they swear fealty to Manticorps!"

He had his lieutenants gather the supers who were now powerless. They should have a natural affinity to their own abilities, if the research was correct. If there were any *untoward* effects, it would be better to know now. He reassured himself that he was not acting out of fear, but of calculated risk. There would be chaos if this fell into one of the hands of the mercs, better that they not know everything until they had sworn fealty. Then they would be bound to him and Manticorps.

When the neutered supers had assembled, he started the ceremony. Archon had shown him the value of presentation and he had absorbed the lessons well. He pulled up a tab in his display to make sure he got the wording correct, then he had the supers swear fealty upon their powers.

One by one they stepped forward, gladly accepting any

agreement if they could once again touch the powers that had become such an integral part of who they were. Little did they know the bargain that they were making.

Basileus marveled at how the supers absorbed their lost powers so quickly, their familiarity making the powers instantly available. He was certain that the general theory was that abilities needed to be assimilated first, but perhaps this only applied to new abilities.

"*Hey!*" someone shouted, bringing Basileus out of his musings. An augment who had reconnected to his electronic minions had released them and was pointing to a balcony above where he caught a glimpse of a familiar face that simultaneously filled him with rage and eagerness.

Good, he saved me the trouble of retrieving him.

CHAPTER FORTY-FOUR

I've Got the Power

"You again!" Basileus roared.

How did he get free? one voice demanded.

That trap was supposed to be inescapable, another added.

Someone is working against us! a fearful voice shrieked.

With a growl he pushed the voices from the fore. He vowed that he would find out once they had sworn fealty; they wouldn't be able to lie to him then.

Sensing they might lose their chance, supers rushed forward, hurriedly repeating the words and touching the crystal, expecting this to be required to regain their abilities. In the moment of distraction, Gus had managed to descend to the landing below.

Basileus fired a plasma ball at Gus, who dodged to one side. At the last second, the ball expanded, forming a large net that draped over him, immediately burning part of his outfit and the skin on his neck before a gray mercurial substance flowed over the areas of contact, separating them from his skin. Gus made a quick shield to push the net away from him, and managed to create a little space, but overall the net held.

Basileus turned his fist, so that his palm faced upwards and the net began to constrict.

Weak to this kind of attack, Gus' shields kept popping with minimal effort. He had to keep spamming shields, each one getting smaller and smaller as the net ate up the space as it constricted between shields.

Basileus was unrelenting, tightening the space and it was all Gus could do to keep generating shield layers while his MP was burning up quickly.

Finally he stopped, with Gus contorted with his arms pressed up in front of him. Basileus turned his attention to the core. "At last, brothers and sisters, the world will see the dawning of a new age. We shall be gods among men. Gods among supers!" A cheer sounded from the group. He placed his hands on the core and his eyes opened wide, the pupils dilating. "There's so much…" he moaned as he began to absorb abilities.

Gus held as still as possible while his MP slowly began to refill. Without the constant need to reform shields, he found that his armor was protecting him and a shield was unnecessary. It interposed itself between the crackling energy, not even heating up. If only he could reach his pocket, he could down a couple blue gels and be at full power. If only he wasn't trapped with his arms in front of him like a, like a…

Like a T-rex! Or a **T-Wrecks** in Gus' case. He had just enough MP. Activating the skill, a terrorizing roar reverberated off the walls of the small chamber. Chaos ensued and supers scattered as the dinosaur rampaged through the room.

Basileus was oblivious to the disturbance as he was so enraptured with the core and absorbing abilities.

Gus took the opportunity to activate his **Energy Absorption** skill and slurped up the energy in the net. The construct thinned and unraveled into nothingness as the energy powering it dissipated.

Free to move again, Gus felt in his left pocket and drew out the last three MP gels he had. Chewing into them, he found that Aurora must have notified the chef; this batch tasted like coconut instead of blue raspberry.

Much better. With his MP restored to seventy-five percent, he formed a shield around the core, breaking Basileus' contact with it. He slapped against the glassy surface, frustrated until he realized that the core hadn't stopped functioning but that there was a barrier there.

He turned and looked at Gus, his eyes glowing with a blue aura. Waves emanated off his exposed skin, like heat shimmering on an Arizona highway in August. Gus couldn't tell if that was steam, excess MP, or a heat mirage, but the effect made Basileus appear more otherworldly and menacing than he ever had. His usual cocky sneer had evolved into a maniacal rictus.

Supers dashed around in the background, getting out of the reach of the stampeding dinosaur. They jumped up to the next tier or down to a lower one as the creature pursued them relentlessly.

Gus hit his fists together and with a thought his armor shifted. It was now studded with spikes, interspersed with small ridges that were razor sharp. Basileus hopped in the air slightly and shot forward in a blur with a punch to Gus' shoulder. There was a muted *thud* and even with his armor absorbing a huge amount of the force, he still was spun around.

Basileus looked at the mangled wreck that was his hand after hitting the newly-studded armor and watched as the bones regenerated, broken tarsals reforming as muscles weaved back over them and the skin rolled over like a new coat of paint, pristine and whole again. He threw back his head and laughed, and Gus could see areas of his skin bubbling and protruding as his body worked to assimilate the powers.

In addition to fighting Basileus, there were a good number of supers who glared daggers at Gus, waiting for their chance to attack. Some were visibly confused that their powers would not activate at all if their attacks were too close to Basileus, but Gus found it difficult to focus on both Basileus and that many opponents.

With a loud crack, Jet appeared behind three supers as they fell forward, hit from behind by the haft of the weapon like a blackjack to the base of the skull. The agile weapon dipped and twirled, easily evading shots taken at it. Someone threw up a shield and Jet was blocked from attacking. Changing it up, Jet spun the tip of its blade like a drill in one area of the shield. The effect popped the entire shield as the polearm spun. The super in question kept throwing up shields but the group was retreating back.

I know how that feels, Gus thought wryly, **TimeSight** guiding him to move. Turning his attention back to Basileus, he barely sidestepped a lunging attack, feeling the brush of air moving around the fist that almost brushed his nose, causing him to flinch back and blink.

Gus attempted to grapple Basileus as he passed, but he had covered himself with a plasma shield. Gus' hands rebounded off without getting purchase, sparking as the energy cascaded off his hybrid-Nth armor. No contact meant **Leech** was off the table.

Faster than expected, Basileus twisted around and grabbed Gus by the neck and then by the waist, lifting him high overhead. Despite the armor's protection, the constriction on his neck made it difficult to breathe.

Gus grit his teeth. *Two can play that game.* He activated **Incapacitate** and made an ether weave around Basileus' face, pulling it tight as he could.

Basileus raised Gus high overhead, flipping him to face the ceiling of the chamber.

Gus clenched tightly to the weave, hoping he could outlast the super.

Basileus appeared to double down on the pressure and Gus felt pain in his hip as the iron grip grated against the bone, and his airway was closed off.

Flailing in desperation, he pulled open his abilities, trying to find anything to get loose. He almost fired **Xyzzy**, but realized before wasting the MP that would transport them both and burn more MP with no release. Being unable to aim, he couldn't use some of his abilities.

In desperation, he landed upon **Chi Pulse** and activated it. His stamina bar dropped to a fourth of its length but an unearthly hollow **boom** flung them apart.

Gus pulled in ragged breaths, watching Basileus panting as well. His haunted eyes looked feral as he stared at Gus like prey. Being close to the crystal, Gus tried to rush to touch it.

Basileus let loose an unearthly howl and thrust his fists forward. Two constructs projected from his outstretched arms and ran towards Gus, intercepting him. They resolved into growling wolves snarling and snapping.

Basileus cocked his head and growled, "Mine…" pointing to the crystal. The tone of his voice fluctuated in pitch, reminding Gus of Bobcat Goldthwaite. He twitched with multiple facial tics and his eyes appeared not to blink as he stared almost through Gus.

"Not for long. You've overloaded yourself! Your body can't handle all of those powers!" Gus **Bounded** over the crystal, trying to access the crystal from that direction, but the wolves adjusted again and he could get no closer. Trying **It's All in the Tips**, Gus swiped with the beams and cleaved through the constructs, but they managed to reform again as Basileus pumped more energy into the thin streams trailing off the wolves. With everything that Gus tried, Basileus matched or exceeded his speed and strength. His eyes flitted from the crystal to Basileus then the wolves. He had to break this standoff.

"Gus, I'm in position," a female voice whispered on the comms.

He had almost forgotten about her part in the plan with the rush of battle. Basileus wrinkled his forehead and squinted his eyes as Gus smiled and began charging a **Krackle** burst, adopting a hadouken pose, his demeanor losing the consternation and stress of before. Gus poured more energy into the ability, stacking three activations into one burst, struggling to keep them focused as he awaited the signal.

CHAPTER FORTY-FIVE

You Ruined Everything

"Gus, when you see my signal, get to the core. You probably won't have much time. The surprise won't last long. Ready?"

In answer to her question Gus let loose the charged **Krackle** burst. An angry nebula of purple-colored energy shot towards Basileus. Before it crossed half the distance, a large boom echoed off the sides of the chamber. Everybody looked up and froze, stunned by the effect of what they saw. The distraction split Basileus' attention just enough that he was caught in the majority of the blast, falling back. The constructs evaporated as his concentration failed and Gus saw his chance.

Averting his eyes from the lightshow above, Gus flew to the far side of the core and activated **Hyper**, doubling his Agility. He then began touching the core repeatedly, alternating hands. As he got into a rhythm, his hands began to blur as he synchronized his movements, faster and faster.

Touch, **Leech** a block of twenty abilities, release, touch with the other hand, **Leech** a block of twenty-five, release. Back and forth, the new upgrade on his **Leech** ability allowing him to maximize his buffer without consciously thinking about it. He tore abilities into him without even knowing what they were. Over and over.

His hands sped up, taking hundreds of abilities in seconds. Time seemed to stretch again, everyone around appearing to slow. The core was Gus' world and all he could see.

He wasn't sure what type of aliens lived on the planet the Mandrite core was formed from, but he felt himself moving faster and faster, reducing the space between his hands and the core as he released to push the transfer even more quickly. As **Leech** leveled up, the regular pinging of a chime increased to a near-constant tone. The buffer grew more and more; the speed with which he pulled powers increased exponentially. The tone changed timbre and stretched out as his **TimeSight** sped his perception to a higher level and he continued on, pulling as much as he could in desperation.

The core appeared to be shrinking as Gus drank in the powers. At first, he worried he was compressing the core and damaging it, but the effect continued even though he modulated his touches to be feather light. Pressing more lightly also increased his speed, shaving tiny slivers of time away from each contact.

When the core had shrunk to the size of a basketball, a high-pitched whine began to emanate from the crystal, resonating in an ever-higher tone. Gus pushed on, oblivious to his surroundings or how much time had elapsed. It must have been ear-shattering to anyone who hadn't been operating at such a high speed.

All that mattered for Gus was keeping these abilities out of Basileus' hands. The whine increased to an ear-piercing screech and suddenly the core imploded to a bright pinpoint of light. There was an aftershock that exploded back outwards, flinging Gus away like a rag doll.

Gus twitched on the floor, his body struggling to make sense of the new information within him. It was excruciating euphoria. His blood was on fire and powers coursed through him, recklessly trying to exert their effects.

Gus lifted his head from the gritty concrete floor and saw Basileus frozen in the act of reaching for the core, but bending backward as the force of the blast was pushing him backward. In Gus' current state, nothing appeared to move, and he took in the scene as his body refused to listen to his commands, shivering and shaking.

Jet was in mid-slice, slashing the end off a gun-arm hybrid from one of the cyborg supers. Glowing orange outlined the severed metal while sparks hung in the air around the cut.

Looking up, he could see Aurora above, raining down ionized death in the largest stream of energy he had ever seen her generate. Supers cowered underneath her as she looked like a vengeful goddess, descending in glory to punish the unworthy.

Slowly time reverted back to normal and chaos resumed. All Gus could do was lie there and watch as Jet flipped and flailed. Hitting supers in the face with the butt end and destroying equipment as the weapon focused on supers who used any sort of electronic augment.

Aurora touched down and began attacking with gusto. Gus watched in admiration as she disabled super after super, the relatively diminutive woman taking out men larger and apparently stronger with ease. Gus smiled, enjoying the show when a boot stepped in front of his view. A polished gold boot, with some new scuff marks on the toe.

The boot suddenly disappeared until it made its reappearance in his side, flipping him over onto his back from the force. Gus barely felt it, his body numb from the near-constant shocks he was feeling as he jittered on the floor.

Seeing his state, Basileus stepped over him crouched down. "You idiot!" he screamed. "All that work, all that time, waiting for my moment and you *took that from me!*" A thin line of drool hung out one side of his mouth, suspended for a second, then dropping to the floor next to Gus.

Aurora was right, this guy was unhinged and was quickly becoming worse.

"At least I was able to pull more power to me than any super has before…" He stood, raising his fists in triumph.

That's debatable, Gus thought, wishing he could vocalize the jibe.

"Now I will be able to pull Manticorps out of obscurity and establish it as a new fourth Faction that others will flock to. It will be glorious!"

Yep, he's definitely losing it. Did absorbing all that power fry his mind? Or at least the part that kept him sane? Gus could feel the first hints of control returning to him, being able to very slightly move his neck, but he was still trapped in his own body.

Basileus leaned in close, his hand beginning to crackle and pop with energy. Sparks flared as dust particles entered the field and were immediately burned away. He moved the ball of energy closer to Gus' face and visions of Graviton sliding by reminded Gus of what was about to happen next. His face began to redden from the intense heat and energy pouring off the madman's hand.

"You don't know how much I am enjoying watching you suffer; I'll make sure to prolong—"

Gus thrust his neck forward into Basileus' hand. Gus' face exploded with pain as he pushed it into the plasma. His vision winked out with indescribable pain but it allowed him to activate **Energy Absorption** and drink. He pulled energy inside and opened himself up. The plasma ball fizzled and sputtered out.

Gus continued to pull, feeling multiple channels he had never noticed before open up. His glove disintegrated as Gus pulled and allowed **Leech** to activate. It grabbed at Basileus' new abilities, the **Absorb** ability from Ash kicked in and he took energy from Basileus' very body, breaking apart the bonds that comprised his muscles, bones, from his every cell and lapping up the energy.

He felt sudden cold in his hand and he felt the filigree on Jet's guard had slid into his hand. He jabbed the naginata in

Basileus' side and drank even deeper as **_Vampire's Kiss_** activated. His face felt a refreshing wave like a cool mist and his skin was suddenly whole. Blinding light appeared as his eyes reformed and were restored. Still he pulled more, feeding the black hole within him, trying to fill the void.

He locked eyes with Basileus, seeing the terror there as he was now just as paralyzed as Gus was, in the throes of the **_Leech_** effect. Gus took and took, stripping the new powers from Basileus that he had just obtained and added them to the myriad others. At that moment, he was a leech, a vampire, a parasite. And he was okay with that.

Basileus opened his mouth to scream but could find no words as Gus continued to draw everything. He saw Basileus appear to visibly age, his skin becoming furrowed and sallow. His hair became limp and lifeless, a dull gray mess matted to his bony skull with fervent sweat. His cheeks sank as his features became more gaunt.

Sensing he had almost taken everything, Gus forced himself to stop. It took a brief moment to stop the massive momentum and influx of power. Gus stopped just shy of killing the man, who toppled over to the side. His now brittle bones made a crunch as he fell to the side. The infusion had restored Gus' ability to move, although he still felt like he was vibrating uncontrollably.

Taking pity on the husk of a man before him, he fished in his pocket for a red gel and popped it between the man's teeth. There was a rough scraping noise and Basileus remained there curled up on the floor weeping.

"What have you done?" He looked at his liver-spotted, withered hands, suit hanging off his shrunken frame. "Father can only restore me to where I was before death...what now?"

Gus turned away from the pitiful sight, not sorry in the least.

Looking around, Gus saw many supers standing in awe, their leader summarily deposed. Many turned to flee, and Gus sped into motion. He flew toward each and stripped their powers away with the velocity of the best speedsters. The process was much quicker now and in less than a minute he had reached them and sapped away what remained of their powers, for good.

CHAPTER FORTY-SIX

Shake It Up

When he had finished running, he noticed that his hands were trembling. No—it was his whole body, as if he had an uncontrollable shivering fit.

"What have I done, Aurora? I think the effect isn't stabilizing. There's no way I can assimilate this many powers." Gus could feel a fatigue starting to creep in, so intense that he began to ache. He dropped to his knees, and the deluge of powers felt like it was literally crushing him, burying him with their enormity. The perimeter of his vision started to fade to blackness.

"Gus!" a voice called.

It felt so far away. It sounded insistent but it could have been his imagination.

"*Gus!*"

The voice was screaming now, but Gus found it difficult to focus through the grogginess. He felt cold. Or did he? *Why am I shaking so much?* He took a deep breath in and subconsciously activated his **Energy Absorption** skill.

The temperature of the room dropped ten degrees as the ambient heat was converted into something Gus could use.

With the infusion of energy, Gus rose out of the fog briefly, enough to realize what had happened and he pulled more at the energy.

Aurora stepped back as a rime of frost formed in a widening circle around Gus' body.

"You must use **Energy Absorption** at full blast to maintain yourself while you hold those powers. It will take an enormous amount of energy to make the changes your sudden increase in stats is trying to implement on your body. It will take some time for your body and Nth to catch up," Nick urged.

Finding the ability in his display, he opened the tab and maxed out the ability, pushing the slider to the far end. His fatigue dropped to a manageable level, but he still felt worn out. He ached everywhere. Even the back of his hand hurt. He began noticing pain from overexertion from the most unlikely of places. His eyelids ached each time he blinked. *How do eyelids get sore?*

Oddly, Gus welcomed the pain. It drove away the desire to sleep. He knew that if he allowed himself to doze off, he would not survive the process as his body and Nth tried to assimilate thousands of abilities simultaneously.

Even with that being done, the shaking he had been experiencing began to intensify. His ears began to ring as the vibration increased.

"This is going to be bad," he said as he could feel the resonating become more and more pronounced. His teeth began to hurt as it hit a certain pitch. He checked his logs to see if he was taking damage; he felt like he would literally vibrate himself to shreds.

In desperation, he opened his stat and ability tabs to see if anything could help him.

Aurora looked on from far across the room, flustered that she could do nothing to help.

Gus clicked on his logs and message after message streamed by, listing the abilities he had acquired. Somewhere along the stream of messages he hit level twenty. The messages continued to stream by as nothing happened. At last the euphoria hit, but still the resonance ramped up.

Gus' watch spun to life again, emitting a beam out to the side and then reflecting back, enveloping him.

Requirements met...
Dimensional unfolding progressing...
Fractal unfolding level two...

There was an odd quiet as the pitch from the resonance was absent. He felt compression, and this time it embraced him and he felt no pain. He knew what to expect and flung his arms out to the side as he was lifted into the air. He felt the tightening of his clothes as he was stretched, feeling pain, but the severity was blunted.

It felt like the comfortable ache after a good workout, a reward for a job well done instead of a punishment. Gus breathed deeply, looking at his body. Green disks encircled his torso and arms and legs within the beam from the watch. Orange and red beams played across his body as he watched himself become visibly more muscular and larger. There was a brief spike of pain as the ring played across his head then it was gone as the process finished and time reverted again and Gus dropped to the floor, falling to his hands and knees with the abrupt end of the effect.

The whine of the resonance was jarring as time returned to normal, but it quickly diminished, like the power to a siren had been cut and it settled to a stop.

At long last, it was over. Gus looked to the side and noticed his obviously beefier shoulders and down at his torso. Were those abs? He had always been trim, but more of a runner's build than a weightlifter. *Dang, they look like Poppin' Fresh Muffins!*

"Do you need some alone time?" Aurora asked as she saw him gawking at his own body.

He looked up and saw her sardonic expression as she leaned against a large icicle.

"Ain't no shame in it," he said. "I thought we had a no-judgment zone thing going here!" The deeper tone of his voice sounded alien to his own ears.

"Okay, but there's a little shame in it," she teased. Holding her fingers an inch apart.

"Yeah, but it's very little," he bragged.

"That's what she said," she countered, folding her arms and cocking her head.

"I give up. I bow to your superior verbal sparring skills," Gus said, dropping to one knee and waving his arms in obeisance.

"You seem better. I take it that, whatever 'that' was, took care of your overload problem?" she said, waving at his watch.

"I think so. I still have no idea what it's all about. Nick doesn't even know why it happens."

"Well, I'm glad it does," she said and punched him in the arm. "You scared the hell out of me!"

"I didn't know you cared."

"I don't. But I need you to get off this island, so I have to put up with you."

Things seemed to be back to normal with Aurora, but the flame didn't ignite for him again. She felt more like a bratty sister than a potential girlfriend. *Probably for the best.*

"While I think I'm stable for now, I don't think I can ever go to sleep and allow these powers to attempt to assimilate all at once. What am I going to do from here? It's going to be a weird life from here on out. Correction, weirder."

Gus tasted pear, not like the actual fruit, but more like the juicy pear flavor of Jelly Belly jelly beans. Along with the sensation he also felt a nuance of the meaning, which was new.

"The hybrid-Nth say—"

"Hold on, I think I'm getting it." Gus focused on the taste and he could see. In his mind, Gus could see himself touching other people, regs as well as supers and gifting them Nth with his 'wasted' upgrade. The transfer not only gave them Nth, but gave them abilities, turning regs into supers and strengthening others who already had powers. Gus saw himself building up his own force of supers of like-minded individuals and the manor populated with thousands of people, all working together for a common goal.

He saw himself addressing them all, leading them, which was a strange sight to his eyes. He had never thought of himself as a leader. The taste and the vision faded away simultaneously, their message delivered.

"I could get used to that," Gus said.

"What happened?" Aurora asked.

"Here, let me show you. You know how you always wanted a crafting ability? Which one exactly did you want the most?"

"Um, I've always liked seeing how things work, but I end up breaking the things I take apart rather than fixing them."

Gus closed his eyes and focused on the requirements. Like a magic 8-ball, an ability surfaced, floating in the void. He combined this with some free Nth and opened his eyes. Reaching out, he traced a line on Aurora's cheekbone, following the contours and leaving a silver streak on her smooth skin. She reached up to touch it as it began to soak in.

"Oh!" she said as she saw a display and slid the message over so Gus could read it:

You have been gifted the ability **Tinker, Tailor, Soldier, Spy:** *Instinctive ability to create, repair, and improve inventions relating to cloth- ing, battle, and espionage.*

"I can create my own group of supers, hopefully one that can actually do some real good in the world. I even have my own lair already!" he said, gesturing to the manor.

Aurora just smiled, still amazed, and began to plan how she would use her new ability.

"But first, I'm starving. Let's head to the cafeteria and eat something and restock our gels." Gus sighed and rubbed his empty stomach. When was the last time he had eaten a good meal? It felt like forever. Aurora shrugged and did a mock bow indicating 'after you.' Gus strode forward and she just shook her head.

"Men and their stomachs," she muttered.

CHAPTER FORTY-SEVEN

Comeback

Gus and Aurora stepped out of the manor, needing the feeling of space and fresh air after they finished cleaning up everything. After hauling the supers to the brig, resetting Gus' access in the control room, and eating a well-deserved meal, the world was back in order. He took in a deep breath, enjoying the change from the stuffy chamber on level twenty-three. Warm sunlight played across Gus' features as he closed his eyes and basked in the afternoon sun. A shadow covered his face, interrupting his respite.

"Hey, cut it out, I'm trying to relax," Gus laughed, expecting Aurora to be messing with him.

"Who are you?" she warned from *beside* him.

Snapping his eyes open, Gus saw a large mecha floating silently in midair in front of him, making his already seven-foot frame even more imposing.

"I am Voltekka. Ah. There it is," the robot intoned, and without saying more, the super flung out a hand with fingers splayed.

Gus felt a wrenching throughout his body, then the imploding pressure increased, causing Gus to collapse. The gunmetal hybrid-Nth that made his armor began to pull away from him. His solid armor began to dissolve into grain-like particles as the mecha activated some ability, pulling them towards his outstretched hand somehow. The individual hybrid-Nth were pulled as grains of sand caught in a powerful vacuum, revealing Gus' plain jumpsuit beneath.

Gus would have protested but was in immense pain from the same process happening to hybrid-Nth inside his body as well, driving him to his knees. Blood welled up as Nth were pulled out like tiny bullets, perforating everything in their path.

As the miniature swarm of Nth touched the mecha, he cocked his head.

Through tears of agony, Gus lifted his head and saw that the ripped swarm was flooding back towards him, resisting the effect. Bit by bit, his armor reformed, and as it did, the pull on his internal hybrid-Nth lessened significantly, though he felt as if his insides had been thoroughly torn up.

"Interesting," the large mecha responded. "This is... curious."

Voltekka processed the reality he'd just seen at play. He knew that he needed more of this Endurium, but he had never experienced this before. The metal had refused to meld with him and had chosen to return to its original host. The rumors of semi-sentience must be true! This one had somehow earned the Endurium's favor, and as such, must be monitored. So strange for one who had not ascended. Nodding in respect, he addressed the entity known simply as Gus.

"We share goals. You are... notable. An anomaly."

"Thanks, I guess," Gus rasped, coughing up a little blood. "But what goals could we possibly share?" Gus blurted, not expecting an answer as he shakily got back to his feet, defiance in his eyes.

"Absorption. Reappropriation. Equality," Voltekka responded, as if this explained everything. He pointed at Gus. "They told me."

With another nod, Voltekka took off towards space, heading

for the station to continue his plans, utilizing the small triangular bit of Endurium he had procured. He had big plans that had waited far too long to implement. There were other sources, and they would be acquired.

Gus and Aurora watched the robot leave, white contrail evaporating and slowly floating away.

"What in the *hell* was that!?" Aurora shrieked when the shock of the moment wore off.

Gus only shrugged, staring upwards. When the robot was out of sight, Gus dropped to the ground. He managed to burble out, "Gels," from bloody lips.

Snapping to herself, she fished out a gel and popped it in Gus' mouth. He didn't know how he had been able to hold it together with his Nth practically yanked out of his body. Aurora kept the supply of red gels coming as Gus was able to take them, and after four he'd lost the internal bleeding debuffs as well as a nasty brain bleed. He wasn't at full HP, but he was stable and not losing any more HP.

She kept feeding him until he had regained most of his health, the gels losing efficacy as more and more were eaten. Aurora then helped him walk to the elevator, hitting the level to his room. By the time they reached the floor with living quarters, he was standing on his own.

"Make sure you get some rest, you've been through a lot," she advised, evaluating him leaning against the wall of the elevator as she stepped out.

"No. I can't sleep; I've absorbed too many abilities. Don't look at me like that, I'll be fine. I just need some time to recuperate. Trust me." Gus smiled weakly then hit the button to the control room.

Aurora surveyed Gus' haggard appearance, biting the inside of her cheek. She was exhausted herself, and felt guilty she was going to sleep.

"Okay, but keep the comm open. If you need anything, let me know right away. Nick, don't let him sleep, okay?" Aurora asked.

"That will be difficult for this lazy boy."

Gus groaned. Chiun was back. He waved wearily as the doors started to close.

"Take care of yourself," she urged.

Gus just nodded and shooed her away and the doors closed, cutting her off.

She stood staring for a moment after the doors closed, then shrugged and made her way to her room, the strain of the day and captivity hitting her more fully. Despite her concerns, when she reached her room and laid down, she fell asleep almost instantly, and slept more deeply than she had in a while.

———

"Aurora, come meet me in the control room, I have more good news."

"Whizza-what?" Aurora exclaimed, sitting up in bed with her hair sticking up on one side. She blinked and coughed, trying to make her thoughts coherent.

"You sound like hammered heck. Get ready for the day and meet me in the control room when you're ready. I should do the same, meet in a little bit, then?"

"Okay, I might be a bit, though," she murmured in affirmation, and rubbed her eyes. One thing Aurora liked and was unwilling to compromise was her long showers. She didn't allow herself a lot of indulgences but this was incontrovertible. It was one of the first things that separated her old childhood from her new life as a super.

When her mom had been around, she only got an occasional shower, and it was always cold. Later, when she stayed with Auntie, the large shower head that heated the water as it came out only worked intermittently. So once again cold showers more often than not.

Plus she had the added fun of possibly shocking herself to death if she reached up and touched the bare wiring that fed into the contraption if she forgot while washing under her arms.

She had earned her hot showers. Gus sounded back to normal, he could wait.

Half an hour later, she rolled into the control room, hair still wet. "Okay, what was this good news?"

Gus was excitedly looking through the facility's console. Gone was the tired, rough appearance she had seen just a few hours ago.

"When Basileus and crew took over the manor, they unlocked a *ton* of things. They must have used over a hundred-thousand legacy FP!" he exulted, like a kid on Christmas day.

"Did they get anything good?"

"Take a look." He slid his chair to the side to show the list of recent upgrades.

A siren sounded and they both looked at each other, Gus eyes shifting from jubilant to a harder stare she hadn't seen on his usually placid face.

"You think that's more of Manticorps' men?" Gus snarled as he checked the monitors.

"Maybe. It could be Purple Faction, if they happened to get my distress message."

Gus' heart tensed a little as he wondered which way Aurora would go if it came to a choice between him and Purple Faction. He had a pretty good idea where her loyalties would lie.

"This island is getting as busy as Grand Central Station. Let's go see who's here now, I'm getting tired of this," Gus growled.

He pushed his chair away, clearly upset about another intrusion and stomped out of the room. He made a beeline to the beach and they stood ready to meet the next challengers.

CHAPTER FORTY-EIGHT

Father Figure

Gus stood watching with his arms folded across his chest as they approached. He zoomed in his display, as he noticed the color of their uniforms. "You were right, it's Purple Faction. Wait, is that Tempest?"

They awaited the group of ten supers who landed on the beach, all having the ability to fly on their own. As Tempest landed, he raised his hands up in a placating gesture. Recognizing Aurora, he turned and addressed her.

"Aurora, I'm so glad you're okay. I got your message right before... *changes* happened within the Faction. I came as soon as I could, and brought a few of the supers loyal to me to come assist you. I would have been here sooner, but the message was corrupted and I had to work on it a while to recompile. Then there was the hassle of requisitioning a transport. I was getting stonewalled until Rory helped with that when he found out you were in trouble. How can I help? I seem to have a lot of extra time on my hands as of late," Tempest said, a little edge in his voice.

Aurora looked at Tempest, then at Gus, confused that he had not recognized his own son. "Um, we're fine, we defeated

Manticorps yesterday. Are you here to let us know you're taking the island?" She put her hands on her hips in a way that Gus wondered if she was being defiant.

"Hmm. That sounds like something I would do, doesn't it?" Tempest rubbed his chin, and Gus squinted as he noticed some rough stubble there. His father usually had dogged insistence on maintaining an immaculate appearance. "That might have been my role in the past, but I've been reevaluating a lot of things." His voice was grim. He stood there with his hands on his hips staring at the sand, thinking. At last he responded, "No, for now I'm just here to help you out and find out anything about what happened to my—"

Tempest looked up and saw Gus, finally recognizing his son. He was so different in appearance and demeanor that his brain struggled to assimilate what he was seeing. Gus could see the cogs working, trying to associate the confident individual who stood before him that was nothing like the lanky gamer son with poor posture Tempest knew. "How long has it been? It feels like another lifetime ago."

"A couple years, at least."

"Gus? How long have you had powers?" he stammered.

"For about a month," Gus replied stiffly.

Tempest nodded, wincing slightly at the obvious edge in his words. "Still, I'd like to get caught up and see how you've been. I really am glad to see you alive and well. I held out hope when the station crashed and escape pods were launched, but we've found nothing in our searches so far."

Gus began to respond but Tempest raised a hand. "Please, let me finish. I've wanted to tell you so much but I was advised that I couldn't."

Gus pressed his lips into a firm line. *This better be good.*

"You should know that your brother challenged me and took my position within Purple Faction. I worry about him too, especially because I know he's being manipulated. We will have to deal with that at some point. There's something bigger going on here that I need to puzzle out, but we can focus on that later. You need to know the most important thing."

"Sure, sure," Gus said folding his arms. *Was he fishing for sympathy?*

"Your mother is alive."

Gus stood there stunned, so many bombs had been dropped and he was trying to sort through them all.

"Count me in, if you'll have me," Aurora chipped in.

Tempest let a smile crease one side of his mouth. "They're never going to know what hit them."

Gus heard none of it as he processed it all.

EPILOGUE

Rampage double checked the locks on his private bunker, then activated the comms, wringing his hands in anticipation. A hooded figure illuminated the dark space, his holographic projection glowing blue. The figure leaned forward, awaiting his report in silence.

"We have established Cyclone in the leadership of Purple Faction, just as you asked." Rampage stammered out, his chubby jowls jiggling. "It will take some time to groom him and solidify his position there, but he is very pliant. We can mold him however we want."

The corpulent man stared into the dark space under the cowl, unnerved by the inability to read his master's disposition.

The figure leaned back and steepled his fingers. Rampage had assumed to see bony, thin fingers but these hands were strong and bore the signs of hard toil and struggle.

"At last! We now have operatives in the leadership of every major Faction. Another phase of the plan is complete," the voice grated as if being used for the first time in years. "You have your orders. Make sure the boy is ready when I need him."

Rampage nodded obediently as the communication winked

out and he was left there in the dark, sweat covering his skin. In the ensuing silence, he could hear his heart beating madly. His master was not known for his leniency toward failure. He would have to start working with the boy immediately.

As he left his hideout, a wicked smile stole across his face as he imagined how things would soon change. He would finally get what he had worked so hard for, and so many would pay. So many!

ABOUT CARL STUBBLEFIELD

The author began his plans for world domination by first becoming a dentist. It is a well-known fact that dentists have unearthed the ancient secrets of how to crush the hearts of men and to hear the lamentations of women and children. When this was insufficient, he created worlds where he could torment the good guys before moving to the next phase of his plans. Known for nefarious accomplishments that involve crippling dad-jokes and debilitating puns.

From his secret lair hidden in the Pacific Northwest, he lives with his wife and three children. They haven't left yet, but the mountain is covered with genetically altered wolves and other creatures. I'm sure that's just a coincidence, though.

Connect with Carl:
HenchmenUnite.com
Patreon.com/Henchmen_Unite
Twitter.com/ouroboros999
Facebook.com/groups/CarlStubblefield

ABOUT MOUNTAINDALE PRESS

Dakota and Danielle Krout, a husband and wife team, strive to create as well as publish excellent fantasy and science fiction novels. Self-publishing *The Divine Dungeon: Dungeon Born* in 2016 transformed their careers from Dakota's military and programming background and Danielle's Ph.D. in pharmacology to President and CEO, respectively, of a small press. Their goal is to share their success with other authors and provide captivating fiction to readers with the purpose of solidifying Mountaindale Press as the place 'Where Fantasy Transforms Reality.'

Connect with Mountaindale Press:
MountaindalePress.com
Facebook.com/MountaindalePress
Twitter.com/_Mountaindale
Instagram.com/MountaindalePress

MOUNTAINDALE PRESS TITLES
GameLit and LitRPG

The Completionist Chronicles,
The Divine Dungeon, and
Full Murderhobo by Dakota Krout

King's League by Jason Anspach and J.N. Chaney

A Touch of Power by Jay Boyce

Red Mage by Xander Boyce

Space Seasons by Dawn Chapman

Ether Collapse and
Ether Flows by Ryan DeBruyn

Bloodgames by Christian J. Gilliland

Wolfman Warlock by James Hunter and Dakota Krout

Axe Druid and
Mephisto's Magic Online by Christopher Johns

Skeleton in Space by Andries Louws

Chronicles of Ethan by John L. Monk

Pixel Dust by David Petrie

Henchman by Carl Stubblefield

Artorian's Archives by Dennis Vanderkerken and Dakota Krout

APPENDIX

Gus' stats and abilities at the end of book 2

Agility: 57 (52+5)
Constitution: 61 (56+5)
Charisma: 33 (28+5)
Strength: 42 (37+5)
Perception: 41 (36+5)
Intelligence: 64 (59+5)
Luck: 42 (37+5)
HP: 1200/1200
MP: 1180/1180
Stamina: 1200/1200

MARTIAL SKILLS:

Wreck-tums! (Level 3): *5% critical chance that will damn near kill the enemy from the opposing forces of chaos the blade unleashes along its edge. Blade also is auto-sharpening due to this effect. After receiving wear or damage to blade edge, chaos forces will re-balance the fineness of the blade. This item has hidden skills only discovered through use.*

Two-Handed Weapons (Level 3): *+10% damage when using two-handed weapons.*

Polearms (Level 7): *+1 to initiative when fighting enemies without polearms.*

Backstab (Level 2): *Unnoticed attacks from behind deal double damage!*

Sweep the Leg! (Level 3): *Upon successfully blocking an attack, have a 25% chance of knocking an opponent off their feet, stunning them for 5 seconds.*

Counter-Attack (Level 1): *After completion of a successful parry of an enemy attack, 5% chance of following through with an attack that deals double the damage! Success rates increase with higher levels.*

Chained Attack (Level 1): *Hit a second target when a successful* **Counter-Attack** *triggers without receiving any damage by either attacker. 50% chance of activating a chained attack with direct attack if no damage is taken.*

Incapacitate (Level 1): *Subdue an attacker by restricting their oxygen flow through an ether weave. Success rates decrease by 10% for every level above originator of skill.*

ENERGY MANIPULATION:

Intermediate Shielding (Level 16) [10MP/minute]: *Form barriers around the host. Can be enlarged to encompass more people but will drain MP at an accelerated rate. Energy attacks will weaken shielding and destabilize it.*

Absorb (Level 26) [20 MP]: *Extract energy and store for later use, most effective when directly draining MP and HP from others.*

Transfer (Level 13) [15MP]: *Distribute energy from Absorb. Cannot change its form or convert energy into another medium. If energy is absorbed, it will be transferred in the same form.*

Warp (Level 12[30MP]): *Distort reality in a localized area, either crushing or expanding items in a 1-meter diameter sphere.*

Zeno Effect (Level 29) [30 MP]: *Focusing on the quantum state of an object or target at will freeze its passage through time, preventing physical movement or skill activation while observed.*

Krackle (Level 6) [30 MP]: *High energy burst attack of concentrated cascading spheres of energy.*

It's All in the Tips (Level 22) [10 MP]: *Fire beams of energy from fingertips.*

Chi Pulse (Level 29) [150 MP]: *Drain internal stored energy to create an intense pulse of energy causing intense damage. Target will also be sapped of stamina regeneration after activation for 10 minutes.*

Dick in a Box (Level 12) [25 MP]: *Encase an enemy in an* *invisible, impenetrable box of ether. Can be sustained by continuous MP drain. Duration at current level: 5 minutes.*

Photoelectric Shielding (Level 11): *Energy below a certain threshold state will be absorbed by shielding, sufficient energy will result in a retaliatory burst of photoelectrons causing radiation damage.*

MATTER MANIPULATION:

Wreck-luse (Level 10): *Upon touching an enemy, with weapon or physical touch, a toxin is released which causes them to flee away from friend and foe. Necrotizing damage at site of touch that continues to spread outward, dealing damage until healed. Gives poisoned debuff, -20% movement speed, -20% attack damage.*

Indi-Wreckt (Level 1): *Allows you to destroy items not directly in physical contact with you, given they are suffused with enough energy.*

Range of effect: 10 feet.

Damage done: 1:2 ratio of MP invested to HP damage.

WRECK-LESS (Level 2): *This skill dramatically increases the durability of used items, weapons and armor. (+50%) It extends to vehicles you directly use, or are a passenger in, and lowers critical failures rates (30% reduction).*

Smol (Level 13) [45MP/minute]: *Controls quantum field fluctuations to reduce the space between fundamental particles, using modified quantum chromodynamics to stabilize quark/gluon interactions. TL;DR: Reduces size by a factor of up to 30 times.*

Cleanse (Level 17) [50 MP]: *Eliminate toxins of all types from self or others who possess Nth. At higher levels, can create remote effects on those who do not possess Nth.*

Shake (Level 21) [30 MP]: *Cause an intense vibration that causes disorientation and dizziness.*

Shatter (Level 11) [20 MP/minute]: *Vibrate at a frequency that will cause stress-hardening weakness in metals and polymers, causing their failure. Vibrations will cause glasses and ceramics to propagate any weaknesses and break.*

Kitty's Got Claws (Level 7) [20 MP]: *Increased damage and poison transmitted to wounds for continued damage over time.*

Meld (Level 8) [40 MP]: *Temporarily gain properties of a selected item. Duration depends on the type of material utilized and energy requirements to affect transformation.*

Ice Shard (Level 16) [15 MP]: *Use ambient moisture to create dagger-like weapons. MP cost doubled if insufficient ambient moisture and ether must be converted to water to create effects.*

Amber (Level 8) [20MP]: *Create a viscous substance that rapidly hardens, trapping enemies inside.*

MINMAX:

Enhanced Strength (Level 36) [Passive]: *Every level of this ability gives a (1.7 x level) permanent increase to Strength stat. Each allocated point into Strength yields 1.7 points in addition to skill boost (not retroactive).*

Hyper (Level 17) [20MP]: *Doubles a stat for 5 minutes per activation.*

Cat-Like Reflexes (Level 34) [Passive]: *More intuitive reactions and Agility. Increases Agility by 20 points.*

ENHANCEMENTS:

Physical:

Resilience (Level 11) [Passive]: *Grants extraordinary resistance to projectiles and explosive damage due to a passive ether shield that absorbs and deflects attacks above melee speeds.*

Mental:

Wreck-ord (Level 3): *Everyone marches to the beat of their own drum, but you use this to your advantage! When you songify your life in apropos ways, you will get a bonus to stats. Bonus depends on the aptness of your choice and stats relevant to the situation. Rock on!*

Note: Each song can only be used once for effect. Unlike most abilities, as you increase in your personal level, this ability loses its potency. Use this ability wisely.

For levels 10-19:

Multiplier Progression: Geometric progression x2.

Cooldown: 12 hours.

Vivid (Level 4) [Passive]: *Enhanced dreams, often providing special benefits, including: temporary stat increases, insights, crafting epiphanies.*

Command (Level 17) [10MP]: *Compel targets to obey instructions. Success rates increase with higher levels of Intelligence.*

Electronic Mind (Level 36): *Facilitated communication with non-biologic entities, as well as intuition in construction and repair of all constructs meant to interface with biologic tissues.*

Aim-Assist (Level 8) [10 MP/minute]: *Display augment to aid in targeting, allows the host to lock-on at higher levels. Once a lock is achieved, can be maintained even after target is out of the line of sight or uses stealth skills.*

Coerce (Level 11) [50MP]: *Compels a target to agree with instruction. Success calculated based on the delta between the target's base Intelligence stat compared to caster.*

Telepathy (Level 21) [10 MP/minute]: *Send and receive mental messages, images and information.*

Mindfulness (Level 8/42).

True Sight (Level 1): *You have looked beyond what is false for long enough to gain a certain sense of clarity. You now can perceive truth more readily. Improved understanding of how the universe truly functions and increased perception of truth in communication, dispelling illusions, and your environment. Increased levels allow greater success in seeing things as they truly are.*

TimeSight (Level 7): *You can now access some relativistic effects that will compensate and increase reaction time while traveling at excessive speeds.*

TRANSPORT:

Dash (Level 12): *Speed forward a distance of 650 feet or less. Distance increases with skill level (50ft +(n x50ft)).*

Bound (Level 5) [20 MP]: *Jump with increased ability, energy stored upon landing, aiding height and power of successive jumps.*

Advanced Flight (Level 47) [30 MP/minute]: *Can control trajectory and speed of flight. Lowered MP cost to maintain flight as levels increase. As levels increase, carry capacity during flight increased.*

Xyzzy (Level 3) [75MP]: *Bamf! Form wormholes to create portals and transport from one location to another. Base range is 5 feet. Each additional level extends this range another 5 feet.*

Lightskate (Level 8): *Move effortlessly on any surface on photonically charged ether.*

Drafting (Level 34): *Creates a wake behind you that allows teammates to travel at the same speed.*

STEALTH:

Camouflage (Level 5) [3 MP/minute]: *Blend seamlessly into your environment. Note: At your current level you will be detectable during movement.*

Phase-Shift (Level 4) [10 MP/minute]: *Shift partially out of the current dimension to avoid detection. During shifts, cannot be damaged by projectiles or melee damage, but will still be susceptible to area-of-effect damage.*

Gemini (Level 11) [40 MP/copy]: *Create an illusory copy of self that acts independently based on mental commands. Shares no actual abilities and can cause no physical damage.*

Shapeshift (Level 18): *Change your physical form at will by temporarily reconfiguring connective and hard tissues.*

Mimic (Level 5) [20 MP]: *Impersonate others by adopting their outward appearance. At higher levels can match vocal patterns and mannerisms.*